THE SILENT BULLET

THE ADVENTURES OF CRAIG KENNEDY, SCIENTIFIC DETECTIVE

ARTHUR B. REEVE

Edited, with an introduction and notes,
by Leslie S. Klinger

LIBRARY
LIBRARY
OF CONGRESS

Poisoned Pen
PRESS

Published by Poisoned Pen Press, an imprint of Sourcebooks,
in association with the Library of Congress
P.O. Box 4410, Naperville, Illinois 60567-4410
(630) 961-3900
sourcebooks.com

This edition of *The Silent Bullet* is based on the first edition in the Library
of Congress's collection, originally published in 1912 by Dodd, Mead and
Company. The illustrations, by Will Foster, are original to the book.

Library of Congress Cataloging-in-Publication Data
Names: Reeve, Arthur B. (Arthur Benjamin), author.
Title: The silent bullet : the adventures of Craig Kennedy, scientific
  detective / Arthur B. Reeve.
Description: Naperville, Illinois : Library of Congress/Poisoned Pen Press,
  [2021] | Series: Library of Congress crime classics | "This edition of
  The Silent Bullet is based on the first edition in the Library of
  Congress's collection, originally published in 1912 by Dodd, Mead and
  Company." | Includes bibliographical references.
Identifiers: LCCN 2020048810 | (trade paperback) | (epub)
Subjects: LCSH: Detective and mystery stories, American. | Chemistry
  teachers--Fiction. | LCGFT: Short stories.
Classification: LCC PS3535.E354 S55 2021 | DDC 813/.52--dc23
LC record available at https://lccn.loc.gov/2020048810

Printed and bound in the United States of America.
SB 10 9 8 7 6 5 4 3 2 1

CONTENTS

FOREWORD

Crime writing as we know it first appeared in 1841, with the publication of "The Murders in the Rue Morgue." Written by American author Edgar Allan Poe, the short story introduced C. Auguste Dupin, the world's first wholly fictional detective. Other American and British authors had begun working in the genre by the 1860s, and by the 1920s, we had officially entered the golden age of detective fiction.

Throughout this short history, many authors who paved the way have been lost or forgotten. Library of Congress Crime Classics bring back into print some of the finest American crime writing from the 1860s to the 1960s, showcasing rare and lesser-known titles that represent a range of genres, from cozies to police procedurals. With cover designs inspired by images from the Library's collections, each book in this series includes the original text, reproduced faithfully from an early edition in the Library's collections and complete with strange spellings and unorthodox punctuation. Also included are a contextual introduction, a brief biography of the author, notes, recommendations for further reading, and suggested discussion questions. Our hope is for these books to start conversations, inspire further research, and bring obscure works to a new generation of readers.

Early American crime fiction is not only entertaining to read, but it also sheds light on the culture of its time. While many of the titles in this series include outmoded language and stereotypes now considered offensive, these books give readers the opportunity to reflect on how our society's perceptions of race, gender, ethnicity, and social standing have evolved over more than a century.

More dark secrets and bloody deeds lurk in the massive collections of the Library of Congress. I encourage you to explore these works for yourself, here in Washington, DC, or online at www.loc.gov.

—Carla D. Hayden, Librarian of Congress

INTRODUCTION

In Arthur Conan Doyle's *A Study in Scarlet* (1887), Dr. Watson
tells Sherlock Holmes: "You have brought detection as near
an exact science as it ever will be brought in this world."[*] But
Holmes does not deserve credit for being the first to apply science (in the sense of current technology) to crime detection. As
early as 1865, Mr. Furbush, in the eponymous tale by English
writer Harriet Spofford, used photographic enlargement to solve
a crime, and a year later, the Australian writer Mary Fortune
employed the same technique in her tale "The Dead Witness."
William Russell (who wrote as "Waters") used blood analysis in
his "Murder under the Microscope"—which was included in his
1863 collection *Autobiography of an English Detective*. And an
anonymous story called "A Tell-Tale Ink Mark" in 1886 focused
on fingerprints.[†]

Science, in the fields of chemistry and medicine, was

---

[*] Arthur Conan Doyle, *The New Annotated Sherlock Holmes: The Novels*, ed. Leslie S.
Klinger (New York: W. W. Norton, 2005), 69.

[†] The story—one of many similar stories—appeared in the *Iowa State Reporter* on
June 17, 1886. Only a few years later, Mark Twain made fingerprints a key point in
Pudd'nhead Wilson, serialized in *The Century Magazine* in 1893–94.

the principal basis for detection in the stories written by the English writer L. T. Meade and her collaborators Robert Eustace and Clifford Halifax, especially the Meade-Halifax *Stories from A Doctor's Diary* (1894). In 1904, English author R. Austin Freeman began a long series of tales about forensic scientist Dr. John Thorndyke and his colleagues (the last of Freeman's stories about Thorndyke appeared in 1927), and the American writer Samuel Hopkins Adams, in his *Average Jones* stories (1911), followed in Meade's footsteps with a private detective who uses knowledge of science and technology to detect scams.

The American school of "scientific detection," emphasizing actual science and technology rather than themes of horror, truly began with *The Achievements of Luther Trant* (1909–1910), by William MacHarg and Edwin Balmer, which emphasized new technology.* The stories' hero is a clean-cut psychologist who works as a criminologist. Cleveland Moffett's *Through the Wall* (1909) also contains a pioneering American look at scientific crime fighting.

Science came to stay in American crime fiction, however, with the appearance of Professor Craig Kennedy, the "scientific detective" created by journalist Arthur B. Reeve. The first published story featuring Kennedy, "The Case of Helen Bond," appeared in *Cosmopolitan* magazine in December 1910, with a subtitle that read "The First of a Series of Unusual Detective Stories in Which the Professor of Criminal Science Adopts the New Method of Making the Criminal Discover Himself." It was the first of 23 consecutive appearances in *Cosmopolitan*. In all, 86 stories about Kennedy appeared in that magazine; the stories appeared almost monthly until 1918, then again in 1924 and

---

* Arthur Reeve later acknowledged his debt to MacHarg and Ballmer in a newspaper interview, though he could not remember their names.

1925.* *The Silent Bullet* (1912) was the first published collection of Craig Kennedy short stories, and in 1918, Harper & Brothers published a 12-volume set titled the Craig Kennedy Stories.

Kennedy's "career" was not limited to print: in 1915, an unsuccessful stage play (christened *The Bannock Mystery*) appeared based on the stories. A number of films were produced between 1914 and 1936, including a silent serial, *The Exploits of Elaine*, cowritten by Reeve, which made Kennedy's fame. Kennedy also surfaced in the funny papers, with 156 strips appearing in 1926 and another four arcs of six daily strips in 1929. Even after Reeve's death, as late as 1952, a 26-episode television series, *Craig Kennedy, Criminologist*, appeared.

Kennedy's mission was clear: "I am going to apply science to the detection of crime, the same sort of methods by which you trace out the presence of a chemical, or run an unknown germ to earth."† Though Kennedy was not an *innovator* of forensic technology, he was quick to see the application of various new inventions—small microphones, blood tests, thermite, acetylene torches, and the like—to crimes and the detection of crime.

Reeve's stories were not much different in format from the Holmes-Watson partnership model created by Conan Doyle. Kennedy's partner in most of the stories is newspaperman Walter Jameson, and like many other writers who came before him, Reeve was content to appeal to readers with cleverness and

---

* For a full bibliography of Reeve's magazine fiction, see John Locke, ed., *From Ghouls to Gangsters: The Career of Arthur B. Reeve* (Elkhorn, CA: Off-Trail Publications, 2007), 2:153–63.

---

† See page 3. This quote first appeared in Reeve's short story "The Case of Helen Bond," *Cosmopolitan* 50, no. 1 (December 1910): 113. "Helen Bond" was eventually split into two parts: the first five hundred words appeared at the beginning of *The Silent Bullet*, and the remainder became the story in this collection titled "The Scientific Cracksman" (see page 27).

novelty, rather than character. Kennedy is never more than an archetypal detective (at least until he falls in love in *The Exploits of Elaine*, the first stories from which appeared in 1914), and Jameson an archetypal sidekick. Kennedy set out to become the first professor of criminal science, not a private detective, but when tastes changed in the 1920s, the stories depicted him as a man of action, more like Dashiell Hammett's protagonist Continental Op than an academic.

Why did Kennedy become so popular? The answer is probably because science itself was popular. The era's newspapers were filled with accounts of the inventions and discoveries of Thomas Edison, Nikola Tesla, and Guglielmo Marconi,* among others, and Kennedy, never described by Reeve as a discoverer or inventor himself, cleverly saw how the popular science of the day could be adapted to crime solving. This was not limited to hard science, as in the case of Holmes's chemical experiments or crime scene investigations, but also encompassed medicine and psychology— even "pseudoscience" like lie detectors. Reeve must have read widely to come up with ideas for these stories.

The critics were not universally kind to Reeve's work. For example, in H. Douglas Thomson's *Masters of Mystery: A Study of the Detective Story*, after he waxes eloquent on the successes of Anna Katharine Green, he writes, "Then the plague of sensational, ill-written thrillers filled the land. Mr. Arthur B. Reeve, who now controls the prosperous fortunes of a group of detective story magazines, is the most notorious representative of this legion. His pseudo-scientific detective, Craig Kennedy, has

---

* Edison's continued activities in the first years of the twentieth century included development of the motion picture and a car battery for Henry Ford; Tesla continued to promote the wireless transmission of energy and free power; and Marconi was developing the "wireless" (radio).

always swayed Teutonic affections.... He is...rather strong and silent, athletic and egregiously resourceful. This last quality was essential owing to Mr. Arthur B. Reeve's ingenuity in devising original methods of destruction the scientific possibility of which is often problematical."* Mystery historian LeRoy Lad Panek, in *After Sherlock Holmes: The Evolution of British and American Detective Stories, 1891–1914*, complained only of the stories' formulaic structure. "Invariably, at the end of the stories suspects gather (usually in the lab at Columbia) and watch Professor Kennedy perform a demonstration with scientific apparatus that answers the questions of how and who raised in the story. Wonderful new scientific machines [are introduced] mysteriously at the visit to the crime scene and then [explained] later at the demonstration."† Rosemary Herbert, in the *Oxford Companion to Crime and Mystery Writing*, rendered the most succinct judgment: "Reeve held a place in the top rank of genre writers, although his dependence upon apparatus that came to seem gimmicky makes his work dated in a way that the stories of Holmes have never become."‡

Today, accurate scientific methods are commonly applied to crime solving. But this was not always so. Crime solving was generally a matter of good luck or relied on informants. This began to change in 1893, when Austrian criminal jurist Hans Gross (1847–1915) published his seminal *Handbuch für Untersuchungsrichter* (usually referred to as *Criminal Investigations*). Gross pulled together wide fields of knowledge,

---

* H. Douglas Thomson, *Masters of Mystery: A Study of the Detective Story* (London: W. Collins and Sons, 1931), 259–60.

---

† LeRoy Lad Panek, *After Sherlock Holmes: The Evolution of British and American Detective Stories, 1891–1914* (Jefferson, NC: McFarland, 2014), 122.

---

‡ Rosemary Herbert, *The Oxford Companion to Crime and Mystery Writing* (Oxford: Oxford University Press, 1999), 398.

including psychology and physical science, that could be successfully used against crime and suggested how to adapt techno-
logical developments, such as photography, to the crime scene.
In 1912, Gross founded the Institute of Criminalistics as part
of the law school of the University of Graz, and other academic
institutions followed Gross's lead. In America, in 1909, August
Vollmer, who admired Gross's work, became chief of police in
Berkeley, California, and implemented formal police training.*
By the 1920s, Edward Oscar Heinrich, one of America's pioneering forensic scientists, was instrumental in capturing the
perpetrators of an unsuccessful train robbery and the murder
of four members of the train crew and became known as the
"American Sherlock Holmes."† Laboratories began to be part of
every major police department, and the public began to expect
that forensic science would be a routine part of the work of the
police. Of course, in the 1980s, when DNA profiling was first
developed, everything accelerated, and as television and fiction
began to promote what is now called the "*CSI* effect," the public
began to expect immediate and near-miraculous identifications
of criminals within hours of the commission of a crime.

As a result, the "scientific detective" is now a well-appreciated
figure in crime writing. Temperance "Bones" Brennan, the forensic anthropologist protagonist of Kathy Reichs's long-running
series; Lincoln Rhyme, a quadriplegic forensic criminalist whose
adventures are penned by Jeffery Deaver; and Dr. Kay Scarpetta,
a medical examiner created by Patricia Cornwell, are just a few
of the latest band of such investigators. While Craig Kennedy's
science and technology are all outdated today (or in some cases,

---

* See first note, page 1.

---

† For more on the incredible life and work of Heinrich, see Kate Winkler Dawson,
American Sherlock: Murder, Forensics, and the Birth of American CSI (New York: G. P.
Putnam's Sons, 2020).

proven to be useless), the immense popularity of Reeve's writing laid the groundwork for a substantial portion of modern crime fiction.

—Leslie S. Klinger

CRAIG KENNEDY'S THEORIES

"It has always seemed strange to me that no one has ever endowed a professorship in criminal science in any of our large universities."*

Craig Kennedy laid down his evening paper and filled his pipe with my tobacco. In college we had roomed together, had shared everything, even poverty, and now that Craig was a professor of chemistry and I was on the staff of the *Star*,† we had continued the arrangement. Prosperity found us in a rather neat bachelor apartment on the Heights, not far from the university.‡

"Why should there be a chair in criminal science?" I remarked argumentatively, settling back in my chair. "I've done my turn

---

* August Vollmer, who became chief of police in Berkeley, California, in 1909, is credited with being the first to implement formal police training. Vollmer was influenced by key European works on the subject, in particular *Criminal Investigations, A Practical Textbook* (1893) by Hans Gross, an Austrian criminologist (a book known to Sherlock Holmes and mentioned in "The Problem of Thor Bridge" [1922]), and the memoirs of Eugène Vidocq (1834), head of the French Sûreté nationale. Starting in 1916, Vollmer led a brand-new criminal justice program at the University of California, Berkeley. One of Vollmer's students, O. W. Wilson, established the first police science degree at Municipal University of Wichita (now Wichita State University) in 1937.

† A fictional newspaper; the actual *New York Star* ceased publication in 1891.

‡ Reeve never identifies which university includes Kennedy on its faculty. New York University was originally located on a hilltop in the Bronx section of New York City and was later referred to as the "University Heights" campus; however, Columbia University was located in Morningside Heights, popularly called "the Heights." *Encyclopedia of Mystery and Detection* by Chris Steinbrunner and Otto Penzler, Bruce F. Murphy's *Encyclopedia of Murder and Mystery*, and William L. DeAndrea's *Encyclopedia Mysteriosa* all simply state flatly that Kennedy was a professor at Columbia, while Rosemary Herbert's *Oxford Companion to Crime and Mystery Writing* more cautiously says merely that he is a professor "at a New York university." Even J. K. Van Dover, who has studied the Kennedy stories in more depth than any other scholars (see *You Know My Method: The Science of the Detective*, Bowling Green, OH: Bowling Green State University Popular Press, 1994, 159–89), can only say that Kennedy is a professor "at, apparently, Columbia University." Reeve himself attended New York Law School, founded by a group of professors and scholars who left Columbia, and so it would be natural for him to mean Columbia when he refers to "the University." Reeve (and, as he reveals in the 1924 story "Water," both Kennedy and Jameson) received an undergraduate degree from Princeton University, but it is clear that Kennedy resides in New York City.

at police headquarters reporting, and I can tell you, Craig, it's no place for a college professor. Crime is just crime. And as for dealing with it, the good detective is born and bred to it. College professors for the sociology of the thing, yes; for the detection of it, give me a Byrnes."*

"On the contrary," replied Kennedy, his clean-cut features betraying an earnestness which I knew indicated that he was leading up to something important, "there is a distinct place for science in the detection of crime. On the Continent they are far in advance of us in that respect. We are mere children beside a dozen crime-specialists in Paris, whom I could name."

"Yes, but where does the college professor come in?" I asked, rather doubtfully.

"You must remember, Walter," he pursued, warming up to his subject, "that it's only within the last ten years or so that we have had the really practical college professor who could do it. The silk-stockinged variety is out of date now. To-day it is the college professor who is the third arbitrator in labour disputes, who reforms our currency, who heads our tariff commissions, and conserves our farms and forests. We have professors of everything—why not professors of crime?"

Still, as I shook my head dubiously, he hurried on to clinch his point. "Colleges have gone a long way from the old ideal of pure culture. They have got down to solving the hard facts of life—pretty nearly all, except one. They still treat crime in the old way, study its statistics and pore over its causes and the theories of how it can be prevented. But as for running the criminal himself down, scientifically, relentlessly—bah! we haven't made

---

* The near-legendary Thomas F. Byrnes (1842–1910) was an Irish-born American police officer who was the chief detective of the New York City Police Department from 1880 until 1895; his *Professional Criminals of America* (1886) was essential reading for every police detective.

an inch of progress since the hammer and tongs method of your Byrnes."

"Doubtless you will write a thesis on this most interesting subject," I suggested, "and let it go at that."

"No, I am serious," he replied, determined for some reason or other to make a convert of me. "I mean exactly what I say. I am going to apply science to the detection of crime, the same sort of methods by which you trace out the presence of a chemical, or run an unknown germ to earth. And before I have gone far, I am going to enlist Walter Jameson as an aide. I think I shall need you in my business."

"How do I come in?"

"Well, for one thing, you will get a scoop, a beat,—whatever you call it in that newspaper jargon of yours."

I smiled in a sceptical way, such as newspapermen are wont to affect toward a thing until it is done—after which we make a wild scramble to exploit it.

Nothing more on the subject passed between us for several days.

I

THE SILENT BULLET

"Detectives in fiction nearly always make a great mistake," said Kennedy one evening after our first conversation on crime and science. "They almost invariably antagonise the regular detective force. Now in real life that's impossible—it's fatal."

"Yes," I agreed, looking up from reading an account of the failure of a large Wall Street brokerage house, Kerr Parker & Co., and the peculiar suicide of Kerr Parker. "Yes, it's impossible, just as it is impossible for the regular detectives to antagonise the newspapers. Scotland Yard found that out in the Crippen case."*

"My idea of the thing, Jameson," continued Kennedy, "is that the professor of criminal science ought to work with, not against, the regular detectives. They're all right. They're indispensable, of course. Half the secret of success nowadays is organisation. The professor of criminal science should be merely what the professor in a technical school often is—a sort of consulting

---

* Hawley Harvey Crippen (1862–1910), usually known as Dr. Crippen, was an American ear and eye specialist living in London. He was convicted for the murder of his wife, Cora Henrietta Crippen. The newspapers were vocal in clamoring for Scotland Yard to produce a suspect, and some suggest that Crippen was innocent.

engineer. For instance, I believe that organisation plus science would go far toward clearing up that Wall Street case I see you are reading."

I expressed some doubt as to whether the regular police were enlightened enough to take that view of it.

"Some of them are," he replied. "Yesterday the chief of police in a Western city sent a man East to see me about the Price murder—you know the case?"

Indeed I did. A wealthy banker of the town had been murdered on the road to the golf club, no one knew why or by whom. Every clue had proved fruitless, and the list of suspects was itself so long and so impossible as to seem most discouraging.

"He sent me a piece of a torn handkerchief with a deep blood-stain on it," pursued Kennedy. "He said it clearly didn't belong to the murdered man, that it indicated that the murderer had himself been wounded in the tussle, but as yet it had proved utterly valueless as a clue. Would I see what I could make of it?

"After his man had told me the story I had a feeling that the murder was committed by either a Sicilian labourer on the links or a negro waiter at the club. Well, to make a short story shorter, I decided to test the blood-stain. Probably you didn't know it, but the Carnegie Institution has just published a minute, careful, and dry study of the blood of human beings and of animals. In fact, they have been able to reclassify the whole animal kingdom on this basis, and have made some most surprising additions to our knowledge of evolution. Now I don't propose to bore you with the details of the tests, but one of the things they showed was that the blood of a certain branch of the human race gives a reaction much like the blood of a certain group of monkeys, the chimpanzees, while the blood of another branch gives a reaction like that of the gorilla.[*] Of course there's lots more to it, but this is all that need concern us now.

"I tried the tests. The blood on the handkerchief conformed strictly to the latter test. Now the gorilla was, of course, out of the question—this was no *Rue Morgue* murder.[†] Therefore it was the negro waiter."

"But," I interrupted, "the negro offered a perfect alibi at the start, and—"

"No buts, Walter. Here's a telegram I received at dinner: 'Congratulations. Confronted Jackson your evidence as wired. Confessed.'"

"Well, Craig, I take off my hat to you," I exclaimed. "Next you'll be solving this Kerr Parker case for sure."

"I would take a hand in it if they'd let me," said he simply.

That night, without saying anything, I sauntered down to the imposing new police building amid the squalor of Centre Street.[‡] They were very busy at headquarters, but, having once had that assignment for the *Star*, I had no trouble in getting in. Inspector Barney O'Connor of the Central Office carefully shifted a cigar from corner to corner of his mouth as I poured forth my suggestion to him.

"Well, Jameson," he said at length, "do you think this professor fellow is the goods?"

---

[*] This is nonsense. Great apes—including gorillas and chimpanzees—have the same blood types (A, B, AB, and O) as humans. (Blood typing, it may be recalled, was only discovered in 1900–01 by Karl Landsteiner.) Historically, America's segregation policies were applied to blood donations as late as 1972, in the State of Louisiana. Is there such a thing as "Black blood"? No, but there are ethnic and racial differences in the antigens found in blood, a fact increasingly important in finding donor matches. Rose George, "The Intersection of Race and Blood," *New York Times*, May 14, 2019.

[†] "The Murders in the Rue Morgue" (1841) by Edgar Allan Poe may be said to be the first mystery story in the English language. Famously, the murders are committed by an orangutan.

[‡] 240 Centre Street was the location of the former New York City Police Headquarters building, built from 1905 to 1909. It served as the headquarters from 1909 to 1973.

I didn't mince matters in my opinion of Kennedy. I told him of the Price case and showed him a copy of the telegram. That settled it.

"Can you bring him down here to-night?" he asked quickly.

I reached for the telephone, found Craig in his laboratory finally, and in less than an hour he was in the office.

"This is a most baffling case, Professor Kennedy, this case of Kerr Parker," said the inspector, launching at once into his subject. "Here is a broker heavily interested in Mexican rubber. It looks like a good thing—plantations right in the same territory as those of the Rubber Trust. Now in addition to that he is branching out into coastwise steamship lines; another man associated with him is heavily engaged in a railway scheme from the United States down into Mexico. Altogether the steamships and railroads are tapping rubber, oil, copper, and I don't know what other regions. Here in New York they have been pyramiding stocks, borrowing money from two trust companies which they control. It's a lovely scheme—you've read about it, I suppose. Also you've read that it comes into competition with a certain group of capitalists whom we will call 'the System.'

"Well, this depression in the market comes along. At once rumours are spread about the weakness of the trust companies; runs start on both of them. The System,—you know them—make a great show of supporting the market. Yet the runs continue. God knows whether they will spread or the trust companies stand up under it to-morrow after what happened to-day. It was a good thing the market was closed when it happened.

"Kerr Parker was surrounded by a group of people who were in his schemes with him. They are holding a council of war in the directors' room. Suddenly Parker rises, staggers toward the window, falls, and is dead before a doctor can get to him. Every effort is made to keep the thing quiet. It is given out that he committed suicide. The papers don't seem to accept the suicide theory, however. Neither do we. The coroner, who is working with us, has kept his mouth shut so far, and will say nothing till the inquest. For, Professor Kennedy, my first man on the spot found that—Kerr—Parker—was—murdered.

"Now here comes the amazing part of the story. The doors to the offices on both sides were open at the time. There were lots of people in each office. There was the usual click of typewriters, and the buzz of the ticker, and the hum of conversation. We have any number of witnesses of the whole affair, but as far as any of them knows no shot was fired, no smoke was seen, no noise was heard, nor was any weapon found. Yet here on my desk is a thirty-two-calibre bullet. The coroner's physician probed it out of Parker's neck this afternoon and turned it over to us."

Kennedy reached for the bullet, and turned it thoughtfully in his fingers for a moment. One side of it had apparently struck a bone in the neck of the murdered man, and was flattened. The other side was still perfectly smooth. With his inevitable magnifying-glass he scrutinised the bullet on every side. I watched his face anxiously, and I could see that he was very intent and very excited.

"Extraordinary, most extraordinary," he said to himself as he turned it over and over. "Where did you say this bullet struck?"

"In the fleshy part of the neck, quite a little back of and below his ear and just above his collar. There wasn't much bleeding. I think it must have struck the base of his brain."

"It didn't strike his collar or hair?"

"No," replied the inspector.

"Inspector, I think we shall be able to put our hands on the murderer—I think we can get a conviction, sir, on the evidence that I shall get from this bullet in my laboratory."

"That's pretty much like a story-book," drawled the inspector incredulously, shaking his head.

"Perhaps," smiled Kennedy. "But there will still be plenty of work for the police to do, too. I've only got a clue to the murderer. It will tax the whole organisation to follow it up, believe me. Now, Inspector, can you spare the time to go down to Parker's office and take me over the ground? No doubt we can develop something else there."

"Sure," answered O'Connor, and within five minutes we were hurrying down-town in one of the department automobiles.

We found the office under guard of one of the Central Office men, while in the outside office Parker's confidential clerk and a few assistants were still at work in a subdued and awed manner. Men were working in many other Wall Street offices that night during the panic, but in none was there more reason for it than here. Later I learned that it was the quiet tenacity of this confidential clerk that saved even as much of Parker's estate as was saved for his widow—little enough it was, too. What he saved for the clients of the firm no one will ever know. Somehow or other I liked John Downey, the clerk, from the moment I was introduced to him. He seemed to me, at least, to be the typical confidential clerk who would carry a secret worth millions and keep it.

The officer in charge touched his hat to the inspector, and Downey hastened to put himself at our service. It was plain that the murder had completely mystified him, and that he was as anxious as we were to get at the bottom of it.

"Mr. Downey," began Kennedy, "I understand you were present when this sad event took place."

"Yes, sir, sitting right here at the directors' table," he replied, taking a chair, "like this."

"Now can you recollect just how Mr. Parker acted when he

was shot? Could you—er—could you take his place and show us just how it happened?"

"Yes, sir," said Downey. "He was sitting here at the head of the table. Mr. Bruce, who is the 'Co.' of the firm, had been sitting here at his right; I was at the left. The inspector has a list of all the others present. That door to the right was open, and Mrs. Parker and some other ladies were in the room—"

"Mrs. Parker?" broke in Kennedy.

"Yes. Like a good many brokerage firms we have a ladies' room. Many ladies are among our clients. We make a point of catering to them. At that time I recollect the door was open— all the doors were open. It was not a secret meeting. Mr. Bruce had just gone into the ladies' department, I think to ask some of them to stand by the firm—he was an artist at smoothing over the fears of customers, particularly women. Just before he went in I had seen the ladies go in a group toward the far end of the room—to look down at the line of depositors on the street, which reached around the corner from one of the trust companies, I thought. I was making a note of an order to send into the outside office there on the left, and had just pushed this button here under the table to call a boy to carry it. Mr. Parker had just received a letter by special delivery, and seemed considerably puzzled over it. No, I don't know what it was about. Of a sudden I saw him start in his chair, rise up unsteadily, clap his hand on the back of his head, stagger across the floor—like this—and fall here."

"Then what happened?"

"Why, I rushed to pick him up. Everything was confusion. I recall someone behind me saying, 'Here, boy, take all these papers off the table and carry them into my office before they get lost in the excitement.' I think it was Bruce's voice. The next moment I heard someone say, 'Stand back, Mrs. Parker has fainted.' But

I didn't pay much attention, for I was calling to someone not to get a doctor over the telephone, but to go down to the fifth floor where one has an office. I made Mr. Parker as comfortable as I could. There wasn't much I could do. He seemed to want to say something to me, but he couldn't talk. He was paralysed, at least his throat was. But I did manage to make out finally what sounded to me like, 'Tell her I don't believe the scandal, I don't believe it.' But before he could say whom to tell he had again become unconscious, and by the time the doctor arrived he was dead. I guess you know everything else as well as I do."

"You didn't hear the shot fired from any particular direction?" asked Kennedy.

"No, sir."

"Well, where do you think it came from?"

"That's what puzzles me, sir. The only thing I can figure out is that it was fired from the outside office—perhaps by some customer who had lost money and sought revenge. But no one out there heard it either, any more than they did in the directors' room or the ladies' department."

"About that message," asked Kennedy, ignoring what to me seemed to be the most important feature of the case, the mystery of the silent bullet. "Didn't you see it after all was over?"

"No, sir; in fact I had forgotten about it till this moment when you asked me to reconstruct the circumstances exactly. No, sir, I don't know a thing about it. I can't say it impressed itself on my mind at the time, either."

"What did Mrs. Parker do when she came to?"

"Oh, she cried as I have never seen a woman cry before. He was dead by that time, of course. Mr. Bruce and I saw her down in the elevator to her car. In fact, the doctor, who had arrived, said that the sooner she was taken home the better she would be. She was quite hysterical."

"Did she say anything that you remember?"

Downey hesitated.

"Out with it, Downey," said the inspector. "What did she say as she was going down in the elevator?"

"Nothing."

"Tell us. I'll arrest you if you don't."

"Nothing about the murder, on my honour," protested Downey.

Kennedy leaned over suddenly and shot a remark at him, "Then it was about the note."

Downey was surprised, but not quickly enough. Still he seemed to be considering something, and in a moment he said:

"I don't know what it was about, but I feel it is my duty, after all, to tell you. I heard her say, 'I wonder if he knew.'"

"Nothing else?"

"Nothing else."

"What happened after you came back?"

"We entered the ladies' department. No one was there. A woman's automobile-coat was thrown over a chair in a heap. Mr. Bruce picked it up. 'It's Mrs. Parker's,' he said. He wrapped it up hastily, and rang for a messenger."

"Where did he send it?"

"To Mrs. Parker, I suppose. I didn't hear the address."

We next went over the whole suite of offices, conducted by Mr. Downey. I noted how carefully Kennedy looked into the directors' room through the open door from the ladies' department. He stood at such an angle that had he been the assassin he could scarcely have been seen except by those sitting immediately next to Mr. Parker at the directors' table. The street windows were directly in front of him, and back of him was the chair on which the motor-coat had been found.

In Parker's own office we spent some time, as well as in

Bruce's. Kennedy made a search for the note, but finding nothing in either office, turned out the contents of Bruce's scrapbasket. There didn't seem to be anything in it to interest him, however, even after he had pieced several torn bits of scraps together with much difficulty, and he was about to turn the papers back again, when he noticed something sticking to the side of the basket. It looked like a mass of wet paper, and that was precisely what it was.

"That's queer," said Kennedy, picking it loose. Then he wrapped it up carefully and put it in his pocket. "Inspector, can you lend me one of your men for a couple of days?" he asked, as we were preparing to leave. "I shall want to send him out of town to-night, and shall probably need his services when he gets back."

"Very well. Riley will be just the fellow. We'll go back to headquarters, and I'll put him under your orders."

It was not until late in the following day that I saw Kennedy again. It had been a busy day on the *Star*. We had gone to work that morning expecting to see the very financial heavens fall. But just about five minutes to ten, before the Stock Exchange opened, the news came in over the wire from our financial man on Broad Street: "The System has forced James Bruce, partner of Kerr Parker, the dead banker, to sell his railroad, steamship, and rubber holdings to it. On this condition it promises unlimited support to the market."

"Forced!" muttered the managing editor, as he waited on the office 'phone to get the composing-room, so as to hurry up the few lines in red ink on the first page and beat our rivals on the streets with the first extras. "Why, he's been working to bring that about for the past two weeks. What that System doesn't control isn't worth having—it edits the news before our men get it, and as for grist for the divorce courts, and tragedies, well—Hello, Jenkins, yes, a special extra. Change the big heads—copy is on the way up—rush it."

"So you think this Parker case is a mess?" I asked.

"I know it. That's a pretty swift bunch of females that have been speculating at Kerr Parker & Co.'s. I understand there's one Titian-haired* young lady—who, by the way, has at least one husband who hasn't yet been divorced—who is a sort of ring-leader, though she rarely goes personally to her brokers' offices. She's one of those up-town plungers, and the story is that she has a whole string of scalps of alleged Sunday-school superin-tendents at her belt. She can make Bruce do pretty nearly any-thing, they say. He's the latest conquest. I got the story on pretty good authority, but until I verified the names, dates, and places, of course I wouldn't dare print a line of it. The story goes that her husband is a hanger-on of the System, and that she's been work-ing in their interest, too. That was why he was so complacent over the whole affair. They put her up to capturing Bruce, and after she had acquired an influence over him they worked it so that she made him make love to Mrs. Parker. It's a long story, but that isn't all of it. The point was, you see, that by this devious route they hoped to worm out of Mrs. Parker some inside information about Parker's rubber schemes, which he hadn't divulged even to his partners in business. It was a deep and carefully planned plot, and some of the conspirators were pretty deeply in the mire, I guess. I wish I'd had all the facts about who this red-haired female Machiavelli was—what a piece of muckraking it would have made! Oh, here comes the rest of the news story over the wire. By Jove, it is said on good authority that Bruce will be taken in as one of the board of directors. What do you think of that?"

---

* According to the *Oxford English Dictionary*, this refers to a bright golden-auburn color, which occurs often in many paintings by the Italian painter Titian, who flourished in the Venetian school of the sixteenth century.

So that was how the wind lay—Bruce making love to Mrs. Parker and she presumably betraying her husband's secrets. I thought I saw it all: the note from somebody exposing the scheme, Parker's incredulity, Bruce sitting by him and catching sight of the note, his hurrying out into the ladies' department, and then the shot. But who fired it? After all, I had only picked up another clue.

Kennedy was not at the apartment at dinner, and an inquiry at the laboratory was fruitless also. So I sat down to fidget for a while. Pretty soon the buzzer on the door sounded, and I opened it to find a messenger-boy with a large brown paper parcel.

"Is Mr. Bruce here?" he asked.

"Why, no, he doesn't—" then I checked myself and added: "He will be here presently. You can leave the bundle."

"Well, this is the parcel he telephoned for. His valet told me to tell him that they had a hard time to find it, but he guesses it's all right. The charges are forty cents. Sign here."

I signed the book, feeling like a thief, and the boy departed. What it all meant I could not guess.

Just then I heard a key in the lock, and Kennedy came in.

"Is your name Bruce?" I asked.

"Why?" he replied eagerly. "Has anything come?"

I pointed to the package. Kennedy made a dive for it and unwrapped it. It was a woman's pongee automobile-coat. He held it up to the light. The pocket on the right-hand side was scorched and burned, and a hole was torn clean through it. I gasped when the full significance of it dawned on me.

"How did you get it?" I exclaimed at last in surprise.

"That's where organisation comes in," said Kennedy. "The police at my request went over every messenger call from Parker's office that afternoon, and traced every one of them up. At last they found one that led to Bruce's apartment. None of them led to Mrs. Parker's home. The rest were all business calls and satisfactorily accounted for. I reasoned that this was the one that involved the disappearance of the automobile-coat. It was a chance worth taking, so I got Downey to call up Bruce's valet. The valet of course recognised Downey's voice and suspected nothing. Downey assumed to know all about the coat in the package received yesterday. He asked to have it sent up here. I see the scheme worked."

"But, Kennedy, do you think she—" I stopped, speechless, looking at the scorched coat.

"Nothing to say—yet," he replied laconically. "But if you could tell me anything about that note Parker received I'd thank you."

I related what our managing editor had said that morning. Kennedy only raised his eyebrows a fraction of an inch.

"I had guessed something of that sort," he said merely. "I'm glad to find it confirmed even by hearsay evidence. This red-haired young lady interests me. Not a very definite description, but better than nothing at all. I wonder who she is. Ah, well, what do you say to a stroll down the White Way before I go to my laboratory? I'd like a breath of air to relax my mind."

We had got no further than the first theatre when Kennedy slapped me on the back. "By George, Jameson, she's an actress, of course."

"Who is? What's the matter with you, Kennedy? Are you crazy?"

"The red-haired person—she must be an actress. Don't you remember the auburn-haired leading lady in the 'Follies'—the girl who sings that song about 'Mary, Mary, quite contrary'? Her stage name, you know, is Phœbe La Neige. Well, if it's she who is concerned in this case I don't think she'll be playing to-night. Let's inquire at the box-office."

She wasn't playing, but just what it had to do with anything in particular I couldn't see, and I said as much.

"Why, Walter, you'd never do as a detective. You lack intuition. Sometimes I think I haven't quite enough of it, either. Why didn't I think of that sooner? Don't you know she is the wife of Adolphus Hesse, the most inveterate gambler in stocks in the System? Why, I had only to put two and two together and the whole thing flashed on me in an instant. Isn't it a good hypothesis that she is the red-haired woman in the case, the tool of the System in which her husband is so heavily involved? I'll have to add her to my list of suspects."

"Why, you don't think she did the shooting?" I asked, half hoping, I must admit, for an assenting nod from him.

"Well," he answered dryly, "one shouldn't let any preconceived hypothesis stand between him and the truth. I've made a guess at the whole thing already. It may or it may not be right. Anyhow she will fit into it. And if it's not right, I've got to be prepared to make a new guess, that's all."

When we reached the laboratory on our return, the inspector's man Riley was there, waiting impatiently for Kennedy.

"What luck?" asked Kennedy.

"I've got a list of purchasers of that kind of revolver," he said. "We have been to every sporting-goods and arms-store in the city which bought them from the factory, and I could lay my hands on pretty nearly every one of those weapons in twenty-four hours—provided, of course, they haven't been secreted or destroyed."

"Pretty nearly all isn't good enough," said Kennedy. "It will have to be all, unless—"

"*That* name is in the list," whispered Riley hoarsely.

"Oh, then it's all right," answered Kennedy, brightening up. "Riley, I will say that you're a wonder at using the organisation in ferreting out such things. There's just one more thing I want you to do. I want a sample of the notepaper in the private desks of every one of these people." He handed the policeman a list of his "suspects," as he called them. It included nearly every one mentioned in the case.

Riley studied it dubiously and scratched his chin thoughtfully. "That's a hard one, Mr. Kennedy, sir. You see, it means getting into so many different houses and apartments. Now you don't want to do it by means of a warrant, do you, sir? Of course not. Well, then, how can we get in?"

"You're a pretty good-looking chap yourself, Riley," said Kennedy. "I should think you could jolly a housemaid, if necessary. Anyhow, you can get the fellow on the beat to do it—if he isn't already to be found in the kitchen. Why, I see a dozen ways of getting the notepaper."

"Oh, it's me that's the lady-killer, sir," grinned Riley. "I'm a regular Blarney stone[*] when I'm out on a job of that sort. Sure, I'll have some of them for you in the morning."

"Bring me what you get, the first thing in the morning, even if you've landed only a few samples," said Kennedy, as Riley departed, straightening his tie and brushing his hat on his sleeve.

"And now, Walter, you too must excuse me to-night," said Craig. "I've got a lot to do, and sha'n't be up to our apartment till very late—or early. But I feel sure I've got a strangle-hold on this mystery. If I get those papers from Riley in good time to-morrow I shall invite you and several others to a grand demonstration here to-morrow night. Don't forget. Keep the whole evening free. It will be a big story."

Kennedy's laboratory was brightly lighted when I arrived

---

[*] According to E. Cobham Brewer's *Dictionary of Phrase and Fable* (London: Cassell, 1898), whoever kisses the Blarney Stoney "shall be able to persuade to anything." Riley means that he can talk his way into getting some notepaper.

early the next evening. One by one his "guests" dropped in. It was evident that they had little liking for the visit, but the coroner had sent out the "invitations," and they had nothing to do but accept. Each one was politely welcomed by the professor and assigned a seat, much as he would have done with a group of students. The inspector and the coroner sat back a little. Mrs. Parker, Mr. Downey, Mr. Bruce, myself, and Miss La Neige sat in that order in the very narrow and uncomfortable little armchairs used by the students during lectures.

At last Kennedy was ready to begin. He took his position behind the long, flat-topped table which he used for his demonstrations before his classes. "I realise, ladies and gentlemen," he began formally, "that I am about to do a very unusual thing; but, as you all know, the police and the coroner have been completely baffled by this terrible mystery and have requested me to attempt to clear up at least certain points in it. I will begin what I have to say by remarking that the tracing out of a crime like this differs in nothing, except as regards the subject-matter, from the search for a scientific truth. The forcing of man's secrets is like the forcing of nature's secrets. Both are pieces of detective work. The methods employed in the detection of crime are, or rather should be, like the methods employed in the process of discovering scientific truth. In a crime of this sort, two kinds of evidence need to be secured. Circumstantial evidence must first be marshalled, and then a motive must be found. I have been gathering facts. But to omit motives and rest contented with mere facts would be inconclusive. It would never convince anybody or convict anybody. In other words, circumstantial evidence must first lead to a suspect, and then this suspect must prove equal to accounting for the facts. It is my hope that each of you may contribute something that will be of service in arriving at the truth of this unfortunate incident."

The tension was not relieved even when Kennedy stopped speaking and began to fuss with a little upright target which he set up at one end of his table. We seemed to be seated over a powder-magazine which threatened to explode at any moment. I, at least, felt the tension so greatly that it was only after he had started speaking again that I noticed that the target was composed of a thick layer of some putty-like material.

Holding a thirty-two-calibre pistol in his right hand and aiming it at the target, Kennedy picked up a large piece of coarse homespun from the table and held it loosely over the muzzle of the gun. Then he fired. The bullet tore through the cloth, sped through the air, and buried itself in the target. With a knife he pried it out.

"I doubt if even the inspector himself could have told us that when an ordinary leaden bullet is shot through a woven fabric the weave of that fabric is in the majority of cases impressed on the bullet, sometimes clearly, sometimes faintly."

Here Kennedy took up a piece of fine batiste and fired another bullet through it.

"Every leaden bullet, as I have said, which has struck such a fabric bears an impression of the threads which is recognisable even when the bullet has penetrated deeply into the body. It is only obliterated partially or entirely when the bullet has been flattened by striking a bone or other hard object. Even then, as in this case, if only a part of the bullet is flattened the remainder may still show the marks of the fabric.* A heavy warp, say of cotton velvet or, as I have here, homespun, will be imprinted

---

* Kennedy is correct. The soft exposed lead nose on non-full-metal-jacketed bullets can be imprinted with anything that is penetrated by the bullet. Wood, glass, fabric, plastic, or tissue may leave marks as well as fragments on the bullet tip. As early as 1902, Oliver Wendell Holmes, testifying as an expert in a court case, compared the marks on a test bullet that he fired into cotton wool to those found on a bullet recovered from a corpse in an autopsy.

well on the bullet, but even a fine batiste, containing one hundred threads to the inch, will show marks. Even layers of goods such as a coat, shirt, and undershirt may each leave their marks, but that does not concern us in this case. Now I have here a piece of pongee silk, cut from a woman's automobile-coat. I discharge the bullet through it—so. I compare the bullet now with the others and with the one probed from the neck of Mr. Parker. I find that the marks on that fatal bullet correspond precisely with those on the bullet fired through the pongee coat."

Startling as was this revelation, Kennedy paused only an instant before the next.

"Now I have another demonstration. A certain note figures in this case. Mr. Parker was reading it, or perhaps re-reading it, at the time he was shot. I have not been able to obtain that note—at least not in a form such as I could use in discovering what were its contents. But in a certain wastebasket I found a mass of wet and pulp-like paper. It had been cut up, macerated, perhaps chewed; perhaps it had been also soaked with water. There was a washbasin with running water in this room. The ink had run, and of course was illegible. The thing was so unusual that I at once assumed that this was the remains of the note in question. Under ordinary circumstances it would be utterly valueless as a clue to anything. But to-day science is not ready to let anything pass as valueless.

"I found on microscopic examination that it was an uncommon linen bond paper, and I have taken a large number of microphotographs of the fibres in it. They are all similar. I have here also about a hundred microphotographs of the fibres in other kinds of paper, many of them bonds. These I have accumulated from time to time in my study of the subject. None of them, as you can see, shows fibres resembling this one in question, so we may conclude that it is of uncommon quality.

Through an agent of the police I have secured samples of the notepaper of every one who could be concerned, as far as I could see, with this case. Here are the photographs of the fibres of these various notepapers, and among them all is just one that corresponds to the fibres in the wet mass of paper I discovered in the scrap-basket. Now lest anyone should question the accuracy of this method I might cite a case where a man had been arrested in Germany charged with stealing a government bond. He was not searched till later. There was no evidence save that after the arrest a large number of spitballs were found around the courtyard under his cell window. This method of comparing the fibres with those of the regular government paper was used, and by it the man was convicted of stealing the bond. I think it is almost unnecessary to add that in the present case we know precisely who—"

At this point the tension was so great that it snapped. Miss La Neige, who was sitting beside me, had been leaning forward involuntarily. Almost as if the words were wrung from her she whispered hoarsely: "They put me up to doing it; I didn't want to. But the affair had gone too far. I couldn't see him lost before my very eyes. I didn't want her to get him. The quickest way out was to tell the whole story to Mr. Parker and stop it. It was the only way I could think of to stop this thing between another man's wife and the man I loved better than my own husband. God knows, Professor Kennedy, that was all—"

"Calm yourself, madame," interrupted Kennedy soothingly. "Calm yourself. What's done is done. The truth must come out. Be calm. Now," he continued, after the first storm of remorse had spent itself and we were all outwardly composed again, "we have said nothing whatever of the most mysterious feature of the case, the firing of the shot. The murderer could have thrust the weapon into the pocket or the folds of this coat"—here he drew forth the automobile-coat and held it aloft, displaying the bullet hole—"and he or she (I will not say which) could have discharged the pistol unseen. By removing and secreting the weapon afterward one very important piece of evidence would be suppressed. This person could have used such a cartridge as I have here, made with smokeless powder, and the coat would have concealed the flash of the shot very effectively. There would have been no smoke. But neither this coat nor even a heavy blanket would have deadened the report of the shot.

"What are we to think of that? Only one thing. I have often wondered why the thing wasn't done before. In fact I have been waiting for it to occur. There is an invention that makes it almost possible to strike a man down with impunity in broad daylight in any place where there is sufficient noise to cover up a click, a slight 'Pouf!' and the whir of the bullet in the air.*

"I refer to this little device of a Hartford inventor.† I place it over the muzzle of the thirty-two-calibre revolver I have so far been using—so. Now, Mr. Jameson, if you will sit at that typewriter over there and write—anything so long as you keep the keys clicking. The inspector will start that imitation stock-ticker in the corner. Now we are ready. I cover the pistol with a cloth. I defy anyone in this room to tell me the exact moment when I discharged the pistol. I could

---

* This is consistent with later depictions of silencers by Hollywood but is in fact an exaggeration: even modern silencers reduce the noise to about 130–150 dB for a supersonic cartridge and 117–130 dB for a subsonic cartridge. For comparison, ambulance sirens produce 100 to 140 dB.

† The professor is referring to Hiram P. Maxim (1869–1936), credited with the invention in 1902 of what became known as the "Maxim Silencer." However, Maxim's silencer only worked with closed-breech rifles and single-shot target pistols, not a .32-caliber revolver, and none were available in 1910. (For more on Maxim, see note on page 289.)

have shot any of you, and an outsider not in the secret would never have thought that I was the culprit. To a certain extent I have reproduced the conditions under which this shooting occurred.

"At once on being sure of this feature of the case I despatched a man to Hartford to see this inventor. The man obtained from him a complete list of all the dealers in New York to whom such devices had been sold. The man also traced every sale of those dealers. He did not actually obtain the weapon, but if he is working on schedule-time according to agreement he is at this moment armed with a search-warrant and is ransacking every possible place where the person suspected of this crime could have concealed his weapon. For, one of the persons intimately connected with this case purchased not long ago a silencer for a thirty-two-calibre revolver, and I presume that that person carried the gun and the silencer at the time of the murder of Kerr Parker."

Kennedy concluded in triumph, his voice high pitched, his eyes flashing. Yet to all outward appearance not a heart-beat was quickened. Someone in that room had an amazing store of self-possession. The fear flitted across my mind that even at the last Kennedy was baffled.

"I had anticipated some such anti-climax," he continued after a moment. "I am prepared for it."

He touched a bell, and the door to the next room opened. One of Kennedy's graduate students stepped in.

"You have the records, Whiting?" he asked.

"Yes, Professor."

"I may say," said Kennedy, "that each of your chairs is wired under the arm in such a way as to betray on an appropriate indicator in the next room every sudden and undue emotion. Though it may be concealed from the eye, even of one like me who stands facing you, such emotion is nevertheless expressed by physical pressure on the arms of the chair.* It is a test that is used frequently with students to demonstrate various points of psychology. You needn't raise your arms from the chairs, ladies and gentlemen. The tests are *all over* now. What did they show, Whiting?"

The student read what he had been noting in the next room. At the production of the coat during the demonstration of the markings of the bullet, Mrs. Parker had betrayed great emotion, Mr. Bruce had done likewise, and nothing more than ordinary emotion had been noted for the rest of us. Miss La Neige's automatic record during the tracing out of the sending of the note to Parker had been especially unfavourable to her; Mr. Bruce showed almost as much excitement; Mrs. Parker very little and Downey very little. It was all set forth in curves drawn by self-recording pens on regular ruled paper. The student had merely noted what took place in the lecture-room as corresponding to these curves.

"At the mention of the noiseless gun," said Kennedy, bending over the record, while the student pointed it out to him and we leaned forward to catch his words, "I find that the curves of Miss La Neige, Mrs. Parker, and Mr. Downey are only so far from normal as would be natural. All of them were witnessing a thing for the first time with only curiosity and no fear. The curve made by Mr. Bruce shows great agitation and—"

---

* There was great interest at this time in the idea that scientific measurements of bodily reactions might reveal emotions—that is, detect lies. Hugo Münsterberg, one of the leading exponents of the use of psychology in the detection of crime, in an essay published in his *On the Witness Stand: Essays on Psychology and Crime* (New York: McClure, 1908), warned that "experiment gives us so far not sufficient hold for the discrimination of the guilty conscience and the emotional excitement of the innocent. The innocent man, especially the nervous man, may grow as much excited on the witness stand as the criminal when the victim and the means of the crime are mentioned; his fear that he may be condemned unjustly may influence his muscles, glands and blood vessels as strongly as if he were guilty" (142).

I heard a metallic click at my side and turned hastily. It was Inspector Barney O'Connor, who had stepped out of the shadow with a pair of hand-cuffs.

"James Bruce, you are under arrest," he said.

There flashed on my mind, and I think on the minds of some of the others, a picture of another electrically wired chair.

II

THE SCIENTIFIC CRACKSMAN

"I'm willing to wager you a box of cigars that you don't know the most fascinating story in your own paper to-night," remarked Kennedy, as I came in one evening with the four or five newspapers I was in the habit of reading to see whether they had beaten the *Star* in getting any news of importance.

"I'll bet I do," I said, "for I was one of about a dozen who worked it up. It's the Shaw murder trial. There isn't another that's even a bad second."

"I am afraid the cigars will be on you, Walter. Crowded over on the second page by a lot of stale sensation that everyone has read for the fiftieth time, now, you will find what promises to be a real sensation, a curious half-column account of the sudden death of John G. Fletcher."

I laughed. "Craig," I said, "when you put up a simple death from apoplexy against a murder trial, and *such* a murder trial,—well, you disappoint me—that's all."

"Is it a simple case of apoplexy?" he asked, pacing up and down the room, while I wondered why he should grow excited over what seemed a very ordinary news item, after all. Then he picked up the paper and read the account slowly aloud.

JOHN G. FLETCHER, STEEL
MAGNATE, DIES SUDDENLY
SAFE OPEN BUT LARGE SUM OF CASH UNTOUCHED

John Graham Fletcher, the aged philanthropist and steel-maker, was found dead in his library this morning at his home at Fletcherwood, Great Neck, Long Island. Strangely, the safe in the library in which he kept his papers and a large sum of cash was found opened, but as far as could be learned nothing is missing.

It had always been Mr. Fletcher's custom to rise at seven o'clock. This morning his housekeeper became alarmed when he had not appeared by nine o'clock. Listening at the door, she heard no sound. It was not locked, and on entering she found the former steel-magnate lying lifeless on the floor between his bedroom and the library adjoining. His personal physician, Dr. W. C. Bryant, was immediately notified.

Close examination of the body revealed that his face was slightly discoloured, and the cause of death was given by the physician as apoplexy. He had evidently been dead about eight or nine hours when discovered.

Mr. Fletcher is survived by a nephew, John G. Fletcher, II., who is the Blake professor of bacteriology at the university, and by a grandniece, Miss Helen Bond. Professor Fletcher was informed of the sad occurrence shortly after leaving a class this morning and hurried out to Fletcherwood. He would make no statement other than that he was inexpressibly shocked. Miss Bond, who has for several years resided with relatives, Mr. and Mrs. Francis Greene of Little Neck, is prostrated by the shock.

"Walter," added Kennedy, as he laid down the paper and, without any more sparring, came directly to the point, "there *was* something missing from that safe."

I had no need to express the interest I now really felt, and Kennedy hastened to take advantage of it.

"Just before you came in," he continued, "Jack Fletcher called me up from Great Neck. You probably don't know it, but it has been privately reported in the inner circle of the university that old Fletcher was to leave the bulk of his fortune to found a great school of preventive medicine, and that the only proviso was that his nephew should be dean of the school. The professor told me over the wire that the will was missing from the safe, and that it was the only thing missing. From his excitement I judge that there is more to the story than he cared to tell over the 'phone. He said his car was on the way to the city, and he asked if I wouldn't come and help him—he wouldn't say how. Now, I know him pretty well, and I'm going to ask you to come along, Walter, for the express purpose of keeping this thing out of the newspapers—understand?—until we get to the bottom of it."

A few minutes later the telephone rang and the hall-boy announced that the car was waiting. We hurried down to it; the chauffeur lounged down carelessly into his seat and we were off across the city and river and out on the road to Great Neck with amazing speed.

Already I began to feel something of Kennedy's zest for the adventure. I found myself half a dozen times on the point of hazarding a suspicion, only to relapse again into silence at the inscrutable look on Kennedy's face. What was the mystery that awaited us in the great lonely house on Long Island?

We found Fletcherwood a splendid estate directly on the bay, with a long driveway leading up to the door. Professor Fletcher met us at the porte cochère, and I was glad to note that, far from taking me as an intruder, he seemed rather relieved that someone who understood the ways of the newspapers could stand between him and any reporters who might possibly drop in.

He ushered us directly into the library and closed the door. It seemed as if he could scarcely wait to tell his story.

"Kennedy," he began, almost trembling with excitement, "look at that safe door."

We looked. It had been drilled through in such a way as to break the combination. It was a heavy door, closely fitting, and it was the best kind of small safe that the state of the art had produced. Yet clearly it had been tampered with, and successfully. Who was this scientific cracksman who had apparently accomplished the impossible? It was no ordinary hand and brain which had executed this "job."

Fletcher swung the door wide, and pointed to a little compartment inside, whose steel door had been jimmied open. Then out of it he carefully lifted a steel box and deposited it on the library table.

"I suppose everybody has been handling that box?" asked Craig quickly.

A smile flitted across Fletcher's features. "I thought of that, Kennedy," he said. "I remembered what you once told me about finger-prints. Only myself has touched it, and I was careful to take hold of it only on the sides. The will was placed in this box, and the key to the box was usually in the lock. Well, the will is gone. That's all; nothing else was touched. But for the life of me I can't find a mark on the box, not a finger-mark. Now on a hot and humid summer night like last night I should say it was pretty likely that anyone touching this metal box would have left finger-marks. Shouldn't you think so, Kennedy?"

Kennedy nodded and continued to examine the place where

the compartment had been jimmied. A low whistle aroused us. Coming over to the table, Craig tore a white sheet of paper off a pad lying there and deposited a couple of small particles on it.

"I found them sticking on the jagged edges of the steel where it had been forced," he said. Then he whipped out a pocket magnifying-glass. "Not from a rubber glove," he commented half to himself. "By Jove, one side of them shows lines that look as if they were the lines on a person's fingers, and the other side is perfectly smooth. There's not a chance of using them as a clue, except—well, I didn't know criminals in America knew that stunt."

"What stunt?"

"Why, you know how keen the new detectives are on the finger-print system? Well, the first thing some of the up-to-date criminals in Europe did was to wear rubber gloves so that they would leave no prints. But you can't work very well with rubber gloves. Last fall in Paris I heard of a fellow who had given the police a lot of trouble. He never left a mark, or at least it was no good if he did. He painted his hands lightly with a liquid rubber which he had invented himself. It did all that rubber gloves would do and yet left him the free use of his fingers with practically the same keenness of touch. Fletcher, whatever is at the bottom of this affair, I feel sure right now that you have to deal with no ordinary criminal."

"Do you suppose there are any relatives besides those we know of?" I asked Kennedy when Fletcher had left to summon the servants.

"No," he replied, "I think not. Fletcher and Helen Bond, his second cousin, to whom he is engaged, are the only two."

Kennedy continued to study the library. He walked in and out of the doors and examined the windows and viewed the safe from all angles. "The old gentleman's bedroom is here," he said, indicating a door. "Now a good smart noise or perhaps even a light shining through the transom from the library might arouse him. Suppose he woke up suddenly and entered by this door. He would see the thief at work on the safe. Yes, that part of reconstructing the story is simple. But who was the intruder?"

Just then Fletcher returned with the servants. The questioning was long and tedious, and developed nothing except that the butler admitted that he was uncertain whether the windows in the library were locked. The gardener was very obtuse, but finally contributed one possibly important fact. He had noted in the morning that the back gate, leading into a disused road closer to the bay than the main highway in front of the house, was open. It was rarely used, and was kept closed only by an ordinary hook. Whoever had opened it had evidently forgotten to hook it. He had thought it strange that it was unhooked, and in closing it he had noticed in the mud of the roadway marks that seemed to indicate that an automobile had stood there.

After the servants had gone, Fletcher asked us to excuse him for a while, as he wished to run over to the Greenes', who lived across the bay. Miss Bond was completely prostrated by the death of her uncle, he said, and was in an extremely nervous condition. Meanwhile if we found any need of a machine we might use his uncle's, or in fact anything around the place.

"Walter," said Craig, when Fletcher had gone, "I want to run back to town to-night, and I have something I'd like to have you do, too."

We were soon speeding back along the splendid road to Long Island City, while he laid out our programme.

"You go down to the *Star* office," he said, "and look through all the clippings on the whole Fletcher family. Get a complete story of the life of Helen Bond, too—what she has done in society, with whom she has been seen mostly, whether she has made any trips abroad, and whether she has ever been engaged—you know, anything likely to be significant. I'm going up to the apartment to get my camera and then to the laboratory to get some rather bulky paraphernalia I want to take out to Fletcherwood. Meet me at the Columbus Circle station at, say half-past-ten."

So we separated. My search revealed the fact that Miss Bond had always been intimate with the ultra-fashionable set, had spent last summer in Europe, a good part of the time in Switzerland and Paris with the Greenes. As far as I could find out she had never been reported engaged, but plenty of fortunes as well as foreign titles had been flitting about the ward of the steel-magnate.

Craig and I met at the appointed time. He had a lot of paraphernalia with him, and it did not add to our comfort as we sped back, but it wasn't much over half an hour before we again found ourselves nearing Great Neck.

Instead of going directly back to Fletcherwood, however, Craig had told the chauffeur to stop at the plant of the local electric light and power company, where he asked if he might see the record of the amount of current used the night before.

The curve sprawled across the ruled surface of the sheet by the automatic registering-needle was irregular, showing the ups and downs of the current, rising sharply from sundown and gradually declining after nine o'clock, as the lights went out. Somewhere between eleven and twelve o'clock, however, the irregular fall of the curve was broken by a quite noticeable upward twist.

Craig asked the men if that usually happened. They were quite sure that the curve as a rule went gradually down until twelve o'clock, when the power was shut off. But they did not see anything remarkable in it. "Oh, I suppose some of the big houses had guests," volunteered the foreman, "and just to show off the place perhaps they turned on all the lights. I don't know, sir, what it was, but it couldn't have been a heavy drain, or we would have noticed it at the time, and the lights would all have been dim."

"Well," said Craig, "just watch and see if it occurs again to-night about the same time."

"All right, sir."

"And when you close down the plant for the night, will you bring the record card up to Fletcherwood?" asked Craig, slipping a bill into the pocket of the foreman's shirt.

"I will, and thank you, sir."

It was nearly half-past eleven when Craig had got his apparatus set up in the library at Fletcherwood. Then he unscrewed all the bulbs from the chandelier in the library and attached in their places connections with the usual green silk-covered flexible wire rope. These were then joined up to a little instrument which to me looked like a drill. Next he muffled the drill with a wad of felt and applied it to the safe door.

I could hear the dull tat-tat of the drill. Going into the bedroom and closing the door, I found that it was still audible to me, but an old man, inclined to deafness and asleep, would scarcely have been awakened by it. In about ten minutes Craig displayed a neat little hole in the safe door opposite the one made by the cracksman in the combination.

"I'm glad you're honest," I said, "or else we might be afraid of you—perhaps even make you prove an alibi for last night's job?"

He ignored my bantering and said in a tone such as he might have used before a class of students in the gentle art of scientific safe-cracking: "Now if the power company's curve is just the same to-night as last night, that will show how the thing was done. I wanted to be sure of it, so I thought I'd try this apparatus which I smuggled in from Paris last year. I believe the old man happened to be wakeful and heard it."

Then he pried off the door of the interior compartment which had been jimmied open. "Perhaps we may learn something by looking at this door and studying the marks left by the jimmy, by means of this new instrument of mine," he said.

On the library table he fastened an arrangement with two upright posts supporting a dial which he called a "dynamometer." The uprights were braced in the back, and the whole thing reminded me of a miniature guillotine.

"This is my mechanical detective," said Craig proudly. "It was devised by Bertillon* himself, and he personally gave me permission to copy his own machine. You see, it is devised to measure pressure. Now let's take an ordinary jimmy and see just how much pressure it takes to duplicate those marks on this door."

Craig laid the piece of steel on the dynamometer in the position it had occupied in the safe, and braced it tightly. Then he took a jimmy and pressed on it with all his strength. The steel door was connected with the indicator, and the needle spun around until it indicated a pressure such as only a strong man could have exerted. Comparing the marks made in the steel in the experiment and by the safe-cracker, it was evident that no such pressure had been necessary. Apparently the lock on the door was only a trifling affair, and the steel itself was not very tough. The safe-makers had relied on the first line of defence to repel attack.

Craig tried again and again, each time using less force. At last he got a mark just about similar to the original marks on the steel.

---

* Alphonse Bertillon (1853–1914) was a French police officer who invented a system of measurements (anthropometry) that could be used to identify persons brought into police custody (known eventually as "Bertillonage"). The system was highly successful in an era before fingerprinting and was widely adopted. He did indeed adapt a dynamometer (a device first commercially manufactured in 1881) to determine the pressure used in forcing an object, such as a door.

"Well, well, what do you think of that?" he exclaimed reflectively. "A child could have done that part of the job."

Just then the lights went off for the night. Craig lighted the oil-lamp, and sat in silence until the electric light plant foreman appeared with the card-record, which showed a curve practically identical with that of the night before.

A few moments later Professor Fletcher's machine came up the driveway, and he joined us with a worried and preoccupied look on his face that he could not conceal. "She's terribly broken up by the suddenness of it all," he murmured as he sank into an armchair. "The shock has been too much for her. In fact, I hadn't the heart to tell her anything about the robbery, poor girl." Then in a moment he asked, "Any more clues yet, Kennedy?"

"Well, nothing of first importance. I have only been trying to reconstruct the story of the robbery so that I can reason out a motive and a few details; then when the real clues come along we won't have so much ground to cover. The cracksman was certainly clever. He used an electric drill to break the combination and ran it by the electric light current."

"Whew!" exclaimed the professor, "is that so? He must have been above the average. That's interesting."

"By the way, Fletcher," said Kennedy, "I wish you would introduce me to your fiancée to-morrow. I would like to know her."

"Gladly," Fletcher replied, "only you must be careful what you talk about. Remember, the death of uncle has been quite a shock to her—he was her only relative besides myself."

"I will," promised Kennedy, "and by the way, she may think it strange that I'm out here at a time like this. Perhaps you had better tell her I'm a nerve specialist or something of that sort—anything not to connect me with the robbery, which you say you haven't told her about."

The next morning found Kennedy out bright and early, for

he had not had a very good chance to do anything during the night except reconstruct the details. He was now down by the back gate with his camera, where I found him turning it end-down and photographing the road. Together we made a thorough search of the woods and the road about the gate, but could discover absolutely nothing.

After breakfast I improvised a dark room and developed the films, while Craig went down the back lane along the shore "looking for clues," as he said briefly. Toward noon he returned, and I could see that he was in a brown study.* So I said nothing, but handed him the photographs of the road. He took them and laid them down in a long line on the library floor. They seemed to consist of little ridges of dirt on either side of a series of regular round spots, some of the spots very clear and distinct on the sides, others quite obscure in the centre. Now and then where you would expect to see one of the spots, just for the symmetry of the thing, it was missing. As I looked at the line of photographs on the floor I saw that they were a photograph of the track made by the tire of an automobile, and I suddenly recalled what the gardener had said.

Next Craig produced the results of his morning's work, which consisted of several dozen sheets of white paper, carefully separated into three bundles. These he also laid down in long lines on the floor, each package in a separate line. Then I began to realise what he was doing, and became fascinated in watching him on his hands and knees eagerly scanning the papers and comparing them with the photographs. At last he gathered up two of the sets of papers very decisively and threw them away. Then he shifted the third set a bit, and laid it closely parallel to the photographs.

---

* "Gloomy meditations" in the words of Samuel Johnson. The phrase is recorded to have been used as early as 1555, according to the *Oxford English Dictionary*.

"Look at these, Walter," he said. "Now take this deep and sharp indentation. Well, there's a corresponding one in the photograph. So you can pick them out one for another. Now here's one missing altogether on the paper. So it is in the photograph."

Almost like a schoolboy in his glee, he was comparing the little round circles made by the metal insertions in an "anti-skid" automobile tire. Time and again I had seen imprints like that left in the dust and grease of an asphalted street or the mud of a road. It had never occurred to me that they might be used in any way. Yet here Craig was, calmly tracing out the similarity before my very eyes, identifying the marks made in the photograph with the prints left on the bits of paper.

As I followed him, I had a most curious feeling of admiration for his genius. "Craig," I cried, "that's the thumb print of an automobile."

"There speaks the yellow journalist," he answered merrily. "'Thumb Print System Applied to Motor Cars'—I can see the Sunday feature story you have in your mind with that headline already. Yes, Walter, that's precisely what this is. The Berlin police have used it a number of times with the most startling results."*

"But, Craig," I exclaimed suddenly, "the paper prints, where did you get them? What machine is it?"

"It's one not very far from here," he answered sententiously, and I saw he would say nothing more that might fix a false suspicion on anyone. Still, my curiosity was so great that if there had been an opportunity I certainly should have tried out his plan on all the cars in the Fletcher garage.

---

* Sherlock Holmes used tire prints (referred to as "tyre-prints") to catch a killer in "The Adventure of the Priory School" (1904) and claimed to be familiar with forty-two distinct impressions left by different types of tires. Of course, Holmes was referring to bicycle tires.

Kennedy would say nothing more, and we ate our luncheon in silence. Fletcher, who had decided to lunch with the Greenes, called Kennedy up on the telephone to tell him it would be all right for him to call on Miss Bond later in the afternoon.

"And I may bring over the apparatus I once described to you to determine just what her nervous condition is?" he asked. Apparently the answer was yes, for Kennedy hung up the receiver with a satisfied, "Good-bye."

"Walter, I want you to come along with me this afternoon as my assistant. Remember I'm now Dr. Kennedy, the nerve specialist, and you are Dr. Jameson, my colleague, and we are to be in consultation on a most important case."

"Do you think that's fair?" I asked hotly—"to take that girl off her guard, to insinuate yourself into her confidence as a medical adviser, and worm out of her some kind of fact incriminating someone? I suppose that's your plan, and I don't like the ethics, or rather the lack of ethics, of the thing."

"Now think a minute, Walter. Perhaps I am wrong; I don't know. Certainly I feel that the end will justify the means. I have an idea that I can get from Miss Bond the only clue that I need, one that will lead straight to the criminal. Who knows? I have a suspicion that the thing I'm going to do is the highest form of your so-called ethics. If what Fletcher tells us is true that girl is going insane over this thing. Why should she be so shocked over the death of an uncle she did not live with? I tell you she knows something about this case that it is necessary for us to know, too. If she doesn't tell someone, it will eat her mind out. I'll add a dinner to the box of cigars we have already bet on this case that what I'm going to do is for the best—for her best."

Again I yielded, for I was coming to have more and more faith in the old Kennedy I had seen made over into a first-class detective, and together we started for the Greenes', Craig carrying something in one of those long black handbags which physicians use.

Fletcher met us on the driveway. He seemed to be very much affected, for his face was drawn, and he shifted from one position to another nervously, from which we inferred that Miss Bond was feeling worse. It was late afternoon, almost verging on twilight, as he led us through the reception-hall and thence onto a long porch overlooking the bay and redolent with honeysuckle.

Miss Bond was half reclining in a wicker chair as we entered. She started to rise to greet us, but Fletcher gently restrained her, saying, as he introduced us, that he guessed the doctors would pardon any informality from an invalid.

Fletcher was a pretty fine fellow, and I had come to like him; but I soon found myself wondering what he had ever done to deserve winning such a girl as Helen Bond. She was what I should describe as the ideal type of "new" woman,—tall and athletic, yet without any affectation of mannishness. The very first thought that struck me was the incongruousness of a girl of her type suffering from an attack of "nerves," and I felt sure it must be as Craig had said, that she was concealing a secret that was having a terrible effect on her. A casual glance might not have betrayed the true state of her feelings, for her dark hair and large brown eyes and the tan of many suns on her face and arms betokened anything but the neurasthenic. One felt instinctively that she was, with all her athletic grace, primarily a womanly woman.

The sun sinking toward the hills across the bay softened the brown of her skin and, as I observed by watching her closely, served partially to conceal the nervousness which was wholly unnatural in a girl of such poise. When she smiled there was a false note in it; it was forced and it was sufficiently evident to me that she was going through a mental hell of conflicting emotions that would have killed a woman of less self-control.

I felt that I would like to be in Fletcher's shoes—doubly so when, at Kennedy's request, he withdrew, leaving me to witness the torture of a woman of such fine sensibilities, already hunted remorselessly by her own thoughts.

Still, I will give Kennedy credit for a tactfulness that I didn't know the old fellow possessed. He carried through the preliminary questions very well for a pseudo-doctor, appealing to me as his assistant on inconsequential things that enabled me to "save my face" perfectly. When he came to the critical moment of opening the black bag, he made a very appropriate and easy remark about not having brought any sharp shiny instruments or nasty black drugs.

"All I wish to do, Miss Bond, is to make a few simple little tests of your nervous condition. One of them we specialists call reaction time, and another is a test of heart action. Neither is of any seriousness at all, so I beg of you not to become excited, for the chief value consists in having the patient perfectly quiet and normal. After they are over I think I'll know whether to prescribe absolute rest or a visit to Newport."

She smiled languidly, as he adjusted a long, tightly fitting rubber glove on her shapely forearm and then encased it in a larger, absolutely inflexible covering of leather. Between the rubber glove and the leather covering was a liquid communicating by a glass tube with a sort of dial. Craig had often explained to me how the pressure of the blood was registered most minutely on the dial, showing the varied emotions as keenly as if you had taken a peep into the very mind of the subject. I think the experimental psychologists called the thing a "plethysmograph."*

---

* A device for measuring the volume of fluids in blood vessels or air in lungs. It continues to be used to determine penile arousal in connection with alleged sexual offences (e.g., pedophilia). A plethysmograph served the same purpose, while a sphygmograph recorded the strength and rate of the subject's pulse. As indicated in a note on page 25 above, devices to detect and record emotions were of great interest at the time but highly suspect.

Then he had an apparatus which measured "association time." The essential part of this instrument was the operation of a very delicate stop-watch, and this duty was given to me. It was nothing more nor less than measuring the time that elapsed between his questions to her and her answers, while he recorded the actual questions and answers and noted the results which I worked out. Neither of us was unfamiliar with the process, for when we were in college these instruments were just coming into use in America. Kennedy had never let his particular branch of science narrow him, but had made a practice of keeping abreast of all the important discoveries and methods in other fields. Besides, I had read articles about the chronoscope,* the plethysmograph, the sphygmograph, and others of the new psychological instruments. Craig carried it off, however, as if he did that sort of thing as an every-day employment.

"Now, Miss Bond," he said, and his voice was so reassuring and persuasive that I could see she was not made even a shade more nervous by our simple preparations, "the game—it is just like a children's parlour game—is just this: I will say a word— take 'dog,' for instance. You are to answer back immediately the first word that comes into your mind suggested by it—say 'cat.' I will say 'chain,' for example, and probably you will answer 'collar,' and so on. Do you catch my meaning? It may seem ridiculous, no doubt, but before we are through I feel sure you'll see how valuable such a test is, particularly in a simple case of nervousness such as yours."

I don't think she found any sinister interpretation in his words, but I did, and if ever I wanted to protest it was then, but my voice seemed to stick in my throat.

He was beginning. It was clearly up to me to give in and not

---

* An instrument for measuring very short intervals of time.

interfere. As closely as I was able I kept my eyes riveted on the watch and other apparatus, while my ears and heart followed with mingled emotions the low, musical voice of the girl.

I will not give all the test, for there was much of it, particularly at the start, that was in reality valueless, since it was merely leading up to the "surprise tests." From the colourless questions Kennedy suddenly changed. It was done in an instant, when Miss Bond had been completely disarmed and put off her guard.

"Night," said Kennedy. "Day," came back the reply from Miss Bond.

"Automobile." "Horse."

"Bay." "Beach."

"Road." "Forest."

"Gate." "Fence."

"Path." "Shrubs."

"Porch." "House."

Did I detect or imagine a faint hesitation?

"Window." "Curtain."

Yes, it was plain that time. But the words followed one another in quick succession. There was no rest. She had no chance to collect herself. I noted the marked difference in the reaction time and, in my sympathy, damned this cold, scientific third degree.

"Paris." "France."

"Quartier Latin." "Students."

"Apaches." Craig gave it its Gallicised pronunciation, "Apash." "Really, Dr. Kennedy," she said, "there is nothing I can associate with them—well, yes, *les vaches*, I believe. You had better count that question out. I've wasted a good many seconds."

"Very well, let us try again," he replied with a forced unconcern, though the answer seemed to interest him, for "*les vaches*" meant "the cows," otherwise known as the police.

No lawyer could have revelled in an opportunity for putting leading questions more ruthlessly than did Kennedy. He snapped out his words sharply and unexpectedly.

"Chandelier." "Light."

"Electric light," he emphasised. "Broadway," she answered, endeavouring to force a new association of ideas to replace one which she strove to conceal.

"Safe." "Vaults." Out of the corner of my eye I could see that the indicator showed a tremendously increased heart action. As for the reaction time, I noted that it was growing longer and more significant. Remorselessly he pressed his words home. Mentally I cursed him.

"Rubber." "Tire."

"Steel." "Pittsburg," she cried at random.

"Strong-box." No answer.

"Lock." Again no answer. He hurried his words. I was leaning forward, tense with excitement and sympathy.

"Key." Silence and a fluttering of the blood-pressure indicator.

"Will."

As the last word was uttered her air of frightened defiance was swept away. With a cry of anguish, she swayed to her feet. "No, no, doctor, you must not, you must not," she cried with outstretched arms. "Why do you pick out those words of all others? Can it be—" If I had not caught her I believe she would have fainted.*

The indicator showed a heart alternately throbbing with feverish excitement and almost stopping with fear. What would Kennedy do next, I wondered, determined to shut him off as soon as I possibly could. From the moment I had seen her I had

---

* The pioneering psychologist Carl G. Jung, in 1910, described a very similar use of the association method in detecting a crime. See "The Association Method," first published in *American Journal of Psychology* 31, 219–69.

been under her spell. Mine should have been Fletcher's place, I knew, though I cannot but say that I felt a certain grim pleasure in supporting even momentarily such a woman in her time of need.

"Can it be that you have guessed what no one in the world, no, not even dear old Jack, dreams? Oh, I shall go mad, mad, mad!"

Kennedy was on his feet in an instant, advancing toward her. The look in his eyes was answer enough for her. She knew that he knew, and she paled and shuddered, shrinking away from him.

"Miss Bond," he said in a voice that forced attention—it was low and vibrating with feeling—"Miss Bond, have you ever told a lie to shield a friend?"

"Yes," she said, her eyes meeting his.

"So can I," came back the same tense voice, "when I know the truth about that friend."

Then for the first time tears came in a storm. Her breath was quick and feverish. "No one will ever believe, no one will understand. They will say that I killed him, that I murdered him."

Through it all I stood almost speechless, puzzled. What did it all mean?

"No," said Kennedy, "no, for they will never know of it."

"Never know?"

"Never—if in the end justice is done. Have you the will? Or did you destroy it?"

It was a bold stroke.

"Yes. No. Here it is. How could I destroy it, even though it was burning out my very soul?"

She literally tore the paper from the bosom of her dress and cast it from her in horror and terror.

Kennedy picked it up, opened it, and glanced hurriedly

through it. "Miss Bond," he said, "Jack shall never know a word of this. I shall tell him that the will has been found unexpectedly in John Fletcher's desk among some other papers. Walter, swear on your honour as a gentleman that this will was found in old Fletcher's desk."

"Dr. Kennedy, how can I ever thank you?" she exclaimed, sinking wearily down into a chair and pressing her hands to her throbbing forehead.

"By telling me just how you came by this will, so that when you and Fletcher are married I may be as good a friend, without suspicion, to you as I am to him. I think a full confession would do you good, Miss Bond. Would you prefer to have Dr. Jameson not hear it?"

"No, he may stay."

"This much I know, Miss Bond. Last summer in Paris with the Greenes you must have chanced to hear of Pillard, the Apache,* one of the most noted cracksmen the world has ever produced. You sought him out. He taught you how to paint your fingers with a rubber composition, how to use an electric drill, how to use the old-fashioned jimmy. You went down to Fletcherwood by the back road about a quarter after eleven the night of the robbery in the Greenes' little electric runabout. You entered the library by an unlocked window, you coupled your drill to the electric light connections of the chandelier. You had to work quickly, for the power would go off at midnight, yet you could not do the job later, when they were sleeping more soundly, for the very same reason."

It was uncanny as Kennedy rushed along in his reconstruction of the scene, almost unbelievable. The girl watched him, fascinated.

---

* A member of the criminal underworld of Paris. The term was first applied in 1904 in an article in a French newspaper that likened the criminal to a member of the well-known Native American tribe.

"John Fletcher was wakeful that night. Somehow or other he heard you at work. He entered the library and, by the light streaming from his bedroom, he saw who it was. In anger he must have addressed you, and his passion got the better of his age—he fell suddenly on the floor with a stroke of apoplexy. As you bent over him he died. But why did you ever attempt so foolish an undertaking? Didn't you know that other people knew of the will and its terms, that you were sure to be traced out in the end, if not by friends, by foes? How did you suppose you could profit by destroying the will, of which others knew the provisions?"

Any other woman than Helen Bond would have been hysterical long before Kennedy had finished pressing home remorselessly one fact after another of her story. But, with her, the relief now after the tension of many hours of concealment seemed to nerve her to go to the end and tell the truth.

What was it? Had she some secret lover for whom she had dared all to secure the family fortune? Or was she shielding someone dearer to her than her own reputation? Why had Kennedy made Fletcher withdraw?

Her eyes dropped and her breast rose and fell with suppressed emotion. Yet I was hardly prepared for her reply when at last she slowly raised her head and looked us calmly in the face.

"I did it because I loved Jack."

Neither of us spoke. I, at least, had fallen completely under the spell of this masterful woman. Right or wrong, I could not restrain a feeling of admiration and amazement.

"Yes," she said as her voice thrilled with emotion, "strange as it may sound to you, it was not love of self that made me do it. I was, I am madly in love with Jack. No other man has ever inspired such respect and love as he has. His work in the university I have fairly gloated over. And yet—and yet, Dr. Kennedy, can you not see that I am different from Jack? What would I do with the income of the wife of even the dean of the new school? The annuity provided for me in that will is paltry. I need millions. From the tiniest baby I have been reared that way. I have always expected this fortune. I have been given everything I wanted. But it is different when one is married—you must have your own money. I need a fortune, for then I could have the town house, the country house, the yacht, the motors, the clothes, the servants that I need—they are as much a part of my life as your profession is of yours. I must have them.

"And now it was all to slip from my hands. True, it was to go in such a way by this last will as to make Jack happy in his new school. I could have let that go, if that was all. There are other fortunes that have been laid at my feet. But I wanted Jack, and I knew Jack wanted me. Dear boy, he never could realise how utterly unhappy intellectual poverty would have made me and how my unhappiness would have reacted on him in the end. In reality this great and beneficent philanthropy was finally to blight both our love and our lives.

"What was I to do? Stand by and see my life and my love ruined or refuse Jack for the fortune of a man I did not love? Helen Bond is not that kind of a woman, I said to myself. I consulted the greatest lawyer I knew. I put a hypothetical case to him, and asked his opinion in such a way as to make him believe he was advising me how to make an unbreakable will. He told me of provisions and clauses to avoid, particularly in making benefactions. That was what I wanted to know. I would put one of those clauses in my uncle's will. I practised uncle's writing till I was as good a forger of that clause as anyone could have become. I had picked out the very words in his own handwriting to practise from.

"Then I went to Paris and, as you have guessed, learned how

to get things out of a safe like that of uncle's. Before God, all I planned to do was to get that will, change it, replace it, and trust that uncle would never notice the change. Then when he was gone, I would have contested the will. I would have got my full share either by court proceedings or by settlement out of court. You see, I had planned it all out. The school would have been founded—I, we would have founded it. What difference, I said, did thirty millions or fifty millions make to an impersonal school, a school not yet even in existence? The twenty million dollars or so difference, or even half of it, meant life and love to me.

"I had planned to steal the cash in the safe, anything to divert attention from the will and make it look like a plain robbery. I would have done the altering of the will that night and have returned it to the safe before morning. But it was not to be. I had almost opened the safe when my uncle entered the room. His anger completely unnerved me, and from the moment I saw him on the floor to this I haven't had a sane thought. I forgot to take the cash, I forgot everything but that will. My only thought was that I must get it and destroy it. I doubt if I could have altered it with my nerves so upset. There, now you have my whole story. I am at your mercy."

"No," said Kennedy, "believe me, there is a mental statute of limitations that as far as Jameson and myself are concerned has already erased this affair. Walter, will you find Fletcher?"

I found the professor pacing up and down the gravel walk impatiently.

"Fletcher," said Kennedy, "a night's rest is all Miss Bond really needs. It is simply a case of overwrought nerves, and it will pass off of itself. Still, I would advise a change of scene as soon as possible. Good afternoon, Miss Bond, and my best wishes for your health."

"Good afternoon, Dr. Kennedy. Good afternoon, Dr. Jameson."

I for one was glad to make my escape.

A half-hour later, Kennedy, with well-simulated excitement, was racing me in the car up to the Greenes' again. We literally burst unannounced into the tête-à-tête on the porch.

"Fletcher, Fletcher," cried Kennedy, "look what Walter and I have just discovered in a tin strong-box poked off in the back of your uncle's desk!"

Fletcher seized the will and by the dim light that shone through from the hall read it hastily. "Thank God," he cried; "the school is provided for as I thought."

"Isn't it glorious!" murmured Helen.

True to my instinct I muttered, "Another good newspaper yarn killed."

III
THE BACTERIOLOGICAL DETECTIVE

Kennedy was deeply immersed in writing a lecture on the chemical compositions of various bacterial toxins and antitoxins, a thing which was as unfamiliar to me as Kamchatka, but as familiar to Kennedy as Broadway and Forty-second Street.

"Really," he remarked, laying down his fountain-pen and lighting his cigar for the hundredth time, "the more one thinks of how the modern criminal misses his opportunities the more astonishing it seems. Why do they stick to pistols, chloroform, and prussic acid when there is such a splendid assortment of refined methods they might employ?"

"Give it up, old man," I replied helplessly, "unless it is because they haven't any imagination. I hope they don't use them. What would become of my business if they did? How would you ever get a really dramatic news feature for the *Star* out of such a thing? 'Dotted line marks route taken by fatal germ; cross indicates spot where antitoxin attacked it'—ha! ha! not much for the yellow journals in that, Craig."

"To my mind, Walter, it would be the height of the dramatic—far more dramatic than sending a bullet into a man. Any fool can shoot a pistol or cut a throat, but it takes brains to be up-to-date."

"It may be so," I admitted, and went on reading, while Kennedy scratched away diligently on his lecture. I mention this conversation both because it bears on my story, by a rather peculiar coincidence, and because it showed me a new side of Kennedy's amazing researches. He was as much interested in bacteria as in chemistry, and the story is one of bacteria.

It was perhaps a quarter of an hour later when the buzzer on our hall door sounded. Imagine my surprise on opening the door to discover the slight figure of what appeared to be a most fascinating young lady who was heavily veiled. She was in a state almost bordering on hysteria, as even I, in spite of my usual obtuseness, noticed.

"Is Professor Kennedy in?" she inquired anxiously.

"Yes, ma'am," I replied, opening the door into our study.

She advanced toward him, repeating her inquiry.

"I am Professor Kennedy. Pray be seated," he said.

The presence of a lady in our apartment was such a novelty that really I forgot to disappear, but busied myself straightening the furniture and opening a window to allow the odour of stale tobacco to escape.

"My name is Eveline Bisbee," she began. "I have heard, Professor Kennedy, that you are an adept at getting at the bottom of difficult mysteries."

"You flatter me," he said in acknowledgment. "Who was so foolish as to tell you that?"

"A friend who has heard of the Kerr Parker case," she replied.

"I beg your pardon," I interrupted, "I didn't mean to intrude. I think I'll go out. I'll be back in an hour or two."

"Please, Mr. Jameson—it is Mr. Jameson, is it not?"

I bowed in surprise.

"If it is possible I wish you would stay and hear my story. I am told that you and Professor Kennedy always work together."

It was my turn to be embarrassed by the compliment.

"Mrs. Fletcher, of Great Neck," she explained, "has told me. I believe Professor Kennedy performed a great service for the Fletchers, though I do not know what it was. At any rate, I have come to you with my case, in which I have small hope of obtaining assistance unless you can help me. If Professor Kennedy cannot solve it—well, I'm afraid nobody can." She paused a moment, then added, "No doubt you have read of the death of my guardian the other day."

Of course we had. Who did not know that "Jim" Bisbee, the southern California oil-magnate, had died suddenly of typhoid fever* at the private hospital of Dr. Bell, where he had been taken from his magnificent apartment on Riverside Drive? Kennedy and I had discussed it at the time. We had commented on the artificiality of the twentieth century. No longer did people have homes; they had apartments, I had said. They didn't fall ill in the good old-fashioned way any more, either—in fact, they even hired special rooms to die in. They hired halls for funeral services. It was a wonder that they didn't hire graves. It was all part of our twentieth-century break-up of tradition. Indeed we did know about the death of Jim Bisbee. But there was nothing mysterious about it. It was just typical in all its surroundings of the first decade of the twentieth century in a great, artificial city—a lonely death of a great man surrounded by all that money could buy.

We had read of his ward, too, the beautiful Miss Eveline Bisbee, a distant relation. As under the heat of the room and her excitement, she raised her veil, we were very much interested

---

* Epidemic typhoid is caused by the spread of the *Rickettsia prowazekii* bacterium, usually through lice and, prior to the discovery of vaccines, had a high fatality rate. A major outbreak occurred in 1903 in Ithaca, New York, and no other took place subsequently in the United States until 1915, when typhoid broke out in New York, and the subsequent year, when a typhoid epidemic was reported in Illinois.

in her. At least, I am sure that even Kennedy had by this time completely forgotten the lecture on toxins.

"There is something about my guardian's death," she began in a tremulous voice, "that I am sure will bear investigating. It may be only a woman's foolish fears, but—but—I haven't told this to a soul till now, except Mrs. Fletcher. My guardian had, as you perhaps know, spent his summer at his country place at Bisbee Hall, New Jersey, from which he returned rather suddenly about a week ago. Our friends thought it merely a strange whim that he should return to the city before the summer was fairly over, but it was not. The day before he returned, his gardener fell sick of typhoid. That decided Mr. Bisbee to return to the city on the following day. Imagine his consternation to find his valet stricken the very next morning. Of course he motored to New York immediately, then he wired to me at Newport, and together we opened his apartment at the Louis Quinze.

"But that was not to be the end of it. One after another, the servants at Bisbee Hall were taken with the disease until five of them were down. Then came the last blow—Mr. Bisbee fell a victim in New York. So far I have been spared. But who knows how much longer it will last? I have been so frightened that I haven't eaten a meal in the apartment since I came back. When I am hungry I simply steal out to a hotel—a different one every time. I never drink any water except that which I have surreptitiously boiled in my own room over a gas-stove. Disinfectants and germicides have been used by the gallon, and still I don't feel safe. Even the health authorities don't remove my fears. With my guardian's death I had begun to feel that possibly it was over. But no. This morning another servant who came up from the hall last week was taken sick, and the doctor pronounces that typhoid, too. Will I be the next? Is it just a foolish fear? Why does it pursue us to New York? Why didn't it stop at Bisbee Hall?"

I don't think I ever saw a living creature more overcome by horror, by an invisible, deadly fear. That was why it was doubly horrible in a girl so attractive as Eveline Bisbee. As I listened I felt how terrible it must be to be pursued by such a fear. What must it be to be dogged by a disease as relentlessly as the typhoid had dogged her? If it had been some great, but visible, tangible peril how gladly I could have faced it merely for the smile of a woman like this. But it was a peril that only knowledge and patience could meet. Instinctively I turned toward Kennedy, my own mind being an absolute blank.

"Is there anyone you suspect of being the cause of such an epidemic?" he asked. "I may as well tell you right now that I have already formed two theories—one perfectly natural, the other diabolical. Tell me everything."

"Well, I had expected to receive a fortune of one million dollars, free and clear, by his will, and this morning I am informed by his lawyer, James Denny, that a new will had been made. It is still one million. But the remainder, instead of going to a number of charities in which he was known to be interested, goes to form a trust fund for the Bisbee School of Mechanical Arts, of which Mr. Denny is the sole trustee. Of course, I do not know much about my guardian's interests while he was alive, but it strikes me as strange that he should have changed so radically, and, besides, the new will is so worded that if I die without children my million also goes to this school—location unnamed. I can't help wondering about it all."

"Why should you wonder—at least what other reasons have you for wondering?"

"Oh, I can't express them. Maybe after all it's only a woman's silly intuition. But often I have thought in the past few days about this illness of my guardian. It was so queer. He was always so careful. And you know the rich don't often have typhoid."

"You have no reason to suppose that it was not typhoid fever of which he died?"

She hesitated. "No," she replied, "but if you had known Mr. Bisbee you would think it strange, too. He had a horror of infectious and contagious diseases. His apartment and his country home were models. No sanitarium could have been more punctilious. He lived what one of his friends called an antiseptic life. Maybe I am foolish, but it keeps getting closer and closer to me now, and—well, I wish you'd look into the case. Please set my mind at rest and assure me that nothing is wrong, that it *is* all natural."

"I will help you, Miss Bisbee. To-morrow night I want to take a trip quietly to Bisbee Hall. You will see that it is all right, that I have the proper letters so I can investigate thoroughly!"

I shall never forget the mute and eloquent thanks with which she said good night after Kennedy's promise.

Kennedy sat with his eyes shaded under his hand for fully an hour after she had left. Then he suddenly jumped up. "Walter," he said, "let us go over to Dr. Bell's. I know the head nurse there. We may possibly learn something."

As we sat in the waiting-room with its thick Oriental rugs and handsome mahagony furniture, I found myself going back to our conversation of the early evening. "By Jove, Kennedy, you were right," I exclaimed. "If there is anything in this germ-plot idea of hers it is, indeed the height of the dramatic—it is diabolical. No ordinary mortal would ever be capable of it."

Just then the head nurse came in, a large woman breathing of germlessness and cheerfulness in her spotless uniform. We were shown every courtesy. There was, in fact, nothing to conceal. The visit set at rest my last suspicion that perhaps Jim Bisbee had been poisoned by a drug. The charts of his temperature and the sincerity of the nurse were absolutely convincing. It had really been typhoid, and there was nothing to be gained by pursuing that inquiry further.

Back at the apartment, Craig began packing his suit-case with the few things he would need for a journey. "I'm going out to Bisbee Hall to-morrow for a few days, Walter, and if you could find it convenient to come along I should like to have your assistance."

"To tell you the truth, Craig, I am afraid to go," I said.

"You needn't be. I'm going down to the army post on Governor's Island first to be vaccinated against typhoid. Then I am going to wait a few hours till it takes effect before going. It's the only place in the city where one can be inoculated against it, so far as I know. While three inoculations are really best, I understand that one is sufficient for ordinary protection, and that is all we shall need, if any."

"You're sure of it?"

"Almost positive."

"Very well, Craig. I'll go."

Down at the army post the next morning we had no difficulty in being inoculated against the disease. The work of immunising our army was going on at that time, and several thousands of soldiers in various parts of the country had already been vaccinated, with the best of results.[*]

"Do many civilians come over to be vaccinated?" asked Craig of Major Carrol, the surgeon in charge.

"Not many, for very few have heard of it," he replied.

---

[*] Sir Almroth Edward Wright, a British bacteriologist, is credited as the first to develop an effective typhoid vaccine, in 1896. The vaccine was used successfully by the British during the Boer War, and at the outset of World War I, Wright convinced the British Army that the troops being sent to the Western Front should also be vaccinated. As a result, the British Army was the only combatant to have its troops fully immunized against typhoid fever when the war started. In 1909, US Army physician Frederick F. Russell adopted Wright's typhoid vaccine, and in 1911, the Army began the process of complete immunization of its military force.

"I suppose you keep a record of them."

"Only their names—we can't follow them up outside the army, to see how it works. Still, when they come to us as you and Mr. Jameson have done we are perfectly willing to vaccinate them. The Army Medical Corps takes the position that if it is good for the army it is good for civil life, and as long as only a few civilians apply we are perfectly willing to do it for a fee covering the cost."

"And would you let me see the list?"

"Certainly. You may look it over in a moment."

Kennedy glanced hurriedly through the short list of names, pulled out his notebook, made an entry, and handed the list back. "Thank you, Major."

Bisbee Hall was a splendid place set in the heart of a great park whose area was measured by square miles rather than by acres. But Craig did not propose to stay there, for he arranged for accommodations in a near-by town, where we were to take our meals also. It was late when we arrived, and we spent a restless night, for the inoculation "took." It wasn't any worse than a light attack of the grippe, and in the morning we were both all right again, after the passing of what is called the "negative phase." I, for one, felt much safer.

The town was very much excited over the epidemic at the hall, and if I had been wondering why Craig wanted me along my wonder was soon set at rest. He had me scouring the town and country looking up every case or rumour of typhoid for miles around. I made the local, weekly paper my headquarters, and the editor was very obliging. He let me read all his news letters from his local correspondent at every crossroads. I waded through accounts of new calves and colts, new fences and barns, who "Sundayed" with his brother, etc., and soon had a list of all the cases in that part of the country. It was not a long one, but it was scattered. After I had traced them out, following Kennedy's instructions, they showed nothing, except that they were unrelated to the epidemic at the hall.

Meanwhile, Kennedy was very busy there. He had a microscope and slides and test-tubes and chemicals for testing things, and I don't know what all, for there was not time to initiate me into all the mysteries. He tested the water from the various driven wells and in the water-tank, and the milk from the cows; he tried to find out what food had come in from outside, though there was practically none, for the hall was self-supporting. There was no stone he left unturned.

When I rejoined him that night he was clearly perplexed. I don't think my report decreased his perplexity, either.

"There is only one thing left as far as I have been able to discover after one day's work," he said, after we had gone over our activities for the day. "Jim Bisbee never drank the water from his own wells. He always drank a bottled water shipped down from a camp of his in New York State, where he had a remarkable mountain spring. I tested a number of the full bottles at the hall, but they were perfectly pure. There wasn't a trace of the bacillus typhosus in any of them. Then it occurred to me that, after all, that was not the thing to do. I should test the empty ones. But there weren't any empty ones. They told me they had all been taken down to the freight station yesterday to be shipped back to the camp. I hope they haven't gone yet. Let's drive around and see if they are there."

The freight-master was just leaving, but when he learned we were from the hall he consented to let us examine the bottles. They were corked and in wooden cases, which protected them perfectly. By the light of the station lamps and the aid of a pocket lens, Kennedy examined them on the outside and satisfied himself that after being replaced in the wooden cases the bottles themselves had not been handled.

"Will you let me borrow some of these bottles to-night?" he asked the agent. "I'll give you my word that they will be returned safely to-morrow. If necessary, I'll get an order for them."

The station-agent reluctantly yielded, especially as a small green banknote figured in the transaction. Craig and I tenderly lifted the big bottles in their cases into our trap and drove back to our rooms in the hotel. It quite excited the hangers-on to see us drive up with a lot of empty five-gallon bottles and carry them up-stairs, but I had long ago given up having any fear of public opinion in carrying out anything Craig wanted.

In our room we worked far into the night. Craig carefully swabbed out the bottom and sides of each bottle by inserting a little piece of cotton on the end of a long wire. Then he squeezed the water out of the cotton swab on small glass slides coated with agar-agar, or Japanese seaweed, a medium in which germ-cultures multiply rapidly. He put the slides away in a little oven with an alcohol-lamp which he had brought along, leaving them to remain over night at blood heat.

I had noticed all this time that he was very particular not to touch any of the bottles on the outside. As for me, I wouldn't have touched them for the world. In fact, I was getting so I hesitated to touch anything. I was almost afraid to breathe, though I knew there was no harm in that. However, it was not danger of infection in touching the bottles that made Craig so careful. He had noted, in the dim light of the station lamps, what seemed to be finger-marks on the bottles, and they had interested him, in fact, had decided him on a further investigation of the bottles.

"I am now going to bring out these very faint finger-prints on the bottles," remarked Craig, proceeding with his examination in the better light of our room. "Here is some powder known to chemists as 'grey powder'—mercury and chalk. I sprinkle it over the faint markings, so, and then I brush it off with a camel's-hair brush lightly. That brings out the imprint much more clearly, as you can see. For instance, if you place your dry thumb on a piece of white paper you leave no visible impression. If grey powder is sprinkled over the spot and then brushed off a distinct impression is seen. If the impression of the fingers is left on something soft, like wax, it is often best to use printers' ink to bring out the ridges and patterns of the finger-marks. And so on for various materials. Quite a science has been built up around finger-prints.*

"I wish I had that enlarging camera which I have in my laboratory. However, my ordinary camera will do, for all I want is to preserve a record of these marks, and I can enlarge the photographs later. In the morning I will photograph these marks and you can do the developing of the films. To-night we'll improvise the bathroom as a dark room and get everything ready so that we can start in bright and early."

We were, indeed, up early. One never has difficulty in getting up early in the country: it is so noisy, at least to a city-bred man. City noise at five A. M. is sepulchral silence compared with bucolic activity at that hour.

There were a dozen negatives which I set about developing after Craig had used up all our films. Meanwhile, he busied himself adjusting his microscope and test-tubes and getting the agar slides ready for examination.

Shirt-sleeves rolled up, I was deeply immersed in my work

---

* Indeed it had: Although the efficacy of fingerprints had been known since the mid-nineteenth century, it wasn't until 1892 that Sir Francis Galton published a book on fingerprinting that pointed out the individuality and uniqueness of fingerprints. In 1901, Sir Edward Henry, an inspector general of police in Bengal, adopted a system of classifying fingerprints that was soon adopted worldwide. In 1905, the United States adopted fingerprinting for military identification, and in 1908, the first official "fingerprint card" was adopted. The information that fingerprints were unique provided some help to law enforcement in confirming the identity of a suspect, but until the development of a database of fingerprints, they were useless as means of detection of a criminal.

when I heard a shout in the next room, and the bathroom door flew open.

"Confound you, Kennedy, do you want to ruin these films?" I cried.

He shut the door with a bang. "Hurrah, Walter!" he exclaimed. "I think I have it, at last. I have just found some most promising colonies of the bacilli on one of my slides."

I almost dropped the pan of acid I was holding, in my excitement. "Well," I said, concealing my own surprise, "I've found out something, too. Every one of these finger-prints so far is from the same pair of hands."

We scarcely ate any breakfast, and were soon on our way up to the hall. Craig had provided himself at the local stationer's with an inking-pad, such as is used for rubber stamps. At the hall he proceeded to get the impressions of the fingers and thumbs of all the servants.

It was quite a long and difficult piece of work to compare the finger-prints we had taken with those photographed, in spite of the fact that writers descant on the ease with which criminals are traced by this system devised by the famous Galton. However, we at last finished the job between us; or rather Craig finished it, with an occasional remark from me. His dexterity amazed me; it was more than mere book knowledge.

For a moment we sat regarding each other hopelessly. None of the finger-prints taken at the hall tallied with the photographed prints. Then Craig rang for the housekeeper, a faithful old soul whom even the typhoid scare could not budge from her post.

"Are you sure I have seen all the servants who were at the hall while Mr. Bisbee was here?" asked Craig.

"Why, no, sir—you didn't ask that. You asked to see all who are here now. There is only one who has left, the cook, Bridget

Fallon. She left a couple of days ago—said she was going back
to New York to get another job. Glad enough I was to get rid of
her, too, for she was drunk most of the time after the typhoid
appeared."

"Well, Walter, I guess we shall have to go back to New York
again, then," exclaimed Kennedy. "Oh, I beg pardon, Mrs.
Rawson, for interrupting. Thank you ever so much. Where did
Bridget come from?"

"She came well recommended, sir. Here is the letter in my
writing-desk. She had been employed by the Caswell-Joneses at
Shelter Island before she came here."

"I may keep this letter?" asked Craig, scanning it quickly.

"Yes."

"By the way, where were the bottles of spring water kept?"

"In the kitchen."

"Did Bridget take charge of them?"

"Yes."

"Did Mr. Bisbee have any guests during the last week that he
was here?"

"Only Mr. Denny one night."

"H'm!" exclaimed Craig. "Well, it will not be so hard for us
to unravel this matter, after all, when we get back to the city. We
must make that noon train, Walter. There is nothing more for
us to do here."

Emerging from the "Tube" at Ninth Street, Craig hustled
me into a taxicab, and in almost no time we were at police
headquarters.

Fortunately, Inspector Barney O'Connor was in and in
an amiable mood, too, for Kennedy had been careful that the
Central Office received a large share of credit for the Kerr
Parker case. Craig sketched hastily the details of this new case.
O'Connor's face was a study. His honest blue Irish eyes fairly

bulged in wonder, and when Craig concluded with a request for help I think O'Connor would have given him anything in the office, just to figure in the case.

"First, I want one of your men to go to the surrogate's office and get the original of the will. I shall return it within a couple of hours—all I want to do is to make a photographic copy. Then another man must find this lawyer, James Denny, and in some way get his finger-prints—you must arrange that yourself. And send another fellow up to the employment offices on Fourth Avenue and have him locate this cook, Bridget Fallon. I want her finger-prints, too. Perhaps she had better be detained, for I don't want her to get away. Oh, and say, O'Connor, do you want to finish this case up like the crack of a whip to-night?"

"I'm game, sir. What of it?"

"Let me see. It is now four o'clock. If you can get hold of all these people in time I think I shall be ready for the final scene to-night—say, at nine. You know how to arrange it. Have them all present at my laboratory at nine, and I promise we shall have a story that will get into the morning papers with leaded type on the front page."

"Now, Walter," he added, as we hurried down to the taxicab again, "I want you to drop off at the Department of Health with this card to the commissioner. I believe you know Dr. Leslie. Well, ask him if he knows anything about this Bridget Fallon. I will go on up-town to the laboratory and get my apparatus ready. You needn't come up till nine, old fellow, for I shall be busy till then, but be sure when you come that you bring the record of this Fallon woman if you have to beg, borrow, or steal it."

I didn't understand it, but I took the card and obeyed implicitly. It is needless to say that I was keyed up to the greatest pitch of excitement during my interview with the health commissioner, when I finally got in to see him. I hadn't talked to him long before a great light struck me, and I began to see what Craig was driving at. The commissioner saw it first.

"If you don't mind, Mr. Jameson," he said, after I had told him as much of my story as I could, "will you call up Professor Kennedy and tell him I'd like very much to be present to-night myself?"

"Certainly I will," I replied, glad to get my errand done in first-class fashion in that way.

Things must have been running smoothly, for while I was sitting in our apartment after dinner, impatiently waiting for half-past eight, when the commissioner had promised to call for me and go up to the laboratory, the telephone rang. It was Craig.

"Walter, might I ask a favour of you?" he said. "When the commissioner comes ask him to stop at the Louis Quinze and bring Miss Bisbee up, too. Tell her it is important. No more now. Things are going ahead fine."

Promptly at nine we were assembled, a curious crowd. The health commissioner and the inspector, being members of the same political party, greeted each other by their first names. Miss Bisbee was nervous, Bridget was abusive, Denny was sullen. As for Kennedy, he was, as usual, as cool as a lump of ice. And I—well, I just sat on my feelings to keep myself quiet.

At one end of the room Craig had placed a large white sheet such as he used in his stereopticon lectures, while at the top of the tier of seats that made a sort of little amphitheatre out of his lecture-room his stereopticon sputtered.

"Moving pictures to-night, eh?" said Inspector O'Connor.

"Not exactly," said Craig, "though—yes, they will be moving in another sense. Now, if we are all ready, I'll switch off the electric lights."

The calcium sputtered some more, and a square of light was thrown on the sheet.

Kennedy snapped a little announcer such as lecturers use. "Let me invite your attention to these enlargements of finger-prints," he began, as a huge thumb appeared on the screen. "Here we have a series of finger-prints which I will show one after another slowly. They are all of the fingers of the same person, and they were found on some empty bottles of spring water used at Bisbee Hall during the two weeks previous to the departure of Mr. Bisbee for New York.

"Here are, in succession, the finger-prints of the various servants employed about the house—and of a guest," added Craig, with a slight change of tone. "They differ markedly from the finger-prints on the glass," he continued, as one after another appeared, "all except this last one. That is identical. It is, Inspector, what we call a composite type of finger-print—in this case a combination of what is called the 'loop' and 'whorl' types."

No sound broke the stillness save the sputtering of the oxygen on the calcium of the stereopticon.

"The owner of the fingers from which these prints were made is in this room. It was from typhoid germs on these fingers that the fever was introduced into the drinking water at Bisbee Hall."

Kennedy paused to emphasise the statement, then continued.

"I am now going to ask Dr. Leslie to give us a little talk on a recent discovery in the field of typhoid fever—you understand, Commissioner, what I mean, I believe?"

"Perfectly. Shall I mention names?"

"No, not yet."

"Well," began Dr. Leslie, clearing his throat, "within the past year or two we have made a most weird and startling discovery in typhoid fever. We have found what we now call 'typhoid carriers'—persons who do not have the disease themselves, perhaps never have had it, but who are literally living test-tubes of the typhoid bacillus.* It is positively uncanny. Everywhere they go they scatter the disease. Down at the department we have the records of a number of such instances, and our men in the research laboratories have come to the conclusion that, far from being of rare occurrence, these cases are comparatively common. I have in mind one particular case of a servant girl, who, during the past five or six years, has been employed in several families.

"In every family typhoid fever has later broken out. Experts have traced out at least thirty cases and several deaths due to this one person. In another case we found an epidemic up in Harlem to be due to a typhoid carrier on a remote farm in Connecticut. This carrier, innocently enough, it is true, contaminated the milk-supply coming from that farm. The result was over fifty cases of typhoid here in this city.

"However, to return to the case of the servant I have mentioned. Last spring we had her under surveillance, but as there was no law by which we could restrain her permanently she is still at large. I think one of the Sunday papers at the time had an account of her—they called her 'Typhoid Bridget,' and in red ink she was drawn across the page in gruesome fashion, frying the skulls of her victims in a frying-pan over a roaring fire. That particular typhoid carrier, I understand—"

---

* It was not until 1907, with the identification of the infamous "Typhoid Mary" Mallon, a cook in a private home, as the source of an outbreak of typhoid fever, that American health officials realized that a healthy person, with no symptoms of the disease, could be a deadly carrier. Initially confined to a government-controlled island in the Bronx's East River, after a legal struggle, Mallon won her release, agreeing to give up her occupation and report to health officials regularly. She proceeded to vanish for five years. When an epidemic of typhus broke out in a Manhattan maternity hospital, Mallon was discovered working there as a cook under a false name. Mallon was again confined to the island facility, where she remained until her death twenty-three years later. The infection of forty-seven people, three of whom died, is attributed to Mallon. At the time of Mallon's first arrest, there was at least one other known carrier in New York, a man called Tony Labella, who had caused more cases of typhoid (120) and deaths (7) than Mallon. Labella fled to New Jersey and was no more cooperative than Mallon.

"Excuse me, Commissioner, if I interrupt, but I think we have carried this part of the programme far enough to be absolutely convincing," said Craig. "Thank you very much for the clear way in which you have put it."

Craig snapped the announcer, and a letter appeared on the screen. He said nothing, but let us read it through:

To whom it may concern:

This is to certify that Bridget Fallon has been employed in my family at Shelter Island for the past season and that I have found her a reliable servant and an excellent cook.

A. St. John Caswell-Jones.

"Before God, Mr. Kennedy, I'm innocent," screeched Bridget. "Don't have me arrested. I'm innocent. I'm innocent."

Craig gently, but firmly, forced her back into her chair.

Again the announcer snapped. This time the last page of Mr. Bisbee's will appeared on the sheet, ending with his signature and the witnesses.

"I'm now going to show these two specimens of handwriting very greatly enlarged," he said, as the stereopticon plates were shifted again.

"An author of many scientific works, Dr. Lindsay Johnson, of London, has recently elaborated a new theory with regard to individuality in handwriting.* He maintains that in certain diseases a person's pulse beats are individual, and that no one

---

* Dr. G. Lindsay Johnson, a "well-known ophthalmic surgeon and author of many scientific works," reported his experiment, described in the succeeding paragraph, to the *Daily Mail* in 1910. Much of this paragraph is copied directly from the article, which was reprinted widely (for example, in the *Western Argus* [Kalgoorlie, Australia] on October 18, 1910).

suffering from any such disease can control, even for a brief space of time, the frequency or peculiar irregularities of his heart's action, as shown by a chart recording his pulsation. Such a chart is obtained for medical purposes by means of a sphygmograph, an instrument fitted to the patient's forearm and supplied with a needle, which can be so arranged as to record automatically on a prepared sheet of paper the peculiar force and frequency of the pulsation. Or the pulsation may be simply observed in the rise and fall of a liquid in a tube. Dr. Johnson holds the opinion that a pen in the hand of a writer serves, in a modified degree, the same end as the needle in the first-named form of the sphygmograph and that in such a person's handwriting one can see by projecting the letters, greatly magnified, on a screen, the scarcely perceptible turns and quivers made in the lines by the spontaneous action of that person's peculiar pulsation.

"To prove this, the doctor carried out an experiment at Charing Cross Hospital. At his request a number of patients suffering from heart and kidney diseases wrote the Lord's Prayer in their ordinary handwriting. The different manuscripts were then taken and examined microscopically. By throwing them, highly magnified, on a screen, the jerks or involuntary motions due to the patient's peculiar pulsations were distinctly visible. The handwriting of persons in normal health, says Dr. Johnson, does not always show their pulse beats. What one can say, however, is that when a document, purporting to be written by a certain person, contains traces of pulse beats and the normal handwriting of that person does not show them, then clearly that document is a forgery.

"Now, in these two specimens of handwriting which we have enlarged it is plain that the writers of both of them suffered from a certain peculiar disease of the heart. Moreover, I am prepared to show that the pulse beats exhibited in the case of certain

"A higher court than those of New York has passed judgment on this astounding criminal."

pen-strokes in one of these documents are exhibited in similar strokes in the other. Furthermore, I have ascertained from his family physician, whose affidavit I have here, that Mr. Bisbee did not suffer from this or any other form of heart disease. Mr. Caswell-Jones, in addition to wiring me that he refused to write Bridget Fallon a recommendation after the typhoid broke out in his country house, also says he does not suffer from heart disease in any form. From the tremulous character of the letters and figures in both these documents, which when magnified is the more easily detected, I therefore conclude that both are forgeries, and I am ready to go farther and say that they are forgeries from the same hand.

"It usually takes a couple of weeks after infection for typhoid to develop, a time sufficient in itself to remove suspicion from acts which might otherwise be scrutinised very carefully if happening immediately before the disease developed. I may add, also, that it is well known that stout people do very poorly when they contract typhoid, especially if they are old. Mr. Bisbee was both stout and old. To contract typhoid was for him a virtual death-warrant. Knowing all these facts, a certain person purposely sought out a crafty means of introducing typhoid fever into Mr. Bisbee's family. That person, furthermore, was inoculated against typhoid three times during the month before the disease was devilishly and surreptitiously introduced into Bisbee Hall, in order to protect himself or herself should it become necessary for that person to visit Bisbee Hall. That person, I believe, is the one who suffered from an aneurism of the heart, the writer, or rather the forger, of the two documents I have shown, by one of which he or she was to profit greatly by the death of Mr. Bisbee and the founding of an alleged school in a distant part of the country—a subterfuge, if you recall, used in at least one famous case for which the convicted perpetrator is now under a life sentence in Sing Sing.

"I will ask Dr. Leslie to take this stethoscope and examine the hearts of everyone in the room and tell me whether there is anyone here suffering from an aneurism."

The calcium light ceased to sputter. One person after another was examined by the health commissioner. Was it merely my imagination, or did I really hear a heart beating with wild leaps as if it would burst the bonds of its prison and make its escape if possible? Perhaps it was only the engine of the commissioner's machine out on the campus driveway. I don't know. At any rate, he went silently from one to the other, betraying not even by his actions what he discovered with the stethoscope. The suspense was terrible. I felt Miss Bisbee's hand involuntarily grasp my arm convulsively. Without disturbing the silence, I reached a glass of water standing near me on Craig's lecture-table and handed it to her.

The commissioner was bending over the lawyer, trying to adjust the stethoscope better to his ears. The lawyer's head was resting heavily on his hand, and he was heaped up in an awkward position in the cramped lecture-room seat. It seemed an age as Dr. Leslie tried to adjust the stethoscope. Even Craig felt the excitement. While the commissioner hesitated, Kennedy reached over and impatiently switched on the electric light in full force.

As the light flooded the room, blinding us for the instant, the large form of Dr. Leslie stood between us and the lawyer.

"What does the stethoscope tell you, Doctor?" asked Craig, leaning forward expectantly. He was as unprepared for the answer as any of us.

"It tells me that a higher court than those of New York has passed judgment on this astounding criminal. The aneurism has burst."

I felt a soft weight fall on my shoulder. The morning *Star* did not have the story, after all. I missed the greatest "scoop" of my life seeing Eveline Bisbee safely to her home after she had recovered from the shock of Denny's exposure and punishment.

IV

THE DEADLY TUBE

"For Heaven's sake, Gregory, what is the matter?" asked Craig Kennedy as a tall, nervous man stalked into our apartment one evening. "Jameson, shake hands with Dr. Gregory. What's the matter, Doctor? Surely your X-ray work hasn't knocked you out like this?"

The doctor shook hands with me mechanically. His hand was icy. "The blow has fallen," he exclaimed, as he sank limply into a chair and tossed an evening paper over to Kennedy.

In red ink on the first page, in the little square headed "Latest News," Kennedy read the caption, "Society Woman Crippled for Life by X-Ray Treatment."

"A terrible tragedy was revealed in the suit begun to-day," continued the article, "by Mrs. Huntington Close against Dr. James Gregory, an X-ray specialist with offices at——Madison Avenue, to recover damages for injuries which Mrs. Close alleges she received while under his care. Several months ago she began a course of X-ray treatment to remove a birthmark on her neck. In her complaint Mrs. Close alleges that Dr. Gregory has carelessly caused X-ray dermatitis,[*] a skin disease of cancerous nature, and that she has also been rendered a nervous wreck through the effects of the rays. Simultaneously with filing the suit she left home and entered a private hospital. Mrs. Close is one of the most popular hostesses in the smart set, and her loss will be keenly felt."

"What am I to do, Kennedy?" asked the doctor imploringly. "You remember I told you the other day about this case—that there was something queer about it, that after a few treatments I was afraid to carry on any more and refused to do so? She really has dermatitis and nervous prostration, exactly as she alleges in her complaint. But, before Heaven, Kennedy, I can't see how she could possibly have been so affected by the few treatments I gave her. And to-night, just as I was leaving the office, I received a telephone call from her husband's attorney, Lawrence, very kindly informing me that the case would be pushed to the limit. I tell you, it looks black for me."

"What can they do?"

"Do? Do you suppose any jury is going to take enough expert testimony to outweigh the tragedy of a beautiful woman? Do? Why, they can ruin me, even if I get a verdict of acquittal. They can leave me with a reputation for carelessness that no mere court decision can ever overcome."

"Gregory, you can rely on me," said Kennedy. "Anything I can do to help you I will gladly do. Jameson and I were on the point of going out to dinner. Join us, and after that we will go down to your office and talk things over."

---

[*] More commonly known today as radiation dermatitis, the condition occurs in almost 95 percent of patients undergoing radiotherapy. The symptoms commonly display within 90 days of the therapy but in cases of chronic radiation dermatitis may occur as long as ten years after the radiation exposure. Acute reactions can impact quality of life and compromise the delivery of cancer treatment; of course, they can also result in significant disfigurement.

"You are really too kind," murmured the doctor. The air of relief that was written on his face was pathetically eloquent.

"Now not a word about the case till we have had dinner," commanded Craig. "I see very plainly that you have been worrying about the blow for a long time. Well, it has fallen. The next thing to do is to look over the situation and see where we stand."

Dinner over, we rode down-town in the subway, and Gregory ushered us into an office-building on Madison Avenue, where he had a very handsome suite of several rooms. We sat down in his waiting-room to discuss the affair.

"It is indeed a very tragic case," began Kennedy, "almost more tragic than if the victim had been killed outright. Mrs. Huntington Close is—or rather I suppose I should say was—one of the famous beauties of the city. From what the paper says, her beauty has been hopelessly ruined by this dermatitis, which, I understand, Doctor, is practically incurable."

Dr. Gregory nodded, and I could not help following his eyes as he looked at his own rough and scarred hands.

"Also," continued Craig, with his eyes half closed and his finger-tips together, as if he were taking a mental inventory of the facts in the case, "her nerves are so shattered that she will be years in recovering, if she ever recovers."

"Yes," said the doctor simply. "I myself, for instance, am subject to the most unexpected attacks of neuritis. But, of course, I am under the influence of the rays fifty or sixty times a day, while she had only a few treatments at intervals of many days."

"Now, on the other hand," resumed Craig, "I know you, Gregory, very well. Only the other day, before any of this came out, you told me the whole story with your fears as to the outcome. I know that that lawyer of Close's has been keeping this thing hanging over your head for a long time. And I also know that you are one of the most careful X-ray operators in the city.

If this suit goes against you, one of the most brilliant men of science in America will be ruined. Now, having said this much, let me ask you to describe just exactly what treatments you gave Mrs. Close."

The doctor led us into his X-ray room adjoining. A number of X-ray tubes were neatly put away in a great glass case, and at one end of the room was an operating-table with an X-ray apparatus suspended over it. A glance at the room showed that Kennedy's praise was not exaggerated.

"How many treatments did you give Mrs. Close?" asked Kennedy.

"Not over a dozen, I should say," replied Gregory. "I have a record of them and the dates, which I will give you presently. Certainly they were not numerous enough or frequent enough to have caused a dermatitis such as she has. Besides, look here. I have an apparatus which, for safety to the patient, has few equals in the country. This big lead-glass bowl, which is placed over my X-ray tube when in use, cuts off the rays at every point except exactly where they are needed."

He switched on the electric current, and the apparatus began to sputter. The pungent odour of ozone from the electric discharge filled the room. Through the lead-glass bowl I could see the X-ray tube inside suffused with its peculiar, yellowish-green light, divided into two hemispheres of different shades. That, I knew, was the cathode ray, not the X-ray, for the X-ray itself, which streams outside the tube, is invisible to the human eye. The doctor placed in our hands a couple of fluoroscopes, an apparatus by which X-rays can be detected. It consists simply of a closed box with an opening to which the eyes are placed. The opposite end of the box is a piece of board coated with a salt such as platino-barium cyanide. When the X-ray strikes this salt it makes it glow, or fluoresce, and objects held between the

X-ray tube and the fluoroscope cast shadows according to the density of the parts which the X-rays penetrate.

With the lead-glass bowl removed, the X-ray tube sent forth its wonderful invisible radiation and made the back of the fluoroscope glow with light. I could see the bones of my fingers as I held them up between the X-ray tube and the fluoroscope. But with the lead-glass bowl in position over the tube, the fluoroscope was simply a black box into which I looked and saw nothing. So very little of the radiation escaped from the bowl that it was negligible—except at one point where there was an opening in the bottom of the bowl to allow the rays to pass freely through exactly on the spot on the patient where they were to be used.

"The dermatitis, they say, has appeared all over her body, particularly on her head and shoulders," added Dr. Gregory. "Now I have shown you my apparatus to impress on you how really impossible it would have been for her to contract it from her treatments here. I've made thousands of exposures with never an X-ray burn before—except to myself. As for myself, I'm as careful as I can be, but you can see I am under the rays very often, while the patient is only under them once in a while."

To illustrate his care he pointed out to us a cabinet directly back of the operating-table, lined with thick sheets of lead. From this cabinet he conducted most of his treatments as far as possible. A little peep-hole enabled him to see the patient and the X-ray apparatus, while an arrangement of mirrors and a fluorescent screen enabled him to see exactly what the X-rays were disclosing, without his leaving the lead-lined cabinet.

"I can think of no more perfect protection for either patient or operator," said Kennedy admiringly. "By the way, did Mrs. Close come alone?"

"No, the first time Mr. Close came with her. After that, she came with her French maid."

The next day we paid a visit to Mrs. Close herself at the private hospital. Kennedy had been casting about in his mind for an excuse to see her, and I had suggested that we go as reporters from the *Star*. Fortunately after sending up my card on which I had written Craig's name we were at length allowed to go up to her room.

We found the patient reclining in an easy chair, swathed in bandages, a wreck of her former self. I felt the tragedy keenly. All that social position and beauty had meant to her had been suddenly blasted.

"You will pardon my presumption," began Craig, "but, Mrs. Close, I assure you that I am actuated by the best of motives. We represent the New York *Star*—"

"Isn't it terrible enough that I should suffer so," she interrupted, "but must the newspapers hound me, too?"

"I beg your pardon, Mrs. Close," said Craig, "but you must be aware that the news of your suit of Dr. Gregory has now become public property. I couldn't stop the *Star*, much less the other papers, from talking about it. But I can and will do this, Mrs. Close. I will see that justice is done to you and all others concerned. Believe me, I am not here as a yellow journalist to make newspaper copy out of your misfortune. I am here to get at the truth sympathetically. Incidentally, I may be able to render you a service, too."

"You can render me no service except to expedite the suit against that careless doctor—I hate him."

"Perhaps," said Craig. "But suppose someone else should be proved to have been really responsible? Would you still want to press the suit and let the guilty person escape?"

She bit her lip. "What is it you want of me?" she asked.

"I merely want permission to visit your rooms at your home and to talk with your maid. I do not mean to spy on you, far from it; but consider, Mrs. Close, if I should be able to get at the bottom of this thing, find out the real cause of your misfortune, perhaps show that you are the victim of a cruel wrong rather than of carelessness, would you not be willing to let me go ahead? I am frank to tell you that I suspect there is more to this affair than you yourself have any idea of."

"No, you are mistaken, Mr. Kennedy. I know the cause of it. It was my love of beauty. I couldn't resist the temptation to get rid of even a slight defect. If I had left well enough alone I should not be here now. A friend recommended Dr. Gregory to my husband, who took me there. My husband wishes me to remain at home, but I tell him I feel more comfortable here in the hospital. I shall never go to that house again—the memory of the torture of sleepless nights in my room there when I felt my good looks going, going"—she shuddered—"is such that I can never forget it. He says I would be better off there, but no, I cannot go. Still," she continued wearily, "there can be no harm in your talking to my maid."

Kennedy noted attentively what she was saying. "I thank you, Mrs. Close," he replied. "I am sure you will not regret your permission. Would you be so kind as to give me a note to her?"

She rang, dictated a short note to a nurse, signed it, and languidly dismissed us.

I don't know that I ever felt as depressed as I did after that interview with one who had entered a living death to ambition, for while Craig had done all the talking I had absorbed nothing but depression. I vowed that if Gregory or anybody else was responsible I would do my share toward bringing on him retribution.

The Closes lived in a splendid big house in the Murray Hill section. The presentation of the note quickly brought Mrs. Close's maid down to us. She had not gone to the hospital because Mrs. Close had considered the services of the trained nurses quite sufficient.

Yes, the maid had noticed how her mistress had been failing, had noticed it long ago, in fact almost at the time when she had begun the X-ray treatment. She had seemed to improve once when she went away for a few days, but that was at the start, and directly after her return she grew worse again, until she was no longer herself.

"Did Dr. Gregory, the X-ray specialist, ever attend Mrs. Close at her home, in her room?" asked Craig.

"Yes, once, twice, he call, but he do no good," she said with her French accent.

"Did Mrs. Close have other callers?"

"But, m'sieur, everyone in society has many. What does m'sieur mean?"

"Frequent callers—a Mr. Lawrence, for instance?"

"Oh, yes, Mr. Lawrence frequently."

"When Mr. Close was at home?"

"Yes, on business and on business, too, when he was not at home. He is the attorney, m'sieur."

"How did Mrs. Close receive him?"

"He is the attorney, m'sieur," Marie repeated persistently.

"And he, did he always call on business?"

"Oh, yes, always on business, but—well, madame, she was a very beautiful woman. Perhaps he like beautiful women—*eh bien*? That was before the Doctor Gregory treated madame. After the doctor treated madame M'sieur Lawrence do not call so often. That's all."

"Are you thoroughly devoted to Mrs. Close? Would you do a favour for her?" asked Craig point-blank.

"Sir, I would give my life, almost, for madame. She was always so good to me."

"I don't ask you to give your life for her, Marie," said Craig, "but you can do her a great service, a very great service."

"I will do it."

"To-night," said Craig, "I want you to sleep in Mrs. Close's room. You can do so, for I know that Mr. Close is living at the St. Francis Club until his wife returns from the sanitarium. To-morrow morning come to my laboratory"—Craig handed her his card—"and I will tell you what to do next. By the way, don't say anything to anyone in the house about it, and keep a sharp watch on the actions of any of the servants who may go into Mrs. Close's room."

"Well," said Craig, "there is nothing more to be done immediately." We had once more regained the street and were walking up-town. We walked in silence for several blocks.

"Yes," mused Craig, "there is something you can do, after all, Walter. I would like you to look up Gregory and Close and Lawrence. I already know something about them. But you can find out a good deal with your newspaper connections. I would like to have every bit of scandal that has ever been connected with them, or with Mrs. Close, or," he added significantly, "with any other woman. It isn't necessary to say that not a breath of it must be published—yet."

I found a good deal of gossip, but very little of it, indeed, seemed to me at the time to be of importance. Dropping in at the St. Francis Club, where I had some friends, I casually mentioned the troubles of the Huntington Closes. I was surprised to learn that Close spent little of his time at the club, none at home, and only dropped into the hospital to make formal inquiries as to his wife's condition. It then occurred to me to drop into the office of *Society Squibs*, whose editor I had long known. The editor told me, with that nameless look of the cynical scandalmonger, that if I wanted to learn anything about Huntington

Close I had best watch Mrs. Frances Tulkington, a very wealthy Western divorcée about whom the smart set were much excited, particularly those whose wealth made it difficult to stand the pace of society as it was going at present.

"And before the tragedy," said the editor with another nameless look, as if he were imparting a most valuable piece of gossip, "it was the talk of the town, the attention that Close's lawyer was paying to Mrs. Close. But to her credit let me say that she never gave us a chance to hint at anything, and—well, you know us; we don't need much to make snappy society news."

The editor then waxed even more confidential, for if I am anything at all, I am a good listener, and I have found that often by sitting tight and listening I can get more than if I were a too-eager questioner.

"It really was a shame the way that man Lawrence played his game," he went on. "I understand that it was he who introduced Close to Mrs. T. They were both his clients. Lawrence had fought her case in the courts when she sued old Tulkington for divorce, and a handsome settlement he got for her, too. They say his fee ran up into the hundred thousands—contingent, you know. I don't know what his game was"—here he lowered his voice to a whisper—"but they say Close owes him a good deal of money. You can figure it out for yourself as you like. Now, I've told you all I know. Come in again, Jameson, when you want some more scandal, and remember me to the boys down on the *Star*."

The following day the maid visited Kennedy at his laboratory while I was reporting to him on the result of my investigations.

She looked worn and haggard. She had spent a sleepless night and begged that Kennedy would not ask her to repeat the experiment.

"I can promise you, Marie," he said, "that you will rest better to-night. But you must spend one more night in Mrs. Close's room. By the way, can you arrange for me to go through the room this morning when you go back?"

Marie said she could, and an hour or so later Craig and I quietly slipped into the Close residence under her guidance. He was carrying something that looked like a miniature barrel, and I had another package which he had given me, both carefully wrapped up. The butler eyed us suspiciously, but Marie spoke a few words to him and I think showed him Mrs. Close's note. Anyhow he said nothing.

Within the room that the unfortunate woman had occupied Kennedy took the coverings off the packages. It was nothing but a portable electric vacuum cleaner, which he quickly attached and set running. Up and down the floor, around and under the bed he pushed the cleaner. He used the various attachments to clean the curtains, the walls, and even the furniture. Particularly did he pay attention to the base board on the wall back of the bed. Then he carefully removed the dust from the cleaner and sealed it up in a leaden box.

He was about to detach and pack up the cleaner when another idea seemed to occur to him. "Might as well make a thorough job of it, Walter," he said, adjusting the apparatus again. "I've cleaned everything but the mattress and the brass bars behind the mattress on the bed. Now I'll tackle them. I think we ought to go into the suction-cleaning business—more money in it than in being a detective, I'll bet."

The cleaner was run over and under the mattress and along every crack and cranny of the brass bed. This done and this dust also carefully stowed away, we departed, very much to the mystification of Marie and, I could not help feeling, of other eyes that peered in through keyholes or cracks in doors.

"At any rate," said Kennedy exultingly, "I think we have stolen a march on them. I don't believe they were prepared for this, not at least at this stage in the game. Don't ask me any questions, Walter. Then you will have no secrets to keep if anyone should try to pry them loose. Only remember that this man Lawrence is a shrewd character."

The next day Marie came, looking even more careworn than before.

"What's the matter, mademoiselle?" asked Craig. "Didn't you pass a better night?"

"Oh, mon Dieu, I rest well, yes. But this morning, while I am at breakfast, Mr. Close send for me. He say that I am discharged. Some servant tell of your visit and he ver-ry angr-ry. And now what is to become of me—will madame his wife give a recommendation now?"

"Walter, we have been discovered," exclaimed Craig with considerable vexation. Then he remembered the poor girl who had been an involuntary sacrifice to our investigation. Turning to her he said: "Marie, I know several very good families, and I am sure you will not suffer for what you have done by being faithful to your mistress. Only be patient a few days. Go live with some of your folks. I will see that you are placed again."

The girl was profuse in her thanks as she dried her tears and departed.

"I hadn't anticipated having my hand forced so soon," said Craig after she had gone, leaving her address. "However, we are on the right track. What was it that you were going to tell me when Marie came in?"

"Something that may be very important, Craig," I said, "though I don't understand it myself. Pressure is being brought to bear on the *Star* to keep this thing out of the papers, or at least to minimise it."

"I'm not surprised," commented Craig. "What do you mean by pressure being brought?"

"Why, Close's lawyer, Lawrence, called up the editor this morning—I don't suppose that you know, but he has some connection with the interests which control the *Star*—and said that the activity of one of the reporters from the *Star*, Jameson by name, was very distasteful to Mr. Close and that this reporter was employing a man named Kennedy to assist him.

"I don't understand it, Craig," I confessed, "but here one day they give the news to the papers, and two days later they almost threaten us with suit if we don't stop publishing it."

"It is perplexing," said Craig, with the air of one who was not a bit perplexed, but rather enlightened.

He pulled down the district telegraph messenger lever three times, and we sat in silence for a while.

"However," he resumed, "I shall be ready for them to-night."

I said nothing. Several minutes elapsed. Then the messenger rapped on the door.

"I want these two notes delivered right away," said Craig to the boy; "here's a quarter for you. Now mind you don't get interested in a detective story and forget the notes. If you are back here quickly with the receipts I'll give you another quarter. Now scurry along."

Then, after the boy had gone, he said casually to me: "Two notes to Close and Gregory, asking them to be present with their attorneys to-night. Close will bring Lawrence, and Gregory will bring a young lawyer named Asche, a very clever fellow. The notes are so worded that they can hardly refuse the invitation."

Meanwhile I carried out an assignment for the *Star*, and telephoned my story in so as to be sure of being with Craig at the crucial moment. For I was thoroughly curious about his next move in the game. I found him still in his laboratory attaching two coils of thin wire to the connections on the outside of a queer-looking little black box.

"What's that?" I asked, eyeing the sinister-looking little box suspiciously. "An infernal machine? You're not going to blow the culprit into eternity, I hope."

"Never mind what it is, Walter. You'll find that out in due time. It may or it may not be an infernal machine—of a different sort than any you have probably ever heard of. The less you know now the less likely you are to give anything away by a look or an act. Come now, make yourself useful as well as ornamental. Take these wires and lay them in the cracks of the floor, and be careful not to let them show. A little dust over them will conceal them beautifully."

Craig now placed the black box back of one of the chairs well down toward the floor, where it could hardly have been perceived unless one were suspecting something of the sort. While he was doing so I ran the wires across the floor, and around the edge of the room to the door.

"There," he said, taking the wires from me. "Now I'll complete the job by carrying them into the next room. And while I'm doing it, go over the wires again and make sure they are absolutely concealed."

That night six men gathered in Kennedy's laboratory. In my utter ignorance of what was about to happen I was perfectly calm, and so were all the rest, except Gregory. He was easily the most nervous of us all, though his lawyer Asche tried repeatedly to reassure him.

"Mr. Close," began Kennedy, "if you and Mr. Lawrence will sit over here on this side of the room while Dr. Gregory and Mr. Asche sit on the opposite side with Mr. Jameson in the middle, I think both of you opposing parties will be better suited. For I apprehend that at various stages in what I am about to say both you, Mr. Close, and you, Dr. Gregory, will want to consult your attorneys. That, of course, would be embarrassing, if not impossible, should you be sitting near each other. Now, if we are ready, I shall begin."

Kennedy placed a small leaden casket on the table of his lecture hall. "In this casket," he commenced solemnly, "there is a certain substance which I have recovered from the dust swept up by a vacuum cleaner in the room of Mrs. Close."

One could feel the very air of the room surcharged with excitement. Craig drew on a pair of gloves and carefully opened the casket. With his thumb and forefinger he lifted out a glass tube and held it gingerly at arm's length. My eyes were riveted on it, for the bottom of the tube glowed with a dazzling point of light.

Both Gregory and his attorney and Close and Lawrence whispered to each other when the tube was displayed, as indeed they did throughout the whole exhibition of Kennedy's evidence.

"No infernal machine was ever more subtle," said Craig, "than the tube which I hold in my hand. The imagination of the most sensational writer of fiction might well be thrilled with the mysteries of this fatal tube and its power to work fearful deeds. A larger quantity of this substance in the tube would produce on me, as I now hold it, incurable burns, just as it did on its discoverer before his death.* A smaller amount, of course, would not act so quickly. The amount in this tube, if distributed about, would produce the burns inevitably, providing I remained near enough for a long-enough time."

---

* The discovery of radium in 1898 is generally credited to Pierre Curie (1859–1906) and his former student and wife Marie Skłodowska Curie (1867–1934). Pierre unfortunately died of a cracked skull from a street accident, but both the Curies experienced many radiation burns, and had Pierre not died accidentally, he would likely have eventually died from the effects of the cumulative radiation exposure (as did Marie, their daughter, and their daughter's husband).

Craig paused a moment to emphasise his remarks.

"Here in my hand, gentlemen, I hold the price of a woman's beauty."

He stopped again for several moments, then resumed.

"And now, having shown it to you, for my own safety I will place it back in its leaden casket."

Drawing off his gloves, he proceeded.

"I have found out by a cablegram to-day that seven weeks ago an order for one hundred milligrams of radium bromide at thirty-five dollars a milligram from a certain person in America was filled by a corporation dealing in this substance."

Kennedy said this with measured words, and I felt a thrill run through me as he developed his case.

"At that same time, Mrs. Close began a series of treatments with an X-ray specialist in New York," pursued Kennedy. "Now, it is not generally known outside scientific circles, but the fact is that in their physiological effects the X-ray and radium are quite one and the same. Radium possesses this advantage, however, that no elaborate apparatus is necessary for its use. And, in addition, the emanation from radium is steady and constant, whereas the X-ray at best varies slightly with changing conditions of the current and vacuum in the X-ray tube. Still, the effects on the body are much the same.

"A few days before this order was placed I recall the following despatch which appeared in the New York papers. I will read it:

"*'Liege, Belgium, Oct.—, 1910. What is believed to be the first criminal case in which radium figures as a death-dealing agent is engaging public attention at this university town. A wealthy old bachelor, Pailin by name, was found dead in his flat. A stroke of apoplexy was at first believed to have caused his death, but a close examination revealed a curious discolouration of his skin. A specialist called in to view the body gave as his opinion that the old man had been exposed for a long time to the emanations of X-ray or radium. The police theory is that M. Pailin was done to death by a systematic application of either X-rays or radium by a student in the university who roomed next to him. The student has disappeared.'*

"Now here, I believe, was the suggestion which this American criminal followed, for I cut it out of the paper rather expecting sooner or later that some clever person would act on it. I have thoroughly examined the room of Mrs. Close. She herself told me she never wanted to return to it, that her memory of sleepless nights in it was too vivid. That served to fix the impression that I had already formed from reading this clipping. Either the X-ray or radium had caused her dermatitis and nervousness. Which was it? I wished to be sure that I would make no mistake. Of course I knew it was useless to look for an X-ray machine in or near Mrs. Close's room. Such a thing could never have been concealed. The alternative? Radium! Ah! that was different. I determined on an experiment. Mrs. Close's maid was prevailed on to sleep in her mistress's room. Of course radiations of brief duration would do her no permanent harm, although they would produce their effect, nevertheless. In one night the maid became extremely nervous. If she had stayed under them several nights no doubt the beginning of a dermatitis would have affected her, if not more serious trouble. A systematic application, covering weeks and months, might in the end even have led to death.

"The next day I managed, as I have said, to go over the room thoroughly with a vacuum cleaner—a new one of my own which I had bought myself. But tests of the dust which I got from the floors, curtains, and furniture showed nothing at all. As a last thought I had, however, cleaned the mattress of the bed and the cracks and crevices in the brass bars. Tests of that dust showed it to be extremely radioactive. I had the dust dissolved, by a chemist who understands that sort of thing, recrystallised, and the radium salts were extracted from the refuse. Thus I found that I had recovered all but a very few milligrams of the radium that had been originally purchased in London. Here it is in this deadly tube in the leaden casket.

"It is needless to add that the night after I had cleaned out this deadly element the maid slept the sleep of the just—and would have been all right when next I saw her but for the interference of the unjust on whom I had stolen a march."

Craig paused while the lawyers whispered again to their clients. Then he continued: "Now three persons in this room had an opportunity to secrete the contents of this deadly tube in the crevices of the metal work of Mrs. Close's bed. One of these persons must have placed an order through a confidential agent in London to purchase the radium from the English Radium Corporation. One of these persons had a compelling motive, something to gain by using this deadly element.

"The radium in this tube in the casket was secreted, as I have said, in the metal work of Mrs. Close's bed, not in large enough quantities to be immediately fatal, but mixed with dust so as to produce the result more slowly but no less surely, and thus avoid suspicion. At the same time Mrs. Close was persuaded—I will not say by whom—through her natural pride, to take a course of X-ray treatment for a slight defect. That would further serve to divert suspicion. The fact is that a more horrible plot could hardly have been planned or executed. This person sought to ruin her beauty to gain a most selfish and despicable end."

Again Craig paused to let his words sink into our minds.

"Now I wish to state that anything you gentlemen may say will be used against you. That is why I have asked you to bring your attorneys. You may consult with them, of course, while I am getting ready my next disclosure."

As Kennedy had developed his points in the case I had been more and more amazed. But I had not failed to notice how keenly Lawrence was following him.

With half a sneer on his astute face, Lawrence drawled: "I cannot see that you have accomplished anything by this rather extraordinary summoning of us to your laboratory. The evidence is just as black against Dr. Gregory as before. You may think you're clever, Kennedy, but on the very statement of facts as you have brought them out there is plenty of circumstantial evidence against Gregory—more than there was before. As for anyone else in the room, I can't see that you have anything on us—unless perhaps this new evidence you speak of may implicate Asche, or Jameson," he added, including me in a wave of his hand, as if he were already addressing a jury. "It's my opinion that twelve of our peers would be quite as likely to bring in a verdict of guilty against them as against anyone else even remotely connected with this case, except Gregory. No, you'll have to do better than this in your next case, if you expect to maintain that so-called reputation of yours for being a professor of criminal science."

As for Close, taking his cue from his attorney, he scornfully added: "I came to find out some new evidence against the wretch who wrecked the beauty of my wife. All I've got is a tiresome lecture on X-rays and radium. I suppose what you say is true. Well, it only bears out what I thought before. Gregory treated my wife at home, after he saw the damage his office treatments had done. I guess he was capable of making a complete job out of it—covering up his carelessness by getting rid of the woman who was such a damning piece of evidence against his professional skill."

Never a shade passed Craig's face as he listened to this tirade. "Excuse me a moment," was all he said, opening the door to leave the room. "I have just one more fact to disclose. I will be back directly."

Kennedy was gone several minutes, during which Close and Lawrence fell to whispering behind their hands, with the assurance of those who believed that this was only Kennedy's method of admitting a defeat. Gregory and Asche exchanged a few words similarly, and it was plain that Asche was endeavouring to put a better interpretation on something than Gregory himself dared hope.

As Kennedy re-entered, Close was buttoning up his coat preparatory to leaving, and Lawrence was lighting a fresh cigar.

In his hand Kennedy held a notebook. "My stenographer writes a very legible shorthand; at least I find it so—from long practice, I suppose. As I glance over her notes I find many facts which will interest you later—at the trial. But—ah, here at the end—let me read:

> "'Well, he's very clever, but he has nothing against me, has he?'
>
> "'No, not unless he can produce the agent who bought the radium for you.'
>
> "'But he can't do that. No one could ever have recognised you on your flying trip to London disguised as a diamond merchant who had just learned that he could make his faulty diamonds good by applications of radium and who wanted a good stock of the stuff.'
>
> "'Still, we'll have to drop the suit against Gregory after all, in spite of what I said. That part is hopelessly spoiled.'

"'Yes, I suppose so. Oh, well, I'm free now. She can hardly help but consent to a divorce now, and a quiet settlement. She brought it on herself—we tried every other way to do it, but she—she was too good to fall into it. She forced us to it.'

"'Yes, you'll get a good divorce now. But can't we shut up this man Kennedy? Even if he can't prove anything against us, the mere rumour of such a thing coming to the ears of Mrs. Tulkington would be unpleasant.'

"'Go as far as you like, Lawrence. You know what the marriage will mean to me. It will settle my debts to you and all the rest.'

"'I'll see what I can do, Close. He'll be back in a moment.'"

Close's face was livid. "It's a pack of lies!" he shouted, advancing toward Kennedy, "a pack of lies! You are a fakir and a blackmailer. I'll have you in jail for this, by God—and you too, Gregory."

"One moment, please," said Kennedy calmly. "Mr. Lawrence, will you be so kind as to reach behind your chair? What do you find?"

Lawrence lifted up the plain black box and with it he pulled up the wires which I had so carefully concealed in the cracks of the floor.

"That," said Kennedy, "is a little instrument called the microphone. Its chief merit lies in the fact that it will magnify a sound sixteen hundred times, and carry it to any given point where you wish to place the receiver. Originally this device was invented for the aid of the deaf, but I see no reason why it should not be used to aid the law. One needn't eavesdrop at the keyhole with this little instrument about. Inside that box there is nothing but a series of plugs from which wires, much finer than a thread, are stretched taut. Yet a fly walking near it will make a noise as loud as a draft-horse. If the microphone is placed in any part of the room, especially if near the persons talking—even if they are talking in a whisper—a whisper such as occurred several times during the evening and particularly while I was in the next room getting the notes made by my stenographer—a whisper, I say, is like shouting your guilt from the housetops.

"You two men, Close and Lawrence, may consider yourselves under arrest for conspiracy and whatever other indictments will lie against such creatures as you. The police will be here in a moment. No, Close, violence won't do now. The doors are locked—and see, we are four to two."*

---

* The plot of this story comes across as far-fetched: The villain induces radiation dermatitis in order to disfigure his wife. This will somehow lead to her willingness to grant him a divorce, so that he can marry a wealthy woman and repay his debts. In order to divert suspicion, he arranges for her to have X-ray treatments so that her disfigurement is blamed on the doctor. There surely must have been easier, more certain ways to obtain a divorce; divorcing a disfigured woman could hardly have endeared the villain to his intended.

V

THE SEISMOGRAPH ADVENTURE

"Dr. James Hanson, Coroner's Physician, Criminal Courts Building," read Craig Kennedy, as he held a visitor's card in his hand. Then to the visitor he added, "Take a chair, Doctor."

The physician thanked him and sat down. "Professor Kennedy," he began, "I have been referred to you by Inspector O'Connor of the Detective Bureau. It may seem an impertinence for a city official to call on you for assistance, but—well, you see, I'm completely floored. I think, too, that the case will interest you. It's the Vandam case."

If Dr. Hanson had suddenly turned on the current of an induction coil and I had been holding the handles I don't think the thrill I received could have been any more sudden. The Vandam case was the sensation of the moment, a triple puzzle, as both Kennedy and myself had agreed. Was it suicide, murder, or sudden death? Every theory, so far, had proved unsatisfactory.

"I have read only what the newspapers have published," replied Craig to the doctor's look of inquiry. "You see, my friend Jameson here is on the staff of the *Star*, and we are in the habit of discussing these cases."

"Very glad to meet you, Mr. Jameson," exclaimed Dr. Hanson at the implied introduction. "The relations between my office and your paper have always been very satisfactory, I can assure you."

"Thank you, Doctor. Depend on me to keep them so," I replied, shaking his proffered hand.

"Now, as to the case," continued the doctor slowly. "Here is a beautiful woman in the prime of life, the wife of a very wealthy retired banker considerably older than herself— perhaps nearly seventy—of very fine family. Of course you have read it all, but let me sketch it so you will look at it from my point of view. This woman, apparently in good health, with every luxury money can buy, is certain within a very few years, from her dower rights, to be numbered among the richest women in America. Yet she is discovered in the middle of the night by her maid, seated at the table in the library of her home, unconscious. She never regains consciousness, but dies the following morning.

"The coroner is called in, and, as his physician, I must advise him. The family physician has pronounced it due to natural causes, the uremic coma of latent kidney trouble. Some of the newspapers, I think the *Star* among them, have hinted at suicide. And then there are others, who have flatly asserted it was murder."

The coroner's physician paused to see if we were following him. Needless to say Kennedy was ahead of him.

"Have you any facts in your possession which have not been given to the public yet?" asked Craig.

"I'm coming to that in a moment," replied Dr. Hanson. "Let me sketch the case first. Henry Vandam had become—well, very eccentric in his old age, we will say. Among his eccentricities none seems to have impressed the newspapers more than his devotion to a medium and her manager, Mrs. May Popper and Mr. Howard Farrington. Now, of course, the case does not go into the truth or falsity of spiritualism, you understand.* You have your opinion, and I have mine. What this aspect of the case involves is merely the character of the medium and her manager. You know, of course, that Henry Vandam is completely under their control."

He paused again, to emphasise the point.

"You asked me if I was in possession of any facts which have not been given to the press. Yes, I am. And just there lies the trouble. They are so very conflicting as to be almost worse than useless, as far as I can see. We found near the unfortunate woman a small pill-box with three capsules still in it. It was labelled 'One before retiring' and bore the name of a certain druggist and the initials 'Dr. C. W. H.' Now, I am convinced that the initials are merely a blind and do not give any clue. The druggist says that a maid from the Vandam house brought in the prescription, which of course he filled. It is a harmless enough prescription—contains, among other things, four and a half grains of quinine and one-sixth of a grain of morphine. Six capsules were prepared altogether.

---

* Spiritualism was an important social movement/pseudo-religion that had adherents throughout the world, though it never had any real organization. It was especially popular among the middle and upper classes, with many women followers. After 1916, Sir Arthur Conan Doyle became its leading spokesperson until his death in 1930, traveling extensively to deliver the spiritualist message. Certainly the popularity of the movement in the 1920s was fed in part by the mass numbers of deaths caused by World War I. In brief, spiritualists believed that the spirits of the dead live on after death and have both the ability and the inclination to communicate with the living, typically through a "medium." The medium either communicated telepathically with the spirits or was the instrument used by spirits for "posthumous writing," letters or even books purported to be authored by the spirit. Spiritualists viewed the spirits as having a continuing afterlife.

She is discovered in the middle of the night, seated at the table in the library of her home, unconscious.

"Now, of course my first thought was that she might have taken several capsules at once and that it was a case of accidental morphine poisoning, or it might even be suicide. But it cannot be either, to my mind, for only three of the six capsules are gone. No doubt, also, you are acquainted with the fact that the one invariable symptom of morphine poisoning is the contraction of the pupils of the eyes to a pin-point—often so that they are unrecognisable. Moreover, the pupils are symmetrically contracted, and this symptom is the one invariably present in coma from morphine poisoning and distinguishes it from all other forms of death.

"On the other hand, in the coma of kidney disease one pupil is dilated and the other contracted—they are unsymmetrical. But in this case both the pupils are normal, or only a very little dilated, and they are symmetrical. So far we have been able to find no other poison than the slight traces of morphine remaining in the stomach after so many hours. I think you are enough of a chemist to know that no doctor would dare go on the stand and swear to death from morphine poisoning in the face of such evidence against him. The veriest tyro of an expert toxicologist could too easily confute him."

Kennedy nodded. "Have you the pill-box and the prescription?"

"I have," replied Dr. Hanson, placing them on the table.

Kennedy scrutinised them sharply. "I shall need these," he said. "Of course you understand I will take very good care of them. Is there anything else of importance?"

"Really, I don't know," said the physician dubiously. "It's rather out of my province, but perhaps you would think it important. It's mighty uncanny anyhow. Henry Vandam, as you doubtless know, was much more deeply interested in the work of this medium than was his wife. Perhaps Mrs. Vandam was a bit jealous—I don't know. But she, too, had an interest in spiritualism, though he was much more deeply influenced by Mrs. Popper than she.

"Here's the strange part of it. The old man believes so thoroughly in rappings and materialisations that he constantly keeps a notebook in his pocket in which he records all the materialisations he thinks he sees and the rappings he hears, along with the time and place. Now it so happened that on the night Mrs. Vandam was taken ill, he had retired—I believe in another part of the house, where he has a regular séance-room. According to his story, he was awakened from a profound sleep by a series of rappings. As was his custom, he noted the time at which they occurred. Something made him uneasy, and he said to his 'control'—at least this is his story:

"'John, is it about Mary?'

"Three raps answered 'yes,' the usual code.

"'What is the matter? Is she ill?'

"The three answering raps were so vigorous that he sprang out of bed and called for his wife's maid. The maid replied that Mrs. Vandam had not gone to bed yet, but that there was a light in the library and she would go to her mistress immediately. The next moment the house was awakened by the screams of the maid calling for help, that Mrs. Vandam was dying.

"That was three nights ago. On each of the two succeeding nights Henry Vandam says he has been awakened at precisely the same hour by a rapping, and on each night his 'control' has given him a message from his dead wife. As a man of science, I attribute the whole thing to an overwrought imagination. The original rappings may have been a mere coincidence with the fact of the condition of Mrs. Vandam. However, I give this to you for what it is worth."

Craig said nothing, but, as was his habit, shaded his eyes with the tips of his fingers, resting his elbows on the arms of his chair. "I suppose," he said, "you can give me the necessary authority to enter the Vandam house and look at the scene of these happenings?"

"Certainly," assented the physician, "but you will find it a queer place. There are spirit paintings and spirit photographs in every room, and Vandam's own part of the house—well, it's creepy, that's all I can say."

"And also I suppose you have performed an autopsy on the body and will allow me to drop into your laboratory to-morrow morning and satisfy myself on this morphine point?"

"Certainly," replied the coroner's physician, "at any time you say."

"At ten sharp, then, to-morrow I shall be there," said Craig. "It is now eight-thirty. Do you think I can see Vandam to-night? What time do these rappings occur?"

"Why, yes, you surely will be able to see him to-night. He hasn't stirred from the house since his wife died. He told me he momentarily expected messages from her direct when she had got strong enough in her new world. I believe they had some kind of a compact to that effect. The rappings come at twelve-thirty."

"Ah, then I shall have plenty of time to run over to my laboratory before seeing Mr. Vandam and get some apparatus I have in mind. No, Doctor, you needn't bother to go with me. Just give me a card of introduction. I'll see you to-morrow at ten. Good night—oh, by the way, don't give out any of the facts you have told me."

"Jameson," said Craig, when we were walking rapidly over toward the university, "this promises to be an uncommonly difficult case."

"As I view it now," I said, "I have suspicions of everybody

concerned in it. Even the view of the *Star*, that it is a case of suicide due to overwrought nerves, may explain it."

"It might even be a natural death," Craig added. "And that would make it a greater mystery than ever—a case for psychical research. One thing that I am going to do to-night will tell me much, however."

At the laboratory he unlocked a glass case and took out a little instrument which looked like two horizontal pendulums suspended by fine wires. There was a large magnet near each pendulum, and the end of each pendulum bore a needle which touched a circular drum driven by clockwork. Craig fussed with and adjusted the apparatus, while I said nothing, for I had long ago learned that in applying a new apparatus to doing old things Craig was as dumb as an oyster, until his work was crowned with success.

We had no trouble in getting in to see Mr. Vandam in his séance-room. His face was familiar to me, for I had seen him in public a number of times, but it looked strangely altered. He was nervous, and showed his age very perceptibly.

It was as the coroner's physician had said. The house was littered with reminders of the cult, books, papers, curious daubs of paintings handsomely framed, and photographs; hazy overexposures, I should have called them, but Mr. Vandam took great pride in them, and Kennedy quite won him over by his admiration for them.

They talked about the rappings, and the old man explained where and when they occurred. They proceeded from a little cabinet or closet at one end of the room. It was evident that he was a thorough believer in them and in the messages they conveyed.

Craig carefully noted everything about the room and then fell to admiring the spirit photographs, if such they might be called.

"The best of all I do not display, they are too precious," said the old man. "Would you like to see them?"

Craig assented eagerly, and Vandam left us for a moment to get them. In an instant Craig had entered the cabinet, and in a dark corner on the floor he deposited the mechanism he had brought from the laboratory. Then he resumed his seat, shutting the box in which he had brought the mechanism, so that it would not appear that he had left anything about the room.

Artfully he led the conversation along lines that interested the old man until he seemed to forget the hour. Not so, Craig. He knew it was nearing half-past twelve. The more they talked the more uncanny did this house and room of spirits seem to me. In fact, I was rapidly reaching the point where I could have sworn that once or twice something incorporeal brushed by me. I know now that it was purely imagination, but it shows what tricks the imagination can play on us.

Rap! rap! rap! rap! rap!

Five times came a curiously hollow noise from the cabinet. If it had been possible I should certainly have fled, it was so sudden and unexpected. The hall clock down-stairs struck the half-hour in those chimes written by Handel for St. Paul's.*

Craig leaned over to me and whispered hoarsely, "Keep perfectly still—don't move a hand or foot."

The old man seemed utterly to have forgotten us. "Is that you, John?" he asked expectantly.

Rap! rap! rap! came the reply.

"Is Mary strong enough to speak to me tonight?"

---

* Reeve got the idea a little garbled here: The tune known as the "Westminster chimes," found on many striking clocks, is played on the bells of Westminster Palace. The tune resembles the four notes that make up the fifth and sixth bars of "I know that my Redeemer liveth" from Handel's *Messiah*.

Rap! rap!

"Is she happy?"

Rap! rap!

"What makes her unhappy? What does she want? Will you spell it out?"

Rap! rap! rap!

Then, after a pause, the rapping started slowly and distinctly to spell out words. It was so weird and uncanny that I scarcely breathed. Letter after letter the message came, nineteen raps for "s," eight for "h," five for "e," according to the place in the alphabet, numerically, of the required letter. At last it was complete:

"She thinks you are not well. She asks you to have that prescription filled again."

"Tell her I will do it to-morrow morning. Is there anything else?"

Rap! rap! came back faintly.

"John, John, don't go yet," pleaded the old man earnestly. It was easy to see how thoroughly he believed in "John," as perhaps well he might after the warning of his wife's death three nights before. "Won't you answer one other question?"

Fainter, almost imperceptibly, came a rap! rap!

For several minutes the old man sat absorbed in thought, trance-like. Then, gradually, he seemed to realise that we were in the room with him. With difficulty he took up the thread of the conversation where the rappings had broken it.

"We were talking about the photographs," he said slowly. "I hope soon to get one of my wife as she is now that she is transfigured. John has promised me one soon."

He was gathering up his treasures preparatory to putting them back in their places of safe-keeping. The moment he was out of the room Craig darted into the cabinet and replaced his mechanism in the box. Then he began softly to tap the walls. At last he found the side that gave a noise similar to that which we had heard, and he seemed pleased to have found it, for he hastily sketched on an old envelope a plan of that part of the house, noting on it the location of the side of the cabinet.

Kennedy almost dragged me back to our apartment, he was in such a hurry to examine the apparatus at his leisure. He turned on all the lights, took the thing out of its case, and stripped off the two sheets of ruled paper wound around the two revolving drums. He laid them flat on the table and studied them for some minutes with evidently growing satisfaction.

At last he turned to me and said, "Walter, here is a ghost caught in the act."

I looked dubiously at the irregular up-and-down scrawl on the paper, while he rang up the Homicide Bureau of the Central Office and left word for O'Connor to call him up the first thing in the morning.

Still eyeing with satisfaction the record traced on the sheets of paper, he lighted a cigarette in a matter-of-fact way and added: "It proves to be a very much flesh-and-blood ghost, this 'John.' It walked up to the wall back of that cabinet, rapped, listened to old Vandam, rapped some more, got the answer it wanted, and walked deliberately away. The cabinet, as you may have noticed, is in a corner of the room with one side along the hallway. The ghost must have been in the hall."

"But who was it?"

"Not so fast, Walter," laughed Craig. "Isn't it enough for one night that we have found out that much?"

Fortunately I was tired, or I certainly should have dreamed of rappings and of "John" that night. I was awakened early by Kennedy talking with someone over the telephone. It was Inspector O'Connor.

Of course I heard only one side of the conversation, but as near as I could gather Kennedy was asking the inspector to obtain several samples of ink for him. I had not heard the first part of the conversation, and was considerably surprised when Kennedy hung up the receiver and said:

"Vandam had the prescription filled again early this morning, and it will soon be in the hands of O'Connor. I hope I haven't spoiled things by acting too soon, but I don't want to run the risk of a double tragedy."

"Well," I said, "it is incomprehensible to me. First I suspected suicide. Then I suspected murder. Now I almost suspect a murder and a suicide. The fact is, I don't know just what I suspect. I'm like Dr. Hanson—floored. I wonder if Vandam would voluntarily take all the capsules at once in order to be with his wife?"

"One of them alone would be quite sufficient if the 'ghost' should take a notion, as I think it will, to walk in the daytime," replied Craig enigmatically. "I don't want to run any chances, as I have said. I may be wrong in my theory of the case, Walter, so let us not discuss this phase of it until I have gone a step farther and am sure of my ground. O'Connor's man will get the capsules before Vandam has a chance to take the first one, anyhow. The 'ghost' had a purpose in that message, for O'Connor tells me that Vandam's lawyer visited him yesterday and in all probability a new will is being made, perhaps has already been made."

We breakfasted in silence and later rode down to the office of Dr. Hanson, who greeted us enthusiastically.

"I've solved it at last," he cried, "and it's easy."

Kennedy looked gravely over the analysis which Dr. Hanson shoved into his hand, and seemed very much interested in the probable quantity of morphine that must have been taken to yield such an analysis. The physician had a text-book open on his desk.

"Our old ideas of the infallible test of morphine poisoning are all exploded," he said, excitedly beginning to read a passage he had marked in the book.

> *"'I have thought that inequality of the pupils, that is to say,*
> *where they are not symmetrically contracted, is proof that*
> *a case is not one of narcotism, or morphine poisoning. But*
> *Professor Taylor has recorded a case of morphine poisoning*
> *in which the unsymmetrical contraction occurred.'*

"There, now, until I happened to run across that in one of the authorities I had supposed the symmetrical contraction of the pupils of the eyes to be the distinguishing symptom of morphine poisoning. Professor Kennedy, in my opinion we can, after all, make out our case as one of morphine poisoning."

"Is that case in the book all you base your opinion on?" asked Craig with excessive politeness.

"Yes, sir," replied the doctor reluctantly.

"Well," said Kennedy quietly, "if you will investigate that case quoted from Professor Taylor, you will find that it has been proved that the patient had one glass eye!"

"Then my contention collapses and she was not poisoned?"

"No, I do not say that. All I say is that expert testimony would refute us as far as we have gone. But if you will let me make a few tests of my own I can readily clear up that end of the case, I now feel sure. Let me take these samples to my laboratory."

I was surprised when we ran into Inspector O'Connor waiting for us in the corridor of the Criminal Courts Building as we left the office of the coroner's physician. He rushed up to Kennedy and shoved into his hand a pill-box in which six capsules rattled. Kennedy narrowly inspected the box, opened it, and looked thoughtfully at the six white capsules lying so innocently within.

"One of these capsules would have been worth hundreds of thousands of dollars to 'John,'" said Craig contemplatively, as he shut the box and deposited it carefully in his inside vest pocket. "I don't believe I even said good morning to you, O'Connor," he continued. "I hope I haven't kept you waiting here long. Have you obtained the samples of ink?"

"Yes, Professor. Here they are. As soon as you telephoned this morning I sent my men out separately to get them. There's the ink from the druggist, this is from the Vandam library, this is from Farrington's room, and this is from Mrs. Popper's apartment."

"Thank you, Inspector. I don't know what I'd do without your help," said Kennedy, eagerly taking four small vials from him. "Science is all right, but organisation enables science to work quickly. And quickness is the essence of this case."

During the afternoon Kennedy was very busy in his laboratory, where I found him that night after my hurried dinner, from which he was absent.

"What, is it after dinner-time?" he exclaimed, holding up a glass beaker and watching the reaction of something he poured into it from a test-tube.

"Craig, I believe that when you are absorbed in a case, you would rather work than eat. Did you have any lunch after I left you?"

"I don't think so," he replied, regarding the beaker and not his answer. "Now, Walter, old fellow, I don't want you to be offended with me, but really I can work better if you don't constantly remind me of such things as eating and sleeping. Say, do you want to help me—really?"

"Certainly. I am as interested in the case as you are, but I can't make heads or tails of it," I replied.

"Then, I wish you would look up Mrs. Popper to-night and

have a private séance with her. What I want you to do particularly is to get a good idea of the looks of the room in which she
is accustomed to work. I'm going to duplicate it here in my laboratory as nearly as possible. Then I want you to arrange with
her for a private 'circle' here to-morrow night. Tell her it is with
a few professors at the university who are interested in psychical
research and that Mr. Vandam will be present. I'd rather have
her come willingly than to force her to come. Incidentally watch
that manager of hers, Farrington. By all means he must accompany her."

That evening I dropped casually in on Mrs. Popper. She
was a woman of great brilliance and delicacy, both in her
physical and mental perceptions, of exceptional vivacity and
cleverness. She must have studied me more closely than I was
aware of, for I believe she relied on diverting my attention
whenever she desired to produce one of her really wonderful
results. Needless to say, I was completely mystified by her per-
formance. She did spirit writing that would have done credit
to the immortal Slade,* told me a lot of things that were true,
and many more that were unverifiable or hopelessly vague. It
was really worth much more than the price, and I did not need
to feign the interest necessary to get her terms for a circle in
the laboratory.

Of course I had to make the terms with Farrington. The first
glance aroused my suspicions of him. He was shifty-eyed, and his
face had a hard and mercenary look. In spite of, perhaps rather
because of, my repugnance we quickly came to an agreement, and
as I left the apartment I mentally resolved to keep my eye on him.

---

* Henry Slade (1835–1905) was a medium who was famous for "slate-writing" (a
demonstration in which the spirits record messages on a slate, typically in chalk). In
1885, he was exposed as a fraud by the Seybert Commission, a group of the faculty of
the University of Pennsylvania dedicated to investigating spiritualist claims.

Craig came in late, having been engaged in his chemical analyses all the evening. From his manner I inferred that they had been satisfactory, and he seemed much gratified when I told him that I had arranged successfully for the séance and that Farrington would accompany the medium.

As we were talking over the case a messenger arrived with a note from O'Connor. It was written with his usual brevity: "Have just found from servants that Farrington and Mrs. P. have key to Vandam house. Wish I had known it before. House shadowed. No one has entered or left it to-night."

Craig looked at his watch. It was a quarter after one. "The ghost won't walk to-night, Walter," he said as he entered his bedroom for a much-needed rest. "I guess I was right after all in getting the capsules as soon as possible. The ghost must have flitted unobserved in there this morning directly after the maid brought them back from the druggist."

Again, the next morning, he had me out of bed bright and early. As we descended from the Sixth Avenue "L," he led me into a peculiar little shop in the shadow of the "L" structure. He entered as though he knew the place well; but, then, that air of assurance was Kennedy's stock in trade and sat very well on him.

Few people, I suppose, have ever had a glimpse of this workshop of magic and deception. This little shop of Marina's was the headquarters of the magicians of the country. Levitation and ghostly disappearing hands were on every side. The shelves in the back of the shop were full of nickel, brass, wire, wood, and papier-maché contrivances, new and strange to the eye of the uninitiated. Yet it was all as systematic as a hardware shop.

"Is Signor Marina in?" asked Craig of a girl in the first room, given up to picture post-cards. The room was as deceptive as the trade, for it was only an anteroom to the storeroom I have described above. This storeroom was also a factory, and half a dozen artisans were hard at work in it.

Yes, the signor was in, the girl replied, leading us back into the workshop. He proved to be a short man with a bland, open face and frank eyes, the very antithesis of his trade.

"I have arranged for a circle with Mrs. May Popper," began Kennedy, handing the man his card. "I suppose you know her?"

"Indeed yes," he answered. "I furnished her séance-room."

"Well, I want to hire for to-night just the same sort of tables, cabinets, carpets, everything that she has—only hire, you understand, but I am willing to pay you well for them. It is the best way to get a good sitting, I believe. Can you do it?"

The little man thought a moment, then replied: "Si, signor— yes—very nearly, near enough. I would do anything for Mrs. Popper. She is a good customer. But her manager—"

"My friend here, Mr. Jameson, has had séances with her in her own apartment," interposed Craig. "Perhaps he can help you to recollect just what is necessary."

"I know very well, signor. I have the duplicate bill, the bill which was paid by that Farrington with a check from the banker Vandam. Leave it to me."

"Then you will get the stuff together this morning and have it up to my place this afternoon?"

"Yes, Professor, yes. It is a bargain. I would do anything for Mrs. Popper—she is a fine woman."

Late that afternoon I rejoined Craig at his laboratory. Signor Marina had already arrived with a truck and was disposing the paraphernalia about the laboratory. He had first laid a thick black rug. Mrs. Popper very much affected black carpets, and I had noticed that Vandam's room was carpeted in black, too. I suppose black conceals everything that one oughtn't to see at a séance.

A cabinet with a black curtain, several chairs, a light deal table, several banjos, horns, and other instruments were disposed about the room. With a few suggestions from me we made a fair duplication of the hangings on the walls. Kennedy was manifestly anxious to finish, and at last it was done.

After Marina had gone, Kennedy stretched a curtain over the end of the room farthest from the cabinet. Behind it he placed on a shelf the apparatus composed of the pendulums and magnets. The beakers and test-tubes were also on this shelf.

He had also arranged that the cabinet should be so situated that it was next a hallway that ran past his laboratory.

"To-night, Jameson," he said, indicating a spot on the hall wall just back of the cabinet, "I shall want you to bring my guests out here and do a little spirit rapping—I'll tell you just what to do when the time comes."

That night, when we gathered in the transformed laboratory, there were Henry Vandam, Dr. Hanson, Inspector O'Connor, Kennedy, and myself. At last the sound of wheels was heard, and Mrs. Popper drove up in a hansom, accompanied by Farrington. They both inspected the room narrowly and seemed satisfied. I had, as I have said, taken a serious dislike to the man, and watched him closely. I did not like his air of calm assurance.

The lights were switched off, all except one sixteen-candle-power lamp in the farthest corner, shaded by a deep-red globe. It was just light enough to see to read very large print with difficulty.

Mrs. Popper began immediately with the table. Kennedy and I sat on her right and left respectively, in the circle, and held her hands and feet. I confess to a real thrill when I felt the light table rise first on two legs, then on one, and finally remain suspended in the air, whence it dropped with a thud, as if someone had suddenly withdrawn his support.

The medium sat with her back to the curtain of the cabinet, and several times I could have sworn that a hand reached out and passed close to my head. At least it seemed so. The curtain bulged at times, and a breeze seemed to sweep out from the cabinet.

After some time of this sort of work Craig led gradually up to a request for a materialisation of the control of Vandam, but Mrs. Popper refused. She said she did not feel strong enough, and Farrington put in a hasty word that he, too, could feel that "there was something working against them." But Kennedy was importunate and at last she consented to see if "John" would do some rapping, even if he could not materialise.

Kennedy asked to be permitted to put the questions.

"Are you the 'John' who appears to Mr. Vandam every night at twelve-thirty?"

Rap! rap! rap! came the faint reply from the cabinet. Or rather it seemed to me to come from the floor near the cabinet, and perhaps to be a trifle muffled by the black carpet.

"Are you in communication with Mrs. Vandam?"

Rap! rap! rap!

"Can she be made to rap for us?"

Rap! rap!

"Will you ask her a question and spell out her answer?"

Rap! rap! rap!

Craig paused a moment to frame the question, then shot it out point-blank: "Does Mrs. Vandam know now in the other world whether anyone in this room substituted a morphine capsule for one of those ordered by her three days before she died? Does she know whether the same person has done the same thing with those later ordered by Mr. Vandam?"

"John" seemed considerably perturbed at the mention of capsules. It was a long time before any answer was forthcoming.

Kennedy was about to repeat the question when a faint sound was heard.

Rap!—

Suddenly came a wild scream. It was such a scream as I had never heard before in my life. It came as though a dagger had been thrust into the heart of Mrs. Popper. The lights flashed up as Kennedy turned the switch.

A man was lying flat on the floor—it was Inspector O'Connor. He had succeeded in slipping noiselessly, like a snake, below the curtain into the cabinet. Craig had told him to look out for wires or threads stretched from Mrs. Popper's clothing to the bulging curtain of the cabinet. Imagine his surprise when he saw that she had simply freed her foot from the shoe, which I was carefully holding down, and with a backward movement of the leg was reaching out into the cabinet behind her chair and was doing the rapping with her toes.

Lying on the floor he had grasped her foot and caught her heel with a firm hand. She had responded with a wild yell that showed she knew she was trapped. Her secret was out.

Hysterically Mrs. Popper began to upbraid the inspector as he rose to his feet, but Farrington quickly interposed.

"Something was working against us to-night, gentlemen. Yet you demanded results. And when the spirits will not come, what is she to do? She forgets herself in her trance; she produces, herself, the things that you all could see supernaturally if you were in sympathy."

The mere sound of Farrington's voice seemed to rouse in me all the animosity of my nature. I felt that a man who could trump up an excuse like that when a person was caught with the goods was capable of almost anything.

"Enough, of this fake séance," exclaimed Craig. "I have let it go on merely for the purpose of opening the eyes of a certain deluded gentleman in this room. Now, if you will all be seated I shall have something to say that will finally establish whether Mary Vandam was the victim of accident, suicide, or murder."

With hearts beating rapidly we sat in silence. Craig took the beakers and test-tubes from the shelf behind the curtain and placed them on the little deal table that had been so merrily dancing about the room.

"The increasing frequency with which tales of murder by poison appear in the newspapers," he began formally, "is proof of how rapidly this new civilisation of ours is taking on the aspects of the older civilisations across the seas. Human life is cheap in this country; but the ways in which human life has been taken among us have usually been direct, simple, aboveboard, in keeping with our democratic and pioneer traditions. The pistol and the bowie-knife for the individual, the rope and the torch for the mob, have been the usual instruments of sudden death. But when we begin to use poisons most artfully compounded in order to hasten an expected bequest and remove obstacles in its way—well, we are practising an art that calls up all the memories of sixteenth century Italy.

"In this beaker," he continued, "I have some of the contents of the stomach of the unfortunate woman. The coroner's physician has found that they show traces of morphine. Was the morphine in such quantities as to be fatal? Without doubt. But equally without doubt analysis could not discover and prove it in the face of one inconsistency. The usual test which shows morphine poisoning failed in this case. The pupils of her eyes were not symmetrically contracted. In fact they were normal.

"Now, the murderer must have known of this test. This clever criminal also knew that to be successful in the use of this drug where others had failed, the drug must be skilfully mixed with something else. In that first box of capsules there were six. The druggist compounded them correctly according to the prescription. But between the time when they came into the house from the druggist's and the time when she took the first capsule, that night, someone who had access to the house emptied one capsule of its harmless contents and refilled it with a deadly dose of morphine—a white powder which looks just like the powder already in the capsules.

"Why, then, the normal pupils of the eyes? Simply because the criminal put a little atropine or belladonna, with the morphine. My tests show absolutely the presence of atropine, Dr. Hanson," said Craig, bowing to the physician.

"The best evidence, however, is yet to come. A second box of six capsules, all intact, was discovered yesterday in the possession of Henry Vandam. I have analysed the capsules. One contains no quinine at all—it is all morphine and atropine. It is, without doubt, precisely similar to the capsule which killed Mrs. Vandam. Another night or so, and Henry Vandam would have died the same death."

The old man groaned. Two such exposures had shaken him. He looked from one of us to another as if not knowing in whom he could trust. But Kennedy hurried on to his next point.

"Who was it that gave the prescription to Mrs. Vandam originally? She is dead and cannot tell. The others won't tell, for the person who gave her that prescription was the person who later substituted the fatal capsule in place of the harmless. The original prescription is here. I have been able to discover from it nothing at all by examining the handwriting. Nor does the texture of the paper indicate anything to me. But the ink—ah, the ink.

"Most inks seem very similar, I suppose, but to a person who has made a study of the chemical composition of ink they are very different. Ink is composed of iron tannate, which on exposure to air gives the black of writing. The original pigment—say blue or blue-black ink—is placed in the ink, to make the writing visible at first, and gradually fades, giving place to the black of the tannate which is formed. The dyestuffs employed in the commercial inks of to-day vary in colour from pale greenish blue to indigo and deep violet. No two give identical reactions—at all events not when mixed with the iron tannate to form the pigment in writing.

"It is owing to the difference in these provisional colouring matters that it is possible to distinguish between writing written with different kinds of ink. I was able easily to obtain samples of the inks used by the Vandams, by Mrs. Popper, by Mr. Farrington, and by the druggist. I have compared the writing of the original prescription with a colour scale of my own construction, and I have made chemical tests. The druggist's ink conforms exactly to the writing on the two pill-boxes, but not to the prescription. One of the other three inks conforms by test absolutely to the ink in that prescription signed 'Dr. C. W. H.' as a blind. In a moment my chain of evidence against the owner of that bottle of ink will be complete."

I could not help but think of the two pendulums on the shelf behind the curtain, but Craig said nothing for a moment to indicate that he referred to that apparatus. We sat dazed. Farrington seemed nervous and ill at ease. Mrs. Popper, who had not recovered from the hysterical condition of her exposure, with difficulty controlled her emotion. Vandam was crushed.

"I have not only arranged this laboratory so as to reproduce Mrs. Popper's séance-room," began Craig afresh, "but I have had the cabinet placed in relatively the same position a similar cabinet occupies in Mr. Vandam's private séance-room in the Vandam mansion.

"One night, Mr. Jameson and myself were visiting Mr. Vandam. At precisely twelve-thirty we heard most unaccountable rappings from that cabinet. I particularly noted the position of the cabinet. Back of it ran a hallway. That is duplicated here. Back of this cabinet is a hallway. I had heard of these rappings before we went, but was afraid that it would be impossible for me to catch the ghost red-handed. There is a limit to what you can do the first time you enter a man's house, and, besides, that was no time to arouse suspicion in the mind of anyone. But science has a way out of every dilemma. I determined to learn something of these rappings."

Craig paused and glanced first at Farrington, then at Mrs. Popper, and then at Mr. Vandam.

"Mr. Jameson," he resumed, "will escort the doctor, the inspector, Mr. Farrington, Mrs. Popper, and Mr. Vandam into my imitation hall of the Vandam mansion. I want each of you in turn to tiptoe up that hall to a spot indicated on the wall, back of the cabinet, and strike that spot several sharp blows with your knuckles."

I did as Craig instructed tiptoeing up myself first so that they could not mistake his meaning. The rest followed separately, and after a moment we returned silently in suppressed excitement to the room.

Craig was still standing by the table, but now the pendulums with the magnets and needles and the drums worked by clockwork were before him.

"Another person outside the Vandam family had a key to the Vandam mansion," he began gravely. "That person, by the way, was the one who waited, night by night, until Mrs. Vandam took the fatal capsule, and then when she had taken it apprised the old man of the fact and strengthened an already blind faith in the shadow world."

You could have heard a pin drop. In fact you could almost have felt it drop.

"That other person who, unobserved, had free access to the house," he continued in the breathless stillness, "is in this room now."

He was looking at O'Connor as if for corroboration. O'Connor nodded. "Information derived from the butler," he muttered.

"I did not know this until yesterday," Kennedy continued, "but I suspected that something of the sort existed when I was first told by Dr. Hanson of the rappings. I determined to hear those rappings, and make a record of them. So, the night Mr. Jameson and I visited Mr. Vandam, I carried this little instrument with me."

Almost lovingly he touched the pendulums on the table. They were now at rest and kept so by means of a lever that prevented all vibration whatever.

"See, I release this lever—now, let no one in the room move. Watch the needles on the paper as the clockwork revolves the drums. I take a step—ever so lightly. The pendulums vibrate, and the needles trace a broken line on the paper on each drum. I stop; the lines are practically straight. I take another step and another, ever so lightly. See the delicate pendulums vibrate? See, the lines they trace are jagged lines."

He stripped the paper off the drums and laid it flat on the table before him, with two other similar pieces of paper.

"Just before the time of the rapping I placed this instrument in the corner of the Vandam cabinet, just as I placed it in this cabinet after Mr. Jameson conducted you from the room. In neither case were suspicions aroused. Everything in both cases was perfectly normal—I mean the 'ghost' was in ignorance of the presence, if not the very existence, of this instrument.

"This is an improved seismograph," he explained, "one after a very recent model by Prince Galitzin of the Imperial Academy of St. Petersburg. The seismograph, as you know, was devised to register earthquakes at a distance. This one not only measures the size of a distant earthquake, but the actual direction from which the earth-tremors come. That is why there are two pendulums and two drums.

"The magnetic arrangement is to cut short the vibrations set up in the pendulums, to prevent them from continuing to vibrate after the first shock. Thus they are ready in an instant to record another tremor. Other seismographs continue to vibrate for a long time as a result of one tremor only. Besides, they give little indication of the direction from which the tremors come.

"I think you must all appreciate that your tiptoeing up the hall must cause a far greater disturbance in this delicate seismograph than even a very severe earthquake thousands of miles away, which it was built to record."

He paused and examined the papers sharply.

"This is the record made by the 'ghost's' walk the other night," he said, holding up two of them in his left hand. "Here on the table, on two other longer sheets, I have records of the vibrations set up by those in this room walking tonight.

"Here is Mr. Jameson's—his is not a bit like the ghost's. Nor is Mr. Vandam's. Least of all are Dr. Hanson's and Inspector O'Connor's, for they are heavy men.

"Now here is Mr. Farrington's"—he bent down closely—"he is a light man, and the ghost was light."

Craig was playing with his victim like a cat with a mouse.

Suddenly I felt something brush by me, and with a swish of air and of garments I saw Mrs. Popper fling herself wildly at the table that bore the incriminating records. In another instant Farrington was on his feet and had made a wild leap in the same direction.

It was done so quickly that I must have acted first and thought afterward. I found myself in the midst of a mêlée with my hand

at his throat and his at mine. O'Connor with a jiu-jitsu movement bent Farrington's other arm until he released me with a
cry of pain.

In front of me I saw Craig grasping Mrs. Popper's wrists as in
a vise. She was glaring at him like a tigress.

"Do you suppose for a moment that *that* toy is going to
convince the world that Henry Vandam has been deceived
and that the spirit which visited him was a fraud? Is that why
you have lured me here under false pretences, to play on my
feelings, to insult me, to take advantage of a lone, defence-
less woman, surrounded by hostile men? Shame on you," she
added contemptuously. "You call yourself a gentleman, but I
call you a coward."

Kennedy, always calm and collected, ignored the tirade.
His voice was as cold as steel as he said: "It would do little
good, Mrs. Popper, to destroy this one link in the chain I have
forged. The other links are too heavy for you. Don't forget the
evidence of the ink. It was your ink. Don't forget that Henry
Vandam will not any longer conceal that he has altered his will
in favour of you. To-night he goes from here to his lawyer's
to draw up a new will altogether. Don't forget that you have
caused the Vandams separately to have the prescription filled,
and that you are now caught in the act of a double murder.
Don't forget that you had access to the Vandam mansion, that
you substituted the deadly for the harmless capsules. Don't
forget that your rappings announced the death of one of your
victims and urged the other, a cruelly wronged and credulous
old man, to leave millions to you who had deceived and would
have killed him.

"No, the record of the ghost on the seismograph was not Mr.
Farrington's, as I implied at the moment when you so kindly furnished this additional proof of your guilt by trying to destroy

the evidence. The ghost was you, Mrs. Popper, and you are at liberty to examine the markings as minutely as you please, but you must not destroy them. You are an astute criminal, Mrs. Popper, but to-night you are under arrest for the murder of Mary Vandam and the attempted murder of Henry Vandam."

VI

THE DIAMOND MAKER

"I've called, Professor Kennedy, to see if we can retain you in a case which I am sure will tax even your resources. Heaven knows it has taxed ours."

The visitor was a large, well-built man. He placed his hat on the table and, without taking off his gloves, sat down in an easy chair which he completely filled.

"Andrews is my name—third vice-president of the Great Eastern Life Insurance Company. I am the nominal head of the company's private detective force, and though I have some pretty clever fellows on my staff we've got a case that, so far, none of us has been able to unravel. I'd like to consult you about it."

Kennedy expressed his entire willingness to be consulted, and after the usual formalities were over, Mr. Andrews proceeded:

"I suppose you are aware that the large insurance companies maintain quite elaborate detective forces and follow very keenly such of the cases of their policy-holders as look at all suspicious. This case which I wish to put in your hands is that of Mr. Solomon Morowitch, a wealthy Maiden Lane jeweller. I suppose you have read something in the papers about his sudden death and the strange robbery of his safe?"

"Very little," replied Craig. "There hasn't been much to read."

"Of course not, of course not," said Mr. Andrews with some show of gratification. "I flatter myself that we have pulled the wires so as to keep the thing out of the papers as much as possible. We don't want to frighten the quarry till the net is spread. The point is, though, to find out who is the quarry. It's most baffling."

"I am at your service," interposed Craig quietly, "but you will have to enlighten me as to the facts in the case. As to that, I know no more than the newspapers."

"Oh, certainly, certainly. That is to say, you know nothing at all and can approach it without bias." He paused and then, seeming to notice something in Craig's manner, added hastily: "I'll be perfectly frank with you. The policy in question is for one hundred thousand dollars, and is incontestable. His wife is the beneficiary. The company is perfectly willing to pay, but we want to be sure that it is all straight first. There are certain suspicious circumstances that in justice to ourselves we think should be cleared up. That is all—believe me. We are not seeking to avoid an honest liability."

"What are these suspicious circumstances?" asked Craig, apparently satisfied with the explanation.

"This is in strict confidence, gentlemen," began Mr. Andrews. "Mr. Morowitch, according to the story as it comes to us, returned home late one night last week, apparently from his office, in a very weakened, a semi-conscious, condition. His family physician, Doctor Thornton, was summoned, not at once, but shortly. He pronounced Mr. Morowitch to be suffering from a congestion of the lungs that was very like a sudden attack of pneumonia.

"Mr. Morowitch had at once gone to bed, or at least was in bed, when the doctor arrived, but his condition grew worse so rapidly that the doctor hastily resorted to oxygen, under which treatment he seemed to revive. The doctor had just stepped out to see another patient when a hurry call was sent to him that Mr. Morowitch was rapidly sinking. He died before the doctor could return. No statement whatever concerning the cause of his sudden illness was made by Mr. Morowitch, and the death-certificate, a copy of which I have, gives pneumonia as the cause of death. One of our men has seen Doctor Thornton, but has been able to get nothing out of him. Mrs. Morowitch was the only person with her husband at the time."

There was something in his tone that made me take particular note of this last fact, especially as he paused for an instant.

"Now, perhaps there would be nothing surprising about it all, so far at least, were it not for the fact that the following morning, when his junior partner, Mr. Kahan, opened the place of business, or rather went to it, for it was to remain closed, of course, he found that during the night someone had visited it. The lock on the great safe, which contained thousands of dollars' worth of diamonds, was intact; but in the top of the safe a huge hole was found—an irregular, round hole, big enough to put your foot through. Imagine it, Professor Kennedy, a great hole in a safe that is made of chrome steel, a safe that, short of a safety-deposit vault, ought to be about the strongest thing on earth.

"Why, that steel would dull and splinter even the finest diamond-drill before it made an impression. The mere taking out and refitting of drills into the brace would be a most lengthy process. Eighteen or twenty hours is the time by actual test which it would take to bore such a hole through those laminated plates, even if there were means of exerting artificial pressure. As for the police, they haven't even a theory yet."

"And the diamonds?"

"All gone—everything of any value was gone. Even the

letter-files were ransacked. His desk was broken open, and papers of some nature had been taken out of it. Thorough is no name for the job. Isn't that enough to arouse suspicion?"

"I should like to see that safe," was all Kennedy said.

"So you shall, so you shall," said Mr. Andrews. "Then we may retain you in our service? My car is waiting down-stairs. We can go right down to Maiden Lane if you wish."

"You may retain me on one condition," said Craig without moving. "I am to be free to get at the truth whether it benefits or hurts the company, and the case is to be entirely in my hands."

"Hats on," agreed Mr. Andrews, reaching in his vest pocket and pulling out three or four brevas. "My chauffeur is quite a driver. He can almost beat the subway down."

"First, to my laboratory," interposed Craig. "It will take only a few minutes."

We drove up to the university and stopped on the campus while Craig hurried into the Chemistry Building to get something.

"I like your professor of criminal science," said Andrews to me, blowing a huge fragrant cloud of smoke.

I, for my part, liked the vice-president. He was a man who seemed thoroughly to enjoy life, to have most of the good things, and a capacity for getting out of them all that was humanly possible. He seemed to be particularly enjoying this Morowitch case.

"He has solved some knotty cases," was all I said. "I've come to believe there is no limit to his resourcefulness."

"I hope not. He's up against a tough one this trip, though, my boy."

I did not even resent the "my boy." Andrews was one of those men in whom we newspaper writers instinctively believe. I knew that it would be "pens lifted" only so long as the case was incomplete. When the time comes with such men they are ready to furnish us the best "copy" in the world.

Kennedy quickly rejoined us, carrying a couple of little glass bottles with ground-glass stoppers.

Morowitch & Co. was, of course, closed when we arrived, but we had no trouble in being admitted by the Central Office man who had been detailed to lock the barn door after the horse was stolen. It was precisely as Mr. Andrews had said. Mr. Kahan showed us the safe. Through the top a great hole had been made—I say made, for at the moment I was at a loss to know whether it had been cut, drilled, burned, blown out, or what-not.

Kennedy examined the edges of the hole carefully, and just the trace of a smile of satisfaction flitted over his face as he did so. Without saying a word he took the glass stopper out of the larger bottle which he had brought and poured the contents on the top of the safe near the hole. There it lay, a little mound of reddish powder. Kennedy took a little powder of another kind from the other bottle and lighted it with a match.

"Stand back—close to the wall," he called as he dropped the burning mass on the red powder. In two or three leaps he joined us at the far end of the room.

Almost instantly a dazzling, intense flame broke out, and sizzled and crackled. With bated breath we watched. It was almost incredible, but that glowing mass of powder seemed literally to be sinking, sinking right down into the cold steel. In tense silence we waited. On the ceiling we could still see the reflection of the molten mass in the cup which it had burned for itself in the top of the safe.

At last it fell through into the safe—fell as the burning roof of a frame building would fall into the building. No one spoke a word, but as we cautiously peered over the top of the safe we instinctively turned to Kennedy for an explanation. The Central Office man, with eyes as big as half-dollars, acted almost as if he would have liked to clap the irons on Kennedy. For there in the top of the safe was another hole, smaller but identical in nature with the first one.

"Thermit," was all Kennedy said.

"Thermit?" echoed Andrews, shifting the cigar which he had allowed to go out in the excitement.

"Yes, an invention of a chemist named Goldschmidt, of Essen, Germany. It is a compound of iron oxide, such as comes off a blacksmith's anvil or the rolls of a rolling-mill, and powdered metallic aluminum. You could thrust a red-hot bar into it without setting it off, but when you light a little magnesium powder and drop it on thermit, a combustion is started that quickly reaches fifty-four hundred degrees Fahrenheit. It has the peculiar property of concentrating its heat to the immediate spot on which it is placed. It is one of the most powerful oxidising agents known, and it doesn't even melt the rest of the steel surface.* You see how it ate its way through the steel. Either black or red thermit will do the trick equally well."

No one said anything. There was nothing to say.

"Someone uncommonly clever, or instructed by someone uncommonly clever, must have done that job," added Craig. "Well, there is nothing more to be done here," he added, after a cursory look about the office. "Mr. Andrews, may I have a word with you? Come on, Jameson. Good day, Mr. Kahan. Good day, Officer."

---

* The thermite reaction was discovered in 1893 and patented in 1895 by German chemist Hans Goldschmidt. Goldschmidt was originally looking for a way to purify metals but the prospects of using thermite for welding led him to test it on tram tracks in Essen in 1899. As Kennedy explains, the most common means of ignition—for a high heat is required to set off the reaction—is a strip of magnesium used as a fuse. The composition of modern thermite varies but is always a mixture of a metal oxide and a metal powder, with aluminum the most common and safest source of powder (because of its low cost and high boiling point).

Outside we stopped for a moment at the door of Andrews's car.

"I shall want to see Mr. Morowitch's papers at home," said Craig, "and also to call on Doctor Thornton. Do you think I shall have any difficulty?"

"Not at all," replied Mr. Andrews, "not at all. I will go with you myself and see that you have none. Say, Professor Kennedy," he broke out, "that was marvellous. I never dreamed such a thing was possible. But don't you think you could have learned something more up there in the office by looking around?"

"I did learn it," answered Kennedy. "The lock on the door was intact—whoever did the job let himself in by a key. There is no other way to get in."

Andrews gave a low whistle and glanced involuntarily up at the window with the sign of Morowitch & Co. in gold letters several floors above.

"Don't look up. I think that was Kahan looking out at us," he said, fixing his eyes on his cigar. "I wonder if he knows more about this than he has told! He was the 'company,' you know, but his interest in the business was only very slight. By George—"

"Not too fast, Mr. Andrews," interrupted Craig. "We have still to see Mrs. Morowitch and the doctor before we form any theories."

"A very handsome woman, too," said Andrews, as we seated ourselves in the car. "A good deal younger than Morowitch. Say, Kahan isn't a bad-looking chap, either, is he? I hear he was a very frequent visitor at his partner's house. Well, which first, Mrs. M. or the doctor?"

"The house," answered Craig.

Mr. Andrews introduced us to Mrs. Morowitch, who was in very deep mourning, which served, as I could not help noticing, rather to heighten than lessen her beauty. By contrast it brought out the rich deep colour of her face and the graceful lines of her figure. She was altogether a very attractive young widow.

She seemed to have a sort of fear of Andrews, whether merely because he represented the insurance company on which so much depended or because there were other reasons for fear, I could not, of course, make out. Andrews was very courteous and polite, yet I caught myself asking if it was not a professional rather than a personal politeness. Remembering his stress on the fact that she was alone with her husband when he died, it suddenly flashed across my mind that somewhere I had read of a detective who, as his net was being woven about a victim, always grew more and more ominously polite toward the victim. I know that Andrews suspected her of a close connection with the case. As for myself, I don't know what I suspected as yet.

No objection was offered to our request to examine Mr. Morowitch's personal effects in the library, and accordingly Craig ransacked the desk and the letter-file. There was practically nothing to be discovered.

"Had Mr. Morowitch ever received any threats of robbery?" asked Craig, as he stood before the desk.

"Not that I know of," replied Mrs. Morowitch. "Of course every jeweller who carries a large stock of diamonds must be careful. But I don't think my husband had any special reason to fear robbery. At least he never said anything about it. Why do you ask?"

"Oh, nothing. I merely thought there might be some hint as to the motives of the robbery," said Craig. He was fingering one of those desk-calendars which have separate leaves for each day with blank spaces for appointments.

"'Close deal Poissan,'" he read slowly from one of the entries, as if to himself. "That's strange. It was the correspondence under the letter 'P' that was destroyed at the office, and there is nothing in the letter-file here, either. Who was Poissan?"

Mrs. Morowitch hesitated, either from ignorance or from a desire to evade the question. "A chemist, I think," she said doubtfully. "My husband had some dealings with him—some discovery he was going to buy. I don't know anything about it. I thought the deal was off."

"The deal?"

"Really, Mr. Kennedy, you had better ask Mr. Kahan. My husband talked very little to me about business affairs."

"But what was the discovery?"

"I don't know. I only heard Mr. Morowitch and Mr. Kahan refer to some deal about a discovery regarding diamonds."

"Then Mr. Kahan knows about it?"

"I presume so."

"Thank you, Mrs. Morowitch," said Kennedy when it was evident that she either could not or would not add anything to what she had said. "Pardon us for causing all this trouble."

"No trouble at all," she replied graciously, though I could see she was intent on every word and motion of Kennedy and Andrews.

Kennedy stopped the car at a drug-store a few blocks away and asked for the business telephone directory. In an instant, under chemists, he put his finger on the name of Poissan—"Henri Poissan, electric furnaces,—William St.," he read. "I shall visit him to-morrow morning. Now for the doctor."

Doctor Thornton was an excellent specimen of the genus physician to the wealthy—polished, cool, suave. One of Mr. Andrews's men, as I have said, had seen him already, but the interview had been very unsatisfactory. Evidently, however, the doctor had been turning something over in his mind since then and had thought better of it. At any rate, his manner was cordial enough now.

As he closed the doors to his office, he began to pace the floor. "Mr. Andrews," he said, "I am in some doubt whether I had better tell you or the coroner what I know. There are certain professional secrets that a doctor must, as a duty to his patients, conceal. That is professional ethics. But there are also cases when, as a matter of public policy, a doctor should speak out."

He stopped and faced us.

"I don't mind telling you that I dislike the publicity that would attend any statement I might make to the coroner."

"Exactly," said Andrews. "I appreciate your position exactly. Your other patients would not care to see you involved in a scandal—or at least you would not care to have them see you so involved, with all the newspaper notoriety such a thing brings."

Doctor Thornton shot a quick glance at Andrews, as if he would like to know just how much his visitor knew or suspected.

Andrews drew a paper from his pocket. "This is a copy of the death-certificate," he said. "The Board of Health has furnished it to us. Our physicians at the insurance company tell me it is rather extraordinary—vague. A word from us calling the attention of the proper authorities to it would be sufficient, I think. But, Doctor, that is just the point. We do not desire publicity any more than you do. We could have the body of Mr. Morowitch exhumed and examined, but I prefer to get the facts in the case without resorting to such extreme measures."

"It would do no good," interrupted the doctor hastily. "And if you'll save me the publicity, I'll tell you why."

Andrews nodded, but still held the death-certificate where the doctor was constantly reminded of it.

"In that certificate I have put down the cause of death as congestion of the lungs due to an acute attack of pneumonia. That is substantially correct, as far as it goes. When I was summoned to see Mr. Morowitch I found him in a semi-conscious state and scarcely breathing. Mrs. Morowitch told me that he had been brought home in a taxicab by a man who had picked him up on William Street. I'm frank to say that at first sight I thought it was a case of plain intoxication, for Mr. Morowitch sometimes indulged a little freely when he made a splendid deal. I smelled his breath, which was very feeble. It had a sickish sweet odour, but that did not impress me at the time. I applied my stethoscope to his lungs. There was a very marked congestion, and I made as my working diagnosis pneumonia. It was a case for quick and heroic action. In a very few minutes I had a tank of oxygen from the hospital.

"In the meantime I had thought over that sweetish odour, and it flashed on my mind that it might, after all, be a case of poisoning. When the oxygen arrived I administered it at once. As it happens, the Rockefeller Institute has just published a report of experiments with a new antidote for various poisons, which consists simply in a new method of enforced breathing and throwing off the poison by oxidising it in that way. In either case—the pneumonia theory or the poison theory—this line of action was the best that I could have adopted on the spur of the moment. I gave him some strychnin to strengthen his heart and by hard work I had him resting apparently a little easier. A nurse had been sent for, but had not arrived when a messenger came to me telling of a very sudden illness of Mrs. Morey, the wife of the steel-magnate. As the Morey home is only a half-block away, I left Mr. Morowitch, with very particular instructions to his wife as to what to do.

"I had intended to return immediately, but before I got back Mr. Morowitch was dead. Now I think I've told you all. You see, it was nothing but a suspicion—hardly enough to warrant making a fuss about. I made out the death-certificate, as you see. Probably that would have been all there was to it if I hadn't heard of this incomprehensible robbery. That set me thinking again. There, I'm glad I've got it out of my system. I've thought about it a good deal since your man was here to see me."

"What do you suspect was the cause of that sweetish odour?" asked Kennedy.

The doctor hesitated. "Mind, it is only a suspicion. Cyanide of potassium or cyanogen gas; either would give such an odour."

"Your treatment would have been just the same had you been certain?"

"Practically the same, the Rockefeller treatment."

"Could it have been suicide?" asked Andrews.

"There was no motive for it, I believe," replied the doctor.

"But was there any such poison in the Morowitch house?"

"I know that they were much interested in photography. Cyanide of potassium is used in certain processes in photography."

"Who was interested in photography, Mr. or Mrs. Morowitch?"

"Both of them."

"Was Mrs. Morowitch?"

"Both of them," repeated the doctor hastily. It was evident how Andrews's questions were tending, and it was also evident that the doctor did not wish to commit himself or even to be misunderstood.

Kennedy had sat silently for some minutes, turning the thing over in his mind. Apparently disregarding Andrews entirely, he now asked, "Doctor, supposing it had been cyanogen gas which caused the congestion of the lungs, and supposing it had not been inhaled in quantities large enough to kill outright, do you nevertheless feel that Mr. Morowitch was in a weak enough condition to die as a result of the congestion produced by the gas after the traces of the cyanogen had been perhaps thrown off?"

"That is precisely the impression which I wished to convey."

"Might I ask whether in his semi-conscious state he said anything that might at all serve as a clue?"

"He talked ramblingly, incoherently. As near as I can remember it, he seemed to believe himself to have become a millionaire, a billionaire. He talked of diamonds, diamonds, diamonds. He seemed to be picking them up, running his fingers through them, and once I remember he seemed to want to send for Mr. Kahan and tell him something. 'I can make them, Kahan,' he said, 'the finest, the largest, the whitest—I can make them.'"

Kennedy was all attention as Dr. Thornton added this new evidence.

"You know," concluded the doctor, "that in cyanogen poisoning there might be hallucinations of the wildest kind. But then, too, in the delirium of pneumonia it might be the same."

I could see by the way Kennedy acted that for the first time a ray of light had dawned upon him in tracing out the case. As we rose to go, the doctor shook hands with us. His last words were said with an air of great relief, "Gentlemen, I have eased my conscience considerably."

As we parted for the night Kennedy faced Andrews. "You recall that you promised me one thing when I took up this case?" he asked.

Andrews nodded.

"Then take no steps until I tell you. Shadow Mrs. Morowitch and Mr. Kahan, but do not let them know you suspect them of anything. Let me run down this Poissan clue. In other words, leave the case entirely in my hands in other respects. Let me know any new facts you may unearth, and some time to-morrow I shall call on you, and we will determine what the next step is to be. Good night. I want to thank you for putting me in the way of this case. I think we shall all he surprised at the outcome."

It was late the following afternoon before I saw Kennedy again. He was in his laboratory winding two strands of platinum wire carefully about a piece of porcelain and smearing on it some peculiar black glassy granular substance that came in a sort of pencil, like a stick of sealing-wax. I noticed that he was very particular to keep the two wires exactly the same distance from each other throughout the entire length of the piece of porcelain, but I said nothing to distract his attention, though a thousand questions about the progress of the case were at my tongue's end.

Instead I watched him intently. The black substance formed a sort of bridge connecting and covering the wires. When he had finished he said: "Now you can ask me your questions, while I heat and anneal this little contrivance. I see you are bursting with curiosity."

"Well, did you see Poissan?" I asked.

Kennedy continued to heat the wire-covered porcelain. "I did, and he is going to give me a demonstration of his discovery to-night."

"His discovery?"

"You remember Morowitch's 'hallucination,' as the doctor called it? That was no hallucination; that was a reality. This man Poissan says he has discovered a way to make diamonds artificially out of pure carbon in an electric furnace.* Morowitch, I believe, was to buy his secret. His dream of millions was a reality—at least to him."

"And did Kahan and Mrs. Morowitch know it?" I asked quickly.

---

* The dream of producing diamonds artificially was first pursued in the mid-nineteenth century. Not until the 1940s, however, did systematic research begin into using the practical methods known as chemical vapor deposition (CVD) and high-pressure high-temperature (HPHT), both of which worked well. The first consistent synthesis of diamonds took place in 1955, and diamonds are regularly made today—using the CVD and HPHT processes—for a variety of purposes, including of course jewelry.

"I don't know yet," replied Craig, finishing the annealing. The black glassy substance was now a dull grey.

"What's that stuff you were putting on the wire?" I asked.

"Oh, just a by-product made in the manufacture of sulphuric acid," answered Kennedy airily, adding, as if to change the subject: "I want you to go with me to-night. I told Poissan I was a professor in the university and that I would bring one of our younger trustees, the son of the banker, T. Pierpont Spencer, who might put some capital into his scheme. Now, Jameson, while I'm finishing up my work here, run over to the apartment and get my automatic revolver. I may need it to-night. I have communicated with Andrews, and he will be ready. The demonstration will take place at half-past-eight at Poissan's laboratory. I tried to get him to give it here, but he absolutely refused."

Half an hour later I rejoined Craig at his laboratory, and we rode down to the Great Eastern Life Building.

Andrews was waiting for us in his solidly furnished office. Outside I noted a couple of husky men, who seemed to be waiting for orders from their chief.

From the manner in which the vice-president greeted us it was evident that he was keenly interested in what Kennedy was about to do. "So you think Morowitch's deal was a deal to purchase the secret of diamond-making?" he mused.

"I feel sure of it," replied Craig. "I felt sure of it the moment I looked up Poissan and found that he was a manufacturer of electric furnaces. Don't you remember the famous Lemoine case in London and Paris?"

"Yes, but Lemoine was a fakir of the first water," said Andrews. "Do you think this man is, too?"

"That's what I'm going to find out to-night before I take another step," said Craig. "Of course there can be no doubt that by proper use the electric furnace will make small, almost microscopic diamonds. It is not unreasonable to suppose that some day someone will be able to make large diamonds synthetically by the same process."

"Maybe this man has done it," agreed Andrews. "Who knows? I'll wager that if he has and that if Morowitch had bought an interest in his process Kahan knew of it. He's a sharp one. And Mrs. Morowitch doesn't let grass grow under her feet, when it comes to seeing the main chance as to money. Now just supposing Mr. Morowitch had bought an interest in a secret like that and supposing Kahan was in love with Mrs. Morowitch and that they—"

"Let us suppose nothing, Mr. Andrews," interrupted Kennedy. "At least not yet. Let me see; it is now ten minutes after eight. Poissan's place is only a few blocks from here. I'd like to get there a few minutes early. Let's start."

As we left the office, Andrews signalled to the two men outside, and they quietly followed a few feet in the rear, but without seeming to be with us.

Poissan's laboratory was at the top of a sort of loft building a dozen stories or so high. It was a peculiar building, with several entrances besides a freight-elevator at the rear and fire-escapes that led to adjoining lower roofs.

We stopped around the corner in the shadow, and Kennedy and Andrews talked earnestly. As near as I could make out Kennedy was insisting that it would be best for Andrews and his men not to enter the building at all, but wait down-stairs while he and I went up. At last the arrangement was agreed on.

"Here," said Kennedy, undoing a package he had carried, "is a little electric bell with a couple of fresh dry batteries attached to it, and wires that will reach at least four hundred feet. You and the men wait in the shadow here by this side entrance for five minutes after Jameson and I go up. Then you must engage the night watchman in some way. While he is away you will find two wires dangling down the elevator shaft. Attach them to these wires from the bell and the batteries—these two—you know how to do that. The wires will be hanging in the third shaft— only one elevator is running at night, the first. The moment you hear the bell begin to ring, jump into the elevator and come up to the twelfth floor—we'll need you."

As Kennedy and I rode up in the elevator I could not help thinking what an ideal place a down-town office-building is for committing a crime, even at this early hour of the evening. If the streets were deserted, the office-buildings were positively uncanny in their grim, black silence with only here and there a light.

The elevator in the first shaft shot down again to the ground floor, and as it disappeared Kennedy took two spools of wire from his pocket and hastily shoved them through the lattice work of the third elevator shaft. They quickly unrolled, and I could hear them strike the top of the empty car below in the basement. That meant that Andrews on the ground floor could reach the wires and attach them to the bell.

Quickly in the darkness Kennedy attached the ends of the wires to the curious little coil I had seen him working on in the laboratory, and we proceeded down the hall to the rooms occupied by Poissan. Kennedy had allowed for the wire to reach from the elevator shaft up this hall, also, and as he walked he paid it out in such a manner that it fell on the floor close to the wall, where, in the darkness, it would never be noticed or stumbled over.

Around an "L" in the hall I could see a ground-glass window with a light shining through it. Kennedy stopped at the window and quickly placed the little coil on the ledge, close up against the glass, with the wires running from it down the hall. Then we entered.

"On time to the minute, Professor," exclaimed Poissan, snapping his watch. "And this, I presume, is the banker who is interested in my great discovery of making artificial diamonds of any size or colour?" he added, indicating me.

"Yes," answered Craig, "as I told you, a son of Mr. T. Pierpont Spencer."

I shook hands with as much dignity as I could assume, for the role of impersonation was a new one to me.

Kennedy carelessly laid his coat and hat on the inside ledge of the ground-glass window, just opposite the spot where he had placed the little coil on the other side of the glass. I noted that the window was simply a large pane of wire-glass set in the wall for the purpose of admitting light in the daytime from the hall outside.

The whole thing seemed eerie to me—especially as Poissan's assistant was a huge fellow and had an evil look such as I had seen in pictures of the inhabitants of quarters of Paris which one does not frequent except in the company of a safe guide. I was glad Kennedy had brought his revolver, and rather vexed that he had not told me to do likewise. However, I trusted that Craig knew what he was about.

We seated ourselves some distance from a table on which was a huge, plain, oblong contrivance that reminded me of the diagram of a parallelopiped which had caused so much trouble in my solid geometry at college.

"That's the electric furnace, sir," said Craig to me with an assumed deference, becoming a college professor explaining things to the son of a great financier. "You see the electrodes at either end? When the current is turned on and led through them into the furnace you can get the most amazing temperatures in the crucible. The most refractory of chemical compounds can be broken up by that heat. What is the highest temperature you have attained, Professor?"

"Something over three thousand degrees Centigrade," replied Poissan, as he and his assistant busied themselves about the furnace.

We sat watching him in silence.

"Ah, gentlemen, now I am ready," he exclaimed at length, when everything was arranged to his satisfaction. "You see, here is a lump of sugar carbon—pure amorphous carbon. Diamonds, as you know, are composed of pure carbon crystallised under enormous pressure. Now, my theory is that if we can combine an enormous pressure and an enormous heat we can make diamonds artificially. The problem of pressure is the thing, for here in the furnace we have the necessary heat. It occurred to me that when molten cast iron cools it exerts a tremendous pressure. That pressure is what I use."

"You know, Spencer, solid iron floats on molten iron like solid water—ice—floats on liquid water," explained Craig to me.

Poissan nodded. "I take this sugar carbon and place it in this soft iron cup. Then I screw on this cap over the cup, so. Now I place this mass of iron scraps in the crucible of the furnace and start the furnace."

He turned a switch, and long yellowish-blue sheets of flame spurted out from the electrodes on either side. It was weird, gruesome. One could feel the heat of the tremendous electric discharge.

As I looked at the bluish-yellow flames they gradually changed to a beautiful purple, and a sickish sweet odour filled the room. The furnace roared at first, but as the vapors increased it became a better conductor of the electricity, and the roaring ceased.

In almost no time the mass of iron scraps became molten. Suddenly Poissan plunged the cast-iron cup into the seething mass. The cup floated and quickly began to melt. As it did so he waited attentively until the proper moment. Then with a deft motion he seized the whole thing with a long pair of tongs and plunged it into a vat of running water. A huge cloud of steam filled the room.

I felt a drowsy sensation stealing over me as the sickish sweet smell from the furnace increased. Gripping the chair, I roused myself and watched Poissan attentively. He was working rapidly. As the molten mass cooled and solidified he took it out of the water and laid it on an anvil.

Then his assistant began to hammer it with careful, sharp blows, chipping off the outside.

"You see, we have to get down to the core of carbon gently," he said, as he picked up the little pieces of iron and threw them into a scrap-box. "First rather brittle cast iron, then hard iron, then iron and carbon, then some black diamonds, and in the very centre the diamonds.

"Ah! we are getting to them. Here is a small diamond. See, Mr. Spencer—gently François—we shall come to the large ones presently."

"One moment, Professor Poissan," interrupted Craig; "let your assistant break them out while I stand over him."

"Impossible. You would not know when you saw them. They are just rough stones."

"Oh, yes, I would."

"No, stay where you are. Unless I attend to it the diamonds might be ruined."

There was something peculiar about his insistence, but after he picked out the next diamond I was hardly prepared for Kennedy's next remark.

"Let me see the palms of your hands."

Poissan shot an angry glance at Kennedy, but he did not open his hands.

"I merely wish to convince you, Mr. Spencer," said Kennedy to me, "that it is no sleight-of-hand trick and that the professor has not several uncut stones palmed in his hand like a prestidigitator."

The Frenchman faced us, his face livid with rage. "You call me a prestidigitator, a fraud—you shall suffer for that! *Sacrebleu! Ventre du Saint Gris!* No man ever insults the honour of Poissan. François, water on the electrodes!"

The assistant dashed a few drops of water on the electrodes. The sickish odour increased tremendously. I felt myself almost going, but with an effort I again roused myself. I wondered how Craig stood the fumes, for I suffered an intense headache and nausea.

"Stop!" Craig thundered. "There's enough cyanogen in this room already. I know your game—the water forms acetylene with the carbon, and that uniting with the nitrogen of the air under the terrific heat of the electric arc forms hydrocyanic acid. Would you poison us, too? Do you think you can put me unconscious out on the street and have a society doctor diagnose my case as pneumonia? Or do you think we shall die quietly in some hospital as a certain New York banker did last year after he had watched an alchemist make silver out of apparently nothing?"

The effect on Poissan was terrible. He advanced toward Kennedy, the veins in his face fairly standing out. Shaking his forefinger, he shouted: "You know that, do you? You are no professor, and this is no banker. You are spies, spies. You come from the friends of Morowitch, do you? You have gone too far with me."

Kennedy said nothing, but retreated and took his coat and

---

* E. Cobham Brewer's *Dictionary of Phrase and Fable* (1898) identifies the phrase as a favorite of King Henri IV of France and attributes the meaning as essentially "the body of Christ." "*Sacrebleu*" means "Holy God."

hat off the window ledge. The hideous penetrating light of the tongues of flame from the furnace played on the ground-glass window.

Poissan laughed a hollow laugh.

"Put down your hat and coat, Mistair Kennedy," he hissed. "The door has been locked ever since you have been here. Those windows are barred, the telephone wire is cut, and it is three hundred feet to the street. We shall leave you here when the fumes have overcome you. François and I can stand them up to a point, and when we reach that point we are going."

Instead of being cowed Kennedy grew bolder, though I, for my part, felt so weakened that I feared the outcome of a hand-to-hand encounter with either Poissan or François, who appeared as fresh as if nothing had happened. They were hurriedly preparing to leave us.

"That would do you no good," Kennedy rejoined, "for we have no safe full of jewels for you to rob. There are no keys to offices to be stolen from our pockets. And let me tell you—you are not the only man in New York who knows the secret of thermit. I have told the secret to the police, and they are only waiting to find who destroyed Morowitch's correspondence under the letter 'P' to apprehend the robber of his safe. Your secret is out."

"Revenge! revenge!" Poissan cried. "I will have revenge. François, bring out the jewels—ha! ha!—here in this bag are the jewels of Mr. Morowitch. To-night François and I will go down by the back elevator to a secret exit. In two hours all your police in New York cannot find us. But in two hours you two impostors will be suffocated—perhaps you will die of cyanogen, like Morowitch, whose jewels I have at last."

He went to the door into the hall and stood there with a mocking laugh. I moved to make a rush toward them, but Kennedy raised his hand.

"You will suffocate," Poissan hissed again.

Just then we heard the elevator door clang, and hurried steps came down the long hall.

Craig whipped out his automatic and began pumping the bullets out in rapid succession. As the smoke cleared I expected to see Poissan and François lying on the floor. Instead, Craig had fired at the lock of the door. He had shattered it into a thousand bits. Andrews and his men were running down the hall.

"Curse you!" muttered Poissan as he banged the now useless lock, "who let those fellows in? Are you a wizard?"

Craig smiled coolly as the ventilation cleared the room of the deadly cyanogen.

"On the window-sill outside is a selenium cell. Selenium is a bad conductor of electricity in the dark, and an excellent conductor when exposed to light. I merely moved my coat and hat, and the light from the furnace which was going to suffocate us played through the glass on the cell, the circuit was completed without your suspecting that I could communicate with friends outside, a bell was rung on the street, and here they are. Andrews, there is the murderer of Morowitch, and there in his hands are the Morowitch—"

Poissan had moved toward the furnace. With a quick motion he seized the long tongs. There was a cloud of choking vapor. Kennedy leaped to the switch and shut off the current. With the tongs he lifted out a shapeless piece of valueless black graphite.

"All that is left of the priceless Morowitch jewels," he exclaimed ruefully. "But we have the murderer."

"And to-morrow a certified check for one hundred thousand dollars goes to Mrs. Morowitch with my humblest apologies and sympathy," added Andrews. "Professor Kennedy, you have earned your retainer."

VII

THE AZURE RING

Files of newspapers and innumerable clippings from the press bureaus littered Kennedy's desk in rank profusion. Kennedy himself was so deeply absorbed that I had merely said good evening as I came in and had started to open my mail. With an impatient sweep of his hand, however, he brushed the whole mass of newspapers into the wastebasket.

"It seems to me, Walter," he exclaimed in disgust, "that this mystery is considered insoluble for the very reason which should make it easy to solve—the extraordinary character of its features."

Inasmuch as he had opened the subject, I laid down the letter I was reading. "I'll wager I can tell you just why you made that remark, Craig," I ventured. "You're reading up on that Wainwright-Templeton affair."

"You are on the road to becoming a detective yourself, Walter," he answered with a touch of sarcasm. "Your ability to add two units to two other units and obtain four units is almost worthy of Inspector O'Connor. You are right, and within a quarter of an hour the district attorney of Westchester County will be here. He telephoned me this afternoon and sent an assistant with this mass of dope. I suppose he'll want it back," he added, fishing the newspapers out of the basket again. "But, with all due respect to your profession, I'll say that no one would ever get on speaking terms with the solution of this case if he had to depend solely on the newspaper writers."

"No?" I queried, rather nettled at his tone.

"No," he repeated emphatically. "Here one of the most popular girls in the fashionable suburb of Williston,* and one of the leading younger members of the bar in New York, engaged to be married, are found dead in the library of the girl's home the day before the ceremony. And now, a week later, no one knows whether it was an accident due to the fumes from the antique charcoal-brazier, or whether it was a double suicide, or suicide and murder, or a double murder, or—or—why, the experts haven't even been able to agree on whether they have discovered poison or not," he continued, growing as excited as the city editor did over my first attempt as a cub reporter.

"They haven't agreed on anything except that on the eve of what was, presumably, to have been the happiest day of their lives two of the best known members of the younger set are found dead, while absolutely no one, as far as is known, can be proved to have been near them within the time necessary to murder them. No wonder the coroner says it is simply a case of asphyxiation. No wonder the district attorney is at his wits' end. You fellows have hounded them with your hypotheses until they can't see the facts straight. You suggest one solution and before—"

The door-bell sounded insistently, and without waiting for an answer a tall, spare, loose-jointed individual stalked in and laid a green bag on the table.

---

* A fictional town.

"Good evening, Professor Kennedy," he began brusquely. "I am District Attorney Whitney, of Westchester. I see you have been reading up on the case. Quite right."

"Quite wrong," answered Craig. "Let me introduce my friend, Mr. Jameson, of the *Star*. Sit down. Jameson knows what I think of the way the newspapers have handled this case. I was about to tell him as you came in that I intended to disregard everything that had been printed, to start out with you as if it were a fresh subject and get the facts at first hand. Let's get right down to business. First tell us just how it was that Miss Wainwright and Mr. Templeton were discovered and by whom."

The district attorney loosened the cords of the green bag and drew out a bundle of documents. "I'll read you the affidavit of the maid who found them," he said, fingering the documents nervously. "You see, John Templeton had left his office in New York early that afternoon, telling his father that he was going to visit Miss Wainwright. He caught the three-twenty train, reached Williston all right, walked to the Wainwright house, and, in spite of the hustle of preparation for the wedding, the next day, he spent the rest of the afternoon with Miss Wainwright. That's where the mystery begins. They had no visitors. At least, the maid who answers the bell says they had none. She was busy with the rest of the family, and I believe the front door was not locked—we don't lock our doors in Williston, except at night."

He had found the paper and paused to impress these facts on our minds.

"Mrs. Wainwright and Miss Marian Wainwright, the sister, were busy about the house. Mrs. Wainwright wished to consult Laura about something. She summoned the maid and asked if Mr. Templeton and Miss Wainwright were in the house. The maid replied that she would see, and this is her affidavit. Ahem! I'll skip the legal part:

"'I knocked at the library door twice, but obtaining no answer, I supposed they had gone out for a walk or perhaps a ride across country as they often did. I opened the door partly and looked in. There was a silence in the room, a strange, queer silence. I opened the door further and, looking toward the davenport in the corner, I saw Miss Laura and Mr. Templeton in such an awkward position. They looked as if they had fallen asleep. His head was thrown back against the cushions of the davenport, and on his face was a most awful look. It was discoloured. Her head had fallen forward on his shoulder, sideways, and on her face, too, was the same terrible stare and the same discolouration. Their right hands were tightly clasped.

"'I called to them. They did not answer. Then the horrible truth flashed on me. They were dead. I felt giddy for a minute, but quickly recovered myself, and with a cry for help I rushed to Mrs. Wainwright's room, shrieking that they were dead. Mrs. Wainwright fainted. Miss Marian called the doctor on the telephone and helped us restore her mother. She seemed perfectly cool in the tragedy, and I do not know what we servants should have done if she had not been there to direct us. The house was frantic, and Mr. Wainwright was not at home.

"'I did not detect any odour when I opened the library door. No glasses or bottles or vials or other receptacles which could have held poison were discovered or removed by me, or to the best of my knowledge and belief by anyone else.'"

"What happened next?" asked Craig eagerly.

"The family physician arrived and sent for the coroner immediately, and later for myself. You see, he thought at once of murder."

"But the coroner, I understand, thinks differently," prompted Kennedy.

"Yes, the coroner has declared the case to be accidental. He says that the weight of evidence points positively to asphyxiation. Still, how can it be asphyxiation? They could have escaped from the room at any time; the door was not locked. I tell you, in spite of the fact that the tests for poison in their mouths, stomachs, and blood have so far revealed nothing, I still believe that John Templeton and Laura Wainwright were murdered."

Kennedy looked at his watch thoughtfully. "You have told me just enough to make me want to see the coroner himself," he mused. "If we take the next train out to Williston with you, will you engage to get us a half-hour talk with him on the case, Mr. Whitney?"

"Surely. But we'll have to start right away. I've finished my other business in New York. Inspector O'Connor—ah, I see you know him—has promised to secure the attendance of anyone whom I can show to be a material witness in the case. Come on, gentlemen: I'll answer your other questions on the train."

As we settled ourselves in the smoker, Whitney remarked in a low voice, "You know, someone has said that there is only one thing more difficult to investigate and solve than a crime whose commission is surrounded by complicated circumstances and that is a crime whose perpetration is wholly devoid of circumstances."

"Are you so sure that this crime is wholly devoid of circumstances?" asked Craig.

"Professor," he replied, "I'm not sure of anything in this case. If I were I should not require your assistance. I would like the credit of solving it myself, but it is beyond me. Just think of it: so far we haven't a clue, at least none that shows the slightest promise, although we have worked night and day for a week. It's all darkness. The facts are so simple that they give us nothing to work on. It is like a blank sheet of paper."

Kennedy said nothing, and the district attorney proceeded:

"I don't blame Mr. Nott, the coroner, for thinking it an accident. But to my mind, some master criminal must have arranged this very baffling simplicity of circumstances. You recall that the front door was unlocked. This person must have entered the house unobserved, not a difficult thing to do, for the Wainwright house is somewhat isolated. Perhaps this person brought along some poison in the form of a beverage, and induced the two victims to drink. And then, this person must have removed the evidences as swiftly as they were brought in and by the same door. That, I think, is the only solution."

"That is not the only solution. It is one solution," interrupted Kennedy quietly.

"Do you think someone in the house did it?" I asked quickly.

"I think," replied Craig, carefully measuring his words, "that if poison was given them it must have been by someone they both knew pretty well."

No one said a word, until at last I broke the silence. "I know from the gossip of the *Star* office that many Williston people say that Marian was very jealous of her sister Laura for capturing the catch of the season. Williston people don't hesitate to hint at it."

Whitney produced another document from that fertile green bag. It was another affidavit. He handed it to us. It was a statement signed by Mrs. Wainwright, and read:

"Before God, my daughter Marian is innocent. If you wish to find out all, find out more about the past history of Mr. Templeton before he became engaged to Laura. She would never in the world have committed suicide. She was too bright and cheerful for that, even if Mr. Templeton had been about to break off the engagement. My daughters Laura and Marian were always treated by Mr. Wainwright and myself exactly alike. Of course they had their quarrels, just as all sisters do, but there was never, to my certain knowledge, a serious disagreement, and I was always close enough to my girls to know. No, Laura was murdered by someone outside."

Kennedy did not seem to attach much importance to this statement. "Let us see," he began reflectively. "First, we have a young woman especially attractive and charming in both person and temperament. She is just about to be married and, if the reports are to be believed, there was no cloud on her happiness. Secondly, we have a young man whom everyone agrees to have been of an ardent, energetic, optimistic temperament. He had everything to live for, presumably. So far, so good. Everyone who has investigated this case, I understand, has tried to eliminate the double-suicide and the suicide-and-murder theories. That is all right, providing the facts are as stated. We shall see, later, when we interview the coroner. Now, Mr. Whitney, suppose you tell us briefly what you have learned about the past history of the two unfortunate lovers."

"Well, the Wainwrights are an old Westchester family, not very wealthy, but of the real aristocracy of the county. There were only two children, Laura and Marian. The Templetons were much the same sort of family. The children all attended a private school at White Plains, and there also they met Schuyler Vanderdyke. These four constituted a sort of little aristocracy in the school. I mention this, because Vanderdyke later became Laura's first husband. This marriage with Templeton was a second venture."

"How long ago was she divorced?" asked Craig attentively.

"About three years ago. I'm coming to that in a moment. The sisters went to college together, Templeton to law school, and Vanderdyke studied civil engineering. Their intimacy was pretty well broken up, all except Laura's and Vanderdyke's. Soon after he graduated he was taken into the construction department of the Central Railroad by his uncle, who was a vice-president, and Laura and he were married. As far as I can learn he had been a fellow of convivial habits at college, and about two years after their marriage his wife suddenly became aware of what had long been well known in Williston, that Vanderdyke was paying marked attention to a woman named Miss Laporte in New York.

"No sooner had Laura Vanderdyke learned of this intimacy of her husband," continued Whitney, "than she quietly hired private detectives to shadow him, and on their evidence she obtained a divorce. The papers were sealed, and she resumed her maiden name.

"As far as I can find out, Vanderdyke then disappeared from her life. He resigned his position with the railroad and joined a party of engineers exploring the upper Amazon. Later he went to Venezuela. Miss Laporte also went to South America about the same time, and was for a time in Venezuela, and later in Peru.

"Vanderdyke seems to have dropped all his early associations completely, though at present I find he is back in New York raising capital for a company to exploit a new asphalt concession in the interior of Venezuela. Miss Laporte has also reappeared in New York as Mrs. Ralston, with a mining claim in the mountains of Peru."

"And Templeton?" asked Craig. "Had he had any previous matrimonial ventures?"

"No, none. Of course he had had love affairs, mostly with the country-club set. He had known Miss Laporte pretty well, too, while he was in law school in New York. But when he settled down to work he seems to have forgotten all about the girls for a couple of years or so. He was very anxious to get ahead, and let nothing stand in his way. He was admitted to the bar and taken in by his father as junior member of the firm of Templeton, Mills & Templeton. Not long ago he was appointed a special master to take testimony in the get-rich-quick-company prosecutions, and I happen to know that he was making good in the investigation."

Kennedy nodded. "What sort of fellow personally was Templeton?" he asked.

"Very popular," replied the district attorney, "both at the country club and in his profession in New York. He was a fellow of naturally commanding temperament—the Templetons were always that way. I doubt if many young men even with his chances could have gained such a reputation at thirty-five as his. Socially he was very popular, too, a great catch for all the sly mamas of the country club who had marriageable daughters. He liked automobiles and outdoor sports, and he was strong in politics, too. That was how he got ahead so fast.

"Well, to cut the story short, Templeton met the Wainwright girls again last summer at a resort on Long Island. They had just returned from a long trip abroad, spending most of the time in the Far East with their father, whose firm has business interests in China. The girls were very attractive. They rode and played tennis and golf better than most of the men, and this fall Templeton became a frequent visitor at the Wainwright home in Williston.

"People who know them best tell me that his first attentions were paid to Marian, a very dashing and ambitious young woman. Nearly every day Templeton's car stopped at the house and the girls and some friend of Templeton's in the country club went for a ride. They tell me that at this time Marian always sat with Templeton on the front seat. But after a few weeks the gossips—nothing of that sort ever escapes Williston—said that the occupant of the front seat was Laura. She often drove the car herself and was very clever at it. At any rate, not long after that the engagement was announced."

As he walked up from the pretty little Williston station Kennedy asked: "One more question, Mr. Whitney. How did Marian take the engagement?"

The district attorney hesitated. "I will be perfectly frank, Mr. Kennedy," he answered. "The country-club people tell me that the girls were very cool toward each other. That was why I got that statement from Mrs. Wainwright. I wish to be perfectly fair to everyone concerned in this case."

We found the coroner quite willing to talk, in spite of the fact that the hour was late. "My friend, Mr. Whitney, here, still holds the poison theory," began the coroner, "in spite of the fact that everything points absolutely toward asphyxiation. If I had been able to discover the slightest trace of illuminating-gas in the room I should have pronounced it asphyxia at once. All the symptoms accorded with it. But the asphyxia was not caused by escaping illuminating-gas.

"There was an antique charcoal-brazier in the room, and I have ascertained that it was lighted. Now, anything like a brazier will, unless there is proper ventilation, give rise to carbonic oxide or carbon monoxide gas, which is always present in the products of combustion, often to the extent of from five to ten per cent. A very slight quantity of this gas, insufficient even to cause an odour in a room, will give a severe headache, and a case is recorded where a whole family in Glasgow was poisoned without knowing it by the escape of this gas. A little over one per cent of it in the atmosphere is fatal, if breathed for any length of time. You know, it is a product of combustion, and is very deadly—it is the much-dreaded white damp or afterdamp of a mine explosion.*

---

* A mixture of poisonous gases—predominately carbon monoxide—commonly found to be present in and after mine explosions (the "afterdamp" is the cloud resulting from the explosion). Of course, with the advent of the internal combustion engine in automobiles and the use of oil-based fuels for home heating, carbon monoxide poisoning would soon become much more common.

"I'm going to tell you a secret which I have not given out to the press yet. I tried an experiment in a closed room to-day, lighting the brazier. Some distance from it I placed a cat confined in a cage so it could not escape. In an hour and a half the cat was asphyxiated."

The coroner concluded with an air of triumph that quite squelched the district attorney.

Kennedy was all attention. "Have you preserved samples of the blood of Mr. Templeton and Miss Wainwright?" he asked.

"Certainly. I have them in my office."

The coroner, who was also a local physician, led us back into his private office.

"And the cat?" added Craig.

Doctor Nott produced it in a covered basket.

Quickly Kennedy drew off a little of the blood of the cat and held it up to the light along with the human samples. The difference was apparent.

"You see," he explained, "carbon monoxide combines firmly with the blood, destroying the red colouring matter of the red corpuscles. No, Doctor, I'm afraid it wasn't carbonic oxide that killed the lovers, although it certainly killed the cat."

Doctor Nott was crestfallen, but still unconvinced. "If my whole medical reputation were at stake," he repeated, "I should still be compelled to swear to asphyxia. I've seen it too often, to make a mistake. Carbonic oxide or not, Templeton and Miss Wainwright were asphyxiated."

It was now Whitney's chance to air his theory. "I have always inclined toward the cyanide-of-potassium theory, either that it was administered in a drink or perhaps injected by a needle," he said. "One of the chemists has reported that there was a possibility of slight traces of cyanide in the mouths."

"If it had been cyanide," replied Craig, looking reflectively at the two jars before him on the table, "these blood specimens would be blue in colour and clotted. But they are not. Then, too, there is a substance in the saliva which is used in the process of digestion. It gives a reaction which might very easily be mistaken for a slight trace of cyanide. I think that explains what the chemist discovered; no more, no less. The cyanide theory does not fit."

"One chemist hinted at nux vomica,"* volunteered the coroner. "He said it wasn't nux vomica, but that the blood test showed something very much like it. Oh, we've looked for morphine, chloroform, ether, all the ordinary poisons, besides some of the little-known alkaloids. Believe me, Professor Kennedy, it *was* asphyxia."

I could tell by the look that crossed Kennedy's face that at last a ray of light had pierced the darkness. "Have you any spirits of turpentine in the office?" he asked.

The coroner shook his head and took a step toward the telephone as if to call the drug-store in town.

"Or ether?" interrupted Craig. "Ether will do."

"Oh, yes, plenty of ether."

Craig poured a little of one of the blood samples from the jar into a tube and added a few drops of ether. A cloudy dark precipitate formed. He smiled quietly and said, half to himself, "I thought so."

"What is it?" asked the coroner eagerly. "Nux vomica?"

Craig shook his head as he stared at the black precipitate. "You were perfectly right about the asphyxiation, Doctor," he remarked slowly, "but wrong as to the cause. It wasn't carbon monoxide or illuminating-gas. And you, Mr. Whitney, were right about the poison, too. Only it is a poison neither of you ever heard of."

---

* More commonly known as strychnine.

"What is it?" we asked simultaneously.

"Let me take these samples and make some further tests. I am sure of it, but it is new to me. Wait till to-morrow night, when my chain of evidence is completed. Then you are all cordially invited to attend at my laboratory at the university. I'll ask you, Mr. Whitney, to come armed with a warrant for John or Jane Doe. Please see that the Wainwrights, particularly Marian, are present. You can tell Inspector O'Connor that Mr. Vanderdyke and Mrs. Ralston are required as material witnesses—anything so long as you are sure that these five persons are present. Good night, gentlemen."

We rode back to the city in silence, but as we neared the station, Kennedy remarked: "You see, Walter, these people are like the newspapers. They are floundering around in a sea of unrelated facts. There is more than they think back of this crime. I've been revolving in my mind how it will be possible to get some inkling about this concession of Vanderdyke's, the mining claim of Mrs. Ralston, and the exact itinerary of the Wainwright trip in the Far East. Do you think you can get that information for me? I think it will take me all day to-morrow to isolate this poison and get things in convincing shape on that score. Meanwhile if you can see Vanderdyke and Mrs. Ralston you can help me a great deal. I am sure you will find them very interesting people."

"I have been told that she is quite a female high financier," I replied, tacitly accepting Craig's commission. "Her story is that her claim is situated near the mine of a group of powerful American capitalists, who are opposed to having any competition, and on the strength of that story she has been raking in the money right and left. I don't know Vanderdyke, never heard of him before, but no doubt he has some equally interesting game."

"Don't let them think you connect them with the case, however," cautioned Craig.

Early the next morning I started out on my quest for facts, though not so early but that Kennedy had preceded me to his work in his laboratory. It was not very difficult to get Mrs. Ralston to talk about her troubles with the government. In fact, I did not even have to broach the subject of the death of Templeton. She volunteered the information that in his handling of her case he had been very unjust to her, in spite of the fact that she had known him well a long time ago. She even hinted that she believed he represented the combination of capitalists who were using the government to aid their own monopoly and prevent the development of her mine. Whether it was an obsession of her mind, or merely part of her clever scheme, I could not make out. I noted, however, that when she spoke of Templeton it was in a studied, impersonal way, and that she was at pains to lay the blame for the governmental interference rather on the rival mine-owners.

It quite surprised me when I found from the directory that Vanderdyke's office was on the floor below in the same building. Like Mrs. Ralston's, it was open, but not doing business, pending the investigation by the Post-Office Department.

Vanderdyke was a type of which I had seen many before. Well dressed to the extreme, he displayed all those evidences of prosperity which are the stock in trade of the man with securities to sell. He grasped my hand when I told him I was going to present the other side of the post-office cases and held it between both of his as if he had known me all his life. Only the fact that he had never seen me before prevented his calling me by my first name. I took mental note of his stock of jewellery, the pin in his tie that might almost have been the Hope diamond, the heavy watchchain across his chest, and a very brilliant seal ring of lapis lazuli on the hand that grasped mine. He saw me looking at it and smiled.

"My dear fellow, we have deposits of that stuff that would make a fortune if we could get the machinery to get at it. Why, sir, there is lapis lazuli enough on our claim to make enough ultramarine paint to supply all the artists to the end of the world. Actually we could afford to crush it up and sell it as paint. And that is merely incidental to the other things on the concession. The asphalt's the thing. That's where the big money is. When we get started, sir, the old asphalt trust will simply melt away, melt away."

He blew a cloud of tobacco smoke and let it dissolve significantly in the air.

When it came to talking about the suits, however, Vanderdyke was not so communicative as Mrs. Ralston, but he was also not so bitter against either the post-office or Templeton.

"Poor Templeton," he said. "I used to know him years ago when we were boys. Went to school with him and all that sort of thing, you know, but until I ran across him, or rather he ran across me, in this investigation I hadn't heard much about him. Pretty clever fellow he was, too. The state will miss him, but my lawyer tells me that we should have won the suit anyhow, even if that unfortunate tragedy hadn't occurred. Most unaccountable, wasn't it? I've read about it in the papers for old time's sake, and can make nothing out of it."

I said nothing, but wondered how he could pass so light-heartedly over the death of the woman who had once been his wife. However, I said nothing. The result was he launched forth again on the riches of his Venezuelan concession and loaded me down with "literature," which I crammed into my pocket for future reference.

My next step was to drop into the office of a Spanish-American paper whose editor was especially well informed on South American affairs.

"Do I know Mrs. Ralston?" he repeated, thoughtfully lighting one of those black cigarettes that look so vicious and are so mild. "I should say so. I'll tell you a little story about her. Three or four years ago she turned up in Caracas. I don't know who Mr. Ralston was—perhaps there never was any Mr. Ralston. Anyhow, she got in with the official circle of the Castro government and was very successful as an adventuress. She has considerable business ability and represented a certain group of Americans. But, if you recall, when Castro was eliminated pretty nearly everyone who had stood high with him went, too. It seems that a number of the old concessionaires played the game on both sides. This particular group had a man named Vanderdyke on the anti-Castro side. So, when Mrs. Ralston went, she just quietly sailed by way of Panama to the other side of the continent, to Peru—they paid her well—and Vanderdyke took the title role.

"Oh, yes, she and Vanderdyke were very good friends, very, indeed. I think they must have known each other here in the States. Still they played their parts well at the time. Since things have settled down in Venezuela, the concessionaires have found no further use for Vanderdyke either, and here they are, Vanderdyke and Mrs. Ralston, both in New York now, with two of the most outrageous schemes of financing ever seen on Broad Street. They have offices in the same building, they are together a great deal, and now I hear that the state attorney-general is after both of them."

With this information and a very meagre report of the Wainwright trip to the Far East, which had taken in some out-of-the-way places apparently, I hastened back to Kennedy. He was surrounded by bottles, tubes, jars, retorts, Bunsen burners, everything in the science and art of chemistry, I thought.

I didn't like the way he looked. His hand was unsteady, and

his eyes looked badly, but he seemed quite put out when I suggested that he was working too hard over the case. I was worried about him, but rather than say anything to offend him I left him for the rest of the afternoon, only dropping in before dinner to make sure that he would not forget to eat something. He was then completing his preparations for the evening. They were of the simplest kind, apparently. In fact, all I could see was an apparatus which consisted of a rubber funnel, inverted and attached to a rubber tube which led in turn into a jar about a quarter full of water. Through the stopper of the jar another tube led to a tank of oxygen.

There were several jars of various liquids on the table and a number of chemicals. Among other things was a sort of gourd, encrusted with a black substance, and in a corner was a box from which sounds issued as if it contained something alive.

I did not trouble Kennedy with questions, for I was only too glad when he consented to take a brisk walk and join me in a thick porterhouse.

It was a large party that gathered in Kennedy's laboratory that night, one of the largest he had ever had. Mr. and Mrs. Wainwright and Miss Marian came, the ladies heavily veiled. Doctor Nott and Mr. Whitney were among the first to arrive. Later came Mr. Vanderdyke and last of all Mrs. Ralston with Inspector O'Connor. Altogether it was an unwilling party.

"I shall begin," said Kennedy, "by going over, briefly, the facts in this case."

Tersely he summarised it, to my surprise laying great stress on the proof that the couple had been asphyxiated.

"But it was no ordinary asphyxiation," he continued. "We have to deal in this case with a poison which is apparently among the most subtle known. A particle of matter so minute as to be hardly distinguishable by the naked eye, on the point of a needle or a lancet, a prick of the skin scarcely felt under any circumstances and which would pass quite unheeded if the attention were otherwise engaged, and not all the power in the world—unless one was fully prepared—could save the life of the person in whose skin the puncture had been made."

Craig paused a moment, but no one showed any evidence of being more than ordinarily impressed.

"This poison, I find, acts on the so-called endplates of the muscles and nerves. It produces complete paralysis, but not loss of consciousness, sensation, circulation, or respiration until the end approaches. It seems to be one of the most powerful sedatives I have ever heard of. When introduced in even a minute quantity it produces death finally by asphyxiation—by paralysing the muscles of respiration. This asphyxia is what so puzzled the coroner.

"I will now inject a little of the blood serum of the victims into a white mouse."

He took a mouse from the box I had seen, and with a needle injected the serum. The mouse did not even wince, so lightly did he touch it, but as we watched, its life seemed gently to ebb away, without pain and without struggle. Its breath simply seemed to stop.

Next he took the gourd I had seen on the table and with a knife scraped off just the minutest particle of the black licorice-like stuff that encrusted it. He dissolved the particle in some alcohol and with a sterilised needle repeated his experiment on a second mouse. The effect was precisely similar to that produced by the blood on the first.

It did not seem to me that anyone showed any emotion except possibly the slight exclamation that escaped Miss Marian Wainwright. I fell to wondering whether it was prompted by a soft heart or a guilty conscience.

We were all intent on what Craig was doing, especially Doctor Nott, who now broke in with a question.

"Professor Kennedy, may I ask a question? Admitting that the first mouse died in an apparently similar manner to the second, what proof have you that the poison is the same in both cases? And if it is the same can you show that it affects human beings in the same way, and that enough of it has been discovered in the blood of the victims to have caused their death? In other words, I want the last doubt set aside. How do you know absolutely that this poison which you discovered in my office last night in that black precipitate when you added the ether— how do you know that it asphyxiated the victims?"

If ever Craig startled me it was by his quiet reply. "I've isolated it in their blood, extracted it, sterilised it, and I've tried it on myself."

In breathless amazement, with eyes riveted on Craig, we listened.

"Altogether I was able to recover from the blood samples of both of the victims of this crime six centigrams of the poison," he pursued. "Starting with two centigrams of it as a moderate dose, I injected it into my right arm subcutaneously. Then I slowly worked my way up to three and then four centigrams. They did not produce any very appreciable results other than to cause some dizziness, slight vertigo, a considerable degree of lassitude, and an extremely painful headache of rather unusual duration. But five centigrams considerably improved on this. It caused a degree of vertigo and lassitude that was most distressing, and six centigrams, the whole amount which I had recovered from the samples of blood, gave me the fright of my life right here in this laboratory this afternoon.

"Perhaps I was not wise in giving myself so large an injection on a day when I was overheated and below par otherwise because of the strain I have been under in handling this case. However that may be, the added centigram produced so much more on top of the five centigrams previously taken that for a time I had reason to fear that that additional centigram was just the amount needed to bring my experiments to a permanent close.

"Within three minutes of the time of injection the dizziness and vertigo had become so great as to make walking seem impossible. In another minute the lassitude rapidly crept over me, and the serious disturbance of my breathing made it apparent to me that walking, waving my arms, anything, was imperative. My lungs felt glued up, and the muscles of my chest refused to work. Everything swam before my eyes, and I was soon reduced to walking up and down the laboratory with halting steps, only preventing falling on the floor by holding fast to the edge of this table. It seemed to me that I spent hours gasping for breath. It reminded me of what I once experienced in the Cave of the Winds of Niagara, where water is more abundant in the atmosphere than air. My watch afterward indicated only about twenty minutes of extreme distress, but that twenty minutes is one never to be forgotten, and I advise you all, if you ever are so foolish as to try the experiment, to remain below the five-centigram limit.

"How much was administered to the victims, Doctor Nott, I cannot say, but it must have been a good deal more than I took. Six centigrams, which I recovered from these small samples, are only nine-tenths of a grain. Yet you see what effect it had. I trust that answers your question?"

Doctor Nott was too overwhelmed to reply.

"And what is this deadly poison?" continued Craig, anticipating our thoughts. "I have been fortunate enough to obtain a sample of it from the Museum of Natural History. It comes in a little gourd, or often a calabash. This is in a gourd. It is black-ish brittle stuff encrusting the sides of the gourd just as if it was poured in in the liquid state and left to dry. Indeed, that is just what has been done by those who manufacture this stuff after a lengthy and somewhat secret process."

He placed the gourd on the edge of the table where we could all see it. I was almost afraid even to look at it.

"The famous traveller, Sir Robert Schomburgk, first brought it into Europe, and Darwin has described it. It is now an article of commerce and is to be found in the United States Pharmacopœia as a medicine, though of course it is used in only very minute quantities, as a heart stimulant."

Craig opened a book to a place he had marked.

"At least one person in this room will appreciate the local colour of a little incident I am going to read—to illustrate what death from this poison is like. Two natives of the part of the world whence it comes were one day hunting. They were armed with blowpipes and quivers full of poisoned darts made of thin charred pieces of bamboo tipped with this stuff. One of them aimed a dart. It missed the object overhead, glanced off the tree, and fell down on the hunter himself. This is how the other native reported the result:

"'Quacca takes the dart out of his shoulder. Never a word. Puts it in his quiver and throws it in the stream. Gives me his blowpipe for his little son. Says to me good-bye for his wife and the village. Then he lies down. His tongue talks no longer. No sight in his eyes. He folds his arms. He rolls over slowly. His mouth moves without sound. I feel his heart. It goes fast and then slow. It stops. Quacca has shot his last woorali dart.'"

We looked at each other, and the horror of the thing sank deep into our minds. Woorali. What was it? There were many travellers in the room who had been in the Orient, home of poisons, and in South America. Which one had run across the poison?

"Woorali, or curare," said Craig slowly, "is the well-known poison with which the South American Indians of the upper Orinoco tip their arrows. Its principal ingredient is derived from the Strychnos toxifera tree, which yields also the drug nux vomica."*

A great light dawned on me. I turned quickly to where Vanderdyke was sitting next to Mrs. Ralston, and a little behind her. His stony stare and laboured breathing told me that he had read the purport of Kennedy's actions.

"For God's sake, Craig," I gasped. "An emetic, quick— Vanderdyke."

A trace of a smile flitted over Vanderdyke's features, as much as to say that he was beyond our interference.

"Vanderdyke," said Craig, with what seemed to me a brutal calmness, "then it was you who were the visitor who last saw Laura Wainwright and John Templeton alive. Whether you shot a dart at them I do not know. But you are the murderer."

Vanderdyke raised his hand as if to assent. It fell back limp, and I noted the ring of the bluest lapis lazuli.

Mrs. Ralston threw herself toward him. "Will you not do something? Is there no antidote? Don't let him die!" she cried.

"You are the murderer," repeated Kennedy, as if demanding a final answer.

Again the hand moved in confession, and he feebly moved the finger on which shone the ring.

---

* Curare was soon to be well known among mystery readers: Sherlock Holmes knew of its existence in "The Adventure of the Sussex Vampire" (1925, collected in *The Case-Book of Sherlock Holmes*, London: John Murray, 1927), in which a mother, caught sucking the poison from her child's wound, is accused of being a vampire. Pharmacologist Rudolf Boehm included curare in his 1895 classification of various alkaloid poisons. The poison is only effective if directly introduced into the bloodstream; it is harmless if taken orally.

Our attention was centred on Vanderdyke. Mrs. Ralston, unobserved, went to the table and picked up the gourd. Before O'Connor could stop her she had rubbed her tongue on the black substance inside. It was only a little bit, for O'Connor quickly dashed it from her lips and threw the gourd through the window, smashing the glass.

"Kennedy," he shouted frantically, "Mrs. Ralston has swallowed some of it."

Kennedy seemed so intent on Vanderdyke that I had to repeat the remark.

Without looking up he said: "Oh, one can swallow it—it's strange, but it is comparatively inert if swallowed even in a pretty good-sized quantity. I doubt if Mrs. Ralston ever heard of it before except by hearsay. If she had, she'd have scratched herself with it instead of swallowing it."

If Craig had been indifferent to the emergency of Vanderdyke before, he was all action now that the confession had been made. In an instant Vanderdyke was stretched on the floor and Craig had taken out the apparatus I had seen during the afternoon.

"I am prepared for this," he exclaimed quickly. "Here is the apparatus for artificial respiration. Nott, hold that rubber funnel over his nose, and start the oxygen from the tank. Pull his tongue forward so it won't fall down his throat and choke him. I'll work his arms. Walter, make a tourniquet of your handkerchief and put it tightly on the muscles of his left arm. That may keep some of the poison in his arm from spreading into the rest of his body. This is the only antidote known—artificial respiration."

Kennedy was working feverishly, going through the motions of first aid to a drowned man. Mrs. Ralston was on her knees beside Vanderdyke, kissing his hands and forehead whenever Kennedy stopped for a minute, and crying softly.

"Schuyler, poor boy, I wonder how you could have done it. I

was with him that day. We rode up in his car, and as we passed through Williston he said he would stop a minute and wish Templeton luck. I didn't think it strange, for he said he had nothing any longer against Laura Wainwright, and Templeton only did his duty as a lawyer against us. I forgave John for prosecuting us, but Schuyler didn't, after all. Oh, my poor boy, why did you do it? We could have gone somewhere else and started all over again—it wouldn't have been the first time."

At last came the flutter of an eyelid and a voluntary breath or two. Vanderdyke seemed to realise where he was. With a last supreme effort he raised his hand and drew it slowly across his face. Then he fell back, exhausted by the effort.

But he had at last put himself beyond the reach of the law. There was no tourniquet that would confine the poison now in the scratch across his face. Back of those lack-lustre eyes he heard and knew, but could not move or speak. His voice was gone, his limbs, his face, his chest, and, last, his eyes. I wondered if it were possible to conceive a more dreadful torture than that endured by a mind which so witnessed the dying of one organ after another of its own body, shut up, as it were, in the fulness of life, within a corpse.

I looked in bewilderment at the scratch on his face. "How did he do it?" I asked.

Carefully Craig drew off the azure ring and examined it. In that part which surrounded the blue lapis lazuli, he indicated a hollow point, concealed. It worked with a spring and communicated with a little receptacle behind, in such a way that the murderer could give the fatal scratch while shaking hands with his victim.

I shuddered, for my hand had once been clasped by the one wearing that poison ring, which had sent Templeton, and his fiancée and now Vanderdyke himself, to their deaths.

VIII
"SPONTANEOUS COMBUSTION"

Kennedy and I had risen early, for we were hustling to get off for a week-end at Atlantic City. Kennedy was tugging at the straps of his grip and remonstrating with it under his breath, when the door opened and a messenger-boy stuck his head in.

"Does Mr. Kennedy live here?" he asked.

Craig impatiently seized the pencil, signed his name in the book, and tore open a night letter. From the prolonged silence that followed I felt a sense of misgiving. I, at least, had set my heart on the Atlantic City outing, but with the appearance of the messenger-boy I intuitively felt that the board walk would not see us that week.

"I'm afraid the Atlantic City trip is off, Walter," remarked Craig seriously. "You remember Tom Langley in our class at the university? Well, read that."

I laid down my safety razor and took the message. Tom had not spared words, and I could see at a glance at the mere length of the thing that it must be important. It was from Camp Hang-out in the Adirondacks.

"Dear old K.," it began, regardless of expense, "can you arrange to come up here by next train after you receive this?

Uncle Lewis is dead. Most mysterious. Last night after we retired noticed peculiar odour about house. Didn't pay much attention. This morning found him lying on floor of living-room, head and chest literally burned to ashes, but lower part of body and arms untouched. Room shows no evidence of fire, but full of sort of oily soot. Otherwise nothing unusual. On table near body siphon of seltzer, bottle of imported gin, limes, and glass for rickeys. Have removed body, but am keeping room exactly as found until you arrive. Bring Jameson. Wire if you cannot come, but make every effort and spare no expense. Anxiously, Tom Langley."

Craig was impatiently looking at his watch as I hastily ran through the letter.

"Hurry, Walter," he exclaimed. "We can just catch the Empire State. Never mind shaving—we'll have a stop-over at Utica to wait for the Montreal express. Here, put the rest of your things in your grip and jam it shut. We'll get something to eat on the train—I hope. I'll wire we're coming. Don't forget to latch the door."

Kennedy was already half-way to the elevator, and I followed ruefully, still thinking of the ocean and the piers, the bands and the roller chairs.

It was a good ten-hour journey up to the little station nearest Camp Hang-out and at least a two-hour ride after that. We had plenty of time to reflect over what this death might mean to Tom and his sister and to speculate on the manner of it. Tom and Grace Langley were relatives by marriage of Lewis Langley, who, after the death of his wife, had made them his protégés. Lewis Langley was principally noted, as far as I could recall, for being a member of some of the fastest clubs of both New York and London. Neither Kennedy nor myself had shared in the world's opinion of him, for we knew how good he had been to Tom in college and, from Tom, how good he had been to Grace.

In fact, he had made Tom assume the Langley name, and in every way had treated the brother and sister as if they had been his own children.

Tom met us with a smart trap at the station, a sufficient indication, if we had not already known, of the "roughing it" at such a luxurious Adirondack "camp" as Camp Hang-out. He was unaffectedly glad to see us, and it was not difficult to read in his face the worry which the affair had already given him.

"Tom, I'm awfully sorry to—" began Craig when, warned by Langley's look at the curious crowd that always gathers at the railroad station at train time, he cut it short. We stood silently a moment while Tom was arranging the trap for us.

As we swung around the bend in the road that cut off the little station and its crowd of lookers-on, Kennedy was the first to speak. "Tom," he said, "first of all, let me ask that when we get to the camp we are to be simply two old classmates whom you had asked to spend a few days before the tragedy occurred. Anything will do. There may be nothing at all to your evident suspicions, and then again there may. At any rate, play the game safely—don't arouse any feeling which might cause unpleasantness later in case you are mistaken."

"I quite agree with you," answered Tom. "You wired, from Albany, I think, to keep the facts out of the papers as much as possible. I'm afraid it is too late for that. Of course the thing became vaguely known in Saranac, although the county officers have been very considerate of us, and this morning a New York *Record* correspondent was over and talked with us. I couldn't refuse, that would have put a very bad face on it."

"Too bad," I exclaimed. "I had hoped, at least, to be able to keep the report down to a few lines in the *Star*. But the *Record* will have such a yellow story about it that I'll simply have to do something to counteract the effect."

"Yes," assented Craig. "But—wait. Let's see the *Record* story first. The office doesn't know you're up here. You can hold up the *Star* and give us time to look things over, perhaps get in a beat on the real story and set things right. Anyhow, the news is out. That's certain. We must work quickly. Tell me, Tom, who are at the camp—anyone except relatives?"

"No," he replied, guardedly measuring his words. "Uncle Lewis had invited his brother James and his niece and nephew, Isabelle and James, junior—we call him Junior. Then there are Grace and myself and a distant relative, Harrington Brown, and—oh, of course, uncle's physician, Doctor Putnam."

"Who is Harrington Brown?" asked Craig.

"He's on the other side of the Langley family, on Uncle Lewis's mother's side. I think, or at least Grace thinks, that he is quite in love with Isabelle. Harrington Brown would be quite a catch. Of course he isn't wealthy, but his family is mighty well connected. Oh, Craig," sighed Langley, "I wish he hadn't done it—Uncle Lewis, I mean. Why did he invite his brother up here now when he needed to recover from the swift pace of last winter in New York? You know—or you don't know, I suppose, but you'll know it now—when he and Uncle Jim got together there was nothing to it but one drink after another. Doctor Putnam was quite disgusted, at least he professed to be, but, Craig," he lowered his voice to a whisper, as if the very forest had ears, "they're all alike—they've been just waiting for Uncle Lewis to drink himself to death. Oh," he added bitterly, "there's no love lost between me and the relatives on that score, I can assure you."

"How did you find him that morning?" asked Kennedy, as if to turn off this unlocking of family secrets to strangers.

"That's the worst part of the whole affair," replied Tom, and even in the dusk I could see the lines of his face tighten. "You know Uncle Lewis was a hard drinker, but he never seemed to show it much. We had been out on the lake in the motor-boat fishing all the afternoon and—well, I must admit both my uncles had had frequent recourse to 'pocket pistols,' and I remember they referred to it each time as 'bait.' Then after supper nothing would do but fizzes and rickeys. I was disgusted, and after reading a bit went to bed. Harrington and my uncles sat up with Doctor Putnam—according to Uncle Jim—for a couple of hours longer. Then Harrington, Doctor Putnam, and Uncle Jim went to bed, leaving Uncle Lewis still drinking.

"I remember waking in the night, and the house seemed saturated with a peculiar odour. I never smelt anything like it in my life. So I got up and slipped into my bathrobe. I met Grace in the hall. She was sniffing.

"'Don't you smell something burning?' she asked.

"I said I did and started down-stairs to investigate. Everything was dark, but that smell was all over the house. I looked in each room down-stairs as I went, but could see nothing. The kitchen and dining-room were all right. I glanced into the living-room, but, while the smell was more noticeable there, I could see no evidence of a fire except the dying embers on the hearth. It had been coolish that night, and we had had a few logs blazing. I didn't examine the room—there seemed no reason for it. We went back to our rooms, and in the morning they found the gruesome object I had missed in the darkness and shadows of the living-room."

Kennedy was intently listening. "Who found him?" he asked.

"Harrington," replied Tom. "He roused us. Harrington's theory is that uncle set himself on fire with a spark from his cigar—a charred cigar-butt was found on the floor."

We found Tom's relatives a saddened, silent party in the face of the tragedy. Kennedy and I apologised very profusely for our intrusion, but Tom quickly interrupted, as we had agreed, by explaining that he had insisted on our coming, as old friends on whom he felt he could rely, especially to set the matter right in the newspapers.

I think Craig noticed keenly the reticence of the family group in the mystery—I might almost have called it suspicion. They did not seem to know just whether to take it as an accident or as something worse, and each seemed to entertain a reserve toward the rest which was very uncomfortable.

Mr. Langley's attorney in New York had been notified, but apparently was out of town, for he had not been heard from. They seemed rather anxious to get word from him.

Dinner over, the family group separated, leaving Tom an opportunity to take us into the gruesome living-room. Of course the remains had been removed, but otherwise the room was exactly as it had been when Harrington discovered the tragedy. I did not see the body, which was lying in an anteroom, but Kennedy did, and spent some time in there.

After he rejoined us, Kennedy next examined the fireplace. It was full of ashes from the logs which had been lighted on the fatal night. He noted attentively the distance of Lewis Langley's chair from the fireplace, and remarked that the varnish on the chair was not even blistered.

Before the chair, on the floor where the body had been found, he pointed out to us the peculiar ash-marks for some space around, but it really seemed to me as if something else interested him more than these ash-marks.

We had been engaged perhaps half an hour in viewing the room. At last Craig suddenly stopped.

"Tom," he said, "I think I'll wait till daylight before I go any further. I can't tell with certainty under these lights, though perhaps they show me some things the sunlight wouldn't show. We'd better leave everything just as it is until morning."

So we locked the room again and went into a sort of library across the hall.

We were sitting in silence, each occupied with his own thoughts on the mystery, when the telephone rang. It proved to be a long-distance call from New York for Tom himself. His uncle's attorney had received the news at his home out on Long Island and had hurried to the city to take charge of the estate. But that was not the news that caused the grave look on Tom's face as he nervously rejoined us.

"That was uncle's lawyer, Mr. Clark, of Clark & Burdick," he said. "He has opened uncle's personal safe in the offices of the Langley estate—you remember them, Craig—where all the property of the Langley heirs is administered by the trustees. He says he can't find the will, though he knows there was a will and that it was placed in that safe some time ago. There is no duplicate."

The full purport of this information at once flashed on me, and I was on the point of blurting out my sympathy, when I saw by the look which Craig and Tom exchanged that they had already realised it and understood each other. Without the will the blood-relatives would inherit all of Lewis Langley's interest in the old Langley estate. Tom and his sister would be penniless.

It was late, yet we sat for nearly an hour longer, and I don't think we exchanged a half-dozen sentences in all that time. Craig seemed absorbed in thought. At length, as the great hall clock sounded midnight, we rose as if by common consent.

"Tom," said Craig, and I could feel the sympathy that welled up in his voice, "Tom, old man, I'll get at the bottom of this mystery if human intelligence can do it."

"I know you will, Craig," responded Tom, grasping each of us by the hand. "That's why I so much wanted you fellows to come up here."

Early in the morning Kennedy aroused me. "Now, Walter, I'm going to ask you to come down into the living-room with me, and we'll take a look at it in the daytime."

I hurried into my clothes, and together we quietly went down. Starting with the exact spot where the unfortunate man had been discovered, Kennedy began a minute examination of the floor, using his pocket lens. Every few moments he would stop to examine a spot on the rug or on the hardwood floor more intently. Several times I saw him scrape up something with the blade of his knife and carefully preserve the scrapings, each in a separate piece of paper.

Sitting idly by, I could not for the life of me see just what good it did for me to be there, and I said as much. Kennedy laughed quietly.

"You're a material witness, Walter," he replied. "Perhaps I shall need you some day to testify that I actually found these spots in this room."

Just then Tom stuck his head in. "Can I help?" he asked. "Why didn't you tell me you were going at it so early?"

"No, thanks," answered Craig, rising from the floor. "I was just making a careful examination of the room before anyone was up so that nobody would think I was too interested. I've finished. But you can help me, after all. Do you think you could describe exactly how everyone was dressed that night?"

"Why, I can try. Let me see. To begin with, uncle had on a shooting-jacket—that was pretty well burnt, as you know. Why, in fact, we all had our shooting-jackets on. The ladies were in white."

Craig pondered a little, but did not seem disposed to pursue the subject further, until Tom volunteered the information that since the tragedy none of them had been wearing their shooting-jackets.

"We've all been wearing city clothes," he remarked.

"Could you get your Uncle James and your Cousin Junior to go with you for an hour or two this morning on the lake, or on a tramp in the woods?" asked Craig after a moment's thought.

"Really, Craig," responded Tom doubtfully, "I ought to go to Saranac to complete the arrangements for taking Uncle Lewis's body to New York."

"Very well, persuade them to go with you. Anything, so long as you keep me from interruption for an hour or two."

They agreed on doing that, and as by that time most of the family were up, we went in to breakfast, another silent and suspicious meal.

After breakfast Kennedy tactfully withdrew from the family, and I did the same. We wandered off in the direction of the stables and there fell to admiring some of the horses. The groom, who seemed to be a sensible and pleasant sort of fellow, was quite ready to talk, and soon he and Craig were deep in discussing the game of the north country.

"Many rabbits about here?" asked Kennedy at length, when they had exhausted the larger game.

"Oh, yes. I saw one this morning, sir," replied the groom.

"Indeed?" said Kennedy. "Do you suppose you could catch a couple for me?"

"Guess I could, sir—alive, you mean?"

"Oh, yes, alive—I don't want you to violate the game laws. This is the closed season, isn't it?"

"Yes, sir, but then it's all right, sir, here on the estate."

"Bring them to me this afternoon, or—no, keep them here in the stable in a cage and let me know when you have them. If anybody asks you about them, say they belong to Mr. Tom."

Craig handed a small treasury note to the groom, who took it with a grin and touched his hat.

"Thanks," he said. "I'll let you know when I have the bunnies."

As we walked slowly back from the stables we caught sight of Tom down at the boat-house just putting off in the motor-boat with his uncle and cousin. Craig waved to him, and he walked up to meet us.

"While you're in Saranac," said Craig, "buy me a dozen or so test-tubes. Only, don't let anyone here at the house know you are buying them. They might ask questions."

While they were gone Kennedy stole into James Langley's room and after a few minutes returned to our room with the hunting-jacket. He carefully examined it with his pocket lens. Then he filled a drinking-glass with warm boiled water and added a few pinches of table salt. With a piece of sterilised gauze from Doctor Putnam's medicine-chest, he carefully washed off a few portions of the coat and set the glass and the gauze soaking in it aside. Then he returned the coat to the closet where he had found it. Next, as silently, he stole into Junior's room and repeated the process with his hunting-jacket, using another glass and piece of gauze.

"While I am out of the room, Walter," he said, "I want you to take these two glasses, cover them, and number them and on a slip of paper which you must retain, place the names of the owners of the respective coats. I don't like this part of it—I hate to play spy and would much rather come out in the open, but there is nothing else to do, and it is much better for all concerned that I should play the game secretly just now. There may be no cause for suspicion at all. In that case I'd never forgive myself for starting a family row. And then again—but we shall see."

After I had numbered and recorded the glasses Kennedy returned, and we went down-stairs again.

"Curious about the will, isn't it?" I remarked as we stood on the wide verandah a moment.

"Yes," he replied. "It may be necessary to go back to New York to delve into that part of it before we get through, but I hope not. We'll wait."

At this point the groom interrupted us to say that he had caught the rabbits. Kennedy at once hurried to the stable. There he rolled up his sleeves, pricked a vein in his arm, and injected a small quantity of his own blood into one of the rabbits. The other he did not touch.

It was late in the afternoon when Tom returned from town with his uncle and cousin. He seemed even more agitated than usual. Without a word he hurried up from the landing and sought us out.

"What do you think of that?" he cried, opening a copy of the *Record*, and laying it flat on the library table.

There on the front page was Lewis Langley's picture with a huge scare-head:

MYSTERIOUS CASE OF
SPONTANEOUS COMBUSTION

"It's all out," groaned Tom, as we bent over to read the account. "And such a story!"

Under the date of the day previous, a Saranac despatch ran:

> *Lewis Langley, well known as sporting man and club member in New York, and eldest son of the late Lewis Langley, the banker, was discovered dead under the most mysterious circumstances this morning at Camp Hang-out, twelve miles from this town.*
> *The Death of "Old Krook" in Dickens's "Bleak House"*

or of the victim in one of Marryat's most thrilling tales was*
not more gruesome than this actual fact. It is without doubt
a case of spontaneous human combustion, such as is recorded
beyond dispute in medical and medico-legal text-books of
the past two centuries. Scientists in this city consulted for the
Record agree that, while rare, spontaneous human combus-
tion is an established fact and that everything in this curious
case goes to show that another has been added to the already
well-authenticated list of cases recorded in America and
Europe. The family refuse to be interviewed, which seems
to indicate that the rumours in medical circles in Saranac
have a solid basis of fact.

Then followed a circumstantial account of the life of Langley
and the events leading up to the discovery of the body—fairly
accurate in itself, but highly coloured.

"The *Record* man must have made good use of his time here,"
I commented, as I finished reading the despatch. "And—well,
they must have done some hard work in New York to get this
story up so completely—see, after the despatch follow a lot of
interviews, and here is a short article on spontaneous combustion itself."

Harrington and the rest of the family had just come in.

"What's this we hear about the *Record* having an article?"
Harrington asked. "Read it aloud, Professor, so we can all hear it."

"'Spontaneous human combustion, or *catacausis ebriosus*,'"

---

* In Charles Dickens's *Bleak House* (first published in book form in 1853), "Old Krook,"
a drunk, dies of spontaneous combustion. A controversy erupted, in which many
tried to prove such a phenomenon to be impossible while others adduced evidence of
similar cases. Dickens was not the first to depict an old, sedentary alcoholic erupting
into flames; Washington Irving told a similar tale, and the idea was repeated by Émile
Zola, Mark Twain, and Herman Melville, among many other writers. Captain Frederick
Marryat, in his novel *Jacob Faithful* (1834), writes of the hero's mother spontaneously
combusting, a "visitation of God."

began Craig, "'is one of the baffling human scientific mysteries. Indeed, there can be no doubt but that individuals have in some strange and inexplicable manner caught fire and been partially or almost wholly consumed.

"'Some have attributed it to gases in the body, such as carbureted hydrogen. Once it was noted at the Hôtel Dieu in Paris that a body on being dissected gave forth a gas which was inflammable and burned with a bluish flame. Others have attributed the combustion to alcohol. A toper several years ago in Brooklyn and New York used to make money by blowing his breath through a wire gauze and lighting it. Whatever the cause, medical literature records seventy-six cases of catacausis in two hundred years.

"'The combustion seems to be sudden and is apparently confined to the cavities, the abdomen, chest, and head. Victims of ordinary fire accidents rush hither and thither frantically, succumb from exhaustion, their limbs are burned, and their clothing is all destroyed. But in catacausis they are stricken down without warning, the limbs are rarely burned, and only the clothing in contact with the head and chest is consumed. The residue is like a distillation of animal tissue, grey and dark, with an overpoweringly fetid odour. They are said to burn with a flickering stifled blue flame, and water, far from arresting the combustion, seems to add to it. Gin is particularly rich in inflammable, empyreumatic oils, as they are called, and in most cases it is recorded that the catacausis took place among gin-drinkers, old and obese.

"'Within the past few years cases are on record which seem to establish catacausis beyond doubt. In one case the heat was so great as to explode a pistol in the pocket of the victim. In another, a woman, the victim's husband was asphyxiated by the smoke. The woman weighed one hundred and eighty pounds in life, but the ashes weighed only twelve pounds. In all these cases the proof of spontaneous combustion seems conclusive.'"*

As Craig finished reading, we looked blankly, horrified, at one another. It was too dreadful to realise.

"What do you think of it, Professor?" asked James Langley, at length. "I've read somewhere of such cases, but to think of its actually happening—and to my own brother. Do you really think Lewis could have met his death in this terrible manner?"

Kennedy made no reply. Harrington seemed absorbed in thought. A shudder passed over us as we thought about it. But, gruesome as it was, it was evident that the publication of the story in the *Record* had relieved the feelings of the family group in one respect—it at least seemed to offer an explanation. It was noticeable that the suspicious air with which everyone had regarded everyone else was considerably dispelled.

Tom said nothing until the others had withdrawn. "Kennedy," he burst out, then, "do you believe that such combustion is absolutely *spontaneous*? Don't you believe that something else is necessary to start it?"

"I'd rather not express an opinion just yet, Tom," answered Craig carefully. "Now, if you can get Harrington and Doctor Putnam away from the house for a short time, as you did with your uncle and cousin this morning, I may be able to tell you something about this case soon."

Again Kennedy stole into another bedroom, and returned to our room with a hunting-jacket. Just as he had done before, he carefully washed it off with the gauze soaked in the salt solution

---

* The term "spontaneous human combustion" was coined in 1746 by Paul Rolli, in an essay "An Extract, by Mr. Paul Rolli, F.R.S. of an Italian Treatise, written by the Reverend Joseph Bianchini, a Prebend in the City of Verona; upon the Death of the Countess Cornelia Zangári & Bandi, of Ceséna," in *Philosophical Transactions of the Royal Society of London*, vol. 21. While many have speculated about psychic or super-natural causes, the consensus is that an external source of ignition has been overlooked.

and quickly returned the coat, repeating the process with Doctor Putnam's coat and, last, that of Tom himself. Finally he turned his back while I sealed the glasses and marked and recorded them on my slip.

The next day was spent mainly in preparations for the journey to New York with the body of Lewis Langley. Kennedy was very busy on what seemed to me to be preparations for some mysterious chemical experiments. I found myself fully occupied in keeping special correspondents from all over the country at bay.

That evening after dinner we were all sitting in the open summer house over the boat-house. Smudges of green pine were burning and smoking on little artificial islands of stone near the lake shore, lighting up the trees on every side with a red glare. Tom and his sister were seated with Kennedy and myself on one side, while some distance from us Harrington was engaged in earnest conversation with Isabelle. The other members of the family were further removed. That seemed typical to me of the way the family group split up.

"Mr. Kennedy," remarked Grace in a thoughtful, low tone, "what do you make of that *Record* article?"

"Very clever, no doubt," replied Craig.

"But don't you think it strange about the will?"

"Hush," whispered Tom, for Isabelle and Harrington had ceased talking and might perhaps be listening.

Just then one of the servants came up with a telegram.

Tom hastily opened it and read the message eagerly in the corner of the summer house nearest one of the glowing smudges. I felt instinctively that it was from his lawyer. He turned and beckoned to Kennedy and myself.

"What do you think of that?" he whispered hoarsely.

We bent over and in the flickering light read the message:

New York papers full of spontaneous combustion story. Record had exclusive story yesterday, but all papers to-day feature even more. Is it true? Please wire additional details at once. Also immediate instructions regarding loss of will. Has been abstracted from safe. Could Lewis Langley have taken it himself? Unless new facts soon must make loss public or issue statement Lewis Langley intestate.

DANIEL CLARK.

Tom looked blankly at Kennedy, and then at his sister, who was sitting alone. I thought I could read what was passing in his mind. With all his faults Lewis Langley had been a good foster-parent to his adopted children. But it was all over now if the will was lost.

"What can I do?" asked Tom hopelessly. "I have nothing to reply to him."

"But I have," quietly returned Kennedy, deliberately folding up the message and handing it back. "Tell them all to be in the library in fifteen minutes. This message hurries me a bit, but I am prepared. You will have something to wire Mr. Clark after that." Then he strode off toward the house, leaving us to gather the group together in considerable bewilderment.

A quarter of an hour later we had all assembled in the library, across the hall from the room in which Lewis Langley had been found. As usual Kennedy began by leaping straight into the middle of his subject.

"Early in the eighteenth century," he commenced slowly, "a woman was found burned to death. There were no clues, and the scientists of that time suggested spontaneous combustion.

This explanation was accepted. The theory always has been that the process of respiration by which the tissues of the body are used up and got rid of gives the body a temperature, and it has seemed that it may be possible, by preventing the escape of this heat, to set fire to the body."

We were leaning forward expectantly, horrified by the thought that perhaps, after all, the *Record* was correct.

"Now," resumed Kennedy, his tone changing, "suppose we try a little experiment—one that was tried very convincingly by the immortal Liebig.* Here is a sponge. I am going to soak it in gin from this bottle, the same that Mr. Langley was drinking from on the night of the—er—the tragedy."

Kennedy took the saturated sponge and placed it in an agate-iron pan from the kitchen. Then he lighted it. The bluish flame shot upward, and in tense silence we watched it burn lower and lower, till all the alcohol was consumed. Then he picked up the sponge and passed it around. It was dry, but the sponge itself had not been singed.

"We now know," he continued, "that from the nature of combustion it is impossible for the human body to undergo spontaneous ignition or combustion in the way the scientific experts of the past century believed. Swathe the body in the thickest of non-conductors of heat, and what happens? A profuse perspiration exudes, and before such an ignition could possibly take place all the moisture of the body would have to be evaporated. As seventy-five per cent or more of the body is water, it

---

* Justus Freiherr von Liebig (1803–1873), a German chemist, studied more than fifty cases of supposed spontaneous combustion in the mid-nineteenth century and concluded that the supposed connection between alcoholism and combustion was untenable. He pointed out that anatomical specimens were typically stored in a 70 percent ethanol solution and yet still would not burn. He actually tried a number of experiments on cadavers and even injected rats with ethanol but was unable to set fire to either the cadavers or the rats. Liebig's "immortality" is not a reference to this work but rather to his role as a founder of organic chemistry.

"Here is a sponge. I am going to soak it in gin from this bottle, the same that Mr. Langley was drinking from on the night of the—er—the tragedy."

is evident that enormous heat would be necessary—moisture is the great safeguard. The experiment which I have shown you could be duplicated with specimens of human organs preserved for years in alcohol in museums. They would burn just as this sponge—the specimen itself would be very nearly uninjured by the burning of the alcohol."

"Then, Professor Kennedy, you maintain that my brother did not meet his death by such an accident?" asked James Langley.

"Exactly that, sir," replied Craig. "One of the most important aspects of the historic faith in this phenomenon is that of its skilful employment in explaining away what would otherwise appear to be convincing circumstantial evidence in cases of accusations of murder."

"Then how do you explain Mr. Langley's death?" demanded Harrington. "My theory of a spark from a cigar may be true, after all."

"I am coming to that in a moment," answered Kennedy quietly. "My first suspicion was aroused by what not even Doctor Putnam seems to have noticed. The skull of Mr. Langley, charred and consumed as it was, seemed to show marks of violence. It might have been from a fracture of the skull or it might have been an accident to his remains as they were being removed to the anteroom. Again, his tongue seemed as though it was protruding. That might have been natural suffocation, or it might have been from forcible strangulation. So far I had nothing but conjecture to work on. But in looking over the living-room I found near the table, on the hardwood floor, a spot—just one little round spot. Now, deductions from spots, even if we know them to be blood, must be made very carefully. I did not know this to be a blood-spot, and so was very careful at first.

"Let us assume it was a blood-spot, however. What did it show? It was just a little regular round spot, quite thick. Now, drops of blood falling only a few inches usually make a round spot with a smooth border. Still the surface on which the drop falls is quite as much a factor as the height from which it falls. If the surface is rough the border may be irregular. But this was a smooth surface and not absorbent. The thickness of a dried blood-spot on a non-absorbent surface is less the greater the height from which it has fallen. This was a thick spot. Now if it had fallen, say, six feet, the height of Mr. Langley, the spot would have been thin—some secondary spatters might have been seen, or at least an irregular edge around the spot. Therefore, if it was a blood-spot, it had fallen only one or two feet. I ascertained next that the lower part of the body showed no wounds or bruises whatever.

"Tracks of blood such as are left by dragging a bleeding body differ very greatly from tracks of arterial blood which are left when the victim has strength to move himself. Continuing my speculations, supposing it to be a blood-spot, what did it indicate? Clearly that Mr. Langley was struck by somebody on the head with a heavy instrument, perhaps in another part of the room, that he was choked, that as the drops of blood oozed from the wound on his head, he was dragged across the floor, in the direction of the fireplace—"

"But, Professor Kennedy," interrupted Doctor Putnam, "have you proved that the spot was a blood-spot? Might it not have been a paint-spot or something of that sort?"

Kennedy had apparently been waiting for just such a question.

"Ordinarily, water has no effect on paint," he answered. "I found that the spot could be washed off with water. That is not all. I have a test for blood that is so delicately sensitive that the blood of an Egyptian mummy thousands of years old will respond to it. It was discovered by a German scientist, Doctor Uhlenhuth, and was no longer ago than last winter applied in

England in connection with the Clapham murder. The suspected murderer declared that stains on his clothes were only spatters of paint, but the test proved them to be spatters of blood. Walter, bring in the cage with the rabbits."

I opened the door and took the cage from the groom, who had brought it up from the stable and stood waiting with it some distance away.

"This test is very simple, Doctor Putnam," continued Craig, as I placed the cage on the table and Kennedy unwrapped the sterilised test-tubes. "A rabbit is inoculated with human blood, and after a time the serum that is taken from the rabbit supplies the material for the test.

"I will insert this needle in one of these rabbits which has been so inoculated and will draw off some of the serum, which I place in this test-tube to the right. The other rabbit has not been inoculated. I draw off some of its serum and place that tube here on the left—we will call that our 'control tube.' It will check the results of our tests.

"Wrapped up in this paper I have the scrapings of the spot which I found on the floor—just a few grains of dark, dried powder. To show how sensitive the test is, I will take only one of the smallest of these minute scrapings. I dissolve it in this third tube with distilled water. I will even divide it in half, and place the other half in this fourth tube.

"Next I add some of the serum of the uninoculated rabbit to the half in this tube. You observe, nothing happens. I add a little of the serum of the inoculated rabbit to the other half in this other tube. Observe how delicate the test is—"

Kennedy was leaning forward, almost oblivious of the rest of us in the room, talking almost as if to himself. We, too, had riveted our eyes on the tubes.

As he added the serum from the inoculated rabbit, a cloudy

milky ring formed almost immediately in the hitherto colourless, very dilute blood-solution.

"That," concluded Craig, triumphantly holding the tube aloft, "that conclusively proves that the little round spot on the hardwood floor was not paint, was not anything in this wide world but blood."

No one in the room said a word, but I knew there must have been someone there who thought volumes in the few minutes that elapsed.

"Having found one blood-spot, I began to look about for more, but was able to find only two or three traces where spots seemed to have been. The fact is that the blood-spots had been apparently carefully wiped up. That is an easy matter. Hot water and salt, or hot water alone, or even cold water, will make quite short work of fresh blood-spots—at least to all outward appearances. But nothing but a most thorough cleaning can conceal them from the Uhlenhuth test, even when they are apparently wiped out. It is a case of Lady Macbeth over again, crying in the face of modern science, 'Out, out, damned spot.'*

"I was able with sufficient definiteness to trace roughly a course of blood-spots from the fireplace to a point near the door of the living-room. But beyond the door, in the hall, nothing."

"Still," interrupted Harrington, "to get back to the facts in the case. They are perfectly in accord either with my theory of the cigar or the *Record's* of spontaneous combustion. How do you account for the facts?"

"I suppose you refer to the charred head, the burned neck, the upper chest cavity, while the arms and legs were untouched?"

---

* The Uhlenhuth test, invented by Paul Uhlenhuth in 1901 and also referred to as the antigen–antibody precipitin test for species, is a test which can determine the species of a blood sample. While Sherlock Holmes developed a similar test as early as 1881, which he demonstrated to Dr. Watson in *A Study in Scarlet* (1887), Conan Doyle did not delineate the details of the test. Scholars suspect that Holmes's test was not unique to hemoglobin and hence useless for forensic applications.

"Yes, and then the body was found in the midst of combustible furniture that was not touched. It seems to me that even the spontaneous-combustion theory has considerable support in spite of this very interesting circumstantial evidence about blood-spots. Next to my own theory, the combustion theory seems most in harmony with the facts."

"If you will go over in your mind all the points proved to have been discovered—not the added points in the *Record* story—I think you will agree with me that mine is a more logical interpretation than spontaneous combustion," reasoned Craig. "Hear me out and you will see that the facts are more in harmony with my less fanciful explanation. No, someone struck Lewis Langley down either in passion or in cold blood, and then, seeing what he had done, made a desperate effort to destroy the evidence of violence. Consider my next discovery."

Kennedy placed the five glasses which I had carefully sealed and labelled on the table before us.

"The next step," he said, "was to find out whether any articles of clothing in the house showed marks that might be suspected of being blood-spots. And here I must beg the pardon of all in the room for intruding in their private wardrobes. But in this crisis it was absolutely necessary, and under such circumstances I never let ceremony stand before justice.

"In these five glasses on the table I have the washings of spots from the clothing worn by Tom, Mr. James Langley, Junior, Harrington Brown, and Doctor Putnam. I am not going to tell you which is which—indeed I merely have them marked, and I do not know them myself. But Mr. Jameson has the marks with the names opposite on a piece of paper in his pocket. I am simply going to proceed with the tests to see if any of the stains on the coats were of blood."

Just then Doctor Putnam interposed. "One question,

Professor Kennedy. It is a comparatively easy thing to recognise a blood-stain, but it is difficult, usually impossible, to tell whether the blood is that of a man or of an animal. I recall that we were all in our hunting-jackets that day, had been all day. Now, in the morning there had been an operation on one of the horses at the stable, and I assisted the veterinary from town. I may have got a spot or two of blood on my coat from that operation. Do I understand that this test would show that?"

"No," replied Craig, "this test would not show that. Other tests would, but not this. But if the spot of human blood were less than the size of a pin-head, it would show—it would show if the spot contained even so little as one twenty-thousandth of a gram of albumin. Blood from a horse, a deer, a sheep, a pig, a dog, could be obtained, but when the test was applied the liquid in which they were diluted would remain clear. No white precipitin, as it is called, would form. But let human blood, ever so diluted, be added to the serum of the inoculated rabbit, and the test is absolute."

A death-like silence seemed to pervade the room. Kennedy slowly and deliberately began to test the contents of the glasses. Dropping into each, as he broke the seal, some of the serum of the rabbit, he waited a moment to see if any change occurred.

It was thrilling. I think no one could have gone through that fifteen minutes without having it indelibly impressed on his memory. I recall thinking as Kennedy took each glass, "Which is it to be, guilt or innocence, life or death?" Could it be possible that a man's life might hang on such a slender thread? I knew Kennedy was too accurate and serious to deceive us. It was not only possible, it was actually a fact.

The first glass showed no reaction. Someone had been vindicated!

The second was neutral likewise—another person in the room had been proved innocent.

The third—no change. Science had released a third.

The fourth—

Almost it seemed as if the record in my pocket burned—spontaneously—so intense was my feeling. There in the glass was that fatal, telltale white precipitate.

"My God, it's the milk ring!" whispered Tom close to my ear.

Hastily Kennedy dropped the serum into the fifth. It remained as clear as crystal.

My hand trembled as it touched the envelope containing my record of the names.

"The person who wore the coat with that blood-stain on it," declared Kennedy solemnly, "was the person who struck Lewis Langley down, who choked him and then dragged his scarcely dead body across the floor and obliterated the marks of violence in the blazing log fire. Jameson, whose name is opposite the sign on this glass?"

I could scarcely tear the seal to look at the paper in the envelope. At last I unfolded it, and my eye fell on the name opposite the fatal sign. But my mouth was dry, and my tongue refused to move. It was too much like reading a death-sentence. With my finger on the name I faltered an instant.

Tom leaned over my shoulder and read it to himself. "For Heaven's sake, Jameson," he cried, "let the ladies retire before you read the name."

"It's not necessary," said a thick voice. "We quarrelled over the estate. My share's mortgaged up to the limit, and Lewis refused to lend me more even until I could get Isabelle happily married. Now Lewis's goes to an outsider—Harrington, boy, take care of Isabelle, fortune or no fortune. Good—"

Someone seized James Langley's arm as he pressed an automatic revolver to his temple. He reeled like a drunken man and dropped the gun on the floor with an oath.

"Beaten again," he muttered. "Forgot to move the ratchet from 'safety' to 'fire.'"

Like a madman he wrenched himself loose from us, sprang through the door, and darted up-stairs. "I'll show you some combustion!" he shouted back fiercely.

Kennedy was after him like a flash. "The will!" he cried.

We literally tore the door off its hinges and burst into James Langley's room. He was bending eagerly over the fireplace. Kennedy made a flying leap at him. Just enough of the will was left unburned to be admitted to probate.

IX

THE TERROR IN THE AIR

"There's something queer about these aeroplane accidents at Belmore Park," mused Kennedy, one evening, as his eye caught a big headline in the last edition of the *Star*, which I had brought up-town with me.

"Queer?" I echoed. "Unfortunate, terrible, but hardly queer. Why, it is a common saying among the aeronauts that if they keep at it long enough they will all lose their lives."

"Yes, I know that," rejoined Kennedy; "but, Walter, have you noticed that all these accidents have happened to Norton's new gyroscope machines?"

"Well, what of that?" I replied. "Isn't it just barely possible that Norton is on the wrong track in applying the gyroscope to an aeroplane? I can't say I know much about either the gyroscope or the aeroplane, but from what I hear the fellows at the office say it would seem to me that the gyroscope is a pretty good thing to keep off an aeroplane, not to put on it."

"Why?" asked Kennedy blandly.

"Well, it seems to me, from what the experts say, that anything which tends to keep your machine in one position is just what you don't want in an aeroplane. What surprises them, they say, is that the thing seems to work so well up to a certain point—that the accidents don't happen sooner. Why, our man on the aviation field tells me that when that poor fellow Browne was killed he had all but succeeded in bringing his machine to a dead stop in the air. In other words, he would have won the Brooks Prize for perfect motionlessness in one place.* And then Herrick, the day before, was going about seventy miles an hour when he collapsed. They said it was heart failure. But to-night another expert says in the *Star*—here, I'll read it: 'The real cause was carbonic-acid-gas poisoning due to the pressure on the mouth from driving fast through the air, and the consequent inability to expel the poisoned air which had been breathed. Air once breathed is practically carbonic-acid-gas. When one is passing rapidly through the air this carbonic-acid-gas is pushed back into the lungs, and only a little can get away because of the rush of air pressure into the mouth. So it is rebreathed, and the result is gradual carbonic-acid-gas poisoning, which produces a kind of narcotic sleep.'"

"Then it wasn't the gyroscope in that case?" said Kennedy with a rising inflection.

"No," I admitted reluctantly, "perhaps not."

I could see that I had been rash in talking so long. Kennedy had only been sounding me to see what the newspapers thought of it. His next remark was characteristic.

"Norton has asked me to look into the thing," he said quietly. "If his invention is a failure, he is a ruined man. All his money is in it, he is suing a man for infringing on his patent, and he is

---

* A fictional award. Early work on helicopters—aircraft that could fly vertically and remain motionless—produced no practical results until after World War I. It was not until 1927 that a helicopter invented by the German engineer Engelbert Zaschka was able to remain stationary at any height. It had two rotors and used a gyroscope to increase stability, as well as to serve as an energy accumulator to permit the helicopter to descend vertically.

liable for damages to the heirs, according to his agreement with Browne and Herrick. I have known Norton some time; in fact, he worked out his ideas at the university physical laboratory. I have flown in his machine, and it is the most marvellous biplane I ever saw. Walter, I want you to get a Belmore Park assignment from the *Star* and go out to the aviation meet with me to-morrow. I'll take you on the field, around the machines— you can get enough local colour to do a dozen *Star* specials later on. I may add that devising a flying-machine capable of remaining stationary in the air means a revolution that will relegate all other machines to the scrap-heap. From a military point of view it is the one thing necessary to make the aeroplane the superior in every respect to the dirigible."

The regular contests did not begin until the afternoon, but Kennedy and I decided to make a day of it, and early the next morning we were speeding out to the park where the flights were being held.

We found Charles Norton, the inventor, anxiously at work with his mechanicians in the big temporary shed that had been accorded him, and was dignified with the name of hangar.

"I knew you would come, Professor," he exclaimed, running forward to meet us.

"Of course," echoed Kennedy. "I'm too much interested in this invention of yours not to help you, Norton. You know what I've always thought of it—I've told you often that it is the most important advance since the original discovery by the Wrights that the aeroplane could be balanced by warping the planes."

"I'm just fixing up my third machine," said Norton. "If anything happens to it, I shall lose the prize, at least as far as this meet is concerned, for I don't believe I shall get my fourth and newest model from the makers in time. Anyhow, if I did I couldn't pay for it—I am ruined, if I don't win that twenty-five-thousand-dollar

Brooks Prize. And, besides, a couple of army men are coming to inspect my aeroplane and report to the War Department on it. I'd have stood a good chance of selling it, I think, if my flights here had been like the trials you saw. But, Kennedy," he added, and his face was drawn and tragic, "I'd drop the whole thing if I didn't know I was right. Two men dead—think of it. Why, even the newspapers are beginning to call me a cold, heartless, scientific crank to keep on. But I'll show them—this afternoon I'm going to fly myself. I'm not afraid to go anywhere I send my men. I'll die before I'll admit I'm beaten."

It was easy to see why Kennedy was fascinated by a man of Norton's type. Anyone would have been. It was not foolhardiness. It was dogged determination, faith in himself and in his own ability to triumph over every obstacle.

We now slowly entered the shed where two men were working over Norton's biplane. One of the men was a Frenchman, Jaurette, who had worked with Farman,* a silent, dark-browed, weather-beaten fellow with a sort of sullen politeness. The other man was an American, Roy Sinclair, a tall, lithe, wiry chap with a seamed and furrowed face and a loose-jointed but very deft manner which marked him a born bird-man. Norton's third aviator, Humphreys, who was not to fly that day, much to his relief, was reading a paper in the back of the shed.

We were introduced to him, and he seemed to be a very companionable sort of fellow, though not given to talking.

"Mr. Norton," he said, after the introduction, "there's quite an account of your injunction against Delanne in this paper. It doesn't seem to be very friendly," he added, indicating the article.

Norton read it and frowned. "Humph! I'll show them yet

---

* Henri Farman (1874–1958) and Maurice Farman (1877–1964) were Anglo-French brothers deeply involved in aviation and aircraft design and manufacture.

that my application of the gyroscope is patentable. Delanne will put me into 'interference' in the patent office, as the lawyers call it, will he? Well, I filed a 'caveat' over a year and a half ago. If I'm wrong, he's wrong, and all gyroscope patents are wrong, and if I'm right, by George, I'm first in the field. That's so, isn't it?" he appealed to Kennedy.

Kennedy shrugged his shoulders non-committally, as if he had never heard of the patent office or the gyroscope in his life. The men were listening, whether or not from loyalty I could not tell.

"Let us see your gyroplane, I mean aeroscope—whatever it is you call it," asked Kennedy.

Norton took the cue. "Now you newspaper men are the first that I've allowed in here," he said. "Can I trust your word of honour not to publish a line except such as I O. K. after you write it?"

We promised.

As Norton directed, the mechanicians wheeled the aeroplane out on the field in front of the shed. No one was about.

"Now this is the gyroscope," began Norton, pointing out a thing encased in an aluminum sheath, which weighed, all told, perhaps fourteen or fifteen pounds. "You see, the gyroscope is really a flywheel mounted on gimbals and can turn on any of its axes so that it can assume any angle in space. When it's at rest like this you can turn it easily. But when set revolving it tends to persist always in the plane in which it was started rotating."

I took hold of it, and it did turn readily in any direction. I could feel the heavy little flywheel inside.

"There is a pretty high vacuum in that aluminum case," went on Norton. "There's very little friction on that account. The power to rotate the flywheel is obtained from this little dynamo here, run by the gas-engine which also turns the propellers of the aeroplane."

"But suppose the engine stops, how about the gyroscope?" I asked sceptically.

"It will go right on for several minutes. You know, the Brennan monorail car* will stand up some time after the power is shut off. And I carry a small storage-battery that will run it for some time, too. That's all been guarded against."

Jaurette cranked the engine, a seven-cylindered affair, with the cylinders sticking out like the spokes of a wheel without a rim. The propellers turned so fast that I could not see the blades—turned with that strong, steady, fierce droning buzz that can be heard a long distance and which is a thrilling sound to hear. Norton reached over and attached the little dynamo, at the same time setting the gyroscope at its proper angle and starting it.

"This is the mechanical brain of my new flier," he remarked, patting the aluminum case lovingly. "You can look in through this little window in the case and see the flywheel inside revolving—ten thousand revolutions a minute. Press down on the gyroscope," he shouted to me.

As I placed both hands on the case of the apparently frail little instrument, he added, "You remember how easily you moved it just a moment ago."

I pressed down with all my might. Then I literally raised myself off my feet, and my whole weight was on the gyroscope. That uncanny little instrument seemed to resent—yes, that's the word, resent—my touch. It was almost human in the resentment, too. Far from yielding to me, it actually rose on the side I was pressing down!

---

* The Irish-born Australian inventor Louis Brennan (1852–1932) patented a gyro monorail car in 1903. Though the British War Office gave Brennan a grant to develop the idea (and Winston Churchill was an enthusiastic backer), it was never commercially produced. A model remains in the National Railway Museum in York, England.

The men who were watching me laughed at the puzzled look on my face.

I took my hands off, and the gyroscope leisurely and nonchalantly went back to its original position.

"That's the property we use, applied to the rudder and the ailerons—those flat planes between the large main planes. That gives automatic stability to the machine," continued Norton. "I'm not going to explain how it is done—it is in the combination of the various parts that I have discovered the basic principle, and I'm not going to talk about it till the thing is settled by the courts.* But it is there, and the court will see it, and I'll prove that Delanne is a fraud—a fraud when he says that my combination isn't patentable and isn't practicable even at that! The truth is that his device as it stands isn't practicable, and, besides, if he makes it so it infringes on mine. Would you like to take a flight with me?"

I looked at Kennedy, and a vision of the wreckage of the two previous accidents, as the *Star* photographer had snapped them, flashed across my mind. But Kennedy was too quick for me.

"Yes," he answered. "A short flight. No stunts."

We took our seats by Norton, I, at least, with some misgiving. Gently the machine rose into the air. The sensation was delightful. The fresh air of the morning came with a stinging rush to my face. Below I could see the earth sweeping past as if it were a moving-picture film. Above the continuous roar of the engine and propeller Norton indicated to Kennedy the automatic balancing of the gyroscope as it bent the ailerons.

---

* It's not clear how Norton's device would have worked. A gyroscopic stabilizer was used soon after, however, in 1914, for the purpose of maintaining stability and control in a Curtiss C-2 biplane. Its inventors Elmer A. Sperry and Lawrence B. Sperry were awarded the Collier Trophy for their invention. The Sperrys' device linked the control surfaces of the airplane with three gyroscopes, allowing flight corrections to be introduced based on the angle of deviation between the flight direction and the original gyroscopic settings.

"Could you fly in this machine without the gyroscope at all?" yelled Kennedy. The noise was deafening, conversation almost impossible. Though sitting side by side he had to repeat his remark twice to Norton.

"Yes," called back Norton. Reaching back of him, he pointed out the way to detach the gyroscope and put a sort of brake on it that stopped its revolutions almost instantly. "It's a ticklish job to change in the air," he shouted. "It can be done, but it's safer to land and do it."

The flight was soon over, and we stood admiring the machine while Norton expatiated on the compactness of his little dynamo.

"What have you done with the wrecks of the other machines?" inquired Kennedy at length.

"They are stored in a shed down near the railroad station. They are just a mass of junk, though there are some parts that I can use, so I'll ship them back to the factory."

"Might I have a look at them?"

"Surely. I'll give you the key. Sorry I can't go myself, but I want to be sure everything is all right for my flight this afternoon."

It was a long walk over to the shed near the station, and, together with our examination of the wrecked machines, it took us the rest of the morning. Craig carefully turned over the wreckage. It seemed a hopeless quest to me, but I fancied that to him it merely presented new problems for his deductive and scientific mind.

"These gyroscopes are out of business for good," he remarked as he glanced at the dented and battered aluminum cases. "But there doesn't seem to be anything wrong with them except what would naturally happen in such accidents."

For my part I felt a sort of awe at the mass of wreckage in which Browne and Herrick had been killed. It was to me more than a tangled mass of wires and splinters. Two human lives had been snuffed out in it.

"The engines are a mass of scrap; see how the cylinders are bent and twisted," remarked Kennedy with great interest. "The gasoline-tank is intact, but dented out of shape. No explosion there. And look at this dynamo. Why, the wires in it are actually fused together. The insulation has been completely burned off. I wonder what could have caused that?"

Kennedy continued to regard the tangled mass thoughtfully for some time, then locked the door, and we strolled back to the grand stand on our side of the field. Already the crowd had begun to collect. Across the field we could see the various machines in front of their hangars with the men working on them. The buzz of the engines was wafted across by the light summer breeze as if a thousand cicadas had broken loose to predict warm weather.

Two machines were already in flight, a little yellow Demoiselle, scurrying around close to the earth like a frightened hen, and a Bleriot, high overhead, making slow and graceful turns like a huge bird.*

Kennedy and I stopped before the little wireless telegraph station of the signal corps in front of the grand stand and watched the operator working over his instruments.

"There it is again," muttered the operator angrily.

"What's the matter?" asked Kennedy. "Amateurs interfering with you?"

The man nodded a reply, shaking his head with the telephone-like receiver, viciously. He continued to adjust his apparatus.

"Confound it!" he exclaimed. "Yes, that fellow has been

---

* The Demoiselle was one of a series of lightweight monoplanes built by the French aviation pioneer Alberto Santos-Dumont. The Bleriot was an aircraft manufactured by Blériot Aéronautique, the company founded by Louis Bleriot. Bleriot later manufactured the popular warplane known as the SPAD for use during World War I.

jamming me for the past two days off and on, every time I get ready to send or receive a message. Williams is going up with a Wright machine equipped with wireless apparatus in a minute, and this fellow won't get out of the way. By Jove, though, those are powerful impulses of his. Hear that crackling? I've never been interfered with so in my experience. Touch that screen door with your knife."

Kennedy did so, and elicited large sparks with quite a tingle of a shock.

"Yesterday and the day before it was so bad we had to give up attempting to communicate with Williams," continued the operator. "It was worse than trying to work in a thunder-shower. That's the time we get our troubles, when the air is overcharged with electricity, as it is now."

"That's interesting," remarked Kennedy.

"Interesting?" flashed back the operator, angrily noting the condition in his "log book." "Maybe it is, but I call it darned mean. It's almost like trying to work in a power station."

"Indeed?" queried Kennedy. "I beg your pardon—I was only looking at it from the purely scientific point of view. Who is it, do you suppose?"

"How do I know? Some amateur, I guess. No professional would butt in this way."

Kennedy took a leaf out of his notebook and wrote a short message which he gave to a boy to deliver to Norton.

"Detach your gyroscope and dynamo," it read. "Leave them in the hangar. Fly without them this afternoon, and see what happens. No use to try for the prize to-day. Kennedy."

We sauntered out on the open part of the field, back of the fence and to the side of the stands, and watched the fliers for a few moments. Three were in the air now, and I could see Norton and his men getting ready.

The boy with the message was going rapidly across the field. Kennedy was impatiently watching him. It was too far off to see just what they were doing, but as Norton seemed to get down out of his seat in the aeroplane when the boy arrived, and it was wheeled back into the shed, I gathered that he was detaching the gyroscope and was going to make the flight without it, as Kennedy had requested.

In a few minutes it was again wheeled out. The crowd, which had been waiting especially to see Norton, applauded.

"Come, Walter," exclaimed Kennedy, "let's go up there on the roof of the stand where we can see better. There's a platform and railing, I see."

His pass allowed him to go anywhere on the field, so in a few moments we were up on the roof.

It was a fascinating vantage-point, and I was so deeply engrossed between watching the crowd below, the bird-men in the air, and the machines waiting across the field that I totally neglected to notice what Kennedy was doing. When I did, I saw that he had deliberately turned his back on the aviation field, and was anxiously scanning the country back of us.

"What are you looking for?" I asked. "Turn around. I think Norton is just about to fly."

"Watch him then," answered Craig. "Tell me when he gets in the air."

Just then Norton's aeroplane rose gently from the field. A wild shout of applause came from the people below us, at the heroism of the man who dared to fly this new and apparently fated machine. It was succeeded by a breathless, deathly calm, as if after the first burst of enthusiasm the crowd had suddenly realised the danger of the intrepid aviator. Would Norton add a third to the fatalities of the meet?

Suddenly Kennedy jerked my arm. "Walter, look over there

across the road back of us—at the old weather-beaten barn. I mean the one next to that yellow house. What do you see?"

"Nothing, except that on the peak of the roof there is a pole that looks like the short stub of a small wireless mast. I should say there was a boy connected with that barn, a boy who has read a book on wireless for beginners."

"Maybe," said Kennedy. "But is that all you see? Look up in the little window of the gable, the one with the closed shutter."

I looked carefully. "It seems to me that I saw a gleam of something bright at the top of the shutter, Craig," I ventured. "A spark or a flash."

"It must be a bright spark, for the sun is shining brightly," mused Craig.

"Oh, maybe it's the small boy with a looking-glass. I can remember when I used to get behind such a window and shine a glass into the darkened room of my neighbours across the street."

I had really said that half in raillery, for I was at a loss to account in any other way for the light, but I was surprised to see how eagerly Craig accepted it.

"Perhaps you are right, in a way," he assented. "I guess it isn't a spark, after all. Yes, it must be the reflection of the sun on a piece of glass—the angles are just about right for it. Anyhow it caught my eye. Still, I believe that barn will bear watching."

Whatever his suspicions, Craig kept them to himself, and descended. At the same time Norton gently dropped back to earth in front of his hangar, not ten feet from the spot where he started. The applause was deafening, as the machine was again wheeled into the shed safely.

Kennedy and I pushed through the crowd to the wireless operator.

"How's she working?" inquired Craig.

"Rotten," replied the operator sullenly. "It was worse than ever about five minutes ago. It's much better now, almost normal again."

Just then the messenger-boy, who had been hunting through the crowd for us, handed Kennedy a note. It was merely a scrawl from Norton:

> *"Everything seems fine. Am going to try her next with the gyroscope. NORTON."*

"Boy," exclaimed Craig, "has Mr. Norton a telephone?"

"No, sir, only that hangar at the end has a telephone."

"Well, you run across that field as fast as your legs can carry you and tell him if he values his life not to do it."

"Not to do what, sir?"

"Don't stand there, youngster. Run! Tell him not to fly with that gyroscope. There's a five-spot in it if you get over there before he starts."

Even as he spoke the Norton aeroplane was wheeled out again. In a minute Norton had climbed up into his seat and was testing the levers.

Would the boy reach him in time? He was half across the field, waving his arms like mad. But apparently Norton and his men were too engrossed in their machine to pay attention.

"Good heavens!" exclaimed Craig. "He's going to try it. Run, boy, run!" he cried, although the boy was now far out of hearing.

Across the field we could hear now the quick staccato chug-chug of the engine. Slowly Norton's aeroplane, this time really equipped with the gyroscope, rose from the field and circled over toward us. Craig frantically signalled to him to come down, but of course Norton could not have seen him in the crowd. As for the crowd, they looked askance at Kennedy, as if he had taken leave of his senses.

I heard the wireless operator cursing the way his receiver was acting.

Higher and higher Norton went in one spiral after another, those spirals which his gyroscope had already made famous.

The man with the megaphone in front of the judge's stand announced in hollow tones that Mr. Norton had given notice that he would try for the Brooks Prize for stationary equilibrium.

Kennedy and I stood speechless, helpless, appalled.

Slower and slower went the aeroplane. It seemed to hover just like the big mechanical bird that it was.

Kennedy was anxiously watching the judges with one eye and Norton with the other. A few in the crowd could no longer restrain their applause. I remember that the wireless back of us was spluttering and crackling like mad.

All of a sudden a groan swept over the crowd. Something was wrong with Norton. His aeroplane was swooping downward at a terrific rate. Would he be able to control it? I held my breath and gripped Kennedy by the arm. Down, down came Norton, frantically fighting by main strength, it seemed to me, to warp the planes so that their surface might catch the air and check his descent.

"He's trying to detach the gyroscope," whispered Craig hoarsely.

The football helmet which Norton wore blew off and fell more rapidly than the plane. I shut my eyes. But Kennedy's next exclamation caused me quickly to open them again.

"He'll make it, after all!"

Somehow Norton had regained partial control of his machine, but it was still swooping down at a tremendous pace toward the level centre of the field.

There was a crash as it struck the ground in a cloud of dust.

With a leap Kennedy had cleared the fence and was running

toward Norton. Two men from the judge's stand were ahead of us, but except for them we were the first to reach him. The men were tearing frantically at the tangled framework, trying to lift it off Norton, who lay pale and motionless, pinned under it. The machine was not so badly damaged, after all, but that together we could lift it bodily off him.

A doctor ran out from the crowd and hastily put his ear to Norton's chest. No one spoke, but we all scanned the doctor's face anxiously.

"Just stunned—he'll be all right in a moment. Get some water," he said.

Kennedy pulled my arm. "Look at the gyroscope dynamo," he whispered.

I looked. Like the other two which we had seen, it also was a wreck. The insulation was burned off the wires, the wires were fused together, and the storage-battery looked as if it had been burned out.

A flicker of the eyelid and Norton seemed to regain some degree of consciousness. He was living over again the ages that had passed during the seconds of his terrible fall.

"Will they never stop? Oh, those sparks, those sparks! I can't disconnect it. Sparks, more sparks—will they never—" So he rambled on. It was fearsome to hear him.

But Kennedy was now sure that Norton was safe and in good hands, and he hurried back in the direction of the grand stand. I followed. Flying was over for that day, and the people were filing slowly out toward the railroad station where the special trains were waiting. We stopped at the wireless station for a moment.

"Is it true that Norton will recover?" inquired the operator.

"Yes. He was only stunned, thank Heaven! Did you keep a record of the antics of your receiver since I saw you last?"

"Yes, sir. And I made a copy for you. By the way, it's working all right now when I don't want it. If Williams was only in the air now I'd give you a good demonstration of communicating with an aeroplane," continued the operator as he prepared to leave.

Kennedy thanked him for the record and carefully folded it. Joining the crowd, we pushed our way out, but instead of going down to the station with them, Kennedy turned toward the barn and the yellow house.

For some time we waited about casually, but nothing occurred. At length Kennedy walked up to the shed. The door was closed and double padlocked. He knocked, but there was no answer.

Just then a man appeared on the porch of the yellow house. Seeing us, he beckoned. As we approached he shouted, "He's gone for the day!"

"Has he a city address—any place I could reach him to-night?" asked Craig.

"I don't know. He hired the barn from me for two weeks and paid in advance. He told me if I wanted to address him the best way was 'Dr. K. Lamar, General Delivery, New York City.'"

"Ah, then I suppose I had better write to him," said Kennedy, apparently much gratified to learn the name. "I presume he'll be taking away his apparatus soon?"

"Can't say. There's enough of it. Cy Smith—he's in the electric light company up to the village—says the doctor has used a powerful lot of current. He's good pay, though he's awful close-mouthed. Flying's over for to-day, ain't it? Was that feller much hurt?"

"No, he'll be all right to-morrow. I think he'll fly again. The machine's in pretty good condition. He's bound to win that prize. Good-bye."

As he walked away I remarked, "How do you know Norton will fly again?"

"I don't," answered Kennedy, "but I think that either he or Humphreys will. I wanted to see that this Lamar believes it anyhow. By the way, Walter, do you think you could grab a wire here and 'phone in a story to the *Star* that Norton isn't much hurt and will probably be able to fly to-morrow? Try to get the City News Association, too, so that all the papers will have it. I don't care about risking the general delivery—perhaps Lamar won't call for any mail, but he certainly will read the papers. Put it in the form of an interview with Norton—I'll see that it is all right and that there is no come-back. Norton will stand for it when I tell him my scheme."

I caught the *Star* just in time for the last edition, and some of the other papers that had later editions also had the story. Of course all the morning papers had it.

Norton spent the night in the Mineola Hospital. He didn't really need to stay, but the doctor said it would be best in case some internal injury had been overlooked. Meanwhile Kennedy took charge of the hangar where the injured machine was. The men had been in a sort of panic; Humphreys could not be found, and the only reason, I think, why the two mechanicians stayed was because something was due them on their pay.

Kennedy wrote them out personal checks for their respective amounts, but dated them two days ahead to insure their staying. He threw off all disguise now and with authority from Norton directed the repairing of the machine. Fortunately it was in pretty good condition. The broken part was the skids, not the essential parts of the machine. As for the gyroscope, there were plenty of them and another dynamo, and it was a very simple thing to replace the old one that had been destroyed.

Sinclair worked with a will, far past his regular hours. Jaurette also worked, though one could hardly say with a will. In fact, most of the work was done by Sinclair and Kennedy, with

Jaurette sullenly grumbling, mostly in French under his breath. I did not like the fellow and was suspicious of him. I thought I noticed that Kennedy did not allow him to do much of the work, either, though that may have been for the reason that Kennedy never asked anyone to help him who seemed unwilling.

"There," exclaimed Craig about ten o'clock. "If we want to get back to the city in any kind of time to-night we had better quit. Sinclair, I think you can finish repairing these skids in the morning."

We locked up the hangar and hurried across to the station. It was late when we arrived in New York, but Kennedy insisted on posting off up to his laboratory, leaving me to run down to the *Star* office to make sure that our story was all right for the morning papers.

I did not see him until morning, when a large touring-car drove up. Kennedy routed me out of bed. In the tonneau of the car was a huge package carefully wrapped up.

"Something I worked on for a couple of hours last night," explained Craig, patting it. "If this doesn't solve the problem then I'll give it up."

I was burning with curiosity, but somehow, by a perverse association of ideas, I merely reproached Kennedy for not taking enough rest.

"Oh," he smiled. "If I hadn't been working last night, Walter, I couldn't have rested at all for thinking about it."

When we arrived at the field Norton was already there with his head bandaged. I thought him a little pale, but otherwise all right. Jaurette was sulking, but Sinclair had finished the repairs and was busily engaged in going over every bolt and wire. Humphreys had sent word that he had another offer and had not shown up.

"We must find him," exclaimed Kennedy. "I want him to make a flight to-day. His contract calls for it."

"I can do it, Kennedy," asserted Norton. "See, I'm all right."

He picked up two pieces of wire and held them at arm's length, bringing them together, tip to tip, in front of him just to show us how he could control his nerves.

"And I'll be better yet by this afternoon," he added. "I can do that stunt with the points of pins then."

Kennedy shook his head gravely, but Norton insisted, and finally Kennedy agreed to give up wasting time trying to locate Humphreys. After that he and Norton had a long whispered conference in which Kennedy seemed to be unfolding a scheme.

"I understand," said Norton at length, "you want me to put this sheet-lead cover over the dynamo and battery first. Then you want me to take the cover off, and also to detach the gyroscope, and to fly without using it. Is that it?"

"Yes," assented Craig. "I will be on the roof of the grand stand. The signal will be three waves of my hat repeated till I see you get it."

After a quick luncheon we went up to our vantage-point. On the way Kennedy had spoken to the head of the Pinkertons engaged by the management for the meet, and had also dropped in to see the wireless operator to ask him to send up a messenger if he saw the same phenomena as he had observed the day before.

On the roof Kennedy took from his pocket a little instrument with a needle which trembled back and forth over a dial. It was nearing the time for the start of the day's flying, and the aeroplanes were getting ready. Kennedy was calmly biting a cigar, casting occasional glances at the needle as it oscillated. Suddenly, as Williams rose in the Wright machine, the needle swung quickly and pointed straight at the aviation field, vibrating through a small arc, back and forth.

"The operator is getting his apparatus ready to signal to

Williams," remarked Craig. "This is an apparatus called an ondometer. It tells you the direction and something of the magnitude of the Hertzian waves used in wireless."

Five or ten minutes passed. Norton was getting ready to fly. I could see through my field-glass that he was putting something over his gyroscope and over the dynamo, but could not quite make out what it was. His machine seemed to leap up in the air as if eager to redeem itself. Norton with his white-bandaged head was the hero of the hour. No sooner had his aeroplane got up over the level of the trees than I heard a quick exclamation from Craig.

"Look at the needle, Walter!" he cried. "As soon as Norton got into the air it shot around directly opposite to the wireless station, and now it is pointing—"

We raised our eyes in the direction which it indicated. It was precisely in line with the weather-beaten barn.

I gasped. What did it mean? Did it mean in some way another accident to Norton—perhaps fatal this time? Why had Kennedy allowed him to try it to-day when there was even a suspicion that some nameless terror was abroad in the air? Quickly I turned to see if Norton was all right. Yes, there he was, circling above us in a series of wide spirals, climbing up, up. Now he seemed almost to stop, to hover motionless. He was motionless. His engine had been cut out, and I could see his propeller stopped. He was riding as a ship rides on the ocean.

A boy ran up the ladder to the roof. Kennedy unfolded the note and shoved it into my hands. It was from the operator.

"Wireless out of business again. Curse that fellow who is butting in. Am keeping record," was all it said.

I shot a glance of inquiry at Kennedy, but he was paying no attention now to anything but Norton. He held his watch in his hand.

"Walter," he ejaculated as he snapped it shut, "it has now been seven minutes and a half since he stopped his propeller. The Brooks Prize calls for five minutes only. Norton has exceeded it fifty per cent. Here goes."

With his hat in his hand he waved three times and stopped. Then he repeated the process.

At the third time the aeroplane seemed to give a start. The propeller began to revolve, Norton starting it on the compression successfully. Slowly he circled down again. Toward the end of the descent he stopped the engine and volplaned, or coasted, to the ground, landing gently in front of his hangar.

A wild cheer rose into the air from the crowd below us. All eyes were riveted on the activity about Norton's biplane. They were doing something to it.

Whatever it was, it was finished in a minute and the men were standing again at a respectful distance from the propellers. Again Norton was in the air. As he rose above the field Kennedy gave a last glance at his ondometer and sprang down the ladder. I followed closely. Back of the crowd he hurried, down the walk to the entrance near the railroad station. The man in charge of the Pinkertons was at the gate with two other men, apparently waiting.

"Come on!" shouted Craig.

We four followed him as fast as we could. He turned in at the lane running up to the yellow house, so as to approach the barn from the rear, unobserved.

"Quietly, now," he cautioned.

We were now at the door of the barn. A curious crackling, snapping noise issued. Craig gently tried the door. It was bolted on the inside. As many of us as could threw ourselves like a human catapult against it. It yielded.

Inside I saw a sheet of flame fifteen or twenty feet long—it

"Lamar," shouted Kennedy, drawing a pistol, "one motion of your hand and you are a dead man. Stand still—where you are."

was a veritable artificial bolt of lightning. A man with a telescope had been peering out of the window, but now was facing us in surprise.

"Lamar," shouted Kennedy, drawing a pistol, "one motion of your hand and you are a dead man. Stand still—where you are. You are caught red-handed."

The rest of us shrank back in momentary fear of the gigantic forces of nature which seemed let loose in the room. The thought, in my mind at least, was: Suppose this arch-fiend should turn his deadly power on us?

Kennedy saw us from the corner of his eye. "Don't be afraid," he said with just a curl to his lip. "I've seen all this before. It won't hurt you. It's a high frequency current. The man has simply appropriated the invention of Mr. Nikola Tesla. Seize him. He won't struggle. I've got him covered."

Two burly Pinkertons leaped forward gingerly into the midst of the electrical apparatus, and in less time than it takes to write it Lamar was hustled out to the doorway, each arm pinioned back of him.

As we stood, half dazed by the suddenness of the turn of events, Kennedy hastily explained: "Tesla's theory is that under certain conditions the atmosphere, which is normally a high insulator, assumes conducting properties and so becomes capable of conveying any amount of electrical energy. I myself have seen electrical oscillations such as these in this room of such intensity that while they could he circulated with impunity through one's arms and chest they would melt wires farther along in the circuit. Yet the person through whom such a current is passing feels no inconvenience. I have seen a loop of heavy copper wire energised by such oscillations and a mass of metal within the loop heated to the fusing point, and yet into the space in which this destructive aerial turmoil was going on

I have repeatedly thrust my hand and even my head, without feeling anything or experiencing any injurious after-effect. In this form all the energy of all the dynamos of Niagara could pass through one's body and yet produce no injury. But, diabolically directed, this vast energy has been used by this man to melt the wires in the little dynamo that runs Norton's gyroscope. That is all.* Now to the aviation field. I have something more to show you."

We hurried as fast as we could up the street and straight out on the field, across toward the Norton hangar, the crowd gaping in wonderment. Kennedy waved frantically for Norton to come down, and Norton, who was only a few hundred feet in the air, seemed to see and understand.

As we stood waiting before the hangar Kennedy could no longer restrain his impatience.

"I suspected some wireless-power trick when I found that the field wireless telegraph failed to work every time Norton's aeroplane was in the air," he said, approaching close to Lamar. "I just happened to catch sight of that peculiar wireless mast of yours. A little flash of light first attracted my attention to it. I thought it was an electric spark, but you are too clever for that, Lamar. Still, you forgot a much simpler thing. It was the glint of the sun on the lens of your telescope as you were watching Norton that betrayed you."

Lamar said nothing.

"I'm glad to say you had no confederate in the hangar here," continued Craig. "At first I suspected it. Anyhow, you

---

* "That is all" is an understatement—Tesla essentially failed to create an effective means of wireless power transmission; Lamar's machine was science fiction. The fault did not lie in Tesla's ideas, however. Experiments in the early twenty-first century have achieved wireless power transmission over short distances, and later work promises to provide power to drone aircraft and to charge cell phones and other battery-powered devices without a plugged-in charger.

succeeded pretty well single handed, two lives lost and two machines wrecked. Norton flew all right yesterday when he left his gyroscope and dynamo behind, but when he took them along you were able to fuse the wires in the dynamo— you pretty nearly succeeded in adding his name to those of Browne and Herrick."

The whir of Norton's machine told us he was approaching. We scattered to give him space enough to choose the spot where he would alight. As the men caught his machine to steady it, he jumped lightly to the ground.

"Where's Kennedy?" he asked, and then, without waiting for a reply, he exclaimed: "Queerest thing I ever saw up there. The dynamo wasn't protected by the sheet-lead shield in this flight as in the first to-day. I hadn't risen a hundred feet before I happened to hear the darndest sputtering in the dynamo. Look, boys, the insulation is completely burned off the wires, and the wires are nearly all fused together."

"So it was in the other two wrecked machines," added Kennedy, coming coolly forward. "If you hadn't had everything protected by those shields I gave you in your first flight to-day you would have simply repeated your fall of yesterday—perhaps fatally. This fellow has been directing the full strength of his wireless high-tension electricity straight at you all the time."

"What fellow?" demanded Norton.

The two Pinkertons shoved Lamar forward. Norton gave a contemptuous look at him. "Delanne," he said, "I knew you were a crook when you tried to infringe on my patent, but I didn't think you were coward enough to resort to—to murder."

Lamar, or rather Delanne, shrank back as if even the protection of his captors was safety compared to the threatening advance of Norton toward him.

"Pouff!" exclaimed Norton, turning suddenly on his heel.

"What a fool I am! The law will take care of such scoundrels as you. What's the grand stand cheering for now?" he asked, looking across the field in an effort to regain his self-control.

A boy from one of the hangars down the line spoke up from the back of the crowd in a shrill, piping voice. "You have been awarded the Brooks Prize, sir," he said.

X

THE BLACK HAND

Kennedy and I had been dining rather late one evening at Luigi's, a little Italian restaurant on the lower West Side. We had known the place well in our student days, and had made a point of visiting it once a month since, in order to keep in practice in the fine art of gracefully handling long shreds of spaghetti. Therefore we did not think it strange when the proprietor himself stopped a moment at our table to greet us. Glancing furtively around at the other diners, mostly Italians, he suddenly leaned over and whispered to Kennedy:

"I have heard of your wonderful detective work, Professor. Could you give a little advice in the case of a friend of mine?"

"Surely, Luigi. What is the case?" asked Craig, leaning back in his chair.

Luigi glanced around again apprehensively and lowered his voice. "Not so loud, sir. When you pay your check, go out, walk around Washington Square, and come in at the private entrance. I'll be waiting in the hall. My friend is dining privately up-stairs."

We lingered a while over our chianti, then quietly paid the check and departed.

True to his word, Luigi was waiting for us in the dark hall.

With a motion that indicated silence, he led us up the stairs to the second floor, and quickly opened a door into what seemed to be a fair-sized private dining-room. A man was pacing the floor nervously. On a table was some food, untouched. As the door opened I thought he started as if in fear, and I am sure his dark face blanched, if only for an instant. Imagine our surprise at seeing Gennaro, the great tenor, with whom merely to have a speaking acquaintance was to argue oneself famous.

"Oh, it is you, Luigi," he exclaimed in perfect English, rich and mellow. "And who are these gentlemen?"

Luigi merely replied, "Friends," in English also, and then dropped off into a voluble, low-toned explanation in Italian.

I could see, as we waited, that the same idea had flashed over Kennedy's mind as over my own. It was now three or four days since the papers had reported the strange kidnapping of Gennaro's five-year-old daughter Adelina, his only child, and the sending of a demand for ten thousand dollars ransom, signed, as usual, with the mystic Black Hand—a name to conjure with in blackmail and extortion.[*]

As Signor Gennaro advanced toward us, after his short talk with Luigi, almost before the introductions were over, Kennedy anticipated him by saying: "I understand, Signor, before you ask me. I have read all about it in the papers. You want someone to help you catch the criminals who are holding your little girl."

---

[*] The "Black Hand" refers not to a gang but to the method of extortion used by New York-based Italian criminals in early twentieth-century America, involving demands adorned by images of skulls, daggers, and black warning hands. According to Mike Dash's *The First Family: Terror, Extortion and the Birth of the American Mafia* (New York: Random House, 2009), in 1907, the legendary tenor Enrico Caruso received a "Black Hand" letter demanding "protection" money. Caruso paid, but when threats persisted, he worked with the police to capture the extortionists in Little Italy. The bizarre form of the demands caught the public's attention, and the extortion racket was dubbed "the Black Hand" by a reporter for the *New York Herald*. The name quickly became synonymous with the principal perpetrators of the racket—the Camorra and the Mafia. (For more on the Camorra, see note on page 236.)

"No, no!" exclaimed Gennaro excitedly. "Not that. I want to get my daughter first. After that, catch them if you can—yes, I should like to have someone do it. But read this first and tell me what you think of it. How should I act to get my little Adelina back without harming a hair of her head?" The famous singer drew from a capacious pocketbook a dirty, crumpled letter, scrawled on cheap paper.

Kennedy translated it quickly. It read:

Honourable sir: Your daughter is in safe hands. But, by the saints, if you give this letter to the police as you did the other, not only she but your family also, someone near to you, will suffer. We will not fail as we did Wednesday. If you want your daughter back, go yourself, alone and without telling a soul, to Enrico Albano's Saturday night at the twelfth hour. You must provide yourself with $10,000 in bills hidden in Saturday's Il Progresso Italiano. *In the back room you will see a man sitting alone at a table. He will have a red flower on his coat. You are to say, "A fine opera is 'I Pagliacci.'"*
If he answers, "Not without Gennaro," lay the newspaper down on the table. He will pick it up, leaving his own, the Bolletino. *On the third page you will find written the place where your daughter has been left waiting for you. Go immediately and get her. But, by the God, if you have so much as the shadow of the police near Enrico's your daughter will be sent to you in a box that night. Do not fear to come. We pledge our word to deal fairly if you deal fairly. This is a last warning. Lest you shall forget we will show one other sign of our power to-morrow.*

La Mano Nera.

The end of this ominous letter was gruesomely decorated with a skull and cross-bones, a rough drawing of a dagger thrust through a bleeding heart, a coffin, and, under all, a huge black hand. There was no doubt about the type of letter that it was. It was such as have of late years become increasingly common in all our large cities, baffling the best detectives.

"You have not showed this to the police, I presume?" asked Kennedy.

"Naturally not."

"Are you going Saturday night?"

"I am afraid to go and afraid to stay away," was the reply, and the voice of the fifty-thousand-dollars-a-season tenor was as human as that of a five-dollar-a-week father, for at bottom all men, high or low, are one.

"'We will not fail as we did Wednesday,'" reread Craig. "What does that mean?"

Gennaro fumbled in his pocketbook again, and at last drew forth a typewritten letter bearing the letter-head of the Leslie Laboratories, Incorporated.

"After I received the first threat," explained Gennaro, "my wife and I went from our apartments at the hotel to her father's, the banker Cesare, you know, who lives on Fifth Avenue. I gave the letter to the Italian Squad of the police. The next morning my father-in-law's butler noticed something peculiar about the milk. He barely touched some of it to his tongue, and he has been violently ill ever since. I at once sent the milk to the laboratory of my friend Doctor Leslie to have it analysed. This letter shows what the household escaped."

"My dear Gennaro," read Kennedy. "The milk submitted to us for examination on the 10th inst. has been carefully analysed, and I beg to hand you herewith the result:

"*Specific gravity 1.036 at 15 degrees Cent.*

Water	*84.60*	*per*	*cent*
Casein	*3.49*	"	"
Albumin	*.56*	"	"
Globulin	*1.32*	"	"
Lactose	*5.08*	"	"
Ash	*.72*	"	"
Fat	*3.42*	"	"
Ricin	*1.19*	"	"

"*Ricin is a new and little-known poison derived from the shell of the castor-oil bean. Professor Ehrlich states that one gram of the pure poison will kill 1,500,000 guinea pigs. Ricin was lately isolated by Professor Robert, of Rostock, but is seldom found except in an impure state, though still very deadly. It surpasses strychnin, prussic acid, and other commonly known drugs. I congratulate you and yours on escaping and shall of course respect your wishes absolutely regarding keeping secret this attempt on your life. Believe me,*
"*Very sincerely yours,*
"*C. W.* LESLIE."

As Kennedy handed the letter back, he remarked significantly: "I can see very readily why you don't care to have the police figure in your case. It has got quite beyond ordinary police methods."

"And to-morrow, too, they are going to give another sign of their power," groaned Gennaro, sinking into the chair before his untasted food.

"You say you have left your hotel?" inquired Kennedy.

"Yes. My wife insisted that we would be more safely guarded

at the residence of her father, the banker. But we are afraid even there since the poison attempt. So I have come here secretly to Luigi, my old friend Luigi, who is preparing food for us, and in a few minutes one of Cesare's automobiles will be here, and I will take the food up to her—sparing no expense or trouble. She is heart-broken. It will kill her, Professor Kennedy, if anything happens to our little Adelina.

"Ah, sir, I am not poor myself. A month's salary at the opera-house, that is what they ask of me. Gladly would I give it, ten thousand dollars—all, if they asked it, of my contract with Herr Schleppencour, the director. But the police—bah!—they are all for catching the villains. What good will it do me if they catch them and my little Adelina is returned to me dead? It is all very well for the Anglo-Saxon to talk of justice and the law, but I am—what you call it?—an emotional Latin. I want my little daughter—and at any cost. Catch the villains afterward—yes. I will pay double then to catch them so that they cannot black-mail me again. Only first I want my daughter back."

"And your father-in-law?"

"My father-in-law, he has been among you long enough to be one of you. He has fought them. He has put up a sign in his banking-house, 'No money paid on threats.' But I say it is fool-ish. I do not know America as well as he, but I know this: the police never succeed—the ransom is paid without their knowl-edge, and they very often take the credit. I say, pay first, then I will swear a righteous vendetta—I will bring the dogs to jus-tice with the money yet on them. Only show me how, show me how."

"First of all," replied Kennedy, "I want you to answer one question, truthfully, without reservation, as to a friend. I am your friend, believe me. Is there any person, a relative or acquain-tance of yourself or your wife or your father-in-law, whom you even have reason to suspect of being capable of extorting money from you in this way? I needn't say that that is the experience of the district attorney's office in the large majority of cases of this so-called Black Hand."

"No," replied the tenor without hesitation. "I know that, and I have thought about it. No, I can think of no one. I know you Americans often speak of the Black Hand as a myth coined originally by a newspaper writer. Perhaps it has no organisation. But, Professor Kennedy, to me it is no myth. What if the real Black Hand is any gang of criminals who choose to use that convenient name to extort money? Is it the less real? My daughter is gone!"

"Exactly," agreed Kennedy. "It is not a theory that confronts you. It is a hard, cold fact. I understand that perfectly. What is the address of this Albano's?"

Luigi mentioned a number on Mulberry Street, and Kennedy made a note of it.

"It is a gambling saloon," explained Luigi. "Albano is a Neapolitan, a Camorrista, one of my countrymen of whom I am thoroughly ashamed, Professor Kennedy."

"Do you think this Albano had anything to do with the letter?"

Luigi shrugged his shoulders.

Just then a big limousine was heard outside. Luigi picked up a huge hamper that was placed in a corner of the room and, followed closely by Signor Gennaro, hurried down to it. As the tenor left us he grasped our hands in each of his.

"I have an idea in my mind," said Craig simply. "I will try to think it out in detail to-night. Where can I find you to-morrow?"

"Come to me at the opera-house in the afternoon, or if you want me sooner at Mr. Cesare's residence. Good night, and a thousand thanks to you, Professor Kennedy, and to you, also, Mr. Jameson. I trust you absolutely because Luigi trusts you."

We sat in the little dining-room until we heard the door of the limousine bang shut and the car shoot off with the rattle of the changing gears.

"One more question, Luigi," said Craig as the door opened again. "I have never been on that block in Mulberry Street where this Albano's is. Do you happen to know any of the shopkeepers on it or near it?"

"I have a cousin who has a drug-store on the corner below Albano's, on the same side of the street."

"Good! Do you think he would let me use his store for a few minutes Saturday night—of course without any risk to himself?"

"I think I could arrange it."

"Very well. Then to-morrow, say at nine in the morning, I will stop here, and we will all go over to see him. Good night, Luigi, and many thanks for thinking of me in connection with this case. I've enjoyed Signor Gennaro's singing often enough at the opera to want to render him this service, and I'm only too glad to be able to be of service to all honest Italians; that is, if I succeed in carrying out a plan I have in mind."

A little before nine the following day Kennedy and I dropped into Luigi's again. Kennedy was carrying a suit-case which he had taken over from his laboratory to our rooms the night before. Luigi was waiting for us, and without losing a minute we sallied forth.

By means of the tortuous twists of streets in old Greenwich village we came out at last on Bleecker Street and began walking east amid the hurly-burly of races of lower New York. We had not quite reached Mulberry Street when our attention was attracted by a large crowd on one of the busy corners, held back by a cordon of police who were endeavouring to keep the people moving with that burly good nature which the six-foot Irish policeman displays toward the five-foot burden-bearers of southern and eastern Europe who throng New York.

Apparently, we saw, as we edged up into the front of the crowd, here was a building whose whole front had literally been torn off and wrecked. The thick plate-glass of the windows was smashed to a mass of greenish splinters on the sidewalk, while the windows of the upper floors and for several houses down the block in either street were likewise broken. Some thick iron bars which had formerly protected the windows were now bent and twisted. A huge hole yawned in the floor inside the doorway, and peering in we could see the desks and chairs a tangled mass of kindling.

"What's the matter?" I inquired of an officer near me, displaying my reporter's fire-line badge, more for its moral effect than in the hope of getting any real information in these days of enforced silence toward the press.

"Black Hand bomb," was the laconic reply.

"Whew!" I whistled. "Anyone hurt?"

"They don't usually kill anyone, do they?" asked the officer by way of reply to test my acquaintance with such things.

"No," I admitted. "They destroy more property than lives. But did they get anyone this time? This must have been a thoroughly overloaded bomb, I should judge by the looks of things."

"Came pretty close to it. The bank hadn't any more than opened when, bang! went this gas-pipe-and-dynamite thing. Crowd collected before the smoke had fairly cleared. Man who owns the bank was hurt, but not badly. Now come, beat it down to headquarters if you want to find out any more. You'll find it printed on the pink slips—the 'squeal book"—by this time. 'Gainst the rules for me to talk," he added with a good-natured

---

* This seems to mean a compilation of records of police investigations. According to the *Oxford English Dictionary*, a "squeal" is a report of a police investigation. Note that "squealer" not only means a police informant but also has taken on the meaning of a police vehicle (with siren). "Pink slips" must be local slang for these records (just as in California, a "pink slip"—actually printed on pink paper—is an official certificate of title to a motor vehicle).

grin, then to the crowd: "G'wan, now. You're blockin' traffic. Keep movin.'"

I turned to Craig and Luigi. Their eyes were riveted on the big gilt sign, half broken, and all askew overhead. It read:

CIRO DI CESARE & CO. BANKERS
NEW YORK, GENOA, NAPLES, ROME, PALERMO

"This is the reminder so that Gennaro and his father-in-law will not forget," I gasped.

"Yes," added Craig, pulling us away, "and Cesare himself is wounded, too. Perhaps that was for putting up the notice refusing to pay. Perhaps not. It's a queer case—they usually set the bombs off at night when no one is around. There must be more back of this than merely to scare Gennaro. It looks to me as if they were after Casare, too, first by poison, then by dynamite."

We shouldered our way out through the crowd and went on until we came to Mulberry Street, pulsing with life. Down we went past the little shops, dodging the children, and making way for women with huge bundles of sweat-shop clothing accurately balanced on their heads or hugged up under their capacious capes. Here was just one little colony of the hundreds of thousands of Italians—a population larger than the Italian population of Rome—of whose life the rest of New York knew and cared nothing.

At last we came to Albano's little wine-shop, a dark, evil, malodorous place on the street level of a five-story, alleged "new-law" tenement. Without hesitation Kennedy entered, and we followed, acting the part of a slumming party. There were a few customers at this early hour, men out of employment and an inoffensive-looking lot, though of course they eyed us sharply. Albano himself proved to be a greasy, low-browed fellow who had a sort of cunning look. I could well imagine such a fellow spreading terror in the hearts of simple folk by merely pressing both temples with his thumbs and drawing his long bony forefinger under his throat—the so-called Black Hand sign that has shut up many a witness in the middle of his testimony even in open court.

We pushed through to the low-ceilinged back room, which was empty, and sat down at a table. Over a bottle of Albano's famous California "red ink" we sat silently. Kennedy was making a mental note of the place. In the middle of the ceiling was a single gas-burner with a big reflector over it. In the back wall of the room was a horizontal oblong window, barred, and with a sash that opened like a transom. The tables were dirty and the chairs rickety. The walls were bare and unfinished, with beams innocent of decoration. Altogether it was as unprepossessing a place as I had ever seen.

Apparently satisfied with his scrutiny, Kennedy got up to go, complimenting the proprietor on his wine. I could see that Kennedy had made up his mind as to his course of action.

"How sordid crime really is," he remarked as we walked on down the street. "Look at that place of Albano's. I defy even the police news reporter on the *Star* to find any glamour in that."

Our next stop was at the corner at the little store kept by the cousin of Luigi, who conducted us back of the partition where prescriptions were compounded, and found us chairs.

A hurried explanation from Luigi brought a cloud to the open face of the druggist, as if he hesitated to lay himself and his little fortune open to the blackmailers. Kennedy saw it and interrupted.

"All that I wish to do," he said, "is to put in a little instrument here and use it to-night for a few minutes. Indeed, there will be no risk to you, Vincenzo. Secrecy is what I desire, and no one will ever know about it."

Vincenzo was at length convinced, and Craig opened his suit-case. There was little in it except several coils of insulated wire, some tools, a couple of packages wrapped up, and a couple of pairs of overalls. In a moment Kennedy had donned overalls and was smearing dirt and grease over his face and hands. Under his direction I did the same.

Taking the bag of tools, the wire, and one of the small packages, we went out on the street and then up through the dark and ill-ventilated hall of the tenement. Half-way up a woman stopped us suspiciously.

"Telephone company," said Craig curtly. "Here's permission from the owner of the house to string wires across the roof."

He pulled an old letter out of his pocket, but as it was too dark to read even if the woman had cared to do so, we went on up as he had expected, unmolested. At last we came to the roof, where there were some children at play a couple of houses down from us.

Kennedy began by dropping two strands of wire down to the ground in the back yard behind Vincenzo's shop. Then he proceeded to lay two wires along the edge of the roof.

We had worked only a little while when the children began to collect. However, Kennedy kept right on until we reached the tenement next to that in which Albano's shop was.

"Walter," he whispered, "just get the children away for a minute now."

"Look here, you kids," I yelled, "some of you will fall off if you get so close to the edge of the roof. Keep back."

It had no effect. Apparently they looked not a bit frightened at the dizzy mass of clothes-lines below us.

"Say, is there a candy-store on this block?" I asked in desperation.

"Yes, sir," came the chorus.

"Who'll go down and get me a bottle of ginger ale?" I asked.

A chorus of voices and glittering eyes was the answer. They all would. I took a half-dollar from my pocket and gave it to the oldest.

"All right now, hustle along, and divide the change."

With the scamper of many feet they were gone, and we were alone. Kennedy had now reached Albano's, and as soon as the last head had disappeared below the scuttle of the roof he dropped two long strands down into the back yard, as he had done at Vincenzo's.

I started to go back, but he stopped me.

"Oh, that will never do," he said. "The kids will see that the wires end here. I must carry them on several houses farther as a blind and trust to luck that they don't see the wires leading down below."

We were several houses down, still putting up wires when the crowd came shouting back, sticky with cheap trust-made candy and black with East Side chocolate. We opened the ginger ale and forced ourselves to drink it so as to excite no suspicion, then a few minutes later descended the stairs of the tenement, coming out just above Albano's.

I was wondering how Kennedy was going to get into Albano's again without exciting suspicion. He solved it neatly.

"Now, Walter, do you think you could stand another dip into that red ink of Albano's?"

I said I might in the interests of science and justice—not otherwise.

"Well, your face is sufficiently dirty," he commented, "so that with the overalls you don't look very much as you did the first time you went in. I don't think they will recognise you. Do I look pretty good?"

"You look like a coal-heaver out of a job," I said. "I can scarcely restrain my admiration."

"All right. Then take this little glass bottle. Go into the back room and order something cheap, in keeping with your looks. Then when you are all alone break the bottle. It is full of gas drippings. Your nose will dictate what to do next. Just tell the proprietor you saw the gas company's wagon on the next block and come up here and tell me."

I entered. There was a sinister-looking man, with a sort of unscrupulous intelligence, writing at a table. As he wrote and puffed at his cigar, I noticed a scar on his face, a deep furrow running from the lobe of his ear to his mouth. That, I knew, was a brand set upon him by the Camorra.* I sat and smoked and sipped slowly for several minutes, cursing him inwardly more for his presence than for his evident look of the "*mala vita*." At last he went out to ask the barkeeper for a stamp.

Quickly I tiptoed over to another corner of the room and ground the little bottle under my heel. Then I resumed my seat. The odour that pervaded the room was sickening.

The sinister-looking man with the scar came in again and sniffed. I sniffed. Then the proprietor came in and sniffed.

"Say," I said in the toughest voice I could assume, "you got

---

* The Camorra was an outgrowth of the Carbonari, an eighteenth-century Italian political organization. In the latter half of the eighteenth century, the Naples-based Camorra, an association that specialized in blackmail, bribery, and smuggling, was encouraged by the corrupt regime of King Ferdinand II of Bourbon that ruled the "Kingdom of the Two Sicilies" to police the city and eliminate the opposition. A crackdown was instituted in the 1880s after the unification of Italy, and the Camorra began to decline in power; its grip on Naples was fatally loosened in 1911, after several of its members were convicted in a high-profile murder trial. Thriving in the poor sections of Naples, the organization followed the waves of Neapolitan immigrants to America; so too did its Sicilian-based cousin, the Mafia, accompany the more-numerous Sicilian immigrants to the US. According to Arthur Train's May 1912 article for *McClure's* magazine, "Imported Crime: The Story of the Camorra in America," the Camorra only preyed on Italians. With the rise of gangsterism after the passage of Prohibition in 1919, however, New York and other major cities became prime territory for the Mafia and Camorra in many fields of criminality, most profitably the liquor business, prostitution, and eventually drugs.

a leak. Wait. I seen the gas company wagon on the next block when I came in. I'll get the man."

I dashed out and hurried up the street to the place where Kennedy was waiting impatiently. Rattling his tools, he followed me with apparent reluctance.

As he entered the wine-shop he snorted, after the manner of gas-men, "Where's de leak?"

"You find-a da leak," grunted Albano. "What-a you get-a you pay for? You want-a me do your work?"

"Well, half a dozen o' you wops get out o' here, that's all. D'youse all wanter be blown ter pieces wid dem pipes and cigarettes? Clear out," growled Kennedy.

They retreated precipitately, and Craig hastily opened his bag of tools.

"Quick, Walter, shut the door and hold it," exclaimed Craig, working rapidly. He unwrapped a little package and took out a round, flat disc-like thing of black vulcanised rubber. Jumping up on a table, he fixed it to the top of the reflector over the gas-jet.

"Can you see that from the floor, Walter?" he asked under his breath.

"No," I replied, "not even when I know it is there."

Then he attached a couple of wires to it and led them across the ceiling toward the window, concealing them carefully by sticking them in the shadow of a beam. At the window he quickly attached the wires to the two that were dangling down from the roof and shoved them around out of sight.

"We'll have to trust that no one sees them," he said. "That's the best I can do at such short notice. I never saw a room so bare as this, anyway. There isn't another place I could put that thing without its being seen."

We gathered up the broken glass of the gas-drippings bottle, and I opened the door.

"It's all right, now," said Craig, sauntering out before the bar. "Only de next time you has anyt'ing de matter call de company up. I ain't supposed to do dis wit'out orders, see?"

A moment later I followed, glad to get out of the oppressive atmosphere, and joined him in the back of Vincenzo's drugstore, where he was again at work. As there was no back window there, it was quite a job to lead the wires around the outside from the back yard and in at a side window. It was at last done, however, without exciting suspicion, and Kennedy attached them to an oblong box of weathered oak and a pair of specially constructed dry batteries.

"Now," said Craig, as we washed off the stains of work and stowed the overalls back in the suit-case, "that is done to my satisfaction. I can tell Gennaro to go ahead safely now and meet the Black-Handers."

From Vincenzo's we walked over toward Centre Street, where Kennedy and I left Luigi to return to his restaurant, with instructions to be at Vincenzo's at half-past eleven that night.

We turned into the new police headquarters and went down the long corridor to the Italian Bureau. Kennedy sent in his card to Lieutenant Giuseppe in charge, and we were quickly admitted. The lieutenant was a short, full-faced, fleshy Italian, with lightish hair and eyes that were apparently dull, until you suddenly discovered that that was merely a cover to their really restless way of taking in everything and fixing the impressions on his mind, as if on a sensitive plate.

"I want to talk about the Gennaro case," began Craig. "I may add that I have been rather closely associated with Inspector O'Connor of the Central Office on a number of cases, so that I think we can trust each other. Would you mind telling me what you know about it if I promise you that I, too, have something to reveal?"

The lieutenant leaned back and watched Kennedy closely without seeming to do so. "When I was in Italy last year," he replied at length, "I did a good deal of work in tracing up some Camorra suspects. I had a tip about some of them to look up their records—I needn't say where it came from, but it was a good one. Much of the evidence against some of those fellows who are being tried at Viterbo was gathered by the Carabinieri as a result of hints that I was able to give them—clues that were furnished to me here in America from the source I speak of. I suppose there is really no need to conceal it, though. The original tip came from a certain banker here in New York."

"I can guess who it was," nodded Craig.

"Then, as you know, this banker is a fighter. He is the man who organised the White Hand—an organisation which is trying to rid the Italian population of the Black Hand.* His society had a lot of evidence regarding former members of both the Camorra in Naples and the Mafia in Sicily, as well as the Black Hand gangs in New York, Chicago, and other cities. Well, Cesare, as you know, is Gennaro's father-in-law.

"While I was in Naples looking up the record of a certain criminal I heard of a peculiar murder committed some years ago. There was an honest old music master who apparently lived the quietest and most harmless of lives. But it became known that he was supported by Cesare and had received handsome presents of money from him. The old man was, as you may have guessed, the first music teacher of Gennaro, the man who discovered him. One might have been at a loss to see how he could have an enemy, but there was one who coveted his small fortune. One

---

* This is a fictitious organization. There was in fact a "White Hand Gang," an aggregation of principally Irish gang members operating along the New York waterfront, that violently opposed the Italian takeover of organized crime in New York. The organization fell apart in 1925 with the death of its leaders, and the Mafia took control of the area.

day he was stabbed and robbed. His murderer ran out into the street, crying out that the poor man had been killed. Naturally a crowd rushed up in a moment, for it was in the middle of the day. Before the injured man could make it understood who had struck him the assassin was down the street and lost in the maze of old Naples where he well knew the houses of his friends who would hide him. The man who is known to have committed that crime—Francesco Paoli—escaped to New York. We are looking for him to-day. He is a clever man, far above the average—son of a doctor in a town a few miles from Naples, went to the university, was expelled for some mad prank—in short, he was the black sheep of the family. Of course over here he is too high-born to work with his hands on a railroad or in a trench, and not educated enough to work at anything else. So he has been preying on his more industrious countrymen—a typical case of a man living by his wits with no visible means of support.

"Now I don't mind telling you in strict confidence," continued the lieutenant, "that it's my theory that old Cesare has seen Paoli here, knew he was wanted for that murder of the old music master, and gave me the tip to look up his record. At any rate Paoli disappeared right after I returned from Italy, and we haven't been able to locate him since. He must have found out in some way that the tip to look him up had been given by the White Hand. He had been a Camorrista, in Italy, and had many ways of getting information here in America."

He paused, and balanced a piece of cardboard in his hand.

"It is my theory of this case that if we could locate this Paoli we could solve the kidnapping of little Adelina Gennaro very quickly. That's his picture."

Kennedy and I bent over to look at it, and I started in surprise. It was my evil-looking friend with the scar on his cheek.

"Well," said Craig, quietly handing back the card, "whether

or not he is the man, I know where we can catch the kidnappers to-night, Lieutenant."

It was Giuseppe's turn to show surprise now.

"With your assistance I'll get this man and the whole gang to-night," explained Craig, rapidly sketching over his plan and concealing just enough to make sure that no matter how anxious the lieutenant was to get the credit he could not spoil the affair by premature interference.

The final arrangement was that four of the best men of the squad were to hide in a vacant store across from Vincenzo's early in the evening, long before anyone was watching. The signal for them to appear was to be the extinguishing of the lights behind the coloured bottles in the druggist's window. A taxicab was to be kept waiting at headquarters at the same time with three other good men ready to start for a given address the moment the alarm was given over the telephone.

We found Gennaro awaiting us with the greatest anxiety at the opera-house. The bomb at Cesare's had been the last straw. Gennaro had already drawn from his bank ten crisp one-thousand-dollar bills, and already had a copy of *Il Progresso* in which he had hidden the money between the sheets.

"Mr. Kennedy," he said, "I am going to meet them to-night. They may kill me. See, I have provided myself with a pistol—I shall fight, too, if necessary for my little Adelina. But if it is only money they want, they shall have it."

"One thing I want to say," began Kennedy.

"No, no, no!" cried the tenor. "I will go—you shall not stop me."

"I don't wish to stop you," Craig reassured him. "But one thing—do exactly as I tell you, and I swear not a hair of the child's head will be injured and we will get the blackmailers, too."

"How?" eagerly asked Gennaro. "What do you want me to do?"

"All I want you to do is to go to Albano's at the appointed time. Sit down in the back room. Get into conversation with them, and, above all, Signor, as soon as you get the copy of the *Bolletino* turn to the third page, pretend not to be able to read the address. Ask the man to read it. Then repeat it after him. Pretend to be overjoyed. Offer to set up wine for the whole crowd. Just a few minutes, that is all I ask, and I will guarantee that you will be the happiest man in New York to-morrow."

Gennaro's eyes filled with tears as he grasped Kennedy's hand. "That is better than having the whole police force back of me," he said. "I shall never forget, never forget."

As we went out Kennedy remarked: "You can't blame them for keeping their troubles to themselves. Here we send a police officer over to Italy to look up the records of some of the worst suspects. He loses his life. Another takes his place. Then after he gets back he is set to work on the mere clerical routine of translating them. One of his associates is reduced in rank. And so what does it come to? Hundreds of records have become useless because the three years within which the criminals could be deported have elapsed with nothing done. Intelligent, isn't it? I believe it has been established that all but about fifty of seven hundred known Italian suspects are still at large, mostly in this city. And the rest of the Italian population is guarded from them by a squad of police in number scarcely one-thirtieth of the number of known criminals. No, it's our fault if the Black Hand thrives."

We had been standing on the corner of Broadway, waiting for a car.

"Now, Walter, don't forget. Meet me at the Bleecker Street station of the subway at eleven-thirty. I'm off to the university.

I have some very important experiments with phosphorescent salts that I want to finish to-day."

"What has that to do with the case?" I asked mystified.

"Nothing," replied Craig. "I didn't say it had. At eleven-thirty, don't forget. By George, though, that Paoli must be a clever one—think of his knowing about ricin. I only heard of it myself recently. Well, here's my car. Good-bye."

Craig swung aboard an Amsterdam Avenue car, leaving me to kill eight nervous hours of my weekly day of rest from the *Star*.

They passed at length, and at precisely the appointed time Kennedy and I met. With suppressed excitement, at least on my part, we walked over to Vincenzo's. At night this section of the city was indeed a black enigma. The lights in the shops where olive oil, fruit, and other things were sold, were winking out one by one; here and there strains of music floated out of wine-shops, and little groups lingered on corners conversing in animated sentences. We passed Albano's on the other side of the street, being careful not to look at it too closely, for several men were hanging idly about—pickets, apparently, with some secret code that would instantly have spread far and wide the news of any alarming action.

At the corner we crossed and looked in Vincenzo's window a moment, casting a furtive glance across the street at the dark empty store where the police must be hiding. Then we went in and casually sauntered back of the partition. Luigi was there already. There were several customers still in the store, however, and therefore we had to sit in silence while Vincenzo quickly finished a prescription and waited on the last one.

At last the doors were locked and the lights lowered, all except those in the windows which were to serve as signals.

"Ten minutes to twelve," said Kennedy, placing the oblong

box on the table. "Gennaro will be going in soon. Let us try this machine now and see if it works. If the wires have been cut since we put them up this morning Gennaro will have to take his chances alone."

Kennedy reached over and with a light movement of his forefinger touched a switch.

Instantly a babel of voices filled the store, all talking at once, rapidly and loudly. Here and there we could distinguish a snatch of conversation, a word, a phrase, now and then even a whole sentence above the rest. There was the clink of glasses. I could hear the rattle of dice on a bare table, and an oath. A cork popped. Somebody scratched a match.

We sat bewildered, looking at Kennedy for an explanation.

"Imagine that you are sitting at a table in Albano's back room," was all he said. "This is what you would be hearing. This is my 'electric ear'—in other words the dictograph, used, I am told, by the Secret Service of the United States.* Wait, in a moment you will hear Gennaro come in. Luigi and Vincenzo, translate what you hear. My knowledge of Italian is pretty rusty."

"Can they hear us?" whispered Luigi in an awe-struck whisper.

Craig laughed. "No, not yet. But I have only to touch this other switch, and I could produce an effect in that room that would rival the famous writing on Belshazzar's wall—only it would be a voice from the wall instead of writing."

"They seem to be waiting for someone," said Vincenzo. "I

---

* The dictograph, consisting of a microphone in one location and a remote listening post, was invented by Kelley M. Turner and patented in 1906. While also marketed as a device that allowed broadcasting of sounds, or dictating text from one room to a typist in another, it was used in several criminal investigations. A popular article in the May 1912 issue of *The World's Work* on "What the Dictograph Is," by French Strother, was subtitled "The Tiny 'Detective's Ear' That Broke Down the McNamara Defense and That Has Convicted Other Criminals" (37–41).

heard somebody say: 'He will be here in a few minutes. Now get out.'"

The babel of voices seemed to calm down as men withdrew from the room. Only one or two were left.

"One of them says the child is all right. She has been left in the back yard," translated Luigi.

"What yard? Did he say?" asked Kennedy.

"No; they just speak of it as the 'yard,'" replied Luigi.

"Jameson, go outside in the store to the telephone booth and call up headquarters. Ask them if the automobile is ready, with the men in it."

I rang up, and after a moment the police central answered that everything was right.

"Then tell central to hold the line clear—we mustn't lose a moment. Jameson, you stay in the booth. Vincenzo, you pretend to be working around your window, but not in such a way as to attract attention, for they have men watching the street very carefully. What is it, Luigi?"

"Gennaro is coming. I just heard one of them say, 'Here he comes.'"

Even from the booth I could hear the dictograph repeating the conversation in the dingy little back room of Albano's, down the street.

"He's ordering a bottle of red wine," murmured Luigi, dancing up and down with excitement.

Vincenzo was so nervous that he knocked a bottle down in the window, and I believe that my heart-beats were almost audible over the telephone which I was holding, for the police operator called me down for asking so many times if all was ready.

"There it is—the signal," cried Craig. "'A fine opera is "I Pagliacci."' Now listen for the answer."

A moment elapsed, then, "Not without Gennaro," came a gruff voice in Italian from the dictograph.

A silence ensued. It was tense.

"Wait, wait," said a voice which I recognised instantly as Gennaro's. "I cannot read this. What is this, 23½ Prince Street?"

"No, 33½. She has been left in the back yard," answered the voice.

"Jameson," called Craig, "tell them to drive straight to 33½ Prince Street. They will find the girl in the back yard—quick, before the Black-Handers have a chance to go back on their word."

I fairly shouted my orders to the police headquarters. "They're off," came back the answer, and I hung up the receiver.

"What was that?" Craig was asking of Luigi. "I didn't catch it. What did they say?"

"That other voice said to Gennaro, 'Sit down while I count this.'"

"Sh! he's talking again."

"If it is a penny less than ten thousand or I find a mark on the bills I'll call to Enrico, and your daughter will he spirited away again," translated Luigi.

"Now, Gennaro is talking," said Craig. "Good—he is gaining time. He is a trump. I can distinguish that all right. He's asking the gruff-voiced fellow if he will have another bottle of wine. He says he will. Good. They must be at Prince Street now—we'll give them a few minutes more, not too much, for word will be back to Albano's like wildfire, and they will get Gennaro after all. Ah, they are drinking again. What was that, Luigi? The money is all right, he says? Now, Vincenzo, out with the lights!"

A door banged open across the street, and four huge dark figures darted out in the direction of Albano's.

With his finger Kennedy pulled down the other switch and

shouted: "Gennaro, this is Kennedy! To the street! *Polizia! Polizia!*"

A scuffle and a cry of surprise followed. A second voice, apparently from the bar, shouted, "Out with the lights, out with the lights!"

Bang! went a pistol, and another.

The dictograph, which had been all sound a moment before, was as mute as a cigar-box.

"What's the matter?" I asked Kennedy, as he rushed past me.

"They have shot out the lights. My receiving instrument is destroyed. Come on, Jameson; Vincenzo, stay back, if you don't want to appear in this."

A short figure rushed by me, faster even than I could go. It was the faithful Luigi.

In front of Albano's an exciting fight was going on. Shots were being fired wildly in the darkness, and heads were popping out of tenement windows on all sides. As Kennedy and I flung ourselves into the crowd we caught a glimpse of Gennaro, with blood streaming from a cut on his shoulder, struggling with a policeman while Luigi vainly was trying to interpose himself between them. A man, held by another policeman, was urging the first officer on. "That's the man," he was crying. "That's the kidnapper. I caught him."

In a moment Kennedy was behind him. "Paoli, you lie. You are the kidnapper. Seize him—he has the money on him. That other is Gennaro himself."

The policeman released the tenor, and both of them seized Paoli. The others were beating at the door, which was being frantically barricaded inside.

Just then a taxicab came swinging up the street. Three men jumped out and added their strength to those who were battering down Albano's barricade.

Gennaro, with a cry, leaped into the taxicab. Over his shoulder I could see a tangled mass of dark brown curls, and a childish voice lisped: "Why didn't you come for me, papa? The bad man told me if I waited in the yard you would come for me. But if I cried he said he would shoot me. And I waited, and waited—"

"There, there, 'Lina; papa's going to take you straight home to mother."

A crash followed as the door yielded, and the famous Paoli gang was in the hands of the law.

XI

THE ARTIFICIAL PARADISE

It was, I recall, at that period of the late unpleasantness in the little Central American republic of Vespuccia,* when things looked darkest for American investors, that I hurried home one evening to Kennedy, bursting with news.

By way of explanation, I may add that during the rubber boom Kennedy had invested in stock of a rubber company in Vespuccia, and that its value had been shrinking for some time with that elasticity which a rubber band shows when one party suddenly lets go his end. Kennedy had been in danger of being snapped rather hard by the recoil, and I knew he had put in an order with his broker to sell and take his loss when a certain figure was reached. My news was a first ray of light in an otherwise dark situation, and I wanted to advise him to cancel the selling order and stick for a rise.

Accordingly I hurried unceremoniously into our apartment with the words on my lips before I had fairly closed the door.

---

* A fictional country. Amerigo Vespucci was a Florentine explorer who made two important voyages of discovery between 1497 and 1504. The "New World" that he identified was named "America" by cartographer Martin Waldseemüller in 1507. (The Library of Congress houses the only known original copy of the Waldseemüller map.) Some have jokingly suggested that the US should instead have been named "Vespuccia."

"What do you think, Craig?" I shouted. "It is rumoured that the revolutionists have captured half a million dollars from the government and are sending it to—" I stopped short. I had no idea that Kennedy had a client, and a girl, too.

With a hastily mumbled apology I checked myself and backed out toward my own room. I may as well confess that I did not retreat very fast, however. Kennedy's client was not only a girl, but a very pretty one, I found, as she turned her head quickly at my sudden entrance and betrayed a lively interest at the mention of the revolution. She was a Latin-American, and the Latin-American type of feminine beauty is fascinating—at least to me. I did not retreat very fast.

As I hoped, Kennedy rose to the occasion. "Miss Guerrero," he said, "let me introduce Mr. Jameson, who has helped me very much in solving some of my most difficult cases. Miss Guerrero's father, Walter, is the owner of a plantation which sells its product to the company I am interested in."

She bowed graciously, but there was a moment of embarrassment until Kennedy came to the rescue.

"I shall need Mr. Jameson in handling your case, Miss Guerrero," he explained. "Would it be presuming to ask you to repeat to him briefly what you have already told me about the mysterious disappearance of your father? Perhaps some additional details will occur to you, things that you may consider trivial, but which, I assure you, may be of the utmost importance."

She assented, and in a low, tremulous, musical voice bravely went through her story.

"We come," she began, "my father and I—for my mother died when I was a little girl—we come from the northern part of Vespuccia, where foreign capitalists are much interested in the introduction of a new rubber plant. I am an only child and have been the constant companion of my father for years, ever since

I could ride a pony, going with him about our hacienda and on business trips to Europe and the States.

"I may as well say at the start, Mr. Jameson, that although my father is a large land-owner, he has very liberal political views and is deeply in sympathy with the revolution that is now going on in Vespuccia. In fact, we were forced to flee very early in the trouble, and as there seemed to be more need of his services here in New York than in any of the neighbouring countries, we came here. So you see that if the revolution is not successful his estate will probably be confiscated and we shall be penniless. He is the agent—the head of the junta, I suppose you would call it—here in New York."

"Engaged in purchasing arms and ammunition," put in Kennedy, as she paused, "and seeing that they are shipped safely to New Orleans as 'agricultural machinery,' where another agent receives them and attends to their safe transit across the Gulf."

She nodded and after a moment resumed: "There is quite a little colony of Vespuccians here in New York, both revolution-ists and government supporters. I suppose that neither of you has any idea of the intriguing that is going on under the peaceful surface right here in your own city. But there is much of it, more than even I know or can tell you. Well, my father lately has been acting very queerly. There is a group who meet frequently at the home of a Señora Mendez—an insurrecto group, of course. I do not go, for they are all much older people than I. I know the señora well, but I—I prefer a different kind of person. My friends are younger and perhaps more radical, more in earnest about the future of Vespuccia.

"For some weeks it has seemed to me that this Señora Mendez has had too much influence over my father. He does not seem like the same man he used to be. Indeed, some of the junta who do not frequent the house of the señora have remarked it.

He seems moody, works by starts, then will neglect his work entirely. Often I see him with his eyes closed, apparently sitting quietly, oblivious to the progress of the cause—the only cause now which can restore us our estate.

"The other day we lost an entire shipment of arms—the Secret Service captured them on the way from the warehouse on South Street to the steamer which was to take them to New Orleans. Only once before had it happened, when my father did not understand all the things to conceal. Then he was frantic for a week. But this time he seems not to care. Ah, señores," she said, dropping her voice, "I fear there was some treachery there."

"Treachery?" I asked. "And have you any suspicions who might have played informer?"

She hesitated. "I may as well tell you just what I suspect. I fear that the hold of Señora Mendez is somehow or other concerned with it all. I even have suspected that somehow she may be working in the pay of the government—that she is a vampire, living on the secrets of the group who so trust her. I suspect anything, everybody—that she is poisoning his mind, perhaps even whispering into his ear some siren proposal of amnesty and his estate again, if he will but do what she asks. My poor father—I must save him from himself if it is necessary. Argument has no effect with him. He merely answers that the señora is a talented and accomplished woman, and laughs a vacant laugh when I hint to him to beware. I hate her."

The fiery animosity of her dark eyes boded ill, I felt, for the señora. But it flashed over me that perhaps, after all, the señora was not a traitress, but had simply been scheming to win the heart and hence the hacienda of the great land-owner, when he came into possession of his estate if the revolution proved successful.

"And finally," she concluded, keeping back the tears by an heroic effort, "last night he left our apartment, promising to return early in the evening. It is now twenty-four hours, and I have heard not a word from him. It is the first time in my life that we have ever been separated so long."

"And you have no idea where he could have gone?" asked Craig.

"Only what I have learned from Señor Torreon, another member of the junta. Señor Torreon said this morning that he left the home of Señora Mendez last night about ten o'clock in company with my father. He says they parted at the subway, as they lived on different branches of the road. Professor Kennedy," she added, springing up and clasping her hands tightly in an appeal that was irresistible, "you know what steps to take to find him. I trust all to you—even the calling on the police, though I think it would be best if we could get along without them. Find my father, señores, and when we come into our own again you shall not regret that you befriended a lonely girl in a strange city, surrounded by intrigue and danger." There were tears in her eyes as she stood swaying before us.

The tenseness of the appeal was broken by the sharp ringing of the telephone bell. Kennedy quickly took down the receiver.

"Your maid wishes to speak to you," he said, handing the telephone to her.

Her face brightened with that nervous hope that springs in the human breast even in the blackest moments. "I told her if any message came for me she might find me here," explained Miss Guerrero. "Yes, Juanita, what is it—a message for me?"

My Spanish was not quite good enough to catch more than a word here and there in the low conversation, but I could guess from the haggard look which overspread her delicate face that the news was not encouraging.

"Oh!" she cried, "this is terrible—terrible! What shall I do? Why did I come here? I don't believe it. I don't believe it."

"Don't believe what, Miss Guerrero?" asked Kennedy reassuringly. "Trust me."

"That he stole the money—oh, what am I saying? You must not look for him—you must forget that I have been here. No, I don't believe it."

"What money?" asked Kennedy, disregarding her appeal to drop the case. "Remember, it may be better that we should know it now than the police later. We will respect your confidence."

"The junta had been notified a few days ago, they say, that a large sum—five hundred thousand silver dollars—had been captured from the government and was on its way to New York to be melted up as bullion at the sub-treasury," she answered, repeating what she had heard over the telephone as if in a dream. "Mr. Jameson referred to the rumour when he came in. I was interested, for I did not know the public had heard of it yet. The junta has just announced that the money is missing. As soon as the ship docked in Brooklyn this morning an agent appeared with the proper credentials from my father and a guard, and they took the money away. It has not been heard of since—and they have no word from my father."

Her face was blanched as she realised what the situation was. Here she was, setting people to run down her own father, if the suspicions of the other members of the junta were to be credited.

"You—you do not think my father—stole the money?" she faltered pitifully. "Say you do not think so."

"I think nothing yet," replied Kennedy in an even voice. "The first thing to do is to find him—before the detectives of the junta do so."

I felt a tinge—I must confess it—of jealousy as Kennedy stood beside her, clasping her hand in both of his and gazing earnestly down into the rich flush that now spread over her olive cheeks.

"Miss Guerrero," he said, "you may trust me implicitly. If your father is alive I will do all that a man can do to find him. Let me act—for the best. And," he added, wheeling quickly toward me, "I know Mr. Jameson will do likewise."

I was pulled two ways at once. I believed in Miss Guerrero, and yet the flight of her father and the removal of the bullion—swallowed up, as it were, instantly, without so much as a trace in New York—looked very black for him. And yet, as she placed her small hand tremblingly in mine to say good-bye, she won another knight to go forth and fight her battle for her, nor do I think that I am more than ordinarily susceptible, either.

When she had gone, I looked hopelessly at Kennedy. How could we find a missing man in a city of four million people, find him without the aid of the police—perhaps before the police could themselves find him?

Kennedy seemed to appreciate my perplexity as though he read my thoughts. "The first thing to do is to locate this Señor Torreon from whom the first information came," he remarked as we left the apartment. "Miss Guerrero told me that he might possibly be found in an obscure boarding-house in the Bronx where several members of the junta live. Let us try, anyway."

Fortune favoured us to the extent that we did find Torreon at the address given. He made no effort to evade us, though I noted that he was an unprepossessing-looking man—undersized and a trifle over-stout, with an eye that never met yours as you talked with him. Whether it was that he was concealing something, or whether he was merely fearful that we might after all be United States Secret Service men, or whether it was simply a lack of command of English, he was uncommonly uncommunicative at first. He repeated sullenly the details of the disappearance of Guerrero, just as we had already heard them.

"And you simply bade him good-bye as you got on a subway train and that is the last you ever saw of him?" repeated Kennedy.

"Yes," he replied.

"Did he seem to be worried, to have anything on his mind, to act queerly in any way?" asked Kennedy keenly.

"No," came the monosyllabic reply, and there was just that shade of hesitation about it that made me wish we had the apparatus we used in the Bond case for registering association time. Kennedy noticed it, and purposely dropped the line of inquiry in order not to excite Torreon's suspicion.

"I understand no word has been received from him at the headquarters on South Street to-day," queried Kennedy.

"None," replied Torreon sharply.

"And you have no idea where he could have gone after you left him last night?"

"No, señor, none."

This answer was given, I thought, with suspicious quickness.

"You do not think that he could he concealed by Señora Mendez, then?" asked Kennedy quietly.

The little man jumped forward with his eyes flashing. "No," he hissed, checking this show of feeling as quickly as he could.

"Well, then," observed Kennedy, rising slowly, "I see nothing to do but to notify the police and have a general alarm sent out."

The fire died in the eyes of Torreon. "Do not do that, señor," he exclaimed. "Wait at least one day more. Perhaps he will appear. Perhaps he has only gone up to Bridgeport to see about some arms and cartridges—who can tell? No, sir, do not call in the police, I beg you—not yet. I myself will search for him. It may be I can get some word, some clue. If I can I will notify Miss Guerrero immediately."

Kennedy turned suddenly. "Torreon," he flashed quickly,

"what do you suspect about that shipment of half a million silver dollars? Where did it go after it left the wharf?"

Torreon kept his composure admirably. An enigma of a smile flitted over his mobile features as he shrugged his shoulders. "Ah," he said simply, "then you have heard that the money is missing? Perhaps Guerrero has not gone to Bridgeport, after all!"

"On condition that I do not notify the police—yet—will you take us to visit Señora Mendez, and let us learn from her what she knows of this strange case?"

Torreon was plainly cornered. He sat for a moment biting his nails nervously and fidgeting in his chair. "It shall be as you wish," he assented at length.

"We are to go," continued Kennedy, "merely as friends of yours, you understand? I want to ask questions in my own way, and you are not to—"

"Yes, yes," he agreed. "Wait. I will tell her we are coming," and he reached for the telephone.

"No," interrupted Kennedy. "I prefer to go with you unexpected. Put down the telephone. Otherwise, I may as well notify my friend Inspector O'Connor of the Central Office and go up with him."

Torreon let the receiver fall back in its socket, and I caught just a glimpse of the look of hate and suspicion which crossed his face as he turned toward Kennedy. When he spoke it was as suavely as if he himself were the one who had planned this little excursion.

"It shall be as you wish," he said, leading the way out to the cross-town surface cars.

Señora Mendez received us politely, and we were ushered into a large music-room in her apartment. There were several people there already. They were seated in easy chairs about the room.

One of the ladies was playing on the piano as we entered. It was a curious composition—very rhythmic, with a peculiar thread of monotonous melody running through it.

The playing ceased, and all eyes were fixed on us. Kennedy kept very close to Torreon, apparently for the purpose of frustrating any attempt at a whispered conversation with the señora.

The guests rose and with courtly politeness bowed as Señora Mendez presented two friends of Señor Torreon, Señor Kennedy and Señor Jameson. We were introduced in turn to Señor and Señora Alvardo, Señor Gonzales, Señorita Reyes, and the player, Señora Barrios.

It was a peculiar situation, and for want of something better to say I commented on the curious character of the music we had overheard as we entered.

The señora smiled, and was about to speak when a servant entered, bearing a tray full of little cups with a steaming liquid, and in a silver dish some curious, round, brown, disc-like buttons, about an inch in diameter and perhaps a quarter of an inch thick. Torreon motioned frantically to the servant to withdraw, but Kennedy was too quick for him. Interposing himself between Torreon and the servant, he made way for her to enter.

"You were speaking of the music," replied Señora Mendez to me in rich, full tones. "Yes, it is very curious. It is a song of the Kiowa Indians of New Mexico which Señora Barrios has endeavoured to set to music so that it can be rendered on the piano. Señora Barrios and myself fled from Vespuccia to Mexico at the start of our revolution, and when the Mexican government ordered us to leave on account of our political activity we merely crossed the line to the United States, in New Mexico. It was there that we ran across this very curious discovery. The monotonous beat of that melody you heard is supposed to represent the beating of the tom-toms of the Indians during their

The Silent Bullet 259

mescal rites. We are having a mescal evening here, whiling away the hours of exile from our native Vespuccia."

"Mescal?" I repeated blankly at first, then feeling a nudge from Kennedy, I added hastily: "Oh, yes, to be sure. I think I have heard of it. It's a Mexican drink, is it not? I have never had the pleasure of tasting it or of tasting that other drink, pulque— poolkay—did I get the accent right?"

I felt another, sharper nudge from Kennedy, and knew that I had only made matters worse. "Mr. Jameson," he hastened to remark, "confounds this mescal of the Indians with the drink of the same name that is common in Mexico."

"Oh," she laughed, to my great relief, "but this mescal is something quite different. The Mexican drink mescal is made from the maguey-plant and is a frightfully horrid thing that sends the peon out of his senses and makes him violent. Mescal as I mean it is a little shrub, a god, a cult, a religion."

"Yes," assented Kennedy; "discovered by those same Kiowa Indians, was it not?"

"Perhaps," she admitted, raising her beautiful shoulders in polite deprecation. "The mescal religion, we found, has spread very largely in New Mexico and Arizona among the Indians, and with the removal of the Kiowas to the Indian reservation it has been adopted by other tribes—even, I have heard, as far north as the Canadian border."

"Is that so?" asked Kennedy. "I understood that the United States government had forbidden the importation of the mescal plant and its sale to the Indians under severe penalties."

"It has, sir," interposed Alvardo, who had joined us, "but still the mescal cult grows secretly. For my part, I think it might be more wise for your authorities to look to the whiskey and beer that unscrupulous persons are selling. Señor Jameson," he added, turning to me, "will you join us in a little cup of this artificial paradise, as one of your English writers—Havelock Ellis, I think—has appropriately called it?"*

I glanced dubiously at Kennedy as Señora Mendez took one of the little buttons out of the silver tray. Carefully paring the fuzzy tuft of hairs off the top of it—it looked to me very much like the tip of a cactus plant, which, indeed, it was—she rolled it into a little pellet and placed it in her mouth, chewing it slowly like a piece of chicle.

"Watch me; do just as I do," whispered Kennedy to me at a moment when no one was looking.

The servant advanced towards us with the tray.

"The mescal plant," explained Alvardo, pointing at the little discs, "grows precisely like these little buttons which you see here. It is a species of cactus which rises only half an inch or so from the ground. The stem is surrounded by a clump of blunt leaves which give it its button shape, and on the top you will see still the tuft of filaments, like a cactus. It grows in the rocky soil in many places in the state of Jalisco, though only recently has it become known to science.† The Indians, when they go out to gather it, simply lop off these little ends as they peep above the earth, dry them, keep what they wish for their own use, and sell the rest for what is to them a fabulous sum. Some people chew the buttons, while a few have lately tried making an infusion or tea out of them. Perhaps to a beginner I had better recommend the infusion."

I had scarcely swallowed the bitter, almost nauseous decoction than I began to feel my heart action slowing up and my pulse

---

* The information imparted by Alvardo is the same as recorded by Havelock Ellis (1859–1939), the English physician and progressive intellectual, in his essay "Mescal: A New Artificial Paradise," appearing in *The Contemporary Review* in January 1898.

---

† Alvardo is speaking of the ritual use of mescaline, a psychedelic drug that occurs naturally in the peyote cactus. Europeans observed the use of the drug in the earliest contacts with Native American rituals. The drug itself was isolated in 1897 and synthesized as early as 1918.

beating fuller and stronger. The pupils of my eyes expanded as with a dose of belladonna; at least, I could see that Kennedy's did, and so mine must have done the same.

I seemed to feel an elated sense of superiority—really I almost began to feel that it was I, not Kennedy, who counted most in this investigation. I have since learned that this is the common experience of mescal-users, this sense of elation; but the feeling of physical energy and intellectual power soon wore off, and I found myself glad to recline in my easy chair, as the rest did, in silent indolence.

Still, the display that followed for an enchanted hour or so was such as I find it hopeless to describe in language which shall convey to others the beauty and splendour of what I saw.

I picked up a book lying on the table before me. A pale blue-violet shadow floated across the page before me, leaving an after-image of pure colour that was indescribable. I laid down the book and closed my eyes. A confused riot of images and colours like a kaleidoscope crowded before me, at first indistinct, but, as I gazed with closed eyes, more and more definite. Golden and red and green jewels seemed to riot before me. I bathed my hands in inconceivable riches of beauty such as no art-glass worker has ever produced. All discomfort ceased. I had no desire to sleep—in fact, was hyper-sensitive. But it was a real effort to open my eyes; to tear myself away from the fascinating visions of shapes and colours.

At last I did open my eyes to gaze at the gas-jets of the chandelier as they flickered. They seemed to send out waves, expanding and contracting, waves of colour. The shadows of the room were highly coloured and constantly changing as the light changed.

Señora Barrios began lightly to play on the piano the

transposed Kiowa song, emphasising the notes that represented the drum-beats. Strange as it may seem, the music translated itself into pure colour—and the rhythmic beating of the time seemed to aid the process. I thought of the untutored Indians as they sat in groups about the flickering camp-fire while others beat the tom-toms and droned the curious melody. What were the visions of the red man, I wondered, as he chewed his mescal button and the medicine man prayed to Hikori, the cactus god, to grant a "beautiful intoxication?"

Under the gas-lights of the chandelier hung a cluster of electric light bulbs which added to the flood of golden effulgence that bathed the room and all things in it. I gazed next intently at the electric lights. They became the sun itself in their steadiness, until I had to turn away my head and close my eyes. Even then the image persisted—I saw the golden sands of Newport, only they were blazing with glory as if they were veritable diamond dust. I saw the waves, of incomparable blue, rolling up on the shore. A vague perfume was wafted on the air. I was in an orgy of vision. Yet there was no stage of maudlin emotion. It was at least elevating.

Kennedy's experiences as he related them to me afterwards were similar, though sufficiently varied to be interesting. His visions took the forms of animals—a Cheshire cat, like that in "Alice in Wonderland," with merely a grin that faded away, changing into a lynx which in turn disappeared, followed by an unknown creature with short nose and pointed ears, then tortoises and guinea pigs, a perfectly unrelated succession of beasts. When the playing began a beautiful panorama unfolded before him—the regular notes in the music enhancing the beauty and changes in the scenes, which he described as a most wonderful kinetoscopic display.

In fact, only De Quincey[*] or Bayard Taylor[+] or Poe could have done justice to the thrilling effects of the drug, and not even they unless an amanuensis had been seated by them to take down what they dictated, for I defy anyone to remember anything but a fraction of the rapid march of changes under its influence. Indeed, in observing its action I almost forgot for the time being the purpose of our visit, so fascinated was I. The music ceased, but not the visions.

Señora Mendez advanced toward us. The spangles on her net dress seemed to give her a fairy-like appearance; she seemed to float over the carpet like a glowing, fleecy, white cloud over a rainbow-tinted sky.

Kennedy, however, had not for an instant forgotten what we were there for, and his attention recalled mine. I was surprised to see that when I made the effort I could talk and think quite as rationally as ever, though the wildest pranks were going on in my mind and vision. Kennedy did not beat about in putting his question, evidently counting on the surprise to extract the truth.

"What time did Señor Guerrero leave last night?"

The question came so suddenly that she had no time to think of a reply that would conceal anything she might otherwise have wished to conceal.

"About ten o'clock," she answered, then instantly was on her guard, for Torreon had caught her eye.

"And you have no idea where he went?" asked Kennedy.

---

[*] Thomas de Quincey (1785–1859), English essayist and author of *Confessions of an English Opium-Eater* (1821). De Quincey's collected output extended to more than twenty volumes, but the *Confessions*—said to have founded a genre of addicts' confessionals, including works by Charles Baudelaire and William S. Burroughs—remains his most widely read work.

[+] Bayard Taylor (1825–1878), American poet and travel writer, known for his romantic descriptions of exotic locations.

"None, unless he went home," she replied guardedly.

I did not at the time notice the significance of her prompt response to Torreon's warning. I did not notice, as did Kennedy, the smile that spread over Torreon's features. The music had started again, and I was oblivious to all but the riot of colour.

Again the servant entered. She seemed clothed in a halo of light and colour, every fold of her dress radiating the most delicate tones. Yet there was nothing voluptuous or sensual about it. I was raised above earthly things. Men and women were no longer men and women—they were brilliant creatures of whom I was one. It was sensuous, but not sensual. I looked at my own clothes. My every-day suit was idealised. My hands were surrounded by a glow of red fire that made me feel that they must be the hands of a divinity. I noticed them as I reached forward toward the tray of little cups.

There swam into my line of vision another such hand. It laid itself on my arm. A voice sang in my ear softly:

"No, Walter, we have had enough. Come, let us go. This is not like any other known drug—not even the famous *Cannabis indica*, hasheesh. Let us go as soon as we politely can. I have found out what I wanted to know. Guerrero is not here."

We rose shortly and excused ourselves and, with general regrets in which all but Torreon joined, were bowed out with the same courtly politeness with which we had been received.

As we left the house, the return to the world was quick. It was like coming out from the matinée and seeing the crowds on the street. They, not the matinée, were unreal for the moment. But, strange to say, I found one felt no depression as a result of the mescal intoxication.

"What is it about mescal that produces such results?" I asked.

"The alkaloids," replied Kennedy as we walked slowly along. "Mescal was first brought to the attention of scientists by explorers employed by our bureau of ethnology. Dr. Weir Mitchell* and Dr. Harvey Wiley† and several German scientists have investigated it since then. It is well known that it contains half a dozen alkaloids and resins of curious and little-investigated nature. I can't recall even the names of them offhand, but I have them in my laboratory."

As the effect of the mescal began to wear off in the fresh air, I found myself in a peculiar questioning state. What had we gained by our visit? Looking calmly at it, I could not help but ask myself why both Torreon and Señora Mendez had acted as if they were concealing something about the whereabouts of Guerrero. Was she a spy? Did she know anything about the loss of the half-million dollars?

Of one thing I was certain. Torreon was an ardent admirer of the beautiful señora, equally ardent with Guerrero. Was he simply a jealous suitor, angry at his rival, and now glad that he was out of the way? Where had Guerrero gone? The question was still unanswered.

Absorbed in these reveries, I did not notice particularly where Kennedy was hurrying me. In fact, finding no plausible answer to my speculations and knowing that it was useless to question Kennedy at this stage of his inquiry, I did not for the moment care where we went but allowed him to take the lead.

We entered one of the fine apartments on the drive and rode up in the elevator. A door opened and, with a start, I found

---

* Silas Weir Mitchell was a pioneering American neurologist (1829–1914), mentioned in Ellis's essay. Mitchell was also the proponent of the "Rest Cure," demonized in Charlotte Perkins Gilman's classic 1892 horror tale "The Yellow Wall-Paper."

+ Dr. Harvey Wile was chief chemist at the US Department of Agriculture, to whom samples of peyote cacti were delivered by James Mooney, the "explorer" whom Kennedy mentions. For more details on the history of the American investigation of peyote, see Alexander S. Dawson's *The Peyote Effect: From the Inquisition to the War on Drugs* (Berkeley: University of California Press, 2018).

myself in the presence of Miss Guerrero again. The questioning look on her face recalled the object of our search, and its ill success so far. Why had Kennedy come back with so little to report?

"Have you heard any thing?" she asked eagerly.

"Not directly," replied Kennedy. "But I have a clue, at least. I believe that Torreon knows where your father is and will let you know any moment now. It is to his interest to clear himself before this scandal about the money becomes generally known. Would you allow me to search through your father's desk?"

For some moments Kennedy rummaged through the drawers and pigeonholes, silently.

"Where does the junta keep its arms stored—not in the meeting-place on South Street does it?" asked Kennedy at length.

"Not exactly; that would be a little too risky," she replied. "I believe they have a loft above the office, hired in someone else's name and not connected with the place down-stairs at all. My father and Señor Torreon are the only ones who have the keys. Why do you ask?"

"I ask," replied Craig, "because I was wondering whether there might not be something that would take him down to South Street last night. It is the only place I can think of his going to at such a late hour, unless he has gone out of town. If we do not hear from Torreon soon I think I will try what I can find down there. Ah, what is this?"

Kennedy drew forth a little silver box and opened it. Inside reposed a dozen mescal buttons.

We both looked quickly at Miss Guerrero, but it was quite evident that she was unacquainted with them.

She was about to ask what Kennedy had found when the telephone rang and the maid announced that Miss Guerrero was wanted by Señor Torreon.

A smile of gratification flitted over Kennedy's face as he leaned over to me and whispered: "It is evident that Torreon is anxious to clear himself. I'll wager he has done some rapid hustling since we left him."

"Perhaps this is some word about my father at last," murmured Miss Guerrero as she nervously hurried to the telephone, and answered. "Yes, this is Señorita Guerrero, Señor Torreon. You are at the office of the junta? Yes, yes, you have word from my father—you went down there to-night expecting some guns to be delivered?—and you found him there—up-stairs in the loft—ill, did you say?—unconscious?"

In an instant her face was drawn and pale, and the receiver fell clattering to the hard-wood floor from her nerveless fingers.

"He is dead!" she gasped as she swayed backward and I caught her. With Kennedy's help I carried her, limp and unconscious, across the room, and placed her in a deep armchair. I stood at her side, but for the moment could only look on helplessly, blankly at the now stony beauty of her face.

"Some water, Juanita, quick!" I cried as soon as I had recovered from the shock. "Have you any smelling-salts or anything of that sort? Perhaps you can find a little brandy. Hurry."

While we were making her comfortable the telephone continued to tinkle.

"This is Kennedy," I heard Craig say, as Juanita came hurrying in with water, smelling-salts, and brandy. "You fool. She fainted. Why couldn't you break it to her gently? What's that address on South Street? You found him over the junta meeting-place in a loft? Yes, I understand. What were you doing down there? You went down expecting a shipment of arms and saw a light overhead—I see—and suspecting something you entered with a policeman. You heard him move across the floor above and fall heavily? All right. Someone will be down directly. Ambulance surgeon has tried everything, you say? No heart action, no breathing? Sure. Very well. Let the body remain just where it is until I get down. Oh, wait. How long ago did it happen? Fifteen minutes? All right. Good-bye."

Such restoratives as we had found we applied faithfully. At last we were rewarded by the first flutter of an eyelid. Then Miss Guerrero gazed wildly about.

"He is dead," she moaned. "They have killed him. I know it. My father is dead." Over and over she repeated: "He is dead. I shall never see him again."

Vainly I tried to soothe her. What was there to say? There could be no doubt about it. Torreon must have gone down directly after we left Señora Mendez. He had seen a light in the loft, had entered with a policeman—as a witness, he had told Craig over the telephone—had heard Guerrero fall, and had sent for the ambulance. How long Guerrero had been there he did not know, for while members of the junta had been coming and going all day in the office below none had gone up into the locked loft.

Kennedy with rare skill calmed Miss Guerrero's dry-eyed hysteria into a gentle rain of tears, which relieved her over-wrought feelings. We silently withdrew, leaving the two women, mistress and servant, weeping.

"Craig," I asked when we had gained the street, "what do you make of it? We must lose no time. Arrest this Mendez woman before she has a chance to escape."

"Not so fast, Walter," he cautioned as we spun along in a taxi-cab. "Our case isn't very complete against anybody yet."

"But it looks black for Guerrero," I admitted. "Dead men tell no tales even to clear themselves."

"It all depends on speed now," he answered laconically.

We had reached the university, which was only a few blocks

away, and Craig dashed into his laboratory while I settled with the driver. He reappeared almost instantly with some bulky apparatus under his arm, and we more than ran from the building to the near-by subway station. Fortunately there was an express just pulling in, as we tumbled down the steps.

To one who knows South Street as merely a river-front street whose glory of other days has long since departed, where an antiquated horsecar now ambles slowly up-town, and trucks and carts all day long are in a perpetual jam, it is peculiarly uninteresting by day, and peculiarly deserted and vicious by night. But there is another fascination about South Street. Perhaps there has never been a revolution in Latin America which has not in some way or other been connected with this street, whence hundreds of filibustering expeditions have started.* Whenever a dictator is to be overthrown, or half a dozen chocolate-skinned generals in the Caribbean become dissatisfied with their portions of gold lace, the arms- and ammunition-dealers of South Street can give, if they choose, an advance scenario of the whole tragedy or comic opera, as the case may be. Real war or opera-bouffé, it is all grist for the mills of these close-mouthed individuals.

Our quest took us to a ramshackle building reminiscent of the days when the street bristled with bowsprits of ships from all over the world, an age when the American merchantman flew our flag on the uttermost of the seven-seas. On the ground floor was an apparently innocent junk-dealer's shop, in reality the meeting-place of the junta. By an outside stairway the

---

* The South Street Seaport, founded in 1625, was originally a major harbor for all kinds of water transport. After the 1880s, when it was too shallow to handle modern ships, it devolved into a locus of smaller, older ships, largely tramp steamers that could be hired to transport anything, including revolutionaries and weapons. By the 1930s, few of the docks continued to function, and it was slowly abandoned, until 1967, when the South Street Seaport Museum was founded.

lofts above were reached, hiding their secrets behind windows opaque with decades of dust.

At the door we were met by Torreon and the policeman. Both appeared to be shocked beyond measure. Torreon was profuse in explanations which did not explain. Out of the tangled mass of verbiage I did manage to extract, however, the impression that, come what might to the other members of the junta, Torreon was determined to clear his own name at any cost. He and the policeman had discovered Señor Guerrero only a short time before, up-stairs. For all he knew, Guerrero had been there some time, perhaps all day, while the others were meeting down-stairs. Except for the light he might have been there undiscovered still. Torreon swore he had heard Guerrero fall; the policeman was not quite so positive.

Kennedy listened impatiently, then sprang up the stairs, only to call back to the policeman: "Go call me a taxicab at the ferry, an electric cab. Mind, now, not a gasoline-cab—electric."

We found the victim lying on a sort of bed of sailcloth in a loft apparently devoted to the peaceful purposes of the junk trade, but really a perfect arsenal and magazine. It was dusty and cobwebbed, crammed with stands of arms, tents, uniforms in bales, batteries of Maxims and mountain-guns, and all the paraphernalia for carrying on a real twentieth-century revolution.

The young ambulance surgeon was still there, so quickly had we been able to get down-town. He had his stomach-pump, hypodermic syringe, emetics, and various tubes spread out on a piece of linen on a packing-case. Kennedy at once inquired just what he had done.

"Thought at first it was only a bad case of syncope,"* he replied, "but I guess he was dead some minutes before I got here. Tried rhythmic traction of the tongue, artificial respiration, stimulants, chest and heart massage—everything, but it was no use."

---

* Fainting, as a result of low blood pressure.

"Have you any idea what caused his death?" asked Craig as he hastily adjusted his apparatus to an electric light socket—a rheostat, an induction coil of peculiar shape, and an "interrupter."

"Poison of some kind—an alkaloid. They say they heard him fall as they came up-stairs, and when they got to him he was blue. His face was as blue as it is now when I arrived. Asphyxia, failure of both heart and lungs, that was what the alkaloid caused."

The gong of the electric cab sounded outside. As Craig heard it he rushed with two wires to the window, threw them out, and hurried downstairs, attaching them to the batteries of the cab.

In an instant he was back again.

"Now, Doctor," he said, "I'm going to perform a very delicate test on this man. Here I have the alternating city current and here a direct, continuous current from the storage-batteries of the cab below. Doctor, hold his mouth open. So. Now, have you a pair of forceps handy? Good. Can you catch hold of the tip of his tongue? There. Do just as I tell you. I apply this cathode to his skin in the dorsal region, under the back of the neck, and this anode in the lumbar region at the base of the spine—just pieces of cotton soaked in salt solution and covering the metal electrodes, to give me a good contact with the body."

I was fascinated. It was gruesome, and yet I could not take my eyes off it. Torreon stood blankly, in a daze. Craig was as calm as if his every-day work was experimenting on cadavers.

He applied the current, moving the anode and the cathode slowly. I had often seen the experiments on the nerves of a frog that had been freshly killed, how the electric current will make the muscles twitch, as discovered long ago by Galvani.* But I

---

* Galvanism, bioelectrical force, was discovered in 1791 by Luigi Galvani (1737–1798), who observed that applying an electric current to a dead frog caused its legs to contract. He was the first scientist to suspect a connection between electricity and life. Galvani's nephew, Giovanni Aldini, subsequently performed experiments with corpses, attempting to reanimate them with electricity.

was not prepared to see it on a human being. Torreon muttered something and crossed himself.

The arms seemed half to rise—then suddenly to fall, flabby again. There was a light hiss like an inspiration and expiration of air, a ghastly sound.

"Lungs react," muttered Kennedy, "but the heart doesn't. I must increase the voltage."

Again he applied the electrodes.

The face seemed a different shade of blue, I thought.

"Good God, Kennedy," I exclaimed, "do you suppose the effect of that mescal on me hasn't worn off yet? Blue, blue—everything blue is playing pranks before my eyes. Tell me, is the blue of that face—his face—is it changing? Do you see it, or do I imagine it?"

"Blood asphyxiated," was the disjointed reply. "The oxygen is clearing it."

"But, Kennedy," I persisted, "his face was dark blue, black a minute ago. The most astonishing change has taken place. Its colour is almost natural now. Do I imagine it or is it real?"

Kennedy was so absorbed in his work that he made no reply at all. He heard nothing, nothing save the slow, forced inspiration and expiration of air as he deftly and quickly manipulated the electrodes.

"Doctor," he cried at length, "tell me what is going on in that heart."

The young surgeon bent his head and placed his ear on the cold breast. As he raised his eyes and they chanced to rest on Kennedy's hands, holding the electrodes dangling idly in the air, I think I never saw a greater look of astonishment on a human face. "It—is—almost—natural," he gasped.

"With great care and a milk diet for a few days Guerrero will live," said Kennedy quietly. "It *is* natural."

"My God, man, but he was dead!" exclaimed the surgeon. "I know it. His heart was stopped and his lungs collapsed."

"To all intents and purposes he was dead, dead as ever a man was," replied Craig, "and would be now, if I hadn't happened to think of this special induction coil loaned to me by a doctor who had studied deeply the process of electric resuscitation developed by Professor Leduc of the Nantes Ecole de Medicin.* There is only one case I know of on record which compares with this—a case of a girl resuscitated in Paris. The girl was a chronic morphine-eater and was 'dead' forty minutes."†

I stood like one frozen, the thing was so incomprehensible, after the many surprises of the evening that had preceded. Torreon, in fact, did not comprehend for the moment.

As Kennedy and I bent over, Guerrero's eyes opened, but

---

* Stéphane Leduc (1853–1939) was a professor of biology at the school and studied the physiological effects of electrical currents, including what he called "the electric sleep" (anesthetic effects of electrical currents). There is no record of Leduc's "process of electric resuscitation."

---

† The first reported use of electric shock as a resuscitative experimental method took place in 1774 and involved a child, Catherine Sophia Greenhill, who fell from a window and was "picked up by a man in a state of apparent death." (The report of the Rev. William Hawes was recorded in *Transactions of the Royal Humane Society of London, 1774*, 31–32.) According to Hawes's report, a Mr. Squires applied electricity to various parts of the body but only when he applied it "through the chest" did he feel "a small pulse, and within a few minutes the child began to breathe with great difficulty." Writing in 1776, John Hunter in a review of an article "Proposal for the recovery of people apparently drowned," remarked, "Electricity is a useful tool and should be used where others have failed...it is likely that this is the only method that we have to stimulate the heart in an instant." This is a remarkable statement, predating Mary Shelley's *Frankenstein* by forty years. In 1850, Dr. Carl Ludwig and Dr. Mauritius Hoffa conducted experiments on dogs that led to the discovery that electrical stimulation was capable of causing ventricular fibrillation. In 1872, surgeon Thomas Green described his use of a galvanic battery to achieve six successful resuscitations (out of seven attempts) following cardiac arrest from chloroform. In 1887, the Scottish physiologist John A. MacWilliam, before the International Medical Congress, demonstrated the interruption of ventricular fibrillation by application of an electric shock, and in 1899, the physiologists Jean-Louis Prévost and Frederic Batelli of the University of Geneva demonstrated on animals that electrical discharges could cause arrhythmias that returned the heart to normal rhythms.

he apparently saw nothing. His hand moved a little, and his lips parted. Kennedy quickly reached into the pockets of the man gasping for breath, one after another. From a vest pocket he drew a little silver case, identical with that he had found in the desk up-town. He opened it, and one mescal button rolled out into the palm of his hand. Kennedy regarded it thoughtfully.

"I suspect there is at least one devotee of the vision-breeding drug who will no longer cultivate its use, as a result of this," he added, looking significantly at the man before us.

"Guerrero," shouted Kennedy, placing his mouth close to the man's ear, but muffling his voice so that only I could distinguish what he said, "Guerrero, where is the money?"

His lips moved trembling again, but I could not make out that he said anything.

Kennedy rose and quietly went over to detach his apparatus from the electric light socket behind Torreon.

"Car-ramba!" I heard as I turned suddenly.

Craig had Torreon firmly pinioned from behind by both arms. The policeman quickly interposed.

"It's all right, officer," exclaimed Craig. "Walter, reach into his inside pocket."

I pulled out a bunch of papers and turned them over.

"What's that?" asked Kennedy as I came to something neatly enclosed in an envelope.

I opened it. It was a power of attorney from Guerrero to Torreon.

"Perhaps it is no crime to give a man mescal if he wants it—I doubt if the penal code covers that," ejaculated Kennedy. "But it is conspiracy to give it to him and extract a power of attorney by which you can get control of trust funds consigned to him. Manuel Torreon, the game is up. You and Señora Mendez have played your parts well. But you have lost. You waited until you thought Guerrero was dead, then you took a policeman along as a witness to clear yourself. But the secret is not dead, after all. Is there nothing else in those papers, Walter? Yes? Ah, a bill of lading dated to-day? Ten cases of 'scrap-iron' from New York to Boston—a long chance for such valuable 'scrap,' señor, but I suppose you had to get the money away from New York, at any risk."

"And Señora Mendez?" I asked as my mind involuntarily reverted to the brilliantly lighted room up-town. "What part did she have in the plot against Guerrero?"

Torreon stood sullenly silent. Kennedy reached in another of Torreon's pockets and drew out a third little silver box of mescal buttons. Holding all three of the boxes, identically the same, before us he remarked: "Evidently Torreon was not averse to having his victim under the influence of mescal as much as possible. He must have forced it on him—all's fair in love and revolution, I suppose. I believe he brought him down here under the influence of mescal last night, obtained the power of attorney, and left him here to die of the mescal intoxication. It was just a case of too strong a hold of the mescal—the artificial paradise was too alluring to Guerrero, and Torreon knew it and tried to profit by it to the extent of half a million dollars."

It was more than I could grasp at the instant. The impossible had happened. I had seen the dead—literally—brought back to life and the secret which the criminal believed buried wrung from the grave.

Kennedy must have noted the puzzled look on my face. "Walter," he said, casually, as he wrapped up his instruments, "don't stand there gaping like Billikin.* Our part in this case

---

* Properly "the Billiken," this was a good-luck totem created in 1908 by Florence Pretz. Said to be "the God of Things as They Ought to Be," it looked like a small, seated Buddha, with pointed ears and head, sparse hair, and a mischievous grin.

is finished—at least mine is. But I suspect from some of the glances I have seen you steal at various times that—well, perhaps you would like a few moments in a real paradise. I saw a telephone down-stairs. Go call up Miss Guerrero and tell her her father is alive—and innocent."

XII
THE STEEL DOOR

It was what, in college, we used to call "good football weather"—a crisp, autumn afternoon that sent the blood tingling through brain and muscle. Kennedy and I were enjoying a stroll on the drive, dividing our attention between the glowing red sunset across the Hudson and the string of homeward-bound automobiles on the broad parkway. Suddenly a huge black touring-car marked with big letters, "P. D. N. Y.," shot past.

"Joy-riding again in one of the city's cars," I remarked. "I thought the last Police Department shake-up had put a stop to that."

"Perhaps it has," returned Kennedy. "Did you see who was in the car?"

"No, but I see it has turned and is coming back."

"It was Inspector—I mean, First Deputy O'Connor. I thought he recognised us as he whizzed along, and I guess he did, too. Ah, congratulations, O'Connor! I haven't had a chance to tell you before how pleased I was to learn you had been appointed first deputy. It ought to have been commissioner, though," added Kennedy.

"Congratulations nothing," rejoined O'Connor. "Just

another new deal—election coming on, mayor must make a show of getting some reform done, and all that sort of thing. So he began with the Police Department, and here I am, first deputy. But, say, Kennedy," he added, dropping his voice, "I've a little job on my mind that I'd like to pull off in about as spectacular a fashion as I—as you know how. I want to make good, conspicuously good, at the start—understand? Maybe I'll be 'broke' for it and sent to pounding the pavements of Dismissalville, but I don't care, I'll take a chance. On the level, Kennedy, it's a big thing, and it ought to be done. Will you help me put it across?"

"What is it?" asked Kennedy with a twinkle in his eye at O'Connor's estimate of the security of his tenure of office.

O'Connor drew us away from the automobile toward the stone parapet overlooking the railroad and river far below, and out of earshot of the department chauffeur. "I want to pull off a successful raid on the Vesper Club," he whispered earnestly, scanning our faces.

"Good heavens, man," I ejaculated, "don't you know that Senator Danfield is interested in—"

"Jameson," interrupted O'Connor reproachfully, "I said 'on the level' a few moments ago, and I meant it. Senator Danfield be—well, anyhow, if I don't do it the district attorney will, with the aid of the Dowling law,* and I am going to beat him to it, that's all. There's too much money being lost at the Vesper Club, anyhow. It won't hurt Danfield to be taught a lesson not to run such a phony game. I may like to put up a quiet bet myself on the ponies now and then—I won't say I don't, but this thing of

---

* New York State Senator Victor J. Dowling (1866–1934) sponsored a bill, enacted in 1904, that amended the New York Penal Code to give immunity to witnesses testifying in prosecutions of violations of the statutes prohibiting gambling and gaming. This was popularly known as the "Dowling law."

Danfield's has got beyond all reason. It's the crookedest gambling joint in the city, at least judging by the stories they tell of losses there. And so beastly aristocratic, too. Read that."

O'Connor shoved a letter into Kennedy's hand, a dainty perfumed and monogramed little missive addressed in a feminine hand. It was such a letter as comes by the thousand to the police in the course of a year, though seldom from ladies of the smart set:

Dear Sir: I notice in the newspapers this morning that you have just been appointed first deputy commissioner of police and that you have been ordered to suppress gambling in New York. For the love that you must still bear toward your own mother, listen to the story of a mother worn with anxiety for her only son, and if there is any justice or righteousness in this great city close up a gambling hell that is sending to ruin scores of our finest young men. No doubt you know or have heard of my family—the DeLongs are not unknown in New York. Perhaps you have also heard of the losses of my son Percival at the Vesper Club. They are fast becoming the common talk of our set. I am not rich, Mr. Commissioner, in spite of our social position, but I am human, as human as a mother in any station of life, and oh, if there is any way, close up that gilded society resort that is dissipating our small fortune, ruining an only son, and slowly bringing to the grave a grey-haired widow, as worthy of protection as any mother of the poor whose plea has closed up a little poolroom or low policy shop.

Sincerely,
(Mrs.) Julia M. DeLong.

P.S.—Please keep this confidential—at least from my son Percival.

J. M. DeL.

"Well," said Kennedy, as he handed back the letter, "O'Connor, if you do it, I'll take back all the hard things I've ever said about the police system. Young DeLong was in one of my classes at the university, until he was expelled for that last mad prank of his. There's more to that boy than most people think, but he's the wildest scion of wealth I have ever come in contact with. How are you going to pull off your raid—is it to be down through the skylight or up from the cellar?"

"Kennedy," replied O'Connor in the same reproachful tone with which he had addressed me, "talk sense. I'm in earnest. You know the Vesper Club is barred and barricaded like the National City Bank. It isn't one of those common gambling joints which depend for protection on what we call 'ice-box doors.' It's proof against all the old methods. Axes and sledge-hammers would make no impression there."

"Your predecessor had some success at opening doors with a hydraulic jack, I believe, in some very difficult raids," put in Kennedy.

"A hydraulic jack wouldn't do for the Vesper Club, I'm afraid," remarked O'Connor wearily. "Why, sir, that place has been proved bomb-proof—bomb-proof, sir. You remember recently the so-called 'gamblers' war' in which some rivals exploded a bomb on the steps? It did more damage to the house next door than to the club. However, I can get past the outer door, I think, even if it is strong. But inside—you must have heard of it—is the famous steel door, three inches thick, made of armour-plate. It's no use to try it at all unless we can pass that door with reasonable quickness. All the evidence we shall get will be of an innocent social club-room down-stairs. The gambling is all on the second floor, beyond this door, in a room without a window in it. Surely you've heard of that famous gambling-room, with its perfect system of artificial ventilation and electric lighting that makes it rival noonday at midnight. And don't tell me I've got to get on the other side of the door by strategy, either. It is strategy-proof. The system of lookouts is perfect. No, force is necessary, but it must not be destructive of life or property—or, by Heaven, I'd drive up there and riddle the place with a fourteen-inch gun," exclaimed O'Connor.

"H'm!" mused Kennedy as he flicked the ashes off his cigar and meditatively watched a passing freight-train on the railroad below us. "There goes a car loaded with tons and tons of scrap-iron. You want me to scrap that three-inch steel door, do you?"

"Kennedy, I'll buy that particular scrap from you at—almost its weight in gold. The fact is, I have a secret fund at my disposal such as former commissioners have asked for in vain. I can afford to pay you well, as well as any private client, and I hear you have had some good fees lately. Only deliver the goods."

"No," answered Kennedy, rather piqued, "it isn't money that I am after. I merely wanted to be sure that you are in earnest. I can get you past that door as if it were made of green baize."

It was O'Connor's turn to look incredulous, but as Kennedy apparently meant exactly what he said, he simply asked, "And will you?"

"I will do it to-night if you say so," replied Kennedy quietly. "Are you ready?"

For answer O'Connor simply grasped Craig's hand, as if to seal the compact.

"All right, then," continued Kennedy. "Send a furniture-van, one of those closed vans that the storage warehouses use, up to my laboratory any time before seven o'clock. How many men will you need in the raid? Twelve? Will a van hold that many comfortably? I'll want to put some apparatus in it, but that won't take much room."

"Why, yes, I think so," answered O'Connor. "I'll get a well-padded van so that they won't be badly jolted by the ride downtown. By George! Kennedy, I see you know more of that side of police strategy than I gave you credit for."

"Then have the men drop into my laboratory singly about the same time. You can arrange that so that it will not look suspicious, so far up-town. It will be dark, anyhow. Perhaps, O'Connor, you can make up as the driver yourself—anyhow, get one you can trust absolutely. Then have the van down near the corner of Broadway below the club, driving slowly along about the time the theatre crowd is out. Leave the rest to me. I will give you or the driver orders when the time comes."

As O'Connor thanked Craig, he remarked without a shade of insincerity, "Kennedy, talk about being commissioner, you ought to be commissioner."

"Wait till I deliver the goods," answered Craig simply. "I may fall down and bring you nothing but a lawsuit for damages for unlawful entry or unjust persecution, or whatever they call it."

"I'll take a chance at that," called back O'Connor as he jumped into his car and directed, "Headquarters, quick."

As the car disappeared, Kennedy filled his lungs with air as if reluctant to leave the drive. "Our constitutional," he remarked, "is abruptly at an end, Walter."

Then he laughed, as he looked about him.

"What a place in which to plot a raid on Danfield's Vesper Club! Why, the nurse-maids have hardly got the children all in for supper and bed. It's incongruous. Well, I must go over to the laboratory and get some things ready to put in that van with the men. Meet me about half-past seven, Walter, up in the room, all togged up. We'll dine at the Cafe Riviera to-night in style. And, by the way, you're quite a man about town—you must know someone who can introduce us into the Vesper Club."

"But, Craig," I demurred, "if there is any rough work as a result, it might queer me with them. They might object to being used—"

"Oh, that will be all right. I just want to look the place over and lose a few chips in a good cause. No, it won't queer any of your *Star* connections. We'll be on the outside when the time comes for anything to happen. In fact I shouldn't wonder if your story would make you all the more solid with the sports. I take all the responsibility; you can have the glory. You know they like to hear the inside gossip of such things, after the event. Try it. Remember, at seven-thirty. We'll be a little late at dinner, but never mind; it will be early enough for the club."

Left to my own devices I determined to do a little detective work on my own account, and not only did I succeed in finding an acquaintance who agreed to introduce us at the Vesper Club that night about nine o'clock, but I also learned that Percival DeLong was certain to be there that night, too. I was necessarily vague about Kennedy, for fear my friend might have heard of some of his exploits, but fortunately he did not prove inquisitive.

I hurried back to our apartment and was in the process of transforming myself into a full-fledged boulevardier, when Kennedy arrived in an extremely cheerful frame of mind. So far, his preparations had progressed very favourably, I guessed, and I was quite elated when he complimented me on what I had accomplished in the meantime.

"Pretty tough for the fellows who are condemned to ride around in that van for four mortal hours, though," he said as he hurried into his evening clothes, "but they won't be riding all the time. The driver will make frequent stops."

I was so busy that I paid little attention to him until he had nearly completed his toilet. I gave a gasp.

"Why, whatever are you doing?" I exclaimed as I glanced into his room.

There stood Kennedy arrayed in all the glory of a sharp-pointed moustache and a goatee. He had put on evening clothes of decidedly Parisian cut, clothes which he had used abroad and had brought back with him, but which I had never known him to wear since he came back. On a chair reposed a chimney-pot hat that would have been pronounced faultless on the "continong,"* but was unknown, except among impresarios, on Broadway.

Kennedy shrugged his shoulders—he even had the shrug.

"Figure to yourself, monsieur," he said. "Ze great Kennedy, ze detectif Américain—to put it tersely in our own vernacular, wouldn't it be a fool thing for me to appear at the Vesper Club where I should surely be recognised by someone if I went in my ordinary clothes and features? *Un faux pas*, at the start? *Jamais!*"

There was nothing to do but agree, and I was glad that I had been discreetly reticent about my companion in talking with the friend who was to gain us entrance to the Avernus† beyond the steel door.

We met my friend at the Riviera and dined sumptuously. Fortunately he seemed decidedly impressed with my friend Monsieur Kay—I could do no better on the spur of the moment than take Kennedy's initial, which seemed to serve.

---

* A comical pronunciation of "the continent" (meaning Europe), dating to Victorian times when the "swells" of London were said to tour "ong continong" (en continent). See, e.g., J. A. Hammerton's *Mr. Punch on the Continong* (1841), a collection of humorous cartoons, articles, and illustrations of the English abroad.

---

† An actual volcanic crater near Cuma, Italy, west of Naples, said to be the legendary entrance to the underworld.

We progressed amicably from oysters and soup down to coffee, cigars, and liqueurs, and I succeeded in swallowing Kennedy's tales of Monte Carlo and Ostend and Ascot without even a smile. He must have heard them somewhere, and treasured them up for just such an occasion, but he told them in a manner that was verisimilitude itself, using perfect English with just the trace of an accent at the right places.

At last it was time to saunter around to the Vesper Club without seeming to be too indecently early. The theatres were not yet out, but my friend said play was just beginning at the club and would soon be in full swing.

I had a keen sense of wickedness as we mounted the steps in the yellow flare of the flaming arc-light on the Broadway corner not far below us. A heavy, grated door swung open at the practised signal of my friend, and an obsequious negro servant stood bowing and pronouncing his name in the sombre mahogany portal beyond, with its green marble pillars and handsome decorations. A short parley followed, after which we entered, my friend having apparently satisfied someone that we were all right.

We did not stop to examine the first floor, which doubtless was innocent enough, but turned quickly up a flight of steps. At the foot of the broad staircase Kennedy paused to examine some rich carvings, and I felt him nudge me. I turned. It was an enclosed staircase, with walls that looked to be of re-enforced concrete. Swung back on hinges concealed like those of a modern burglar-proof safe was the famous steel door.

We did not wish to appear to be too interested, yet a certain amount of curiosity was only proper.

My friend paused on the steps, turned, and came back.

"You're perfectly safe," he smiled, tapping the door with his cane with a sort of affectionate respect. "It would take the police ages to get past that barrier, which would be swung shut and bolted the moment the lookout gave the alarm. But there has never been any trouble. The police know that it is so far, no farther. Besides," he added with a wink to me, "you know, Senator Danfield wouldn't like this pretty little door even scratched. Come up, I think I hear DeLong's voice up-stairs. You've heard of him, monsieur? It's said his luck has changed. I'm anxious to find out."

Quickly he led the way up the handsome staircase and into a large, lofty, richly furnished room. Everywhere there were thick, heavy carpets on the floors, into which your feet sank with an air of satisfying luxury.

The room into which we entered was indeed absolutely windowless. It was a room built within the original room of the old house. Thus the windows overlooking the street from the second floor in reality bore no relation to it. For light it depended on a complete oval of lights overhead so arranged as to be themselves invisible, but shining through richly stained glass and conveying the illusion of a slightly clouded noonday. The absence of windows was made up for, as I learned later, by a ventilating device so perfect that, although everyone was smoking, a most fastidious person could scarcely have been offended by the odour of tobacco.

Of course I did not notice all this at first. What I did notice, however, was a faro-layout and a hazard-board, but as no one was playing at either, my eye quickly travelled to a roulette-table which stretched along the middle of the room. Some ten or a dozen men in evening clothes were gathered watching with intent faces the spinning wheel. There was no money on the table, nothing but piles of chips of various denominations. Another thing that surprised me as I looked was that the tense look on the faces of the players was anything but the feverish, haggard gaze I had expected. In fact, they were sleek, well-fed, typical prosperous New-Yorkers rather inclined to the noticeable in dress and carrying their avoirdupois as if life was an easy game with them. Most of them evidently belonged to the financial and society classes. There were no tragedies; the tragedies were elsewhere—in their offices, homes, in the courts, anywhere, but not here at the club. Here all was life, light, and laughter.

For the benefit of those not acquainted with the roulette wheel—and I may as well confess that most of my own knowledge was gained in that one crowded evening—I may say that it consists, briefly, of a wooden disc very nicely balanced and turning in the centre of a cavity set into a table like a circular washbasin, with an outer rim turned slightly inward. The "croupier" revolves the wheel to the right. With a quick motion of his middle finger he flicks a marble, usually of ivory, to the left. At the Vesper Club, always up-to-date, the ball was of platinum, not of ivory. The disc with its sloping sides is provided with a number of brass rods, some perpendicular, some horizontal. As the ball and the wheel lose momentum the ball strikes against the rods and finally is deflected into one of the many little pockets or stalls facing the rim of the wheel.

There are thirty-eight of these pockets; two are marked "0" and "00," the others numbered from one to thirty-six in an irregular and confusing order and painted alternately red and black. At each end of the table are thirty-six large squares correspondingly numbered and coloured. The "0" and "00" are of a neutral colour. Whenever the ball falls in the "0" or "00" the bank takes the stakes, or sweeps the board. The Monte Carlo wheel has only one "0," while the typical American has two, and the Chinese has four.

To one like myself who had read of the Continental gambling-houses with the clink of gold pieces on the table, and the croupier with his wooden rake noisily raking in the winnings of the bank, the comparative silence of the American game comes as a surprise.

As we advanced, we heard only the rattle of the ball, the click of the chips, and the monotonous tone of the spinner: "Twenty-three, black. Eight, red. Seventeen, black." It was almost like the boys in a broker's office calling off the quotations of the ticker and marking them up on the board.

Leaning forward, almost oblivious to the rest, was Percival DeLong, a tall, lithe, handsome young man, whose boyish face ill comported with the marks of dissipation clearly outlined on it. Such a boy, it flashed across my mind, ought to be studying the possible plays of football of an evening in the field-house after his dinner at the training-table, rather than the possible gyrations of the little platinum ball on the wheel.

"Curse the luck!" he exclaimed, as "17" appeared again.

A Hebrew banker staked a pile of chips on the "17" to come up a third time. A murmur of applause at his nerve ran through the circle. DeLong hesitated, as one who thought, "Seventeen has come out twice—the odds against its coming again are too great, even though the winnings would be fabulous, for a good stake." He placed his next bet on another number.

"He's playing Lord Rosslyn's system, tonight," whispered my friend.

The wheel spun, the ball rolled, and the croupier called again, "Seventeen, black." A tremor of excitement ran through the crowd. It was almost unprecedented.

DeLong, with a stifled oath, leaned back and scanned the faces about the table.

"And '17' has precisely the same chance of turning up in the next spin as if it had not already had a run of three," said a voice at my elbow.

It was Kennedy. The roulette-table needs no introduction when curious sequences are afoot. All are friends.

"That's the theory of Sir Hiram Maxim,"* commented my friend, as he excused himself reluctantly for another appointment. "But no true gambler will believe it, monsieur, or at least act on it."

All eyes were turned on Kennedy, who made a gesture of polite deprecation, as if the remark of my friend were true, but—he nonchalantly placed his chips on the "17."

"The odds against '17' appearing four consecutive times are some millions," he went on, "and yet, having appeared three times, it is just as likely to appear again as before. It is the usual practice to avoid a number that has had a run, on the theory that some other number is more likely to come up than it is.

---

* Sir Hiram Maxim was a renowned inventor-businessman, best remembered for inventing the "Maxim gun," the first portable automatic machine gun, and a partner in the Bleriot aeronautics firm, mentioned in the note on page 205. On September 19, 1908, Maxim and "Lord Rosslyn," mentioned earlier (James Francis Harry St Clair-Erskine, 5th Earl of Rosslyn and a well-known gambler) began a "gambling duel" in which Rosslyn pitted his "system" against the roulette wheel, with Maxim keeping track of the results. Maxim, who had earlier published his analysis of the mathematics of gambling (*Monte Carlo Facts and Fallacies,* 1904) confidently predicted that the house would win. The duel was reported prominently in the *New York Times* ("Maxim Sure Rosslyn Cannot Break Bank," *New York Times,* September 20, 1908). On October 3, Rosslyn conceded, and the following day's *Times* headline read "Rosslyn's Defeat Easy." According to the later *Times* article, Rosslyn's "system" was essentially the same as the notorious "martingale" system that became popular in seventeenth-century France, only with a slower progression. The "martingale" system works like this: Bet one unit; if lost, bet two units; if lost, bet four units; etc. Exponents point out that eventually the gambler will win a bet and recoup all previous losses, winning a net of one unit. Critics point out that the system could result in the gambler betting insane amounts to win a single unit and, in modern casinos, is thwarted quickly by the house limits on bets. For example, if one lost only fifteen times in a row, one would need to bet 16,384 units to win a single unit, and depending on the table limit, that might not be possible. The "martingale" system, while mathematically correct, can only be 100 percent successful if the gambler has an unlimited stake, unlimited time, and unlimited bets.

That would be the case if it were drawing balls from a bag full of red and black balls—the more red ones drawn the smaller the chance of drawing another red one. But if the balls are put back in the bag after being drawn the chances of drawing a red one after three have been drawn are exactly the same as ever. If we toss a cent and heads appear twelve times, that does not have the slightest effect on the thirteenth toss—there is still an even chance that it, too, will be heads. So if '17' had come up five times to-night, it would be just as likely to come the sixth as if the previous five had not occurred, and that despite the fact that before it has appeared at all odds against a run of the same number six times in succession are about two billion, four hundred and ninety-six million, and some thousands. Most systems are based on the old persistent belief that occurrences of chance are affected in some way by occurrences immediately preceding, but disconnected physically. If we've had a run of black for twenty times, system says play the red for the twenty-first. But black is just as likely to turn up the twenty-first as if it were the first play of all. The confusion arises because a run of twenty on the black should happen once in one million, forty-eight thousand, five hundred and seventy-six coups. It would take ten years to make that many coups, and the run of twenty might occur once or any number of times in it. It is only when one deals with infinitely large numbers of coups that one can count on infinitely small variations in the mathematical results. This game does not go on for infinity—therefore anything, everything, may happen. Systems are based on the infinite; we play in the finite."

"You talk like a professor I had at the university," ejaculated DeLong contemptuously as Craig finished his disquisition on the practical fallibility of theoretically infallible systems. Again DeLong carefully avoided the "17," as well as the black.

The wheel spun again; the ball rolled. The knot of spectators around the table watched with bated breath.

Seventeen won!

As Kennedy piled up his winnings superciliously, without even the appearance of triumph, a man behind me whispered, "A foreign nobleman with a system—watch him."

"*Non*, monsieur," said Kennedy quickly, having overheard the remark, "no system, sir. There is only one system of which I know."

"What?" asked DeLong eagerly.

Kennedy staked a large sum on the red to win. The black came up, and he lost. He doubled the stake and played again, and again lost. With amazing calmness Craig kept right on doubling.

"The martingale," I heard the man whisper behind me. "In other words, double or quit."

Kennedy was now in for some hundreds, a sum that was sufficiently large for him, but he doubled again, still cheerfully playing the red, and the red won. As he gathered up his chips he rose.

"That's the only system," he said simply.

"But, go on, go on," came the chorus from about the table.

"No," said Kennedy quietly, "that is part of the system, too— to quit when you have won back your stakes and a little more."

"Huh!" exclaimed DeLong in disgust. "Suppose you were in for some thousands—you wouldn't quit. If you had real sporting blood you wouldn't quit, anyhow!"

Kennedy calmly passed over the open insult, letting it be understood that he ignored this beardless youth.

"There is no way you can beat the game in the long run if you keep at it," he answered simply. "It is mathematically impossible. Consider. We are Crœsuses*—we hire players to stake

---

* The king of Lydia, ca. 550 BCE, who became proverbial for his wealth.

money for us on every possible number at every coup. How do we come out? If there are no '0' or '00,' we come out after each coup precisely where we started—we are paying our own money back and forth among ourselves; we have neither more nor less. But with the '0' and '00' the bank sweeps the board every so often. It is only a question of time when, after paying our money back and forth among ourselves, it has all filtered through the '0' and '00' into the bank. It is not a game of chance for the bank—ah, it is exact, mathematical—*c'est une question d' arithmetique, seulement, n'est-ce pas, messieurs?*"*

"Perhaps," admitted DeLong, "but it doesn't explain why I am losing to-night while everyone else is winning."

"We are not winning," persisted Craig. "After I have had a bite to eat I will demonstrate how to lose—by keeping on playing." He led the way to the café.

DeLong was too intent on the game to leave, even for refreshments. Now and then I saw him beckon to an attendant, who brought him a stiff drink of whiskey. For a moment his play seemed a little better, then he would drop back into his hopeless losing. For some reason or other his "system" failed absolutely.

"You see, he is hopeless," mused Kennedy over our light repast. "And yet of all gambling games roulette offers the player the best odds, far better than horse-racing, for instance. Our method has usually been to outlaw roulette and permit horse-racing; in other words, suppress the more favourable and permit the less favourable. However, we're doing better now; we're suppressing both. Of course what I say applies only to roulette when it is honestly played—DeLong would lose anyhow, I fear."

I started at Kennedy's tone and whispered hastily: "What do you mean? Do you think the wheel is crooked?"

---

* "It is solely a matter of arithmetic, is it not, sirs?"

"I haven't a doubt of it," he replied in an undertone. "That run of '17' *might* happen—yes. But it is improbable. They let me win because I was a new player—new players always win at first. It is proverbial, but the man who is running this game has made it look like a platitude. To satisfy myself on that point I am going to play again—until I have lost my winnings and am just square with the game. When I reach the point that I am convinced that some crooked work is going on I am going to try a little experiment, Walter. I want you to stand close to me so that no one can see what I am doing. Do just as I will indicate to you."

The gambling-room was now fast filling up with the first of the theatre crowd. DeLong's table was the centre of attraction, owing to the high play. A group of young men of his set were commiserating with him on his luck and discussing it with the finished air of roués of double their ages. He was doggedly following his system.

Kennedy and I approached.

"Ah, here is the philosophical stranger again," DeLong exclaimed, catching sight of Kennedy. "Perhaps he can enlighten us on how to win at roulette by playing his own system."

"*Au contraire,* monsieur, let me demonstrate how to lose," answered Craig with a smile that showed a row of faultless teeth beneath his black moustache, decidedly foreign.

Kennedy played and lost, and lost again; then he won, but in the main he lost. After one particularly large loss I felt his arm on mine, drawing me closely to him. DeLong had taken a sort of grim pleasure in the fact that Kennedy, too, was losing. I found that Craig had paused in his play at a moment when DeLong had staked a large sum that a number below "18" would turn up—for five plays the numbers had been between "18" and "36." Curious to see what Craig was doing, I looked cautiously down between us. All eyes were fixed on the wheel. Kennedy was holding an ordinary compass in the crooked-up palm of his hand. The needle pointed at me, as I happened to be standing north of it.

The wheel spun. Suddenly the needle swung around to a point between the north and south poles, quivered a moment, and came to rest in that position. Then it swung back to the north.

It was some seconds before I realised the significance of it. It had pointed at the table—and DeLong had lost again. There was some electric attachment at work.

Kennedy and I exchanged glances, and he shoved the compass into my hand quickly. "You watch it, Walter, while I play," he whispered.

Carefully concealing it, as he had done, yet holding it as close to the table as I dared I tried to follow two things at once without betraying myself. As near as I could make out, something happened at every play. I would not go so far as to assert that whenever the larger stakes were on a certain number the needle pointed to the opposite side of the wheel, for it was impossible to be at all accurate about it. Once I noticed the needle did not move at all, and he won. But on the next play he staked what I knew must be the remainder of his winnings on what seemed a very good chance. Even before the wheel was revolved and the ball set rolling, the needle swung about, and when the platinum ball came to rest Kennedy rose from the table, a loser.

"By George though," exclaimed DeLong, grasping his hand. "I take it all back. You are a good loser, sir. I wish I could take it as well as you do. But then, I'm in too deeply. There are too many 'markers' with the house up against me."

Senator Danfield had just come in to see how things were going. He was a sleek, fat man, and it was amazing to see with what deference his victims treated him. He affected not to have heard what DeLong said, but I could imagine what he was thinking, for I had heard that he had scant sympathy with anyone after he "went broke"—another evidence of the camaraderie and good-fellowship that surrounded the game.

Kennedy's next remark surprised me. "Oh, your luck will change, D. L.,"—everyone referred to him as "D. L.," for gambling-houses have an aversion for real names and greatly prefer initials—"your luck will change presently. Keep right on with your system. It's the best you can do to-night, short of quitting."

"I'll never quit," replied the young man under his breath.

Meanwhile Kennedy and I paused on the way out to compare notes. My report of the behaviour of the compass only confirmed him in his opinion.

As we turned to the stairs we took in a full view of the room. A faro-layout was purchasing Senator Danfield a new touring-car every hour at the expense of the players. Another group was gathered about the hazard-board, deriving evident excitement, though I am sure none could have given an intelligent account of the chances they were taking. Two roulette-tables were now going full blast, the larger crowd still about DeLong's. Snatches of conversation came to us now and then, and I caught one sentence, "DeLong's in for over a hundred thousand now on the week's play, I understand; poor boy—that about cleans him up."

"The tragedy of it, Craig," I whispered, but he did not hear.

With his hat tilted at a rakish angle and his opera-coat over his arm he sauntered over for a last look.

"Any luck yet?" he asked carelessly.

"The devil—no," returned the boy.

"Do you know what my advice to you is, the advice of a man who has seen high play everywhere from Monte Carlo to Shanghai?"

"What?"

"Play until your luck changes if it takes until to-morrow."

A supercilious smile crossed Senator Danfield's fat face.

"I intend to," and the haggard young face turned again to the table and forgot us.

"For Heaven's sake, Kennedy," I gasped as we went down the stairway, "what do you mean by giving him such advice—you?"

"Not so loud, Walter. He'd have done it anyhow, I suppose, but I want him to keep at it. This night means life or death to Percival DeLong and his mother, too. Come on, let's get out of this."

We passed the formidable steel door and gained the street, jostled by the late-comers who had left the after-theatre restaurants for a few moments of play at the famous club that so long had defied the police.

Almost gaily Kennedy swung along toward Broadway. At the corner he hesitated, glanced up and down, caught sight of the furniture-van in the middle of the next block. The driver was tugging at the harness of the horses, apparently fixing it. We walked along and stopped beside it.

"Drive around in front of the Vesper Club slowly," said Kennedy as the driver at last looked up.

The van lumbered ahead, and we followed it casually. Around the corner it turned. We turned also. My heart was going like a sledgehammer as the critical moment approached. My head was in a whirl. What would that gay throng back of those darkened windows down the street think if they knew what was being prepared for them?

On, like the Trojan horse, the van lumbered. A man went into the Vesper Club, and I saw the negro at the door eye the oncoming van suspiciously. The door banged shut.

The next thing I knew, Kennedy had ripped off his disguise,

had flung himself up behind the van, and had swung the doors open. A dozen men with axes and sledge-hammers swarmed out and up the steps of the club.

"Call the reserves, O'Connor," cried Kennedy. "Watch the roof and the back yard."

The driver of the van hastened to send in the call.

The sharp raps of the hammers and the axes sounded on the thick brass-bound oak of the outside door in quick succession. There was a scurry of feet inside, and we could hear a grating noise and a terrific jar as the inner, steel door shut.

"A raid! A raid on the Vesper Club!" shouted a belated passer-by. The crowd swarmed around from Broadway, as if it were noon instead of midnight.

Banging and ripping and tearing, the outer door was slowly forced. As it crashed in, the quick gongs of several police patrols sounded. The reserves had been called out at the proper moment, too late for them to "tip off" the club that there was going to be a raid, as frequently occurs.

Disregarding the mêlée behind me, I leaped through the wreckage with the other raiders. The steel door barred all further progress with its cold blue impassibility. How were we to surmount this last and most formidable barrier?

I turned in time to see Kennedy and O'Connor hurrying up the steps with a huge tank studded with bolts like a boiler, while two other men carried a second tank.

"There," ordered Craig, "set the oxygen there," as he placed his own tank on the opposite side.

Out of the tanks stout tubes led, with stopcocks and gages at the top. From a case under his arm Kennedy produced a curious arrangement like a huge hook, with a curved neck and a sharp beak. Really it consisted of two metal tubes which ran into a sort of cylinder, or mixing chamber, above the nozzle, while parallel to them ran a third separate tube with a second nozzle of its own. Quickly he joined the ends of the tubes from the tanks to the metal hook, the oxygen-tank being joined to two of the tubes of the hook, and the second tank being joined to the other. With a match he touched the nozzle gingerly. Instantly a hissing, spitting noise followed, and an intense blinding needle of flame.

"Now for the oxy-acetylene blowpipe," cried Kennedy as he advanced toward the steel door. "We'll make short work of this."

Almost as he said it, the steel beneath the blowpipe became incandescent.

Just to test it, he cut off the head of a three-quarter-inch steel rivet—taking about a quarter of a minute to do it. It was evident, though, that that would not weaken the door appreciably, even if the rivets were all driven through. Still they gave a starting-point for the flame of the high-pressure acetylene torch.*

It was a brilliant sight. The terrific heat from the first nozzle caused the metal to glow under the torch as if in an open-hearth furnace. From the second nozzle issued a stream of oxygen under which the hot metal of the door was completely consumed. The force of the blast as the compressed oxygen and acetylene were expelled carried a fine spray of the disintegrated metal visibly

---

* French engineers Edmond Fouché and Charles Picard were the first to develop oxygen-acetylene welding in 1903. According to Ralph O. Tribolet's *History of Acetylene* (privately published for Union Carbide, ca. 1990), an English engineer named Walter Roberts was instrumental in promoting the use of the new device. In early 1908, the Quebec Bridge had fallen into the St. Lawrence River, and attempts to dynamite the bridge for removal were unsuccessful. Roberts convinced those in charge to let him cut up the bridge into pieces that could be readily removed, using an oxyacetylene torch. An even more convincing demonstration of the cutting powers of oxy-acetylene involved dismantling boilers in the battleship *Kentucky*. "In 1910," writes Tribolet, "the ship was in Norfolk for overhaul. Workers with cold chisels and hacksaws began cutting the 1 1/8 inch boiler plate to remove the boilers. After three months they were one quarter through the job. Roberts offered to do the job for the Navy and they were skeptical, but Roberts' claim to do it in 10 days got him the job. They set up a generator on shore and started with the torches on one end, challenging a hand crew which was no contest. They removed the boiler in less than 10 days" (8).

before it. And yet it was not a big hole that it made—scarcely an eighth of an inch wide, but clear and sharp as if a buzz-saw were eating its way through a three-inch plank of white pine.

With tense muscles Kennedy held this terrific engine of destruction and moved it as easily as if it had been a mere pencil of light. He was easily the calmest of us all as we crowded about him at a respectful distance.

"Acetylene, as you may know," he hastily explained, never pausing for a moment in his work, "is composed of carbon and hydrogen. As it burns at the end of the nozzle it is broken into carbon and hydrogen—the carbon gives the high temperature, and the hydrogen forms a cone that protects the end of the blowpipe from being itself burnt up."

"But isn't it dangerous?" I asked, amazed at the skill with which he handled the blowpipe.

"Not particularly—when you know how to do it. In that tank is a porous asbestos packing saturated with acetone, under pressure. Thus I can carry acetylene safely, for it is dissolved, and the possibility of explosion is minimised. This mixing chamber by which I am holding the torch, where the oxygen and acetylene mix, is also designed in such a way as to prevent a flashback. The best thing about this style of blowpipe is the ease with which it can be transported and the curious uses—like the present—to which it can be put."

He paused a moment to test the door. All was silence on the other side. The door itself was as firm as ever.

"Huh!" exclaimed one of the detectives behind me, "these new-fangled things ain't all they're cracked up to be. Now if I was runnin' this show, I'd dynamite that door to kingdom come."

"And wreck the house and kill a few people," I returned, hotly resenting the criticism of Kennedy. Kennedy affected not to hear.

"When I shut off the oxygen in this second jet," he resumed as if nothing had been said, "you see the torch merely heats the steel. I can get a heat of approximately sixty-three hundred degrees Fahrenheit, and the flame will exert a pressure of fifty pounds to the square inch."

"Wonderful!" exclaimed O'Connor, who had not heard the remark of his subordinate and was watching with undisguised admiration. "Kennedy, how did you ever think of such a thing?"

"Why, it's used for welding, you know," answered Craig as he continued to work calmly in the growing excitement. "I first saw it in actual use in mending a cracked cylinder in an automobile. The cylinder was repaired without being taken out at all. I've seen it weld new teeth and build up old worn teeth on gearing, as good as new."

He paused to let us see the terrifically heated metal under the flame.

"You remember when we were talking on the drive about the raid, O'Connor? A car-load of scrap-iron went by on the railroad below us. They use this blowpipe to cut it up, frequently. That's what gave me the idea. See. I turn on the oxygen now in this second nozzle. The blowpipe is no longer an instrument for joining metals together, but for cutting them asunder. The steel burns just as you, perhaps, have seen a watch-spring burn in a jar of oxygen. Steel, hard or soft, tempered, annealed, chrome, or Harveyised,* it all burns just as fast and just as easily. And it's cheap too. This raid may cost a couple of dollars, as far as the blowpipe is concerned—quite a difference from the thousands of dollars' loss that would follow an attempt to blow the door in."

---

* The "Harvey process," patented by American engineer Hayward Augustus Harvey in 1888, was used to manufacture steel armor for warships, until it was superseded by better armored steel developed by Krupp in the late 1890s.

The last remark was directed quietly at the doubting detective. He had nothing to say. We stood in awe-struck amazement as the torch slowly, inexorably, traced a thin line along the edge of the door.

Minute after minute sped by, as the line burned by the blow-pipe cut straight from top to bottom. It seemed hours to me. Was Kennedy going to slit the whole door and let it fall in with a crash?

No, I could see that even in his cursory examination of the door he had gained a pretty good knowledge of the location of the bolts imbedded in the steel. One after another he was cutting clear through and severing them, as if with a superhuman knife.

What was going on on the other side of the door, I wondered. I could scarcely imagine the consternation of the gamblers caught in their own trap.

With a quick motion Kennedy turned off the acetylene and oxygen. The last bolt had been severed. A gentle push of the hand, and he swung the once impregnable door on its delicately poised hinges as easily as if he had merely said, "Open Sesame." The robbers' cave yawned before us.

We made a rush up the stairs. Kennedy was first, O'Connor next, and myself scarcely a step behind, with the rest of O'Connor's men at our heels.

I think we were all prepared for some sort of gun-play, for the crooks were desperate characters, and I myself was surprised to encounter nothing but physical force, which was quickly overcome.

In the now disordered richness of the rooms, waving his "John Doe" warrants in one hand and his pistol in the other, O'Connor shouted: "You're all under arrest, gentlemen. If you resist further it will go hard with you."

Crowded now in one end of the room in speechless amazement was the late gay party of gamblers, including Senator

A well directed blow shattered the mechanism of the delicate wheel.

Danfield himself. They had reckoned on toying with any chance but this. The pale white face of DeLong among them was like a spectre, as he stood staring blankly about and still insanely twisting the roulette wheel before him.

Kennedy advanced toward the table with an ax which he had seized from one of our men. A well directed blow shattered the mechanism of the delicate wheel.

"DeLong," he said, "I'm not going to talk to you like your old professor at the university, nor like your recent friend, the Frenchman with a system. This is what you have been up against, my boy. Look."

His forefinger indicated an ingenious, but now tangled and twisted, series of minute wires and electro-magnets in the broken wheel before us. Delicate brushes led the current into the wheel. With another blow of his axe, Craig disclosed wires running down through the leg of the table to the floor and under the carpet to buttons operated by the man who ran the game.

"Wh-what does it mean?" asked DeLong blankly.

"It means that you had little enough chance to win at a straight game of roulette. But the wheel is very rarely straight, even with all the odds in favour of the bank, as they are. This game was electrically controlled. Others are mechanically controlled by what is sometimes called the 'mule's ear,' and other devices. You *can't* win. These wires and magnets can be made to attract the little ball into any pocket the operator desires. Each one of those pockets contains a little electro-magnet. One set of magnets in the red pockets is connected with one button under the carpet and a battery. The other set in the black pockets is connected with another button and the battery. This ball is not really of platinum. Platinum is non-magnetic. It is simply a soft iron hollow ball, plated with platinum. Whichever set of electro-magnets is energised attracts the ball and by this simple method it is in the power of the operator to let the ball go to red or black as he may wish. Other similar arrangements control the odd or even, and other combinations from other push buttons. A special arrangement took care of that '17' freak. There isn't an honest gambling-machine in the whole place—I might almost say the whole city. The whole thing is crooked from start to finish—the men, the machines, the—"

"That machine could be made to beat me by turning up a run of '17' any number of times, or red or black, or odd or even, over '18' or under '18,' or anything?"

"Anything, DeLong."

"And I never had a chance," he repeated, meditatively fingering the wires. "They broke me to-night. Danfield"—DeLong turned, looking dazedly about in the crowd for his former friend, then his hand shot into his pocket, and a little ivory-handled pistol flashed out—"Danfield, your blood is on your own head. You have ruined me."

Kennedy must have been expecting something of the sort, for he seized the arm of the young man, weakened by dissipation, and turned the pistol upward as if it had been in the grasp of a mere child.

A blinding flash followed in the farthest corner of the room and a huge puff of smoke. Before I could collect my wits another followed in the opposite corner. The room was filled with a dense smoke.

Two men were scuffling at my feet. One was Kennedy. As I dropped down quickly to help him I saw that the other was Danfield, his face purple with the violence of the struggle.

"Don't be alarmed, gentlemen," I heard O'Connor shout, "the explosions were only the flashlights of the official police photographers. We now have the evidence complete. Gentlemen, you will now go down quietly to the patrol-wagons below, two by two. If you have anything to say, say it to the magistrate of the night court."

"Hold his arms, Walter," panted Kennedy.

I did. With a dexterity that would have done credit to a pickpocket, Kennedy reached into Danfield's pocket and pulled out some papers.

Before the smoke had cleared and order had been restored, Craig exclaimed: "Let him up, Walter. Here, DeLong, here are the I. O. U.'s against you. Tear them up—they are not even a debt of honour."

THE END

READING GROUP GUIDE

1. All of these stories revolve around scientific discoveries
    or inventions. Which of them was the most interesting
    or novel? Which still have some relevance today? Which
    seem silly in light of today's scientific knowledge?

2. Do you find the characters of Craig Kennedy and Walter
    Jameson appealing? What do you like about them?

3. Some critics have complained that the professor and the
    newspaperman are stock figures with no personalities
    and offer that as an explanation for why these stories have
    faded away. Do you agree?

4. Why do you think that the Craig Kennedy stories were so
    popular in the 1910s through 1930s?

5. Do you like contemporary mysteries that feature science
    or scientists? What interests you about them? How are
    they different from Reeve's stories?

6. What do you think about television shows that glamorize the scientific aspects of police work? Do you think that the lack of realism in these shows has created problems for real law enforcement officers?

FURTHER READING

BY ARTHUR B. REEVE:

The twelve-volume Craig Kennedy Stories, published by
Harper & Bros. in 1918:

The Silent Bullet
The Poisoned Pen
The Dream Doctor
The War Terror
The Social Gangster
The Treasure Train
The Ear in the Wall
The Gold of the Gods
The Exploits of Elaine
The Romance of Elaine
Guy Garrick (Kennedy's name has been changed to "Guy
  Garrick," and other characters' names are changed as well)
Constance Dunlap (Kennedy does not appear)

The Fourteen Points. New York: Harper & Bros., 1925.

CRITICAL STUDIES:

Knight, Stephen. *Crime Fiction since 1800: Detection, Death, Diversity.* 2nd ed. New York: Palgrave Macmillan, 2010.

Locke, John, ed. *From Ghouls to Gangsters: The Career of Arthur B. Reeve.* 2 vols. Elkhorn, CA: Off-Trail Publications, 2007.

Panek, LeRoy Lad. *After Sherlock Holmes: The Evolution of British and American Detective Stories, 1891–1914.* Jefferson, NC: McFarland, 2014.

Van Dover, J. K. *You Know My Methods: The Science of the Detective.* Bowling Green, OH: Bowling Green State University Popular Press, 1994.

BY OTHER WRITERS:

Balmer, Edwin and William MacHarg. *The Achievements of Luther Trant.* Boston: Small, Maynard, 1910.

Cornwell, Patricia. *Postmortem.* New York: Charles Scribner and Sons, 1990. The first of the Dr. Kay Scarpetta novels.

Deaver, Jeffery. *The Bone Collector.* New York: Viking, 1997. The first of the Lincoln Rhyme novels.

Freeman, R. Austin. *The Red Thumb Mark.* London: Collingwood Bros., 1907.

———. *John Thorndyke's Cases.* London: Chatto & Windus, 1909.

Moffett, Cleveland. *Through the Wall.* New York: D. Appleton, 1909.

Reichs, Kathy. *Déjà Dead.* New York: Scribner, 1997. The first of the Temperance "Bones" Brennan novels.

ABOUT THE AUTHOR

Arthur Benjamin Reeve (1880–1936) was born in Patchogue, New York, to Jennie (Henderson) and Walter F. Reeve. As a boy, he read the stories of Nick Carter* and his kind in dime novels, until he discovered Arthur Conan Doyle, after which he "spent hours with Sherlock Holmes."† He graduated from Princeton University in 1903 and then enrolled at New York Law School. Dismayed to learn that there were 16,000 lawyers in New York, however, he dropped out of law school and took a job as assistant editor of *Public Opinion* magazine, where he contributed articles on science and technology. From 1906 to 1910, he edited *Our Own Times*, an annual, and took up freelance journalism, contributing to *Everybody's*, *World's Work Magazine*, *Outlook Magazine*, *The Independent*, and, commencing in 1907, Munsey's *The Scrap Book*. His interests were broad, and he penned articles on science, farming, industry, sports,

* Possibly the second-longest-lived detective in mystery fiction (104 years), Carter made his debut in "dime novels" in 1886, and continued to appear in print until 1990 (though, in the later years, he was known as "Killmaster"). Only Sherlock Holmes, who first appeared in 1887, has a longer "lifespan" (133 years as of 2020).

† *Trenton Sunday Times Advertiser*, May 22, 1932, in an interview about Reeve's move to Trenton, New Jersey.

law, crime, fashion, and social trends. In 1907, he published his first short story, a humorous piece.

His great creation, Craig Kennedy, "scientific detective," was apparently long in his thoughts. He admitted that in law school, he was "fascinated by criminal law. Hence [I] conceived the incongruity of combining science and law with a Nick Carter who should have both the University and Third Avenue Theatre melodrama in his makeup."* Much like how Dr. Joseph Bell was the inspiration for Arthur Conan Doyle's Sherlock Holmes, Kennedy was modeled on Reeve's good friend Dr. Otto Schultze, who was a coroner's physician for New York County. Reeve confirmed this in an interview in 1923.† Unlike Bell, however, who reveled publicly in the limelight of his association with Doyle,‡ Schulze never took credit: "I might have dropped the seed of fact," he reportedly said, "but Arthur made it flower into fiction."§

Reeve's first published story featuring Kennedy was "The Case of Helen Bond," which appeared in the December 1910 issue of *Cosmopolitan*. Though the magazine today is about fashion, then it was filled with literature. Purchased by William Randolph Hearst in 1905, it had already established itself as a promoter of new technology—automobiles, airplanes, and the like—and speculative fiction, such as H. G. Wells's *War of the Worlds*, serialized in the April through December 1897 issues.

---

* *Dime Detective Magazine*, October 1, 1933, quoted in John Locke, ed., *From Ghouls to Gangsters: The Career of Arthur B. Reeve* (Elkhorn, CA: Off-Trail Publications, 2007), 2:32.

† "Craig Kennedy, Scientific Sleuth, Is Tracked Down," *Olean Evening Times* (New York), April 20, 1923.

‡ Bell wrote an essay on the connection for *The Bookman* in December 1892, reproduced in an early reprint edition of the first Holmes story, *A Study in Scarlet* (London: Ward, Lock, 1893), after Holmes's popularity reached its peak in *The Strand Magazine*.

§ "Dr. Schultze Dead, Famed as Coroner," *New York Times*, July 5, 1934.

Though Hearst for a short time tried to make the magazine an outlet for "muckraking" journalism, it soon returned to its literary roots and general fiction. Reeve's timing was excellent, and his stories became an important part of the success of *Cosmopolitan*.

Reeve continued to pursue journalism, writing essays about crime fiction and covering crime stories, but he soon focused on stories about the professor. He sold them to other magazines as well, quite lucratively,* and many of the stories were published in newspapers, producing additional income. In 1912, he cowrote with William J. Burns, former head of the Secret Service, a series of four stories titled *Detective Burns' Great Cases*.† Reeve even repurposed his own work, turning stories that initially featured Craig Kennedy into a novel called *Guy Garrick*, with the character's name and profession changed (as well as the name of his sidekick, who remained a journalist).

By 1914, Reeve may have seen his market diminishing.‡ Fortunately, Reeve proved adaptable. He began to reserve "dramatic rights" and later, specifically, "motion picture rights" to his stories. In late 1914, Pathé, the successful producers of the

---

* Reeve sold five stories to Street & Smith in the years 1911, 1912, and 1913 for $800 each; the stories were all in excess of 30,000 words, with Reeves receiving between 2 and 2.7 cents per word. This was far from top dollar; Conan Doyle sold thirteen Holmes stories to *Collier's* in 1903 for £45,000, which was equivalent to about US$225,000, or US$17,000 per story. However, the $800 was quite good pay for a magazine writer, though not in the league of "celebrity" writers such as Theodore Roosevelt and explorer Frederick Cook, who were paid US$1.00 per word for their writing in 1908 and 1910, respectively.

† These appeared in *McClure's*; Burns cowrote with other authors as well.

‡ The *New York Times*, in its 1914 review of *The Dream Doctor* (Reeve's third collection of Kennedy stories, spliced together into a "novel"), wrote: "The detective, especially the scientific detective, with his array of unpronounceable instruments for his emotional clinics, is becoming a little too pervasive nowadays. His methods are hard to follow, and we begin to distrust his omniscience. These things tend to take the edge off the keenness of appetite with which we were wont to devour anything that called itself a 'detective story.'" "Latest Fiction," *New York Times*, May 24, 1914, 246.

now-legendary silent film serial *The Perils of Pauline*, developed *The Exploits of Elaine*, cowritten by Reeve and Charles W. Goddard (the scenarist for *Pauline*), featuring the character Craig Kennedy. A fourteen-part film, it starred Pearl White (who had made such an impression as Pauline) and featured high production values. Its success was followed in 1915 by a ten-parter, *The New Exploits of Elaine*, and a twelve-parter, *The Romance of Elaine*. Reeve also "novelized" these films to great success.

After 1918, Reeve's magazine fiction writing slowed considerably, but commensurately, his film career and other writing increased. He collaborated on five serials and two features between 1919 and 1920. In early 1920, he signed a deal for four five-reel Craig Kennedy films (whether they were made is unknown), and he wrote a number of magazine articles on prominent crimes of the day. But Reeve was not done with crime fiction. Though by 1924 he had essentially concluded writing for prestigious magazines like *Cosmopolitan*, he had more stories to tell, and he began a highly successful career writing for pulp magazines, some of which made their reputations from his association. The most important of these was his series written for *Flynn's*, a new pulp that was first published in late 1924. Reeve wrote fourteen stories for the magazine, later collected as *The Fourteen Points* (Harper & Bros., 1925).

Reeve's remaining career was a series of successes and failures. He wrote for films; he produced short stories and novels; and he wrote articles on crimes and crime detection. Reeve even took up battling crime himself. In 1930, he created a new radio show for NBC called *Crime Prevention Program*, which featured Reeve as the host. Each episode consisted of a short drama featuring a detective named Thurlow Wade, a guest speaking about crime prevention (guests included police, state attorneys, and judges), and an editorial by Reeve. The show ran for almost a year, then vanished. Undaunted, Reeve announced the creation of the Crime Crusade Foundation, which would devote itself to delivering Reeve's messages. The Foundation idea went nowhere, but Reeve did produce a massive book, titled *The Golden Age of Crime*, that was a history of the impact of Prohibition on crime focused especially on racketeering. This focus would permeate his remaining fiction output as well: he collaborated on a comic strip known as *Craig Kennedy and the Gangsters* and, in 1932, published a novel called *The Kidnap Club*, about the kidnapping of the child of the chair of a crime-prevention league. The latter began a long association with *Complete Detective Novel Magazine*, a successful pulp of the day. This was the end of the "scientific detective," for Reeve's stories shifted to two-fisted investigators focused on action.

Reeve's last fiction to appear in magazine form was a story, "The Death Cry," that appeared in *Weird Tales* in May 1935. That same year, Reeve traveled daily to Flemington, New Jersey, to cover the trial of Bruno Hauptmann (for the kidnapping of the Lindbergh baby) for a Philadelphia newspaper. Reeve seemed to know that his life was ending. In February, as the trial was ending, he was stuck in bed with an attack of what he called "cardiac asthma," a secondary symptom of heart failure, and he described his work on the trial to his friend Leo Margulies as "my last story, a valedictory." Reeve died on August 9, 1936.

Arthur B. Reeve was a competent journalist, and his best stories drew contemporary science into adventurous and exciting contexts, providing thrills to readers along with an education. His shortcoming was in failing to develop the character of Craig Kennedy to outlast the science. "After reading enough stories of his adventures," concluded scholar John Locke, "you realize you will never know him. And perhaps that's why he passed from the limelight."* Though Reeve achieved great success for a while, in the end, he slipped into near obscurity, just one more of the countless pulp writers lost to history.

---

* Locke, *From Ghouls to Gangsters,* 2:49.

LAST SEEN WEARING

No one saw her leave, and no one knows where she went...

It's a perfectly typical day for Lowell Mitchell at her perfectly ordinary university in Massachusetts. She goes to class, chats with friends, and retires to her dorm room. Everything is normal until suddenly it's not—in the blink of an eye, Lowell is gone.

Facts are everything for Police Chief Frank Ford. He's a small-town cop, and he knows only hard evidence and thorough procedure will lead him to the truth. Together with the wise-cracking officer Burt Cameron, the grizzled chief will deal with the distraught family, chase dead-end leads, interrogate shady witnesses, and spend late nights ruminating over black coffee and cigars. Everyone tells him what a good, responsible girl Lowell is. But Ford believes that Lowell had a secret and that if he can discover it, this case will crack wide open.

Considered one of the first-ever police procedurals and hailed as a milestone, *Last Seen Wearing*—based on a true story—is riveting in its accurate portrayal of an official police investigation. Hillary Waugh, who earned the title of Grand Master from the Mystery Writers of America, went on to create several memorable series, but this early novel ranks among his finest work. This installment in the Library of Congress Crime Classics series will keep readers in suspense until the final page.

For more Library of Congress Crime Classics, visit:
sourcebooks.com